Newhall Public Library

WITHDRAWN

P9-BYM-294

DRAGONS
OF DARKNESS

ALSO BY ANTONIA MICHAELIS

Tiger Moon, translated by Anthea Bell

ANTONIA MICHAELIS

DRAGONS
OF DARKNESS

Translated from the German by
ANTHEA BELL

Amulet Books
New York

PUBLISHER'S NOTE: This is a work of fiction. Names,
characters, places, and incidents are either the product of the
author's imagination or are used fictitiously, and any resemblance to
actual persons, living or dead, business establishments, events, or
locales is entirely coincidental.

Library of Congress Cataloging-in-Publication Data

Michaelis, Antonia.
[Drachen der Finsternis. English]
The dragons of darkness / by Antonia Michaelis ; translated by
Anthea Bell.
p. cm.
Summary: Two boys from very different backgrounds are thrown
together by magic, mayhem, and a common foe as they battle deadly
dragons in the wilderness of Nepal.
ISBN 978-0-8109-4074-1
[1. Magic—Fiction. 2. Coming of age—Fiction. 3. Dragons—Fiction.
4. Nepal—Fiction.] I. Bell, Anthea, ill. II. Title.
PZ7.M5798274Dr 2010
[Fic]—dc22
2009003051

First published by Loewe Verlag GmbH
Copyright © 2006 Loewe Verlag, Bindlach, Germany
First published in English in hardcover by Amulet Books in 2008
English translation copyright © 2010 Anthea Bell

Book design by Maria T. Middleton

Published in 2010 by Amulet Books, an imprint of ABRAMS. All
rights reserved. No portion of this book may be reproduced, stored
in a retrieval system, or transmitted in any form or by any means,
mechanical, electronic, photocopying, recording, or otherwise, without
written permission from the publisher. Amulet Books and Amulet
Paperbacks are registered trademarks of Harry N. Abrams, Inc.

Printed and bound in U.S.A.
10 9 8 7 6 5 4 3 2 1

Amulet Books are available at special discounts when purchased
in quantity for premiums and promotions as well as fundraising or
educational use. Special editions can also be created to specification.
For details, contact specialmarkets@abramsbooks.com or the
address below.

ABRAMS
THE ART OF BOOKS SINCE 1949
115 West 18th Street
New York, NY 10011
www.abramsbooks.com

For my father, who may perhaps be able to read the words between the lines, and who was almost lost in the snowstorm over Thorung La—but luckily was persuaded to wait another day to recover from his altitude sickness.

And for Carolin, who should look for the atomic chicken and the pretty five-lobed leaves that we never smoked but swapped for chocolate at Poon Hill.

The consonants are for my father
and the vowels are for Carolin.

Contents

ABOVE THE SNOWLINE

CENTRAL HILL COUNTRY

GERMANY, OCTOBER

THE DAY WHEN ARNE DISAPPEARED was made of gold.

It was one of those late October days when the colors flare brightly once more before finally fading away, one of those days when you seem to catch a last breath of summer, although the streets are full of sweaters and corduroy pants.

Later, whenever he thought of Arne, Christopher would always remember the yellow chestnut leaves in the school yard and the blue sky that day.

Everyone at school had liked Arne.

All the girls, from grade 7 and up, had been in love with him, and at least two thirds of the boys admired him.

Christopher, on the other hand, was the kind of kid who went almost unnoticed.

Sometimes when people recognized his last name, he caught a look of surprise in their eyes. "Hagedorn? Are you related to *Arne* Hagedorn? Are you by any chance his little brother?"

And when Christopher nodded, they would shake their heads as if they thought there must be some mistake. "We didn't imagine you at all like that," they'd say. "You two don't look at all like each other."

That was a fact. They didn't.

Arne was tall and broad-shouldered and strong, and he had very fair hair and a face that no one could ever forget. Christopher was small and slight and dark-haired, and he had inherited their grandmother's features. Neither of them had known her, but ages ago she had come from Nepal to marry a tall, blond German—someone just like Arne.

So of course no one was surprised when Arne decided to spend a year in Nepal after finishing school.

"In search of his roots. Such a serious-minded boy," they murmured, nodding approvingly. He was going to work at an orphanage there. That was so Arne Hagedorn.

Once everyone knew that he was going to Nepal, all the girls who hadn't been in love with him already promptly did fall in love with him, and he had to promise to take dozens of e-mail addresses away with him.

And knowing his brother as Christopher did, he was sure he really would try to write to them all at least once. Arne was like that. He did all the right things. If someone had to save the day in a basketball tournament, Arne was there to do it. If someone had to win a chess championship for the school, Arne won it. Even if a protest against the teachers had to be led because of some injustice, he did that as well—which was why everyone liked Arne.

Christopher liked Arne, too.

Arne was nearly twenty. Christopher himself was only fourteen. He would never have dared to e-mail a girl. He never scored any points in basketball, he would have made a terrible mess of a chess championship, and he'd have chickened out of leading a protest against the teachers.

He admired Arne just as everyone else did.

When people talked to his parents, they said, "You must be very proud of your son!"

And when Christopher's parents asked, "Which son?" the answer was, "Well, Arne, of course. Do you have another son as well?"

That was how things were.

Until Arne disappeared that golden October day.

✦ ✦ ✦

Of course he didn't really disappear that day. He had disappeared earlier, but no one knew it.

However, that was the day when Christopher and his parents heard the news.

The orphanage where Arne was working had given him a few days off, and Arne had gone walking in the Himalayas. On his own. Now, four weeks later, the people who ran the orphanage finally plucked up enough courage to send a message to the Hagedorns saying that he hadn't come back. For three weeks, his parents had been blaming the Internet, the e-mail program, and Arne's love of adventure for his failure to get in touch. "He was only going to be away for a week," said Christopher's father about twenty-seven times. "He was only going to be away for a week, and now, four weeks later, they tell us he never came back!"

And the news was saying that the political situation in Nepal was critical. More and more tanks were assembling outside the palace in Durbar Square. On the German Foreign Ministry's Web site they were advising against traveling to Nepal. They didn't say what you were supposed to do if you were already there. Probably fly home. Probably stay in the capital city. Probably not go walking in the mountains on your own. Because the Maoists were in the mountains.

And they were Communists. Arne had joked about them when he wrote home, saying that they demanded a second payment from tourists who had already paid their fee to visit the Annapurna region, and handed out leaflets in bad English explaining that they were the real government of the country. Apart from that, they were polite but not forthcoming.

For weeks, Christopher had been reading everything he could find about the Maoists. That didn't add up to much, but there was a disturbing fascination about it. Christopher was small and not very strong, and maybe not too brave, but he wasn't stupid. In those days of waiting to hear from Arne, he asked himself for the first time in his life whether maybe *Arne* was stupid. But not in the usual sense of the word. In another, broader sense; one that sent you off walking on your own in the Annapurna region when everyone advised you not to.

And then the news that Arne was missing came. It was a Thursday afternoon.

"Of course no one can be sure," said Christopher's father, turning his narrow-framed glasses around in his hands. "Maybe he's sprained an ankle and he's sitting in a village in the middle of nowhere, teaching the local kids French while they bandage his ankle with jungle leaves. That would be just like Arne."

"You're out of your mind," said Christopher's mother. "Right out of your mind. Bandaging him with jungle leaves! You just sit there in your chair talking about bandaging ankles with jungle leaves! We have to do something! Call someone, the embassy or—"

"I already did," said Christopher's father.

"Then call them again!" cried his mother, knocking over the glass of fruit juice that she'd put down on the table a moment before. Christopher saw how her hands were shaking as she collected the shards. Then she poured herself half a glass of gin, instead of more juice, and Christopher's father stood up, took it away from her after her first sip, and poured the rest down the sink.

"That won't do any good, either," he said.

"Don't be so damn calm about it!" shouted his mother. "I suppose you're not bothered that our son's been abducted by some band of armed Communists! It leaves you cold, am I right? That's it, it leaves you cold, it—"

Then she collapsed on the sofa and dissolved into a flood of tears.

Christopher just stood there watching his parents hugging and trying to comfort each other, and he felt as rigid as a statue. He told himself he ought to be feeling something else. Fear. Horror. Grief. Rage. Even secret guilt for *not* feeling fear, horror, or grief. But there was nothing there. All Christopher's feelings had turned to stone. It was as if Arne had taken these emotions away with him—taken them away to nowhere.

Nothing happened for three days. Then they heard that a Maoist splinter group claimed to be holding three Europeans hostage, but there were no pictures or names, and there was no basis for negotiations, either, because the Maoists couldn't agree with each other on their demands.

Christopher's mother swallowed tranquilizers like candy, and his father spent hours every day phoning people in their offices and embassies who couldn't help him. In school, Christopher felt the other kids' eyes on him. They didn't dare to ask questions, and he avoided them. At home, he did the dishes that were stacking up. He hung out the wash that he found in a musty-smelling washing machine. At one point, he went to the library, borrowed a book full of pictures of Nepal, and took it home and into his room with him. Under the outer shell of the statue he'd become, something slowly began to seethe. Maybe the statue would melt from the inside. If it exploded, there'd be no one left to do the dishes and hang up the wash.

The fact that everyone liked Arne didn't help him much

now, Christopher thought, because obviously nobody was actually ready to do anything practical for him! They were all cracking up, spinning around in circles, while Arne was held prisoner somewhere in the Himalayas.

Christopher sat down on his bed and leafed through the pages of the library book: mountains, ravines, snow-covered peaks, a dry river valley, mules crossing a narrow suspension bridge. Broad-leaved trees and climbing plants, waterfalls, Buddhist monasteries with bright wall paintings and colorful prayer flags above small brown buildings. There was nothing he could do, so he dreamed his way into its pages, over the mountains and through the valleys, past meandering blue rivers, up dazzlingly bright glaciers. At least that way he felt a little closer to Arne. When evening came and no one felt like eating, when the street lights flickered on in the darkness like a string of beads, and October brought fine rain falling on the streets, Christopher's eyes stopped to dwell on one particular picture. It showed the surging green of the tropical jungle, where the mountains were still low and there was hot, humid, motionless air among the trees. You could see a path in the foreground leading into that green world, turning, winding, and finally disappearing into the undergrowth in a mysterious way.

Christopher looked at the picture for a long time, so long

that his eyes were streaming. Everything blurred in front of them, and he saw nothing but the color green.

Green.

GREEN.

The green twilight of an afternoon in the tropical jungle.

Something rustled in the thickets to his left. He spun around, and at that moment, he noticed that his feet were on a springy carpet of leaves. Ahead of him, the path wound on into the undergrowth. Dozens of exotic birds, invisible in the high branches, were making a lot of noise, and cicadas were chirping so loudly that you might have thought you were right next to a power station.

This was impossible. This couldn't be true.

This was—no, no. Stay sensible, Christopher, he told himself. Cracking up was something other people did. There was a perfectly plausible explanation.

He was dreaming.

Something was moving on his left again, and Christopher saw a trail leading away into the jungle—a trail of trodden grass and broken twigs leading away from the path. He wasn't Arne. Arne would have followed the trail right away, without a trace of fear. Christopher did feel fear. Even if he was only dreaming his fear. He didn't understand what was going on, and he was so strung up that his palms felt moist.

All the same, he decided to follow the trail, step by step, very cautiously, and the rustling came closer.

Then a voice he didn't know, a tired, desperate voice, said, "Don't run away. *Please* don't run away. Help me. *Please!*"

Christopher shook his head and took one more step forward to see if he'd miscalculated the distance. Maybe whoever the voice belonged to was hiding somewhere behind a bush . . .

As he stepped forward, he stumbled over someone.

Someone about his own size, who let out a scream when Christopher fell on top of him.

Christopher rolled off and looked around, gasping for air.

But there wasn't anyone there.

NEPAL

THE GARDEN LAY SILENT IN THE MORNING
light, as silent as a secret thought.

The frangipani trees lifted their white, wheel-shaped
blossoms, fanning out toward the sun, and the orange lilies
opened their flowers to greet the dawning day.

A lizard scurried over the wall in a pale green streak of
color.

Sumptuous fragrance rose from thousands upon thousands of flowers, gathering under the glass dome like a cloud,
and in the city they said that sometimes rain fell from that
cloud on the garden, like tears flooding the flowerbeds and
low walls, and that one day it would flood the palace itself in

a deluge of flowery perfume. But that was only one of many rumors. None of the city folk had ever seen the garden. All they saw was its high walls. No one could climb those walls, and when people spoke of what lay behind them, they lowered their voices to a whisper.

For there in the garden, sheltered by walls and shaded by trees, beneath the glass dome and in the middle of the fragrance, the queen slept.

She did not sleep like someone in a fairy tale. She was asleep in real life, and it was better not to say so out loud. Something had happened, and she had fallen into a deep slumber from which no one could wake her. Even the doctors who came from far away, flying over the sea in great airplanes, couldn't wake the queen. They had all just shaken their heads, boarded their planes again, and flown home. It's very likely they have long forgotten the strange case of the queen of Nepal and her deep sleep.

The queen had been asleep for fourteen years.

But on the morning when the pale green lizard scurried over the garden wall, a side door to the palace opened to let someone in, and something began to happen.

Later, people said it should have been possible to foretell it long ago, from the signs in the sky and the sounds in the air, from the lines in a human hand, or perhaps from the weather forecast. But it's always *later* that such things are said.

Jumar Sander Pratap was the first to hear the knocking. The corridor leading to that side door was in the servants' quarters, and Jumar had no business being there, because the heir to a throne ought not to be in a place like that.

However, where he ought or ought not to be had never bothered Jumar. Moreover, it was difficult to forbid him to be here, there, or anywhere. You could never tell exactly where he was, because in all the fourteen years of his life in the palace, no human soul had ever set eyes on Jumar. Not even Jumar himself. Nothing was ever said about him out in the city.

No one there knew.

Not a single person in all Kathmandu knew that there was an heir to the throne at all.

For it was rather embarrassing for the king to have an invisible son. Imagine all the fuss! The rumors. The foreign press. No, invisibility was not right and proper. So Jumar had lived between the walls of the palace all his life, not just unseen but unknown as well. It was a life that was more appearance than reality, or perhaps it really only appeared to be unreal. At this point in his thinking he always got confused.

They had tried to make him visible, but the clothes

that touched his skin behaved as improperly, indeed as outrageously, as his skin itself, disappearing before the servants' very eyes as soon as he put them on. However, any second layer of clothing that didn't come into contact with his skin stayed visible, so on his father's orders, Jumar walked the palace corridors like a silken husk of himself. Ever since he was five, when he made off with a whole dish of rice pudding, he had been required to wear gloves so that the inanimate objects he touched wouldn't also become invisible.

But what do orders mean? Who can order an invisible person around? Suppose that person sometimes took off his second layer of clothes, so as to walk around the palace unseen?

Only the doors and gateways leading out into the city remained closed to the invisible heir to the throne. For the last fourteen years, as few servants as possible had been employed in the palace. And those few were obliged to wear their keys to the outer doors and gates around their necks, and when they unlocked the doors and locked them again, they were sworn to take the greatest care that no one else slipped out into the busy turmoil of the city with them.

Imagine someone invisible but for a second layer of clothing! Heaven forbid! Think of the headlines in the minds of the general public.

"Sightings of Invisible Man."

"Mystery Man Mysteriously Escapes from Palace."

Whose are those unseen eyes? Whose are those disembodied footsteps? Whose is that voice without a mouth?

For fourteen years, the heir to the throne of Nepal had been a prisoner of rumors that had never yet, in fact, begun to circulate.

And anyone who had the key to the outside world—anyone who had seen the faceless heir, had heard the boy without a mouth speak—wore another lock on his own mouth, although that lock, too, was invisible.

But let us return to that corridor near the kitchen in the servants' quarters, back to the noise. Jumar stopped and listened. He wondered what it was and went on listening. The noise was like the scrabbling of a dog. There was something desperate about it.

He had learned that there was unrest outside, and it was growing—although he didn't know the nature of that unrest. He had been told it could be dangerous to be anywhere outside these days. Jumar had never in his life done anything dangerous. His world was full of soft cushions and music lessons, texts in English, sine curves on graph paper, swimming practice in the royal pool (because only in that sport, where the water moved about, could they be for certain, without the two layers of clothing, that he was obeying the rules entirely), computer courses, foreign friends he knew only by e-mail, and books. But there was no danger in any of those.

On that day (the day when the pale green lizard . . . but we know about the lizard already), when he heard the desperate scrabbling at the door in the corridor, an idea ran through his mind, hot and cold at the same time. In short, it was a wonderful idea. And although he knew he should have turned back, he stayed where he was and waited.

Suddenly and unexpectedly, the door flew open.

The person on the other side had finally managed to unlatch it—and fell into Jumar's arms.

Jumar staggered back, and at exactly that moment, his world changed forever. He fell to the floor with the other person, and found himself enveloped in the odor of sweat and dirt and blood, things he had never smelled before. It was so strong that it took his breath away. All the same, he greeted it as one might greet an unknown land, and when he saw that the man half lying on him was his old servant Tapa, and his fingers touched sticky, warm blood, his horror was mingled with a longing for what was new to him, what was dark, the opposite of anything he had known before. He felt ashamed of it later, but he couldn't deny that feeling.

"Tapa!" Jumar gasped, struggling to his feet. He quickly

closed the door and knelt down beside the old man. "What . . . How—?"

The old man's clothes were in rags, torn and discolored with dark stains in so many places that Jumar seriously wondered whether all that blood could really have been in Tapa's body before. He concluded that there couldn't be much left in it, and tried to support the old man.

"Your Highness," whispered Tapa, "I have—I have to speak to your father."

Jumar turned the old man's face toward him, saw the split lips and swollen eyes, the encrusted blood on his nostrils, the dirt sticking his sparse hair together. He felt sickened.

"Who did this?" he whispered.

"They did," replied the old man hoarsely, pointing in some vague direction. "I was visiting my daughter in her village—"

"I know, Tapa, I know." Jumar desperately tried to remember if he had ever learned what to do when injured people fall into your arms.

"They were there, in the village. Someone told them I work in the palace. The people are starving, they say, starving, and there's too much bread in the palace, too much. They're coming. They'll change everything, they said, it won't be long now. They're going to put an end to people like me who eat the king's bread. The king!"

The old man clutched Jumar's shirt, hauled himself up, and got to his feet, staggering. "I must speak to the king. I must tell him what's going on in those villages. I must—"

He struggled for air and reached for the wall to keep himself from falling over. His hand left a mark of blood and dirt on the pure white surface.

And it so happened that a certain key, carefully guarded until then, fell from that hand to the floor. It landed with a slight clink, barely audible, yet very important.

"He's in the garden," said Jumar, and for the first time he detected a certain bitter note in his own voice. "He's always in the garden at this time of day. Watering his plants. You know he won't let anyone else water his plants."

Old Tapa's split lips smiled. "They say he planted them all with his own hands. Is that true?"

"I'm afraid so," replied Jumar. "It's the only thing I've ever seen him do with such enthusiasm. He plants them for my mother . . . What—what are you going to tell him?"

But Tapa did not reply, for he needed what little breath he still had left to limp along the corridors down which Jumar led him. And on their way, Jumar remembered how he had learned to walk in these very same corridors, and at that time he was the one who had held on to Tapa.

It had always been to Tapa that he turned, asking,

"Brother Tapa, why aren't I like other people? Why can I see them but they can't see me? I can't even see myself, although I can feel every part of my body!"

In his memory, he heard Tapa say, "Ask your father."

"But he won't tell me," Jumar had said, tugging at the leg of Tapa's pants. "You tell me!"

And again he heard Tapa saying, "I can't answer that."

Now that he was dragging the old man through the palace, feeling the weight of his wounded body heavy on his shoulder, it was as if everything were coming full circle. Jumar didn't yet understand what death meant, or that it was near. There were still too many confused feelings whirling around in his mind, and the scent of danger and adventure set them dancing wildly.

And the key lay heavy in his pocket.

Jumar found his father in the shade of a rose hedge. He was standing there lost in thought, the hose in one hand, and the water was running away unnoticed into the dark, fragrant earth.

"Father," said Jumar.

"Look," said the king. "See how beautiful the orange lilies are this year. They're lovelier than ever before. I'm almost sure their glowing color makes its way into your mother's dreams."

19

"Father!" Jumar said again. "Someone wants to speak to you!"

"Later," said the king impatiently. "Can't you see the garden needs me? My audiences are between three and five in the afternoon. You know that."

Jumar took the king's arm in his free hand. "Father!" he said for the last time. "Forget the orange lilies for once!"

The king stared at his arm, where his son's invisible fingers had left a mark: a red bloodstain—someone else's red blood, only too visible. And at last, at long last he turned around.

"You're not wearing your second layer of clothes," he told his son reproachfully. But there was more vague inquiry than reproof in his voice.

Old Tapa tried to bow, but Jumar raised him up again. "I don't think this is any time for talking about layers of clothes," he said. "Or for bowing, either."

"I—I bring news from outside," stammered old Tapa. "I thought someone must tell the king. My king, you must know that the people out there are hungry, and the Communists who want to change everything have grown strong. I've seen how strong they are already—there are a great many of them, and they boast of what they'll do—"

Jumar saw the king turn and run his finger down the stem of an orange lily. "My lilies are beautiful," he said. "Beautiful, aren't they?"

Old Tapa hesitated, baffled. "The . . . the lilies?" he murmured, unable to make this out.

The king turned to him again and he smiled.

"It's all right," he said. "There's nothing for anyone to worry about. We're at peace in this country. No need to be uneasy. No need to come disturbing me in my garden. The commanders of my army tell me they have the situation under control."

"What situation?" asked Jumar.

"I'm not in the habit of inquiring into such minor details," replied the king, narrowing his eyes very slightly as he looked at the place where he assumed his son was standing. Jumar opened his mouth and closed it again.

"Go away now," said the king. "Go away and leave me alone."

But it was the king who went away. He picked up the garden hose and walked along the path leading past the rose hedges to the center of the garden, where a woman had been sleeping hidden in her pavilion for fourteen years.

And Jumar knew it was his fault that she was asleep.

Because nothing in her body or her head was sick. They had X-rayed her, they had scanned her, they had used tomography on her, they had measured her brainwaves, and worked out the speed of her nervous reflexes. There was nothing wrong with her.

And the word *coma* that the doctors liked to use wasn't right, either.

However, the doctors didn't know that the queen had given birth to an invisible child. That one fact had been kept from them. Otherwise, and in view of such a terrible, incomprehensible thing, they could hardly have blamed her for preferring to close her eyes to the world and fall into a never-ending slumber.

"It's my fault," whispered Jumar. "It's all my fault, isn't it? And that's why he'll never listen to me. If she wasn't fast asleep, he would never have planted this garden to surround her under that ridiculous glass dome, and then he'd know what's going on outside, and no one would be starving."

He sensed that old Tapa couldn't stay on his feet for long, so he sat down on the ground, in the middle of the carefully swept pathway of polished marble, and held the old man in his arms.

"If I'd always done as my father told me . . . if I'd always worn gloves, and never secretly taken off the second layer of clothes . . . Tapa . . . do you think I'd have turned visible some day? Do you think the queen would have woken up then?"

Tapa's battered face smiled up at him. "You're talking like

the little boy you were so long ago," he said. "Of course not, dear Jumar. Of course not. I don't know if there's any way you can ever be visible. And I don't know if it's anyone's fault." He was whispering now, and his voice was weaker and weaker. "It is not for us to decide these things."

"Tell me," Jumar asked, bending down very close to him, "tell me what's happening outside. Tell me about the people who did this to you!"

"They want to bring the king down," Tapa whispered. "There are many of them, and they go into the villages and find strong young people to join them. More and more of them are coming all the time, and they make fine-sounding speeches. When people are hungry, they're ready to listen to such things. The insurgents hide out in the mountains, and you don't often see them come into a village as they came into my daughter's." He was struggling to speak now, and Jumar saw the pain gnawing at his features and trying to silence his voice. "Or not often, so far," he went on, with difficulty. "In the mountains, in the jungle, that's where they feel secure and where they have their camps. That's where they're preparing for revolution, in those camps. People coming down from the mountains to the valley say they can be heard shooting their guns in practice there."

"Why are they hungry?" asked Jumar. Even the word

"hungry" seemed an adventure to him. He had never felt hungry. He wanted to know what it was like, whether it hurt, and whether it changed your ideas.

"Did no one ever tell you about the dragons?" asked old Tapa.

Jumar shook his head. "All I know is that there aren't any such things as dragons," he replied. "They belong in old fairy tales. All we have today is small reptiles. Lizards, chameleons, frill-necked lizards, and so forth . . ."

"Yes, that's what the clever books say, the books from distant lands," said Tapa. "But there are dragons out there. In the mountains. They don't venture into the city yet, but they're growing bolder every day . . . they . . ."

"Yes?" Jumar leaned even closer to the old man. He could hardly hear what he was saying.

"They eat colors. The rice fields have no color, Your Highness, they're black and white like an old newspaper picture, and colorless rice . . ." His voice sank even lower, and halted, "colorless rice doesn't satisfy hunger. But that's . . . not . . . not all. You . . ."

Jumar put his ear close to Tapa's mouth.

"What else?" he whispered. "What else do they do?"

But old Tapa shook his head very slowly. It was the last thing he ever did.

His head fell to one side, where an invisible arm was holding him, and his eyes took their last glance at the glass dome that rose high above, sheltering the garden from rain and stormy winds. And from the troubles of the outside world.

"Tapa . . . ," Jumar whispered. "Tapa!"

He shook the old man, first gently, then more vigorously.

But he couldn't remember how to do resuscitation, although he must have learned the theory of it in some long-ago lesson from his swimming instructor, but at this moment he realized that lessons in theory can sometimes be pointless.

That morning, Jumar Sander Pratap, crown prince of the kingdom where the highest mountains in the world stand, learned his first lesson in practice: He learned to understand death.

Jumar cried aloud with grief for a long time, pointlessly. The king's ears were closed to his son's pain, just as his heart was closed to everything his son did and thought. But it frightened the pale green lizards in the palace garden, and they all scurried off together into their cracks in the walls.

They didn't venture out again for hours.

By then, the palace garden was abandoned, and so was the palace, although at first no one noticed. It was abandoned by an invisible boy. Only an open side door showed that he had gone away.

The city welcomed Jumar with open arms, but if it sensed his invisible footsteps, it didn't care about either the ancient, noble blood flowing in his veins or his own inexperience. It flung its stench, its dust, its heat, and its colors straight into his face.

Jumar felt its violence, and was pleased.

"I'm free," he whispered into the wind that swept garbage and scraps of paper through the streets. "I'm free. I, Jumar the crown prince of Nepal, am not a prisoner anymore. In fact, I'm freer than anyone else in the world. I can do what I like, I don't have to do anything I don't like, and guess what—I'll never wish to be visible again!"

He took off his gloves and enjoyed feeling air on his fingers.

The pigeons, sensing something that they couldn't see, flew up in surprise. Next came the many temples of Durbar Square, the great open space outside the palace. The scarred, stray dogs asleep in the shade of the temple steps. The beggars. The worshippers. And people, people, people. He had often looked down at them from the windows of the palace, or from its roof, but how different it felt to be right here in the midst of it all! People were pushing and shoving, shouting and laughing, praying and haggling—and whenever any of them collided with Jumar, he enjoyed the bewildered expression on their faces. He climbed the steps of one temple and sat down at the very top of its ancient structure of decaying, dark wooden carvings. From there he could look back into the eyes of the palace, into its windows.

He also saw the three tanks outside it and his father's soldiers, crouched in hidden niches on the second-floor ledges. Their guns had been aimed at the empty air for weeks. Jumar felt cold.

Finally, he cleared his throat and delivered a short speech.

"Right," he said quietly, and the blood sang in his veins with a wonderfully new, disturbing rhythm. "Right, so now everything's going to be different. There you are in your garden, Father, and you have no idea of anything. You just sit there idle, like an old man. And you *are* old, too. You've made yourself old. But I, Jumar Sander Pratap, will not be idle. Not me! I'm going up to the mountains to find the leader of the insurgents, and I'll kill him just the way his men killed old Tapa. I am invisible, and no one knows about me, so it will be easy for me to steal in among them. I have a waterproof backpack from the United States with a top-quality Norwegian flashlight in it, and a fine cashmere blanket. I've packed Indian wax matches, and a Belgian lemonade bottle full of water, and adhesive tape from England, and a bag of Nepalese fruit candies. And I have a box full of money. I've thought of everything. I'll find the dragons, too, and then I'll make sure no one has to starve anymore. Just telling you, Father! I'll find them and defeat them, never mind how. And then you'll have to admit that I'm more than just a stupid child who does his lessons in the palace, and who no one needs to listen to. Then you'll stop denying that I exist. You'll tell people: 'See,' you'll say. 'See what a brave son I have!' And then you can sit in your garden and read a book for all I care—maybe read a book about growing rhododendrons." Here he found himself laughing a little at his own high-flown speech. "And then you'll give me the key, the key to a certain special room, because by the time I get back to Kathmandu, I shall be grown up."

At this point, Jumar Sander Pratap had no idea how right he was.

The pigeons heard his speech with indifference, and went on pecking up the brightly colored rice grains left over from someone's offering to the gods at the foot of the temple pagoda. The dogs yawned and scratched their fleas farther into their coats. And the people went on pushing and shoving each other as they made their way over Durbar Square.

28

No one but an old beggar really listened to Jumar's speech.

"Fine words, resounding words," he said, and Jumar spun around, because he hadn't noticed the old man sitting down beside him. The beggar held a stick between his grazed, bent knees, and seemed too old and fragile to be clambering around on temple pagodas.

"Let me see the face that goes with those words," he said, putting out his hand. Jumar tried to retreat, but the bony brown fingers had found their target already and were moving attentively over his smooth, young skin.

Startled, Jumar sought an explanation in the beggar's eyes. Only when he saw that those eyes were cloudy and white, with no irises, did he realize that the old man was blind. Jumar was as visible as anyone else to him.

"An unmarked face," said the old man, smiling. "So the king with no future has a son whose face bears no marks. I like it when the irony of life is so easily understood."

Jumar jumped up and shook his head, bewildered.

"I don't understand this at all," he said. "May I ask you a stupid question?"

"There's no other kind of question," replied the beggar.

"Can you tell me how to get to the mountains?"

The beggar laughed. "Which mountains, my boy? Which mountains?"

"The ones where the insurgents are hiding out," said Jumar.

The beggar put a thin finger to his lips. "You don't have to say everything out loud in this city," he commented. "And if anyone knew for certain how you could get there, well, much would be improved. But anyone who did know would be living dangerously. If it were me, I'd get on a bus going north. They say the north is already occupied. No police officers go there anymore, and no soldiers. Only the dragons venture into those parts."

A wave of heat passed through Jumar's guts, as if he had chewed a chili pod too quickly.

"Do they really exist, then?" he whispered.

"Do who really exist?" asked the blind beggar. "The police officers or the soldiers?"

"The dragons," whispered Jumar.

The beggar did not reply to that.

And finally, Jumar caught his breath and asked, "Where can I find a bus going north?"

"Why not try the bus station?" suggested the beggar.

Jumar opened his mouth to ask where the bus station was. Why, he thought, had I been taught geography by a private tutor for four years if I don't even know how to find the bus station in my own city? The only bus stations known to Jumar featured in Hollywood movies.

When he climbed down from the temple and asked someone else the way to the bus station, he got only a terrified glance instead of an answer. Finally he squeezed himself into a rickshaw with two women and a lot of baggage, sending up a silent prayer to all the gods of Nepal, and Buddha, and—just to be on the safe side—to the Christian God as well, asking them to make sure that the rickshaw was going to the bus station.

At least one of the gods of those religions heard his prayer.

So on the afternoon of that very day (the day when the pale green lizard scurried over the wall of the palace garden), the crown prince of Nepal was sitting with his knees drawn up in the back of an over-crowded bus, tucked in between a sheep, three large wooden crates, and a woman suckling her baby from her attractively curving breasts, left and right breast in turn, right in front of his interested gaze.

Once—and only because the bus was crammed so extremely full—his bare hand touched the woman's blouse, and its fabric disappeared from view. But only for half a second. After that, Jumar swiftly put his gloves on again, vowing not to take them off again unless he wanted to make something disappear on purpose.

The men in the bus, however, were wondering whether there was anything in the belief that a man could undress a woman with his eyes—even if the trick worked for no more than half a second.

But on that day, a rumor from Kathmandu made its way out into the country, across the terraced green paddy fields of rice, and on up into the mountains. The rumor said that although no one had known it before, the king had a son, and this prince was on his way to his people. And he would change everything that had gone before.

Whispered, murmured, spoken in the shadows, rumors travel faster than the wind, and certainly faster than the rickety buses leaving the city, and so the rumor overtook the invisible crown prince long before he knew anything about it.

It reached the mountains, made itself at home in the villages and in the mud huts and the fields there, and settled down to wait for him in the dust of the alleys. But the rumor had been born with blind, white eyes, and didn't know that the heir to the throne was invisible.

By the time the bus left the constant traffic jams around Kathmandu, Jumar was fast asleep. He woke much, much later when the bus stopped, tires squealing. The woman with the voluptuous breasts was getting out. Jumar pushed the sheep aside so that he could look out of the window. It was night outside, a dark and empty night. In the night, it seemed, you couldn't see the ground. Jumar felt alarmed, but then he realized that he was looking down into a valley: the Kathmandu valley. The bus had stopped on a bend in the road, and Jumar was on his way to the mountains. For the next three hours, the bus edged forward inch by jolting inch. In between jolts, the invisible passenger drifted in a mist between dreaming and waking—he saw his father hovering in the mist, he saw the pavilion in the garden emerge, and his mother's white bed. He saw her sleeping face—but then it turned into the bloodstained face of old Tapa, with his swollen eyes and split lips. Tapa's lips opened as if he were about to say something else, something about the dragons. "And that's not all," he heard Tapa whispering through the mist in his dream. "There's something else you must know . . . Everyone out!"

Jumar woke with a start, but it wasn't Tapa shouting at the passengers to get out of their seats, it was a police officer in a blue-gray uniform. Jumar pushed his way out of the bus with the other passengers, and realized how good it felt to stretch his legs. For the first time in his life, he had been sitting still for a long time in an uncomfortable position.

"Interesting," he remarked to himself. "Very interesting."

The cool night air caressed his cheeks, carrying with it the

33

exciting smells of gasoline, burned rubber, and sheep's dung. The column of vehicles went on and on until far beyond the next curve, and the next moment Jumar saw why they were all waiting in this long line in the middle of nowhere. Ahead of them was one of the checkpoints he'd heard about.

So this was where his father's men looked to see whether there were any Communists in the bus, or anyone taking anything to the Communists, like weapons, papers, or ammunition.

He saw the people standing in line to file past a small table where two more police officers opened their bags and took out the contents. They rummaged around in folded underwear, and seemed annoyed not to find anything. Just watching gave Jumar a bad taste in his mouth, and he was glad when the bus finally drove on and he could get back to where he'd been sitting with the sheep and the crates.

It was time someone did away with these police checkpoints. It was time they were unnecessary. The sheep looked through him with its sad eyes, and nothing at all was reflected in its vertical pupils.

The next morning, Jumar woke up when the sheep, slipping on the smooth floor of the bus, kicked him. He sat up suddenly and rubbed the sleep from his eyes. The bus was almost empty. It had just stopped on the edge of a river valley, and on the other side of that valley, Jumar saw a path winding its way up into the mountains. In fact, he saw only its beginning. A promising beginning, among the lush green of paddy fields and the yellow of flowering trees.

He just managed to jump out of the bus before it drove on again.

That path, Jumar told himself, was the start of his journey. And he tilted his head back to look up at the mountains rising before him, clothed in green by the dense forest, when a strange sensation tugged at his stomach.

"Hunger," said Jumar, and he smiled. He was used to talking to himself, because although until now his life had been simple and sheltered, it had also been lonely. No one likes to spend much time talking to invisible people. And no one seems to like spending much time talking to a crown prince. So you can easily work out how often people talk to invisible crown princes. Particularly if your math lessons have been as strict as Jumar's.

What Jumar's lessons at the palace had not taught him was how to feed yourself if no one serves you a hot meal every five hours, at a table with a view of the garden. There were some wooden stalls at the roadside, where pies were sold. With interest, Jumar watched the flies settling on the pastries, and saw a toddler smearing the contents of his diaper on the floor of a stall right next to where the pastry was made. He gulped and he shooed the flies away, took a pie, and watched it disappear as he touched it. The woman selling the pies, lost in thought, let out a short, sharp scream.

Jumar wasn't used to such reactions, because back in the palace, everyone was accustomed to seeing any inanimate objects that his bare skin touched turn invisible, too. He dropped the pie, and it came into view again. The woman screamed once more.

"Oh, this is just too much," he said out loud, and for the second time, with desperate courage, he picked up the pie. He bit into it, and to his amazement it didn't taste bad at all. He took one of the blue plastic water bottles as well, because after all, Jumar told himself, he was heir to the throne, and he had a certain kind of hereditary right to that bottle of water. Then it occurred to him that he had brought a box full of money from the palace with him, and he put some coins down on the wooden counter.

The woman saw the bottle disappear before her eyes, saw the coins materialize, and was still shaking her head long after the invisible crown prince had gone away. But of course it made no difference to her whether he was there or not.

Unseen, unnoticed, unaccompanied, Jumar set off down

the path to the river valley. He crossed a metal suspension bridge that swayed beneath his feet, crossed the terraced paddy fields where rice grew, and was soon on the way uphill into the forest.

The dense green foliage, the huge leaves and creepers, closed around him like the waves of the sea, and he said, yet again, "Interesting."

Half an hour later, he went behind a bush to do something that even crown princes have to do. On his way back to the path that he had been following before that, something bit his foot.

He gasped in surprise and looked down at his leg. The jaws of a small, strong animal seemed to have closed around it. Jumar tried to tug his foot free, but it was caught. And it hurt. He knelt down and moved the green plants hiding his foot and the little animal aside. There was nothing to be seen. Jumar felt around for a while.

"Interesting," he said for the third time that day. The animal wasn't an animal at all, but a rusty metal structure firmly anchored in the ground with a spring mechanism to work it. He tried to pull its iron jaws apart with his hands, but they wouldn't move. And their tiny teeth dug deeper and deeper into the skin of his ankle.

In his mind, he went through all the useful and international items he had brought in his rucksack: Belgian lemonade bottle. Nepalese fruit candies. A Norwegian flashlight. What he could have used right now was a Swiss Army knife.

"Hey!" he shouted. "Hey! Is there anyone there? Can you hear me?"

There wasn't anyone there.

After a while, Jumar heard footsteps coming along the path. He shouted again, louder and more desperately this time. Before long, the branches parted, and a man with a carrying frame loaded up with crates on his back was staring into Jumar's face.

But he couldn't see Jumar. Of course not. No one could see him. He couldn't even see the trap that had turned invisible once it was in contact with Jumar's skin.

"Please," said Jumar, "get me out of this thing. I walked into it, I don't know how it could happen, but it *did* happen, and now I can't get out on my own."

The man went on staring at him and shook his head. Then he staggered back, turned around and ran for it. Jumar heard things rattling about in the crates on the man's back, and he heard his footsteps dying away as he raced away through the undergrowth again.

Then he heard no more for a long, long time.

And it was a very long time indeed since he had said, "Interesting."

Evergreen
Tropical Forest

· · ✦ · ·

· · ✦ · ·

FLORA

Large-leaved rhododendron (*Rhododendron grande*), tree rhododendron (*Rhododendron arboreum*), epiphitic tree orchid (*Agapetes serpens*), juniper (*Juniper communis*), oak, various tree ferns, giant bamboo, maize, rice grown on terraces

FAUNA

Wild boar, brown bear, lemur monkey, musk ox, mule, common leech, various butterfly genera

CHRISTOPHER
DREAMS

W HO . . . WHO ARE YOU?" CHRISTOPHER gasped. *"Where are you?"*

"My name is Jumar," a voice replied out of the air. "And I would have thought that you just figured out where I am. Hold out your hand."

Christopher hesitated. What would he feel if he obeyed? Scales, fur, claws, teeth? This was a nightmare. It couldn't be real.

"Hold out your hand," the voice repeated rather impatiently. It seemed used to being obeyed.

Christopher felt another hand taking his and guiding it, and the next moment his fingers felt skin, hair . . . a face.

"You see?" asked the voice. It was a silly question, because of course Christopher didn't see anything. "I'm just like you. Only no one can see me."

"Why . . . why not?"

The voice sighed. "No one knows. I was born this way. It has its good points and its bad points. And by the way, I'm the son of the king."

"Oh," said Christopher blankly. "Uh, which king?"

"Well, *the* king!" cried the voice. "Where on earth have you come from if you don't know who the king is?"

"I've come from my room at home," replied Christopher truthfully. "Just now I was sitting on my bed, and then I was here in the jungle."

"You're crazy," said the voice. "But never mind that, so long as you help me. I fell into a trap, a kind of iron thing. I've no idea what kind of animals they catch in it. You'll have to bend the spring open . . . here, can you feel it? It's turned invisible because it's touching my skin. That's one of the other annoying things that happen."

The hand guided Christopher's fingers over rough, rusty iron, and he touched something wet: blood. Christopher flinched back.

"I can't stand seeing blood," he said.

"Great," said Jumar. "You don't. It's invisible,

remember? If you'd pull at this, then I'll pull the other side . . ."

They pulled together at the iron jaws of the trap, working hard, struggling for air together, and finally Christopher felt the pieces of iron moving, inch by inch. "It . . . It's working!" gasped Jumar. "Go on! Go on!"

Christopher narrowed his eyes, gritted his teeth, and pulled as hard as he could. He imagined it was his brother, Arne, in this trap. He braced his legs against the ground and tugged. "Wait," he heard Jumar whispering. "This should do it. A little more . . ."

Christopher felt the bloodstained skin brush against him.

"Now let go," said Jumar. "But carefully, because it will snap shut again."

Christopher obediently withdrew his fingers, and something in front of him gave a metallic click. The next moment, an iron trap was lying on the leaf-strewn ground. When he cautiously touched the interlocking teeth, he felt blood sticking to them—invisible blood. And now he saw the shoe lying beside it. But as soon as he had spotted the shoe, it, too, dissolved into nothing. Nothing was left of it but the soft sound of a buckle on a sandal closing.

His invisible acquaintance had put the shoe back on again.

"Please," said Christopher. "Please explain—does everything you touch turn invisible?"

"Only some inanimate objects," replied Jumar. "Water, for instance, stays the way it was before. Earth and rock, too. It's a question of trial and error. If I walked barefoot, I suppose the dead leaves on the ground here would disappear. But the path would stay where it is. Anyway, I usually wear gloves so that the things I pick up won't vanish. But gloves aren't very practical when you're doing up shoes."

"Interesting," said Christopher.

"Do me a favor," said Jumar, "just don't say that word for a while."

Half an hour later, they were sitting on a rock beside the path together, looking down into the valley through which a river clad in bright blue wound its way.

Actually, Christopher was sitting there on his own. But a voice beside him was telling him an incredible story.

A story about a sleeping woman and a garden under a gigantic glass dome, about dragons who lived in the mountains and ate colors, about a dying servant and a king who had forgotten his country. It would have been a fairy tale if there hadn't been airplanes in it, and doctors, and the crown prince's computer courses, and military tanks.

"So now tell me something about you," said the voice without a name. "I still don't know anything about you. How did you get here?"

You don't know anything about me because you do all the talking yourself, thought Christopher. "My name is Christopher," he said rather stiffly.

"And how did you get here, Cri . . . Cisto . . . Crisho?" asked Jumar.

"Christopher," Christopher put him right, giving himself time to think what to say next.

"Crishnofer. What are you doing here?"

I have no idea, Christopher thought.

He said, "I think I've come looking for my brother, Arne. He's nineteen, and he came to Nepal to work in an orphanage. He does things like that. Everyone likes him."

"Where is he now?"

Christopher sighed. "No one knows for certain," he said. "They think the Maoists have kidnapped him. But no one's sure. He wanted to go walking on his own in the Annapurna region . . . and he didn't come back."

Jumar said nothing for a while. In fact, he said nothing for so long that Christopher began to doubt whether he was real. Perhaps he himself was sitting alone on this rock above this outrageously bright blue river . . .

He put out his hand—and felt another hand take it.

"I'm on my way," said Jumar, "to find the insurgents' camp. And you're on your way to find your brother. So maybe that comes to the same thing. Why don't we travel together?"

Christopher smiled. "Did anyone say we wouldn't be traveling together? I mean, obviously this is a dream, and I'll soon wake up, but while I'm dreaming, I might as well dream along with you."

That was well put, Christopher thought, and it was a pity none of the girls from school had heard him—those girls who always used to spend their days waiting to hear one of Arne's well-turned phrases.

45

The path became steeper, and there were some large stone steps along it. At first, Jumar went ahead, but Christopher kept bumping into him. Being invisible really wasn't so helpful for them.

So Christopher led the way. He heard Jumar's heavy breathing behind him, and sometimes the crack of a twig under his sandals. When the path ran level, they talked to each other. As long as Christopher didn't turn to where Jumar was walking, he could imagine he was on the road with a perfectly normal human being. That felt better than talking to a voice that came out of thin air.

"Where is this insurgents' camp?" asked Christopher. "Do you know the way there? How far is it?"

"Oh, we'll ask the way," said Jumar. "I don't know exactly where it is, of course, and maybe it isn't easy to find. But it's somewhere here in these mountains."

"Ah," said Christopher. "Then it can only be a matter of weeks before we get there."

Maybe it was just as well that he didn't know how true that was.

"Tell me," said Jumar later, "how come you look so . . . well, so normal? Didn't you say you came from the Netherlands or Sweden or somewhere like that?"

"Germany," said Christopher.

"Same thing," said Jumar. "Why aren't you tall and fair-haired?"

"Oh, for goodness' sake! Not all Germans are blond and drink beer in front of the TV around the clock!"

"But you look like the people here," Jumar insisted. "I've often stood at the window watching the tourists crossing Durbar Square. And I've seen lots of your movies. The actors in them are tall and hearty and they move around as elegantly as elephants."

"Oh, really? What about me?"

"You move perfectly normally, I'd say. You're the right

height and size, and your face isn't peculiar. It's the right kind of shape."

Christopher sighed. "Where I come from, they don't see it that way. I had this grandmother, you see. She came from Nepal."

"Is that why you speak our language?"

"*Your* language?" Up to this point Christopher hadn't given it a thought. Was he really speaking Nepali? It felt to him like German.

"It must be something to do with the dream," he muttered, rather confused. "That's all. This is just a dream. I mean, you do sometimes suddenly speak foreign languages in your dreams. It's about time morning came and I woke up."

But morning never came, and the strange workings of Christopher's dream were to grow darker and more disturbing, and the whirlpool of events into which they dragged him down refused to let in the light of an ordinary day.

Far from it. The dream that wasn't a dream grew wilder all the time.

After they had been climbing for what seemed like an eternity, the huge trees, draped in climbing plants, gave way to the view of a high plateau, and a pale green ocean of rice fields stretched out before their eyes. They saw the brown roofs of a village in the distance. A breath of wind passed over the rice plants, and when the blades bowed under the touch of its soft fingers, it was as if the surface of an unusually green sea were rippling. Christopher stopped and listened. He heard the trickling of water, and then there was another sound in the air. He wondered if it was just the wind in the branches of trees in the jungle.

Jumar saw him listening. "What you hear is the irrigation of the fields," he said. "The rice stands in water, and the water runs along channels from field to field. I learned about the system in one of my lessons—"

Christopher put a finger to his lips. "That's not it," he whispered. "Can you hear that other noise? In the air above us?"

"The wind," said Jumar dismissively, his voice wandering past Christopher, out of the forest, and into the paddy fields. "Or the cicadas. You worry too much. Come on! There's a village ahead, and maybe we'll find something to eat there. I'm starving."

Christopher hesitated. The sound in the air seemed to have come closer now. It was like a tiny, angry whisper, a soft rustling, an alarming crackle secretly stealing nearer. In the green of the paddy fields, he saw individual workers who looked like brightly colored dots. Now they, too, straightened up to listen. There was a hissing and fluttering in the air, as if a flock of birds were coming—a huge flock of birds. Hundreds of them, thousands . . .

The wind was stronger now, and all the tiny voices of the forest had fallen silent.

Christopher looked up. There was something like a vague outline high above the treetops that cast a shadow over him. Was it some vast creature moving up there?

Seconds later, he saw the people in the fields begin to run. They were scattering along the narrow paths between the paddy fields and moving toward the village that Christopher had seen in the distance. They stumbled, fell, and struggled up again, and when one of the women, who wore a red blouse, turned around, he thought he saw horror on her face like a mask, distorted and terrifying.

Somewhere inside him, a cold hand closed around his guts.

"Jumar!" called Christopher. "Where are you? Come back!"

But he didn't wait for the answer. He sprinted off, going up the path leading out of the forest, collided with an invisible body, and hauled it back into the shelter of the trees.

Gasping for breath, he stood among the leafy arms of the undergrowth and, with Jumar beside him, stared out at the green expanse of the fields until his eyes were burning.

And his heart was also burning, burning with fear. Fear of the unknown.

And then they saw the shadow on the green surface of the fields. It was moving over them like a gigantic fish, and the blades of rice seemed to shiver at the shadow's touch. Christopher looked up at the sky, but it wasn't blue anymore. Something was blocking it. At first it looked like a colorful cloud, but the cloud had a shape. It had a head and two enormous wings, it had claws and a lashing tail, and now it seemed to be denser than before. It was a dragon.

A dragon like those Jumar had described.

A dragon soaring down from the mountain peaks on brightly colored wings.

A dragon on its way to destroy.

It shimmered as it wound its way through the wind, flew in a curve above the fields, and swiped at the air with huge, flashing claws as if to tear it apart.

"So they do exist," whispered Jumar.

Christopher nodded. The dragons did exist, and here, only a few feet away from him, one of them was displaying its full, gorgeous splendor.

"How beautiful it is," whispered Christopher in surprise. "So beautiful!"

For hidden in the depths of the human mind lies the

conviction that everything bad is ugly and everything good is beautiful, and probably no one will ever find out why we think that way.

The dragon swept over the high plateau and away, and then came down, bending its slender head and graceful neck toward the rice, as if it were about to graze an outsized meadow.

"What . . . what's it doing?" asked Christopher.

"Eating the colors," replied Jumar in a whisper. "Watch!"

And Jumar was right. When the shimmering dragon slowly passed over the fields, it left a black-and-white trail behind it. It was as if everything it touched changed into a clipping from an old-fashioned newspaper printed on cheap, coarse newsprint. The light reflecting off the blades of rice gave way to a dirty pale gray, and the brown wood of the wet irrigation pipes, which had reflected rainbow-colored sunlight here and there only a moment ago, turned to dull black.

"Where are the people?" asked Christopher. "All the people who were in the fields?"

However hard he strained his eyes, he couldn't see the red blouse worn by the woman who had run away, and there was no sign of the other workers in the paddies, either.

"Perhaps they reached their village in time," whispered

Jumar. Everything in Christopher wanted to believe it, but he knew Jumar was wrong. Something had happened to the people, too.

But what?

"And that's not all," old Tapa had warned Jumar. That was how Jumar told the story, anyway. There was something else you had to know about the dragons, something apart from the fact that they ate colors. Something, he thought, to do with human beings.

The dragon was taking its time. Now and then it raised its head, swung its long neck back and forth, and looked at its surroundings. Its eyes were almost the scariest thing about it. They weren't there. Where it ought to have had eyeballs with pupils and irises, there were only dark holes in its head. Everything about it was brightly colored and beautiful, except for those eyes. And yet it seemed to see extremely well. It was as if there were no bottom to the depths of those eyes, as if they went on forever, and everything the dragon saw with them had to disappear into them.

They radiated a sense of suction, and when Christopher saw those eyes, even from a distance, he felt as if he were standing on the edge of an abyss that threatened to swallow him up. He felt for Jumar's hand.

"Do you think it can see us?" he whispered.

"I don't know," Jumar whispered back.

Christopher took a step back, farther into the safety of the trees. Then another step. At the third step, he stepped on a dry twig that broke with a snap. If only the birds had been singing as usual—the thousands upon thousands of birds with their thousands upon thousands of melodies. If only the leaves had been rustling—all those thousands upon thousands of different kinds of leaves. If only the tiny creatures living on the forest floor had been scurrying about as usual with faint scrabbling sounds. Then no one would have heard the twig snap. But the forest was silent. The birds had stopped singing, not one of them raising its voice in song; the leaves were not rustling; the tiny forest creatures were keeping still in their hiding places. A deathly silence had fallen in the evergreen forest.

And in that silence, the snap of the tiny dry twig sounded like a gong. Christopher froze, and he felt the fear of Jumar's hand in his own. The dragon raised its head.

It swung its neck once in an arc, searching the outskirts of the forest. Christopher dared not breathe. He saw the dragon's dark, empty eyes scan across the undergrowth like searchlights, though no light came from them. Instead, they seemed to absorb the light. After an eternity of watching and listening, the dragon began to move. Its movement on the ground was as wonderfully elegant as its flight in the air. It was as if it were flowing through the swaying blades of rice, beautiful and almost weightless. It hardly crushed a single rice plant with its spotless, shimmering, scaly paws. And those spotless paws with their immaculate claws carried the dragon to the outskirts of the forest. There were just two thoughts that repeated in Christopher's mind: Run away. Stay put. Run away. Stay put.

Running away would be noisy. Staying put would be quiet. Running away would be active. Staying put would be passive. Running away would be an attempt to do something—a pointless attempt. Staying put would be pointless, and he wouldn't even have tried anything. He felt Jumar pulling at his hand.

Then the dragon stopped just before it reached the forest.

And Christopher felt that it was looking at him.

Perhaps its empty eyes could see through his. Perhaps they could see right through him and read his thoughts. Perhaps they saw his fear as a bright, pulsating outline. Perhaps they saw his heart beating and the blood pumping violently through his veins. Perhaps they could see the possibility of his death within the next few seconds.

Christopher's mouth was dry and his throat was burning. He wanted to look away from the dragon. He wanted to close his eyes, but he couldn't. The black void had attached itself to him by suction.

After another eternity, the dragon bent its head as if nodding—a greeting?—but it was probably just an involuntary movement of the long, flexible neck. Then it turned suddenly and sank its dragon jaws back into what remained of the green in the paddy field, and it went back to grazing on colors.

Only when Jumar's grasp relaxed did Christopher notice how hard the prince had been clutching his hand. Fear gradually evaporated through every pore in his body, leaving a tingling, empty feeling behind.

And so they stayed there for a long, long time, in the shadow of gigantic jungle leaves: two timid little animals who didn't dare to move out of hiding.

At last, the dragon spread its wings, with a rustling sound like millions of tiny pieces of tissue paper, cast a final look around from the fathomless depths of its black eyes, and hunched its long neck down like a heron's. It was greener now than before.

The claws pushing off from the ground left no marks behind. Christopher watched the dragon rising into the blue sky, soaring higher and higher, and somehow seeming to lose density in a way he couldn't explain.

Finally, it was only a tiny green dot in the afternoon light, green as the paddy fields whose color it had eaten. And then that dot disappeared to the northeast, where the highest peaks of the Himalayas rose, waiting with their frozen, snow-capped summits incredibly far away.

The mountain peaks were waiting for the dragon's return, and for something else, too. But that was only a rumor.

The boys went along the path through the fields in silence.

Behind them lay the green forest; ahead, there was no color at all. The fields glared at them, just expanses of dirty white, and the village rooftops rising in the distance were dull black. Yet the sky was still blue. It looked as if the dragon couldn't harm the sky. It was too far away . . .

Christopher nearly slipped and fell in the water between the rows of rice plants a couple of times, but managed to recover his balance. The water itself was a pale, muddy gray—like the water in a jar where you've been rinsing paint off your paintbrushes.

The rice plants stood motionless and silent like a mere memory of themselves, and the black mud that squelched as it clung to Christopher's sneakers was dull and thick. There was a feeling of desolation in the air that he couldn't explain. It was as if the world mourned for its colors. Christopher looked down at himself. He was wearing a T-shirt with a

Red Hot Chili Peppers logo on it, and blue jeans, and this afternoon his clothes appeared to him the most beautiful and comforting things he had ever seen.

Almost lovingly, he stroked the faded fabric of the T-shirt—and at that moment, he stumbled over something. He swore quietly, although he wasn't very good at swearing (Arne had been better at that), staggered, and held on to Jumar, and the next moment they were both flat on their faces in the gray water. The water should have been refreshingly cold in the hot, sticky air, but it seemed to have lost its temperature, too. It was neither cold nor hot. It was nothing. It didn't even feel particularly wet.

When Christopher struggled to his feet, he was afraid his T-shirt would have lost its color, too, but except for a little mud on it, it was as red as before.

He looked around and suddenly loneliness hit him like a fist, knocking all the life out of him. He stood in the middle of a black-and-white landscape without any joy or life in it, and the only spot of color in this wilderness was himself. He felt terribly alone.

There was no way he could get back to his old life: to his room full of bright posters and wallpaper, where pools of golden October sunlight warmed the floor. He had come to find Arne, but could he do it?

Was it possible? Wasn't he too small, too young, too weak, and too timid?

"Hey, Christopher," said a voice beside him. "What's up? Are you dreaming?"

Christopher smiled. "I'm afraid not," he said. "And I've only just realized . . ."

Warmth slowly came back into his heart. He wasn't alone, even if it looked like it. Here was someone right beside him in the gray water, someone just as young, and just the same size, with no more idea than he had of how things were going to turn out.

"Well, look what you stumbled over!" said Jumar.

"Are you by any chance holding it?"

"Yes. So?"

Christopher sighed. "Then in that case, you'd have to let go of it if you want me to see it."

"Oh."

Jumar let go of what he was holding, and Christopher had a shock, because just for a moment he thought there was someone lying in the water beside him. Then he saw that it wasn't a human being, but a bronze statue. Christopher looked at it, frowning.

"What," he asked slowly, "is a bronze statue doing here?"

"No idea," said Jumar, who had learned, in the course of

the last fourteen years, that it wasn't any good just shrugging his shoulders.

Christopher turned the statue this way and that. It wasn't as heavy as he had expected—it must be hollow inside.

It was the figure of a woman, but there was something wrong with it. The bronze figure wore a simple skirt and blouse, but she didn't have either particularly regular features or a particularly beautiful body—she seemed too *real*. Christopher heaved the statue onto the path and examined it more closely. The woman was shown kneeling, with her face raised to the sky and one arm above her head. She wasn't praying or making any other symbolic gesture: It was a strange position for a statue.

And then he realized that she wasn't really a statue at all.

"Jumar," he said, with a cold, uncomfortable note in his voice. "Did you see that woman who was running away and turned to look back? The woman in the red blouse?"

"No. You were dragging me into the undergrowth."

"Come on," Christopher slowly murmured. "I have a bad feeling about this."

They made their way back from the paddy field and up to the path, and they hadn't gone fifty yards before another fallen bronze statue barred their way. This time, it was a man. He was flat on the ground with his arms over his head as if trying to protect himself from something. But it hadn't done him any good. Right in front of him sat a bronze child, looking as if it, too, had fallen over and was just trying to scramble up. But the child would never stand on two feet again.

It was too late for that.

"They've been turned into bronze," whispered Jumar. "They've all been turned into bronze."

Christopher nodded.

"And now they're hollow inside. Hollow like this whole landscape. There's nothing left of them—no soul, no warmth, just an outer husk. It's like the water that doesn't have any temperature."

"But the bronze isn't black and white," Jumar pointed out. "The dragon wasn't able to feed on the color of these things."

Christopher nodded in silence. It's like a symbol, he wanted to say. A symbol of the people. But he said nothing. Maybe there was an explanation somewhere. Somewhere up there among the mountain peaks where the dragons came from.

They climbed over the two bronze statues lying on the ground, and walked toward the village. Perhaps there was an answer there. Later, people said that on the day when the dragon came, they had seen the tracks of two pairs of shoes, although only one stranger had come walking down that path.

The brown of the huts was a comforting sight for the two young travelers, and the yellow, red, green, and blue of the prayer flags on the rooftops beamed at them like a warm welcome.

Christopher breathed a sigh of relief and glanced back. He saw the dark green leaves of the forest in the distance. The dragon had spared it. This time.

"I never, never want to walk through fields like that again," he said quietly. He had no idea how many such fields, how many forests, and how many mountain slopes, all colorless, still lay ahead of them.

The village seemed deserted, and at first Christopher was afraid all its inhabitants had been in the paddy fields. But then he saw a few children peering around a corner, and something moved in a window. People were still afraid the dragon might come back.

In the middle of the village, there was a house with its doors and window frames painted bright blue, and some lettering had been painted on the white wall. It said:

ELECT TRY CITY HERE.

An enormous white chicken was sitting in front of it,

looking very pleased with herself—as if she personally had written the words.

"Choose a test city here," Jumar translated into Nepalese. He had had lessons with an English tutor, but recently the tutor had decided that it might be safer to leave the country.

"I think the idea is to tell us there's electricity here," said Christopher.

"Hm. Yes, that could be it."

Under ELECT TRY CITY HERE there was more lettering, saying HOT SOUR 24 HOWERS, and Jumar said he thought it meant they sold something hot and sour to eat, but then again it could be offering the use of a shower.

And only then did it dawn on Christopher that they must have come here along the tourist route. He wondered if maybe Arne had been here before them. He wiped his hands, suddenly damp with sweat, on his jeans, and looked around. Maybe Arne had been through this very door. Maybe he had spent the night in this house.

"Let's ask if we can sleep here," he said. "It . . . it's getting dark, and I'm sure it would be better not to go on today . . ."

"Fine by me," said Jumar.

At that moment, the garden gate opened, and a woman carrying a baby peered out from behind a hedge of tall, flowering plants.

"Do you always talk to yourself?" she asked.

"Oh, sometimes," said Jumar, and at the same time Christopher said, "Not often," and the woman smiled uncertainly at him.

"What are you doing here?"

"Looking for a room for the night," explained Jumar, and Christopher realized, rather late in the day, that he would do better to move his own lips when his invisible companion had decided to speak for them both.

"Oh, I have plenty of vacant rooms," said the woman, laughing. "They're all vacant. There've been fewer and fewer tourists for a long time, and none at all have come these last few weeks. You can work out on one finger why. So come on in. It's not expensive."

"Do we have any money?" Christopher asked in a whisper as the woman went ahead through the garden, and then climbed a rickety flight of wooden steps outside the house.

"Don't worry," Jumar whispered back. The woman turned, frowning, but she didn't say anything, and Christopher cleared his throat at great length, as if he had been doing that all the time instead of whispering.

"The—uh—the mountain air," he said. "My throat."

At the top of the steps, the woman stopped on a landing. Christopher counted seven rooms on this floor.

The woman opened the door to the first room, which contained two beds and one window. He looked out, and there before him lay the colorless fields outside the village, as if they wouldn't let him forget them even for a moment.

"Did you see the dragon?" asked the woman quietly.

Christopher nodded, and Jumar said, "No." Christopher tried to kick him, but he only stubbed his foot on the edge of the bed. The woman gave him a funny look.

"It was the first time one of them has come here," she said. "They're venturing farther and farther down from the mountain heights where they live. I was watching the dragon from up here. It was beautiful, but it had such terrible eyes— eyes that seemed to swallow everything up, so dark, so deep. And once a dragon has eaten the color of the rice, its grain won't satisfy anyone. You hear that everywhere. This country is in a bad way. All's far from well with us. Even worse will happen. I sense it in my veins."

The baby in her arms had woken up and it began to cry.

"There, there," the woman told the baby. "You don't know anything about what goes on out there yet, do you? You're all right. They say that anyone who falls under the shadow of the dragons turns to stone. Do you know anything about that? Is it true?"

"No," said Jumar and Christopher at the same moment.

And Christopher felt something congeal inside him. The shadow of the dragons.

What would have happened if he hadn't hauled the invisible heir to the throne of Nepal back into the darkness of the tropical forest? Well, he thought, then Nepal would have been left without an heir to the throne, with nothing but a hollow bronze statue, whether it was invisible or not.

"A woman two villages away was turned into something else. She had the most beautiful garden for miles around, and one day a blue dragon came to eat its colors. It was one of the first dragons to come down from the mountains to these parts. She was just tying up her climbing plants, so I've heard, when the shadow of the dragon fell on her. Then she lay there for forty days and forty nights, like a hollow statue, without a heart or soul. They took the statue out into the fields because it felt so eerie to them. Then the dragon came back to eat the yellow of the corn cobs growing outside the village. And the children watching, at a distance, say they saw its wings brush against the statue as it flew past. When the dragon had gone, the woman stood up and went back to the village and her colorless garden. It looks like the touch of the dragon brought her back to life. But since that day, they say, she just sits in her black-and-white garden and never talks to anyone anymore."

The woman sighed. "Oh, there are too many rumors," she said, "and too many lies. But there's also too much truth. The most dangerous rumors are those that give you hope, because those are the rumors that kill you when the truth is a disappointment. Many say that things will soon change. They say someone will come along and change them. But that's a dangerous rumor, too. They say the king has a son, and no one ever knew about him before. Well, I ask you: How can that be true? How can a king have a son without his people knowing? And even if it *is* true, well, what's this son supposed to do now that the dragons are coming here?"

At this point, Christopher finally found Jumar's foot and stamped on it very heavily, to make him keep his mouth shut.

When the sun set over the flowers in the garden, the boys sat on the kitchen floor with the woman and her three children eating *dhal bhat*. Christopher had read that *dhal bhat* was rice with lentils, but it hadn't said anywhere what it tasted like, which was just as well. He was glad that Jumar was sitting beside him on the faded rug, because Jumar was really hungry, so the mountain of rice gradually disappeared.

Jumar did the talking, too. Christopher thought it would be good to have someone like that next to him in school—

someone who could speak up when he didn't know what to say, someone whose invisible hands would help him out. But then again, when you were playing basketball, the ball would become invisible at Jumar's touch, and that would certainly have been very confusing.

"The rumor you heard about the prince is true," said Jumar, when he had finished off his first helping of *dhal bhat*. "He's here."

"Here?" The little woman looked up from her sewing. "What do you mean?"

"Exactly what I said," replied Jumar, and Christopher imagined him observing the woman's surprised expression with a smile on his invisible face. He began to feel queasy about trying to move his lips in time with Jumar's words. Anyone paying attention would have caught on by now to the trick they were playing.

"You mean . . . ?" She looked Christopher up and down— the faded Red Hot Chili Peppers T-shirt, the jeans, the sneakers—and then tipped her head back and laughed and laughed until tears came to her eyes. Christopher almost laughed, too.

"You don't believe me," said Jumar, sounding hurt.

"Well, it would be difficult to do that," admitted the woman. "You're a nice boy, and I hope you can pay me something for the room, and I don't know what brings you here. But you're certainly not the crown prince who's going to save this country."

"His arms are too thin!" crowed the little girl sitting opposite Christopher. She giggled so much that she choked on her rice and spluttered it all over the table.

"The prince would wear fine clothes," said her brother seriously.

"I can prove it," said Jumar.

The next moment, Christopher felt, to his surprise, a hand taking his and raising it into the air, bending his fingers apart until he was showing the palm of his hand to the woman, as if about to bless her. What is Jumar playing at?

He let go of Christopher, who obediently kept his hand raised, and after a second or so a gold ring appeared in the air in front of it. Christopher stared at it, just as surprised as the woman and her children. The ring was a signet ring, with a big, heavy, and very ornate seal. A little voice at the back of Christopher's head was shouting, "costume jewelry," but although it was not his style, this ring was genuine. At least Christopher thought so.

"It bears the king's crest," he heard Jumar say, and forgot to move his lips. "And there's only one of it."

How does Jumar manage to keep the ring hanging in

the air like that? Why is it visible although he is obviously holding it firmly in place?

The ring floated down to the table in a graceful curve and stayed there.

Hesitantly, the woman put out her hand to touch it—as if she were afraid the metal might be red-hot. Finally, she passed her fingertip over it, looked up, and smiled.

"This is crazy," she said. "This is absolutely crazy. You—you really are the prince. Here I am, sitting in my own kitchen with the king's son!"

"Are you really the king's son?" asked the little girl, staring at Christopher with her mouth open.

No, thought Christopher. I'm nobody. I'm the body that the king's son is borrowing to talk to you. And his lips said, in Jumar's voice, "Yes. I am."

"We've had all kinds of people here," said the boy, who was a little older than his sister. "We had an Englishman who was studying the stars, and a doctor who spent his whole life just curing people's knees. We had a man with fair hair who said his grandmother had come from Nepal. But we've never had a king's son here before."

Christopher almost choked on nothing but the evening air.

"Where did the fair-haired man come from?" he asked in his own voice, and it sounded small and shy and not a bit like

Jumar's. Whatever Jumar said and did, he always seemed 200 percent sure of himself. But the gleam of the gold ring on the table distracted everyone so much that none of them noticed anything odd.

"He came from the country where they had the world football championship," explained the little boy eagerly. "And he played football with me in the garden among the flowers."

The woman smiled. "That German was a nice man. He was still young. He was the last tourist who spent the night here."

"When was he here, and where—where was he going?" asked Christopher quickly. He could sense that Jumar wanted to say something, too, but he wasn't going to let him interrupt.

"Oh, it was some time ago. He was on the usual tour," replied the woman. "Going the way everyone goes, to Poon Hill, where they take photos of the rising sun. From the top of it, you can see all the mountains of the Annapurna massif if the sky's not cloudy." She smiled. "And I hardly need to say that the sky's always cloudy. After that, he was probably going back to the valley. But no one can get to Poon Hill anymore, or take photographs of Poon Hill from the clouds, or climb up there from here. No tourists. *They* would be there. But he said he knew that already, and he had only to pay, after all, the way everyone had done before him. He wouldn't listen when I told him things were different now. And something was starting. Something was ending. And *they* were getting ready."

She was whispering now, as she glanced behind her. It was as if she was afraid that someone could have slipped into the room—someone who mustn't hear those words.

"Up there, at Tatopani where the hot springs flow, they're said to be seen more often than anywhere else. They must have one of their camps around there. My neighbor's son went to join them. His name is Shiva, and he's a good boy. If everything changes . . . If the king is strong again . . . What will happen to those people in the mountains?"

"The Mao—" Jumar began, but the woman put her finger to her lips.

"Hush, hush. Many words are better not spoken aloud. Maybe later, when everything's different. I don't like them, they frighten me with their loud talk and their weapons. But someone like Shiva . . . Would they let a boy like him go again?"

"Don't worry," said Jumar. "You have seen the ring. I am the king's son, and I will make sure that everything ends well. No harm will come to your Shiva."

"Then that's all right," said the woman. "And now you

must sleep, because anyone who's going to change the world, even if he's the son of a king and has powers that I don't understand—well, anyone who's going to change the world needs his sleep."

Her eyes rested on Christopher's T-shirt for a while, then his worn old jeans and his thin body.

"Forgive me," she said. "You're not at all the way I imagined you!"

And Christopher sighed because he had heard people say that too many times in his life.

In the dark, when they were lying in their beds, Christopher asked Jumar about the ring.

"Oh, that's easy," said Jumar, pleased with himself. "I put it on over my glove so that I wasn't touching it directly."

"Wow," said Christopher. "Not a bad idea."

"No," agreed Jumar. "There are plenty of tricks like that."

"If we do find the Maoists—I mean, the insurgents— what are you going to do?"

"We won't find them tomorrow. The mountains are a long way off, and very high. I'll have plenty of time to think about that."

And Christopher thought how odd this invisible boy beside him was. Sometimes he talked like a child, sometimes like one of the old wise men you usually saw on packets of tea. What does Jumar know about the world?

How does he imagine he is going to defeat the rebels?

Does he really think he can impress them with a simple conjuring trick, making a ring appear in the air, or getting something to vanish?

"Christopher," said Jumar softly. "You're thinking about Arne, aren't you?"

"Well . . . ," said Christopher.

"We'll soon find him," said Jumar. "I'm sure we will."

"Mmm," said Christopher.

"Christopher? Are you angry with me for borrowing your body and using my own voice? You're not angry, are you? It's just—more practical this way."

"Mmm."

"Christopher?"

"Mmm."

"What are you thinking about now?"

"Mmm," said Christopher for the last time. "I'm thinking what a long day this has been."

He couldn't bring himself to say what he was really thinking: Their mission was doomed to failure and that they'd better turn back. But Jumar, it was clear to him by now, was not the sort to turn back. Not any more than Arne was.

And Arne had disappeared.

And so Christopher couldn't turn back, either. Not this time.

The darkness was like a cloak wrapped around them both. The cicadas were still singing their songs outside, and thick clouds covered the sky. Christopher pulled the blanket closer around him. How cold it had turned in the night! Had Arne lain in this same bed, and felt the same cold? And where was he now?

Was he cold? Was he hungry or injured? Was he all right? Was he still—but Christopher refused to let himself finish that thought.

From the other side of the room, he heard Jumar's regular breathing coming from an invisible bed. But Christopher couldn't sleep. He was afraid he might dream of the dragon's fathomless eyes. He'd often been afraid of sleep when he was younger.

On such nights he had stolen into Arne's room and got into bed with him, knowing that Arne would put an arm around his little brother.

"You're so close to me now," Arne had whispered, "that you can't dream anything except what I'm dreaming. I'm going to dream of the two of us on the beach together . . . and we'll build the biggest sand castle of all time . . ."

And Christopher had believed him, and everything had been all right.

Later, when he was too old for such things and when he had begun to hate Arne for being so much bigger and stronger and better at everything than he himself—he had had the worst nightmare of all, one he dreamed over and over again. In it, he woke up, made his way along a passage, opened the door of Arne's room—and saw the pale moonlight shining on an empty bed.

Now that dream had come true.

CHRISTOPHER
DISAPPEARS

CHRISTOPHER WOKE UP TO FIND HE wasn't freezing anymore. Yellow light filtered through his closed eyelids, and he tried to lie perfectly still for a moment longer. In the state between sleeping and waking, the no-man's-land between dream and reality, he wished with all his might to see, when he opened his eyes, the edge of his own bed, his desk, his school bag tossed down carelessly in a corner.

And he'd hear Arne singing in the shower, as he liked to do. Arne's disappearance, the invisible prince, the color-eating dragon—all that would have been nothing but a long and bewildering dream.

But then the chirping of the cicadas forced itself into his consciousness, he smelled the smoke of wood fires, he felt the scratchy, woolen blanket he had wrapped around himself, and he had to admit that it had not been a dream.

"Good morning," said Jumar out of the air roughly in the middle of the room. "The sun is shining."

Christopher hid his face in his arms and growled something.

He felt someone pulling the blanket away. It immediately turned invisible.

The sun really was shining. It was hovering on the horizon, large and yellow as an egg yolk just before you stick a fork into it. Christopher realized that he was hungry.

There was *dhal bhat* for breakfast.

He might have known.

The little woman apologized. Such a lack of variety wasn't worthy of a king's son. Christopher managed to swallow a little rice with lentil sauce that tasted of nothing at all.

"You have to eat a lot when you're going to walk for a long time," said Jumar. The little woman nodded, but of course he was talking to his traveling companion. Christopher dipped his spoon dutifully in the rice. The woman was eating with her fingers. When Christopher had a chance, he wanted to ask Jumar how one did that without getting rice all over the floor, but for now he was glad that crown princes were given spoons.

In the garden beyond the blue fence, the flowers turned their faces up to the sun.

On behalf of Jumar, Christopher paid a princely sum for their night's lodging, but the woman looked sad as she took the money. She stood at the garden gate for a long time and watched them walk along the old tourist road that would take them through the village and toward Poon Hill, to the clouds.

The light of the new morning had brought life back to the alleys of the village. Perhaps the people imagined the dragon had been only a nightmare. A goat was standing under the branches of a low-growing tree, nibbling the young shoots. Discordant music from a radio came out of a window. A little boy was rolling a bicycle tire along the uneven road with a stick, and a group of tiny, large-eyed children followed the boy in western clothes for a while. Their own clothes were stiff with dirt, and they were holding on to each other and gurgling happily. It was good to see a tourist in the village again at last, and maybe he'd brought candies or something else with him. A bag was pressed into Christopher's hand out of nowhere, and he handed out brightly colored fruit candies to the children.

A sleepy dog hobbled away on three legs. A rooster crowed, rather late.

You couldn't have wished for a more peaceful morning.

Yet the hollow bronze statues were lying in the fields outside the village, and they would never walk down these alleys in human form again.

Once they were past the village, Christopher and Jumar plunged into the forest again, and the steps started up.

This time they weren't single steps here and there. The whole road was a stairway. An endless, steep, stone stairway. The steps were hacked roughly into the rock and overgrown with moss. They had a slippery gleam in the shade of the trees.

"This is really interesting," said Jumar. "I've never seen such a long stairway before."

After a few more steps, he added, "It's even longer than I thought."

And then he said, "It really is cool to see a stairway like that, but after a while . . ."

"After a while you'd think it might stop," gasped Christopher.

But the stairway didn't stop. Sometimes it pretended it was coming to an end, but that was only a trick. They walked along a level stretch for a little way, turned a corner—and found themselves facing another endless stretch of steps.

Sweat was streaming down Christopher's face, and he felt the blood pulsing in his head. The air was motionless, and now it was as if last night's cold had been an illusion. The mosquitoes liked the smell of the strangers. They came hovering soundlessly out of the shadows, their long legs dangling, as soon as the travelers stopped for a rest. When they settled on Jumar, it looked as if they were settling in the air.

The endless stairway led past a river valley. Sometimes the boys saw the turquoise blue of the water flowing by far below; sometimes they saw snow-covered peaks glinting beyond the tree-covered mountains. Cicadas and birds were competing in the forest to see who could make most noise, and once Christopher saw three gray-bearded monkeys disappearing into the foliage high overhead. Blue butterflies seemed to be looking at their reflections on the edges of puddles; the green leaves of non-flowering tree orchids hung like beards from the forks of branches, and gray lichens drew an intricate pattern on the moldering tree trunks next to outsized fungi. Now and then, they could see a waterfall with the sunlight painting rainbows in its drops.

"Now—now—now I understand," gasped Jumar, reaching a level stretch on the stairway, "what people mean when they talk about a breathtaking landscape."

Too much of Christopher's breath had been taken away for him to answer.

Around midday, they sat down on a particularly tall step in order to rest above another waterfall. In the distance, Christopher saw colorless patches in the forest. Jumar must have seen them, too. But neither of them made any comment about it.

"If I see yet another waterfall," said Christopher, "I'll throw up."

In silence, Jumar handed him the plastic bottle, which had only a little water left in it. When Christopher took it, he noticed that his hand was shaking.

"We've got to eat something," he said. "Anything."

Jumar's backpack, which he had just put down on one of the stone steps, disappeared, and Christopher heard him rummaging around in it.

"Fruit candies," he said, and the plastic bag appeared on Christopher's knees. "That's all we have left. I really brought them for the children. You keep meeting children in this country. But that's all I know about traveling."

Christopher put a lemon candy in his mouth. It had a sour taste, somewhere between shaving cream and nail-polish remover. The people of this country might have the highest mountains in the world, and the bluest rivers, and the most beautiful sunrises, but all of them, he decided, had something the matter with their taste buds.

"Thanks," he said. "I can go a bit farther without eating."

And so they continued an endless upward climb.

Sometimes they thought they were never going to meet another human being. Sometimes they thought they couldn't walk another step. Jumar thought it was interesting to feel exhaustion, and get cramps in his legs, and discover what it felt like when you simply sat down and couldn't get up again. Then Christopher felt for his invisible hand, pulled him up, and made him go on. And when Christopher couldn't go any farther, Jumar did the same for him.

They passed through villages with blue painted doors hanging off their hinges, and notices promising HOT WATER 24 HOURS, although there never was any. Perhaps the hot water had left with the tourists, but it was more likely there never *had* been any.

They saw monkeys and birds on the branches of the trees, creatures that made no attempt to run or fly away. They couldn't. They were made of bronze.

The nights were cold, and in one village they bought heavy woolen jackets, taking turns to carry them in the backpack during the day. When Jumar put his jacket on over his shirt, it looked as if the jacket were hovering through the air by itself, and at first Christopher thought it was useful to be able to see where Jumar was. But in the end, the hovering jacket got on his nerves—you never knew when you might meet some frightened person beyond the next bend in the road, so he asked Jumar to hold the sleeves of the jacket so that it would disappear.

Twice they saw places in the distance where the forest had no color anymore. Christopher tried not to look.

He got used to eating *dhal bhat*, and Jumar got used to Christopher lending him his body when they came to a village and he wanted to talk to the people who lived there. Many of them thought he was crazy when he told them who he was.

But many of them believed him.

The higher they climbed, however, the more often people put a finger to their lips when Jumar told his story. "We haven't seen any king's son," they said. "If you want to stay alive, it's better for you to be nobody, nothing—someone nobody knows."

And then they knew they were on the right track, and Jumar kept his mouth shut.

Five days after they first set out, they had spent the night in Tatopani, the place that the woman had mentioned. Christopher was wearing the prince's long shirt and linen pants now, because in a country where rumors travel so fast, a Western-looking T-shirt could sometimes say who you were without your wanting it to. In the large, empty room where they ate breakfast, the encrusted ketchup bottles and plastic flower arrangements spoke of the past glories of the tourist epoch. Glossy photographs of mountain peaks hung on the walls. Curiously enough, there was also one of a Norwegian fishing port, with the geographically confusing caption HOME SWEET HOME underneath it.

Jumar was in the middle of saying, "Interesting," when the door flew open and a group of men came in. Christopher nodded politely, but the men took no notice of him.

They were wearing green camouflage jackets, and gloves with the fingertips cut off, and they warmed their hands on the stove in the middle of the room. As they did so, they smoked and talked in low voices about something Christopher didn't understand. A large NO SMOKING sign hung over the doorway, but the men didn't seem to care about that—not any more than they bothered about the ashes they dropped on the floor. Christopher shifted uncomfortably on the wooden bench.

"Jumar," he whispered, "we'd better go."

"No," Jumar whispered back. "Wait. I want to hear what they're saying."

And Christopher clearly heard Jumar getting up from the bench.

He looked down at his teacup, as if the men couldn't see him if he wasn't looking at them. The next moment, he heard a chair being pulled up to his table, and when he glanced up, he expected that it would be Jumar coming back. Instead, he was looking into the clear, dark eyes of a young man wearing a red scarf on his head under his cap. His eyes were not unfriendly, but they were hard—hard as stone.

Christopher tried not to notice that the man was leaning on a gun.

"Good morning," he said. His mouth was smiling, but his eyes were not.

"Good morning," replied Christopher. His voice sounded hoarse and cracked.

"Tell me, do you live here?" asked the man.

"Not here, no," said Christopher. "In the next village down the slope. I . . . I'm visiting someone."

The man nodded. "Fine. How old are you?"

"Fourteen." Christopher swallowed. His throat felt really dry.

"And what's your name?"

"Shiva," said Christopher, lying.

"Fine," said the man again. "Tell me, Shiva, would you like to come with us? Fourteen is a good age to learn something new. At fourteen, you have courage and strength. You *are* courageous, Shiva, aren't you?"

"Not . . . not particularly," Christopher admitted.

The man laughed and clapped him on the shoulder. "Think about it, Shiva. We have your own interests in mind. We've already had many courageous boys join us from the village down the slope. They like it with us, and they learn a lot. Wouldn't you like to learn how to use a thing like this?" He lovingly stroked the gleaming black barrel of his gun.

"I . . . I'll think about it," Christopher managed to say.

"We'll think about it, too," said the man. "We'll think about whether or not we can use you. If we can, you'd come and join us, wouldn't you?"

"Sure," replied Christopher. He felt he'd become smaller and smaller on the bench, and he would have liked to merge with it entirely.

"Well then, Shiva," said the man, raising a hand to his cap, "we'll meet again soon. Don't forget to think about us."

He turned back to the others, and Christopher's shoulders were rigid with tension. Then he felt Jumar's hand on his arm, and stood up to follow him outside. He drew the air deep into his lungs—but it wasn't only the cigarette smoke that had made its way inside him. It was fear.

"Just as well we swapped shirts," whispered Jumar. "They're looking for me. Or rather for you. Or both of us."

"They've just tried to recruit me," said Christopher. "It's time we got out of here. And it's time we planned what we're going to do when we find their base camp. Any ideas?"

"Uh . . . no," Jumar admitted. "But I did find out something else. The direct way out of this village is along a broad trail through the forest. And there's been a dragon sitting there since this morning. Those men lost two of their boys when its shadow fell on them."

"Which explains why they need new recruits."

"And why we have to find another route."

"Which route?"

"Apparently there's a secret path that begins at the hot springs. I've no idea exactly where it is, but it exists. We just have to find it."

"I love your optimism," said Christopher, although he didn't feel at all like joking. "So now we're off to find a secret path, we don't know where it begins, and while we're secretly going along it, you'll think up some way for two people to put an army out of commission."

"Exactly," said Jumar.

But something entirely different happened.

It wasn't difficult to find the hot springs that had given this place its name: there were blue-and-white signs that had been put up for tourists, left behind like a peculiar set of footprints. The funny pidgin English on them made Christopher feel sad. They were like possessions left in an abandoned house where the people hadn't had time to pack up.

Christopher wondered if Arne had been this way. He could imagine him setting out in the morning, walking easily along and whistling, blowing his fair hair off his forehead and saying to himself, "Ah, so these are the famous hot springs of Tatopani."

"Ah," said Christopher, "so these are the famous hot springs of Tatopani."

The sun, falling on the boys through the leaves of the forest canopy high above them, painted ornate squiggly shapes on the water of two little basins, and the rocks that rose beyond them glittered in its light. Small channels of water tried to make their way between swaying ferns, and a lethargic spider had caught shimmering drops of water in its web like tiny jewels.

A group of girls was kneeling beside the first basin, wringing the soap out of colored fabrics.

NU ALLOW NUDE FOR SWIM, said a blue notice near

the basins. But it said nothing about washing clothes in the nude. The girls' blouses were so wet that they showed more than they hid, and Christopher stopped and looked at them, fascinated. Then one of them noticed him, and nudged the others. A moment later, they were pushing past him on the narrow path, giggling, and they disappeared around the next bend.

Christopher was weak at the knees as he made his way over to the rocky rim of the basin. His shirt was damp where the last girl's breasts had touched him in passing, and he felt as if the place were burning.

"Don't go falling in the water over a couple of girls," said Jumar.

"Find your own path," Christopher growled.

Feeling slightly dazed, he made his way around the basin to where dozens of tiny waterfalls were cascading down the rock. When he put his hand on the rock itself, it was warm as a human body, as if it were one of the girls he were touching. He couldn't get the sight of them out of his head.

And so he didn't spot it right away.

Or rather, he saw it, but he didn't register it. It was left hanging somewhere, on the way from his eyes to his mind.

"There's no path anywhere here," Jumar said behind him. Christopher turned around.

And then at last the image in his eyes reached the right place in his brain.

He grabbed at where he thought Jumar was and pointed his outstretched arm at the tropical forest, rising green and impassable on the rim of the natural basin.

"There," he whispered.

"The dragon . . . ," Jumar whispered back.

Christopher nodded. In the dark, shady green of the jungle, you hardly saw the great body. It lay there like an enormous cat, eyes closed, apparently asleep. There was nothing colorless near it. It seemed to have come here not to eat but to rest for a while. Or to lie in wait for someone.

The huge body rose and fell in its sleep, and then, very slowly, the dragon opened one eye. A black, empty, fathomless eye. Christopher remembered the dragon in the fields on the outskirts of the forest. He wondered if that dragon had seen them then.

And if this dragon could see them now.

Christopher stepped back, just as he had on the outskirts of the forest. And once again, that was a mistake.

He landed in the water and went under. When he struggled up again, he saw something glittering between the ripples, but could not tell if it was a ray of sunlight or the glitter of a scaly body. He thought he heard a hiss, went under again, and swam as fast as he could. More questions rose in his mind. Had the dragon risen to follow him into the water? What did it want? Was it planning to eat his colors? Turn him into a bronze statue? Where was Jumar?

Christopher tried to come up to the surface, but something was pulling him down, and when he opened his eyes he saw that the water ahead of him was getting darker. He tried to swim against the current coming out of the darkness, but it was too strong. And before he knew what was happening, the dark water seized him with all its power and dragged him into its depths.

The world went black.

There was nothing around him, nothing at all, only darkness and a deafening roar.

Christopher felt cold. He couldn't breathe.

And then—

One Tuesday afternoon the king of Nepal received a man in his garden with a horizontal scar above his right cheekbone.

The man was tall and lean, and he wore a suit without a single crease in it.

It was as if someone had ironed the suit onto his skin.

The man walked down the longest of the gravel paths beside the king, and, from time to time, he flicked an invisible speck of dust off one of his shoulders, because it irritated him not to have epaulettes there. He was used to wearing a uniform, and his uniform, too, was always perfectly pressed. However, this Tuesday afternoon he had come in civilian clothes. That was what the king wanted.

"No one needs to know we've had this little chat," the king said.

The man nodded. His nod was as correct as his upright posture.

Nodding was a European habit, and he had picked it up during his training. People don't nod in Nepal—they move their heads to one side to say yes, as if they couldn't really decide. The man in the suit hated that sideways movement.

"There's something I've been meaning to tell you for a long time," said the king, sighing. They sat down on a bench beneath a cascade of flowers from a flourishing rosebush. "You have been my only close friend over the years, my link to the world, and all the same there's something you don't know."

The man bowed his head, listening attentively.

But first he had something to say himself. He said, "I, on the other hand, am careful to tell you everything that goes on outside, Your Majesty. You know that, I hope. I have heard that there are malicious tongues in the city. But what they say is nonsense. I only wanted you to know that.

The lies are under control. My troops are everywhere they ought to be. It's just a question of time before we get them. We dug out one of their nests last week—a whole village full of them."

"I hope there was no need for too much violence," said the king, looking at his roses.

"Where I am," said the man in the suit, "there is no violence. Where I am there is only discipline."

The king sighed again and waved a hand dismissively. The fragrant petals of the roses rustled.

"I didn't ask you here to talk about that. I asked you to visit me because I have a job for you—a rather unusual job. A job worthy only of a man who leads an army."

"Your Majesty."

"Fourteen years ago," said the king, and you could see how hard it was for him to say these words, "fourteen years ago, when you were still at that training program in America and no one here knew your name, the queen gave me a son. Before she fell asleep. His name is Jumar Sander Pratap, and no one was ever supposed to know he exists, because it is impossible to understand. My son, the heir to the throne of my kingdom, is invisible."

A barely perceptible expression ran over the man's face, which itself looked as if it might have been carefully ironed.

It was difficult to say what that expression was. It was like seeing a breeze blow over a smooth stretch of water and ruffle it into the tiniest of ripples.

The king didn't notice.

"No one knows why he was born invisible," the king went on. "I don't know much about him myself. He was brought up by other people. But those other people were not watchful enough. About a week ago—we know all this only vaguely—Jumar disappeared. He is no longer at the palace. I want you to find him."

"Your Majesty," repeated the man, bowing his head again, "I will track your son down wherever he may be."

And he intended to do just that.

94

Jumar saw Christopher go under, and the water splashing up drenched him from head to foot. Water, curiously enough, did not take on Jumar's invisibility, so a passerby might have seen a strange kind of stain hovering in the air, but as there was no path around the hot springs of Tatopani, there *were* no passersby.

The only other living being was the dragon, which was still lying among the trees a stone's throw away, with one eye lazily open. It blinked, and closed that eye.

Jumar turned back to the water.

"Christopher?" he whispered. But Christopher couldn't hear him. He was somewhere there under the water.

Jumar leaned over the rocky basin and searched for Christopher's shadow. But Christopher's shadow was nowhere to be seen.

Astonished, Jumar picked his way once around the slippery rim of the basin, over to the place where it came up against the rock of the mountain wall. There was no sign of him.

Christopher had vanished completely.

CHRISTOPHER REMEMBERS (AND FORGETS)

I N JUST FIVE DAYS, THE HEIR TO THE throne of Nepal had found out about hunger, thirst, exhaustion, fear, and pain, which was not bad for a cross-section of new experiences. But there was still one experience he hadn't had: total bafflement.

He made up for that when he stood beside the basin of water that morning and his companion didn't come up again. He walked up and down along the side of the basin for exactly fifteen seconds. He clasped his hands behind his back, frowned, and shook his head. Then, at the sixteenth second, he heard a rustling and saw that the dragon had now opened both of its eyes and was beginning to spread its wings.

At this point, he decided it would be a better idea to follow Christopher. He hastily kicked off his borrowed sneakers, stuffed them frantically into his backpack, hoisted the pack on again, and jumped into the water.

Remembering his swimming lessons in the royal pool at home, he swam across the basin with four perfect butterfly strokes. At the fifth stroke, something grabbed him, and he gasped for air in surprise.

This was not a bad move, because what had grabbed him was a strong current coming up from the depths, and for the next few minutes he had no chance of taking a breath. He struggled briefly against the current, but then a voice in his mind said, loud and clear: This current carried Christopher away. Weren't you going to look for him? Then why struggle with it?

Soon after that, Jumar felt himself falling, and there was nothing around him anymore but a deafening rushing sound.

Jumar's arm struck something hard, he cried out, got water in his mouth, and choked, and then there was some kind of impact, but he hadn't fallen to the ground. There was still water everywhere, but now it was carrying him upward. He reached the surface, gasped for air, coughed, spat out water, and struggled in the whirlpool thrashing around him. A strong current was still carrying him, but it was totally dark; he couldn't see an inch of the surface ahead of him.

For a few moments, the rushing sound swelled once more, and even before he could think, he was falling again. As he fell, he began to understand.

He was in the middle of an underground waterfall.

He could not know if this river would ever emerge back into the light of day.

He fought the water pressing him down with its icy fist, flinging him aside, tangling up his arms and legs ruthlessly, until he didn't know where was above and where was below; he fought the water and felt agonizing fear rise in his heart. What he felt around him, and what filled his lungs, was not the water, but the first glimmerings of a possibility.

The possibility that he might die.

He had met Death when old Tapa closed his eyes and died in his arms. But until now it had never occurred to him that he might die himself. His shoulder hit another rock; he screamed and got his mouth full of water yet again. No! he wanted to scream. No, no! I didn't want it to end this way! I'm young, I'm the heir to the throne! Death isn't for me! I still have so much life ahead of me! But the underground river had plans of its own for him. It seemed to have set its heart on teaching Jumar the meaning of fear. Mercilessly, it whirled him around and around the jagged rocks and crippled his strength.

He knew there could be more rocks waiting for him to crash against them. Jumar could already see them in his mind's eye, sharp, angular, pitiless.

And that would be it.

He felt his strength failing and his will ebbing away, like daylight when dusk comes on. He let the water fling him back and forth. It made no difference. There was nothing he could do.

Then he began to get angry.

He hadn't set out on this mission to let some waterfall break his neck! If he really had to die, at least he wanted the cause of death to be a Maoist bullet. His anger gave him strength, and he fought the water more wildly. After a while, he realized that he'd stopped falling. The river was now carrying him straight ahead. Jumar gathered the power of his newfound determination in himself, came up to a surface that promised safety, and gasped for air. The air he was breathing now was musty and stale, moldy and stuffy, yet he felt as if he had never breathed sweeter air in his life.

For a while, he simply let himself drift downstream, breathing deeply in and out.

Then he told himself that every river, even an underground one, must have a bank. Or at least something at the edge of it.

With the last of his strength, Jumar swam across the current and prayed that he wouldn't meet another waterfall. After an eternity, he felt that the water was growing shallower and the river flowed more slowly. Then his hand struck stone, painfully, and he hauled himself up on a rock.

In the distance, he could still hear the rushing of the waterfall.

He lay there motionless for some time, trying to collect his thoughts. He ached in a number of places. His head was throbbing as if part of the waterfall were caught inside it. He found it hard to keep his ideas in the right order, because most of them were whirling around in confusion.

Then one thought forced its way forward, insisted on staying put, and finally let him work out what it meant.

Light.

He needed light.

Jumar sat up, hit his head on another rock, and growled furiously, since none of his many different tutors had taught him any swear words.

Then he extracted himself from the straps of his dripping-wet backpack. After he managed to get the zipper open, his fingers finally found what they were looking for: a large, chunky flashlight with a grooved metal surface. He had found it among old Tapa's things and decided to take it on his journey. He was sure Tapa wouldn't have minded. Now the question was whether the flashlight minded the water.

Jumar sent out a silent prayer to some nameless god, and pushed the switch forward. The nameless god heard him. A wan light came flooding out of the broad head of the flashlight, suddenly transforming the darkness.

Jumar blinked and looked around him.

And then he said, "Interesting."

Christopher opened his eyes to find himself in absolute blackness. He tried to remember what had happened. He was lying on damp gravel, and somewhere near him there was a gurgling that sounded like water flowing by.

A dull, throbbing pain spread through his head.

He remembered. He remembered sunlight.

There was sunlight falling through large, feathery green leaves, painting squiggles on water. What kind of water had it been?

The last thing he remembered seeing clearly was the expression in the hard eyes of the young man with the scarf under his cap and the military jacket. Stony as two marbles, they stared through his memory.

"Shiva," he heard the man say again. "Wouldn't you like to learn how to use a gun?"

He couldn't figure out what had happened then. Had they taken him away with them? But where to? Christopher tried to shake his head so as to escape those eyes. A sharp pain raced through his brain like a rocket and exploded behind his forehead, and he slipped back into the soft cotton wadding of unconsciousness.

Only the splashing of the water penetrated those mists, and another memory emerged from the darkness—a pleasant memory full of light: splashing water in a lake in a flooded gravel pit. One summer.

Arne.

It was as if the Arne he remembered came to his aid, as if he were sending him those golden afternoons so that Christopher's body wouldn't give up in the cold and the dark. The sunlight of that memory, soft and warm, surrounded him.

There he was: Arne by the lake, on the lifeguard's chair, with the girls in their tiny bikinis sunbathing as close as they could get to him—the smell of suntan lotion and cigarette smoke filled the warm air—Christopher himself unnoticed, watching, in the shadow of his brother, content just to watch. And then Arne in the lake, fountains of water shooting up around him.

He tried to focus on what had happened out there in the quiet ultramarine water of the lake in the old gravel pit.

A punctured air mattress. A sinking inflatable raft. A capsized rubber dinghy. A cramp in a girl's slender foot. Whatever it was, Arne would come to the rescue.

It was a good thing he had aced the course he took in first aid! So many young ladies had near-death experiences in his arms, and urgently needed the kiss of life . . .

Christopher's memory faded. Back came the pain in his head. He felt himself shaking. He wished he were back with Arne by the lake in the old gravel pit, back on one of those long summer afternoons, but something brought him abruptly back to reality. It was as if someone were calling his name from very far away.

The beam of Jumar's flashlight fell on an underground landscape of curiously shaped rocks. There was a kind of stone hall above the river, although its roof was too far off for the light to reach it. Where it came lower, armies of stalactites hung from it, and Jumar instinctively shrank back close to the wall. It was as if someone had pinned their sharp points in place, intending them to fall on an unfortunate passerby, and in the unsteady beam of the old flashlight, it seemed to him as if they were moving, shifting slightly, coming closer to him . . .

"Echo?" called Jumar experimentally.

"Co-oo-oo," the sound echoed back from the walls.

"Christopher?" asked Jumar.

"Opher-opher-opher," the echo whispered. There was something harsh and sarcastic about its whispering—an undertone of malice—and Jumar narrowed his eyes and stared fiercely in its direction. But the echo was nowhere you could stare fiercely at it. It wasn't impressed.

He let the beam of the flashlight slide over the water of the river. It lay smooth and leaden here, moving past him like a lazy snake. A damp, gleaming rocky landscape reached along the bank before Jumar's eyes.

Time had smoothed the edges of the rocks, as if they had been lovingly shaped by a potter. Slender stalagmites also grew from the floor of the cave, and Jumar wondered if he had those names the right way around, but he couldn't remember.

Perhaps the light of Jumar's flashlight was the first ever to fall on that rocky landscape. It seemed to welcome the light. Shining like mother-of-pearl, and smooth as silk, the natural interior of the cave could be seen in the beam, enjoying its own newly discovered beauty, giving itself up to a whole dimension of unreality.

It was the kind of landscape that makes some feel an urgent wish to write poetry. Others might be inspired to pick up paintbrush and canvas, capturing the underground scene in plenty of pink paint to represent the unspeakably lovely light.

Jumar swallowed and cleared his throat to get rid of the taste of that beauty, because something just didn't feel quite right. The echo cleared its throat, too; it sounded like a menacing chuckle multiplying itself a million times, as if the crevices and shadows among the rocks were all full of tiny creatures with sharp teeth.

"We'll see about that," Jumar said out loud. "We'll see who can scare the crown prince of Nepal."

He was forgetting that the river had already done just that.

Remembering that the rock on which he had climbed was near the bank, Jumar deduced that Christopher must have crawled to land somewhere, as he had, but farther downstream.

Jumar began clambering over the smooth rocks, and held on to the stalactites and stalagmites. They left his fingers feeling slimy, perhaps from the tiny algae stoically ignoring the absence of light, or perhaps it was just his imagination. More than once, Jumar jumped in alarm, flinched back against the wall, and switched off the flashlight, thinking he had seen a shadow move. Then he heard his own labored breathing at unnatural volume in the silence, and it was some time before it struck him that there wasn't anyone else there.

105

Jumar would have liked to sing. Singing is a help in the dark, warding off the fear and loneliness. Oddly enough, he had spent his whole life on his own, without ever having a friend, and he had never felt lonely. Now that he knew Christopher, and Christopher wasn't with him anymore, he had a hollow space inside him, and it hurt.

But Jumar didn't sing, because the echo was lurking in the corners, just waiting to distort any tune he sang. In silence, Jumar made his way along the slippery bank of the river, silent as the rock itself. Only the river whispered something to him that he didn't understand.

He wondered what the river had done to Christopher. He wondered where he was.

The beam of the flashlight just proved his absence.

After a while, Jumar lost all sense of time. He had no idea how long he had been down there. An hour? Two hours? A day? And then a new worry made its way into his heart: What if he missed seeing Christopher somewhere? Suppose the pale beam of the flashlight hadn't been strong enough to light up every nook and cranny of the craggy bank on the other side of the river? Suppose Christopher had fallen asleep and hadn't seen his flashlight?

He stopped and considered turning back.

At that moment, he heard the voices. Genuine human

voices, distorted by the effect of the echo. They were behind him, and they were coming closer.

Jumar switched off the flashlight and retreated near the wall of the cave so that whoever was coming wouldn't stumble over him.

One thing he knew: It wasn't Christopher.

These were men's voices, deep and guttural, and there were several of them.

Jumar hoped they hadn't seen his light. He stood perfectly still. The beam of a stronger flashlight than his came closer, dancing up and down through the blackness. Now he could make out what they were saying. Scraps of words reached him and became more distinct:

". . . told him it wasn't a good idea, taking them there today. What's the use of blindfolding them down here? Who are they going to tell, and when? It's ridiculous. Anyway, we should have left them where they were, still able to see, but where there was nothing to be seen . . . Yesterday a whole crowd of soldiers was there, coming from the southern slopes. Who knows where they are today? They could be right above our heads."

"Maybe that's the very reason why he wanted it done today. Prakash is a wily fox. He knows what will happen to him if anything goes wrong, believe you me. The Great T.

is keeping an eye on him. He doesn't make a character like Prakash his right-hand man for nothing."

The shadows of the men stole around the rocky ledge, and Jumar blinked in the bright light. There must be five or six of them.

He saw their cartridge belts glinting. He saw the guns on their backs and their green camouflage jackets. There was something else, too. The three in the middle didn't look like the others. And before he knew it, they had passed and were gone again.

Three of them hadn't belonged with the others. He stared after them in the darkness.

Three of them had been wearing blindfolds—cheap, brightly colored scarves tied tightly to hide their eyes.

Three of them were holding a rope so as not to lose their footing.

Three of them were taller and moved differently, more clumsily—and not just because they couldn't see the way they were going. They were European. And now Jumar understood who "they" were—the people being "taken" somewhere.

One of them, bringing up the rear, had pale blond hair. Jumar saw it in the light.

He thought of Christopher's words.

"And then he disappeared. Everyone liked him."

Arne. Wasn't that his name?

Jumar began moving quietly, following the little group. His footsteps were inaudible, and he was straining his ears.

"Why would I care what happens to that dog Prakash?" cried one of the men.

"Keep your voice down!"

"Who's going to hear me down here? It's true. We're the ones who have to believe in it in the end."

"It's all the same to me."

Only a rocky ledge separated Jumar from them now.

"I had a wife and two daughters," said the man who had spoken last. "The army found out that I was in the mountains—and there's nothing left of my family that you'd want to look at. I have no house to go back to. They burned it down to its foundations. I could still smell blood in the ashes. One of these days, they'll catch me, and I'll laugh at them. I'm not afraid of anyone."

Jumar felt a shiver run down his spine. He didn't understand any of what he had heard, but the hatred in the man's voice stung his heart.

"There!" one of the men said. "Wait! Here—there's something here! Well, I'll be damned if it's not someone lying over there!"

The beam of the flashlight shone on the ground.

"A boy," said the man with the flashlight, surprised. "How did he get here?"

"Is he one of us?" asked the man bringing up the rear.

"I don't think so. Wrong sort of clothes. Although you never know . . ."

Jumar felt something inside him, in a place in between his diaphragm and his liver, go hot and cold, and he didn't know whether to feel glad or afraid.

"Is he still alive?" asked the man at the back.

"I don't know," said the man with the flashlight. Jumar could bear it no longer. He stole around the group. Then he saw Christopher's face.

The man pushed him with his boot, and he moved—only a little. But he was alive. Alive!

"Unconscious. We'd better take him with us," said one of the men. "*If* he's one of us . . ."

"What if he isn't?"

"We can't leave him lying down here! He must be injured—he's fourteen at the most!"

"What difference does that make?"

"For heaven's sake, he's soaked through. Look at him! The river spat him out! He must have been caught in the whirlpool up there."

"That means he's *not* one of us. He's here by chance."

"And that means if he comes back to his senses and finds the way out, he'll tell people about the whirlpool."

"Which means, yes, we have to take him with us."

"Are you going to carry him?"

"He'll never make it anyway. Look at him. He's as good as dead already. He won't get out of here."

"We can't be sure of that."

Jumar saw the two men who were now kneeling beside Christopher look at each other.

"Can't we?" asked one of them, unslinging the gun from his shoulder. He looked at it for a moment, then undid the safety catch and took aim at the body lying on the ground.

Then he screamed.

He screamed in horror, as only a guerrilla fighter can scream when meeting a ghost in the dark beside an underground river.

"There!" he cried. "There was something there! Something grabbed my arm just when I was going to pull the trigger! Don't stare at me like that! I tell you, something grabbed hold of me!"

The others looked at him incredulously.

But then the second man cried, "It touched me, too!" And then the third man felt a soft touch on his cheek. The touch of an invisible hand.

III

"There's something weird going on!" he cried. "That boy lying there is bait! He's not human!"

And then the three men were in a great haste to leave the place where they had met a ghost.

Only the three foreigners were wondering what on earth had happened as the fighters hurried them away.

Later, news of the ghosts by the underground river spread among the guerrillas in the mountains faster than tuberculosis, and almost as fast as Death. And from then on, many of them swore that on a clear day, they could hear the ghosts singing far away underground.

Jumar knelt down beside the body and switched on his flashlight.

It lit up a familiar face, surrounded by damp black hair that fell back to reveal a bad cut on the forehead.

Christopher was lying so still! His chest rose and fell, but his eyes stayed shut. Jumar spoke his name, first whispering, then shouting it. He switched off the flashlight and said nothing for a long time. He sat on the ground beside Christopher, feeling cold and trying to come up with an idea in the darkness. He had to think about what to do next.

What if Christopher never woke up? What if he stopped

breathing? Jumar's throat felt hot. He swallowed and swallowed, but he couldn't swallow his fear.

Finally, he switched on the flashlight again and grabbed the heavy, limp body by the armpits to raise it. He couldn't leave Christopher here, whatever happened. He would find daylight. If Christopher really was going to stop breathing, he must see the light of day again first.

He slung Christopher over his shoulders like a dead animal and started on a long, laborious walk into the unknown, the river rushing along beside him.

He had never felt so lonely in his life as he walked on.

At one point, Jumar thought his burden moved slightly, only a little, hardly perceptibly.

"Christopher?" Jumar asked the body.

He put him down on the ground, and then, at last, Christopher did open his eyes. He looked bewildered, as if he were searching for something where there was nothing in the dark behind Jumar.

And then he said, very quietly, "Could you stop shining that flashlight in my eyes?"

The first thing Christopher took in was light. There was light, light in the darkness, and there was a voice beside him, and then he was fully conscious again.

"Jumar?" he whispered. "What happened? Where are we?"

"A long way underground," Jumar replied. "I jumped in after you. It was all I could do."

"Jumped in . . . after me?" asked Christopher. "Where?"

"Don't you remember?"

"I'm afraid not. Oh, damn it. The last thing I remember is sitting at that table with the vase of plastic flowers, and one of the Maoists trying to recruit me."

Jumar was quiet, thinking. Then Christopher felt an invisible hand swipe the hair back from his forehead.

"That's a nasty injury," he said. "Concussion, if you ask me. Retrograde amnesia."

"Retro what?"

114

Christopher sat up with difficulty. The world seemed to be going around and around. And what a strange world it was! It seemed to consist entirely of fabric, endless lengths of fabric weaving complicated patterns in the darkness. Or no, it wasn't fabric. It was rocks.

"Retrograde amnesia. We've had so many doctors at the palace over the years, because of my mother, that I'm practically a walking medical dictionary. Retrograde amnesia means you can't remember something."

"So what do you do about it?"

"You ask someone else what happened."

Christopher could hear the smile in Jumar's voice. "There was that dragon . . . and you fell into the basin of water. I mean, because of the dragon . . . and then you fell down an underground waterfall—well, two of them, to be precise. I followed you."

"Are you . . . Are you sure you're not the one who got hit on the head? It sounds a little crazy."

Jumar sighed. "Can you stand up?"

As he helped Christopher to his feet, he said, "Oh, and there's news. Good news and bad news."

The world around Christopher slowly stopped turning. "Yes?"

"The good news is: There's a way out of here. The bad news is that I know about it from them: the Mao—the insurgents. They're somewhere ahead of us. This is obviously their secret path. Only we found it. They must have climbed back into daylight somewhere, and so will we."

"How many were there?"

"Three. And they seemed to be in a hurry. Don't worry, they must be some way ahead of us by now."

"Did you hear why they were in a hurry?"

Christopher thought that Jumar seemed to hesitate, just for a tiny moment.

"No," he said then. "They weren't talking much as they went along."

◆ ◆ ◆

Jumar and Christopher walked along the bank in silence. Sometimes Christopher leaned on his invisible companion, although Jumar's feet kept getting in the way. After a while, his dizziness began to fade.

"I wish I knew how long this path was," he whispered. "That would make it easier."

They walked for hours. Now and then, they stopped for a few minutes' rest, but whenever they did, they soon felt freezing cold.

A time came when Christopher felt very weak, and he wondered, almost angrily, whether Jumar ever got tired himself. He thought about falling to the ground and not getting up again! His stomach was rumbling, and his head had begun to throb.

"Could we stop and rest for just a little longer?" he finally asked. "I don't mind if I get cold."

"I'm so glad you said that," whispered Jumar. "I've been feeling I can't go on anymore for quite some time. But I didn't want to be the first to give up."

That made Christopher laugh.

They sat down side by side on a big rock. At least it wasn't wet, and Jumar switched off the flashlight to save the battery. They sat there in the darkness for a long time and listened to each other's breathing.

"I still have those fruit candies," Jumar said. "We have to eat something or we'll never make it out of here."

"Oh, please!" groaned Christopher. "Not those again!"

But his stomach contracted painfully at the thought of food, so he put the sticky lump that Jumar handed him into his mouth. In some mysterious way, the flavor had improved, and he crunched the candy gratefully.

"You know something?" said Jumar after a while. "When all this is over, he'll give me the key."

"Give you what key?" Christopher scraped a piece of the candy out of one molar with his fingernail.

"The key to the room in the palace that's opened only once a year," said Jumar. "Or maybe he opens it in secret. I think he does."

"What are you talking about?"

"Didn't you ever hear of it?"

"No."

"There's a room with a single table in it, and a small ornate box standing on the table. It's covered with gold and decorated with silver."

"About as tasteful as that signet ring, then," remarked Christopher.

"What?"

"Nothing. Go on."

"The lid of the box is set with diamonds and rubies, and it's very, very old. There's a copy in the museum in Kathmandu, but it's only a copy, like I said. The real one is in that locked room. The room is on the third floor, at the very end of a long corridor. All you can see through the keyhole is blackness, because there is no window. There's no window so no one can get in from outside and try to steal the box. Every New Year, there's a procession. The king is in it, with a whole troop of his soldiers, and the special box is carried through the streets in a kind of litter with drapes. The people scatter colored grains of rice and flowers as the procession passes by, and if anyone catches a glimpse of part of the box shining through the drapes of the litter, they say that person will have a lucky year."

"But what . . . What's *in* the box?" asked Christopher.

Jumar's voice turned solemn, and even the echo seemed to be silenced when he said, "The power of the royal house."

"The power? How can power be inside a fancy box?"

"I don't know," replied Jumar. "But when I get back, he'll have to give me the key. I'm sure of it. Because then everything will be different. And I will take the power, and defeat the dragons, and give the fields their colors back. I'll put an end to starvation and hatred among the people, the way all the great kings have done. Until my father withdrew into his garden."

There was silence between them for a while, and all you could hear was the mysterious sound of the river flowing.

"You believe that?" asked Christopher at last. "You believe there's something that fits inside a box and can do all those things? What kind of thing would it be?"

"Maybe a magic weapon?" whispered Jumar. "Or a book? Or maybe it's something invisible, like me."

Christopher sighed. "There are too many fairy tales in this country."

"There are color dragons in this country," said Jumar gravely. "And human beings who get turned into bronze statues."

Christopher didn't know what to say to that, and they fell silent once more.

Maybe it was all just as this strange boy said. Maybe there really was a secret power in a locked room that could put everything right. He hoped so.

Because if there were going to be changes, that power was urgently needed.

They must have dropped off to sleep, because when Christopher woke up, he was frozen stiff and could hardly move.

"I don't think I've ever, ever been so cold," he said, shaking Jumar awake.

"I was dreaming . . ." Jumar murmured. "Dreaming of

glaciers . . . and snow . . . It was so white, Christopher! So white that you couldn't look at it. We climbed up a path, blinded by the dazzle, right up above the clouds . . ."

"You'd better wake up and come with me," said Christopher. "If we stay here any longer, you'll never see any snow."

He sneezed, and they set off again.

The flashlight batteries were getting weaker. Jumar switched it on now only when they couldn't find their way by feel. And then the bank came to an end. It simply stopped.

Christopher stood on the last rock, shivering, and looked around. "We'll have to swim," he said.

"I don't think *they* swam," said Jumar. "They knew their way around here. There has to be a way out somewhere or—"

He went no further because, at that moment, a bang broke through the air. Christopher jumped. Another bang followed, and then another. Jumar switched off the flashlight.

"Shots," he whispered.

The echo played with the sound, threw it back and forth between the walls, split it up, multiplied it again and again. It was impossible to say where it first came from.

Then a fourth shot rang out, and this time Christopher felt as if the sound were coming down from above. He tipped his head back.

"Jumar," he whispered. "Look. Look up there."

Just above them, far, far above, there was a circular patch with bright dots in it. But they weren't dots. Christopher smiled. They were stars.

"*There's* the way out," he said. "It's night outside."

And now all was still.

Jumar let the beam of the flashlight slide along the wall. Above them, the roof narrowed to a kind of rock chimney, and then they saw the stairway, too. Someone had carved a flight of rough-hewn steps in the rock.

Christopher went up first. He held on to the ledges jutting out from the rock wall, and was careful not to look down.

"Arne could do this kind of thing," he said. "There was this cool gym near us, and he was always climbing the artificial rock wall there. He took me with him once, but I was too scared to try it. I just stood and watched him."

"You're getting in some practice now, then," said Jumar.

The steps came to an end where the narrow rock chimney began.

"Now what?" asked Jumar.

"Did you sometimes climb door frames when you were little?"

"Door frames? No, never."

"Well, maybe palaces don't have that kind of door frame. But where I come from you can climb them. You push off with your bottom from behind, you brace your legs against either side of the frame, and you slowly work your way up."

"Aren't you afraid of that, then?"

"Afraid of a door frame?" Christopher snorted with laughter. Then he looked up, and the starlight above him seemed endlessly far away, while a fall of many feet lay below.

"Show me," Jumar asked. "Show me how to climb a door frame."

"Okay, then," said Christopher.

And he began working his way up the chimney through the rock, bit by bit.

"It's . . . it's really easy," he said. "You don't . . . You don't have to feel scared."

He closed his eyes and saw before him the kitchen at home. He was six again, and Arne was standing at the stove making pancakes and singing to himself, and the sound of the wind in the branches of the trees in the garden came in from outside. Arne turned around and gave him a wide grin. "Watch out! Mind you don't push that door frame apart climbing it," he said. "Or the door won't fit properly, and we'll have to roll it out with the rolling pin to make it wider."

And six-year-old Christopher laughed. All was well with the world.

Then Arne turned back to the pan, and when he turned

around again, he wasn't Arne anymore. Christopher started in alarm. The man now standing at the stove had dark eyes, hard as granite, and he wore a military cap over his head-scarf.

Christopher opened his eyes.

Above him, he felt the night wind blowing. He pushed off from the rock wall with his feet one last time and sat on the stone rim of a well. He heard Jumar breathing heavily as he hauled himself up.

His memories had brought him up through the rock chimney into the starlight.

The night air felt almost warm to Christopher, compared with the damp chill down underground. He sat there for a moment, still dazed. Black silhouettes of huts rose all around him. The boys had come out in the middle of a village.

When Christopher swung his legs over the rim of the well, he stepped on something soft and yielding, and cried out.

"Jumar," he whispered. "Jumar, hand me the flashlight."

The weak beam of light fell on the outstretched body of a man lying lifeless beside the well, facedown. It was warm, but it didn't move. Christopher thought of the shots. Everything in him fought against the idea of touching the body lying there at his feet. When they were children, he and Arne had once found a dead cat lying in the road in front of their house. Arne had picked it up and carried it to the roadside, but

Christopher had just stood there as if his feet had rooted him to the ground. Now he finally forced himself to kneel down and roll the body aside.

The last faint beam of the flashlight fell on a face staring up at Christopher, eyes open wide. But those eyes saw nothing now. They were cold and dull. The head-scarf holding back the dark hair had slipped off, the man had lost his cap, and his gun and cartridge belt had been taken from him.

His clothes were dark with blood. Blood that was now also sticking to Christopher's hands.

Christopher felt for a pulse, couldn't find one, and stood up. He felt dizzy again. He staggered a few steps away and threw up.

On the night when the shots rang out, a stranger came to the village below the steep slope.

There was blood on his hands, and what he said was all confused.

Sometimes the sound of his voice changed, barely perceptibly, as if he had not one but two tongues, but later no one could be quite sure of that.

The stranger was young and wore expensive clothes, but they were ragged now, and there was an open wound on his forehead. He knocked on the door of the last house in the village just before midnight. At first the people inside were scared and didn't want to open it. The shots had woken them, and they hadn't gone back to bed. They were sitting in the kitchen around the open fire, taking turns putting fuel on the flames, and making soup.

There were twelve of them, all related to each other in various ways, young and old, a blind old lady, and a tiny baby. In just two months of life, the baby had learned that when you heard shots in the distance, it was better to keep quiet and not to cry.

The baby's father looked out of the little window beside the door.

"It's a boy," he murmured. "Not much more than fourteen years old, I'd say. He doesn't look like one of them. And he's frightened."

So they let the stranger in, and when they saw that his clothes were wet, they found others for him, and hung his own up to dry.

"Where do you come from?" the man asked the boy.

"Up from the well," he said. "And there's a dead man with stony eyes lying beside it—"

Then he was shaken by a coughing fit, as if he had been out in the cold too long, and they knew he was talking wildly in a fever. They found him a place to lie down beside the fire and gave him some soup. Later, the old lady, who had lost her eyesight and heard only noises, would insist that there had been two boys there, keeping close together and sharing the soup. But there's no point in listening to what old people say.

That night by the fire, Christopher and Jumar heard a fairy tale that they would remember for a long time. It was told by the blind lady. Her spidery fingers wandered unsteadily through the air as she told the story, and the shadows of her movements drew shapes on the mud wall of the low-roofed room.

Christopher was clutching the metal bowl of soup in both hands, and he was sorry he couldn't let Jumar hold it, because Jumar had taken off his gloves along with the rest of his wet clothes. And when no one was looking, the clothes had appeared beside the fire with Christopher's—as if they had hung themselves up. A blanket had disappeared, unnoticed; Jumar must have put it around his bare shoulders.

There were thin noodles in the soup, like threads that could be spun into stories.

Christopher saw large supplies of brightly printed plastic packets on a rather rickety shelf, and with some surprise he saw the word RAMEN.

The soup was the best thing he'd tasted since arriving

in such a surprising way in this surprising country, and he wondered how on earth these instant noodles had found their way up into these lonely mountains.

Well, they *had*, anyway, and that was what mattered.

"When no one can sleep, it's time to tell stories," the old woman whispered hoarsely. "No one can listen for shots while a story's being told. Once upon a time, a long time ago . . ." Her fingers twined together as she thought. "A long time ago, when fairy tales were still true, and even I had not been born, there was a beautiful princess in a faraway land. She was so lovely that the mountains trembled when she went walking on their slopes, and the cicadas fell silent at the sight of her. So lovely that the court poets had no words for her beauty, and the musicians all ran away because, compared to her beauty, the most wonderful of their songs sounded ugly and ordinary, like the crunching of cartwheels on sand. All the birds of the kingdom sang about her grace. And it was also the birds who brought the fame of the king's daughter into the mountains, far up to the heights where no one lives and no one dares to go. It surprised the birds to find a traveler there, and they sang their song of the princess to him with special care, because he looked so lost and lonely."

Christopher saw the clothes by the stove disappearing for a moment—just like a flicker in the air, something imaginary, an optical illusion. Jumar had better be careful, thought Christopher. Sooner or later, someone was going to notice something odd. And then rumors would reach the villages ahead of them, or follow them, or walk beside them and circle them like a pack of hungry dogs. You never knew what rumor could do . . .

"The traveler listened to their song," the old lady went on, and for a moment Christopher was confused and thought of singing rumors. But no, she meant birds. "And the following night, he dreamed of the princess. She was walking in the distance and didn't see him, but when he woke in the morning, he told the birds what he had decided to do. He would go down into the valley so that for once, just once, he could see the princess with his own eyes. The birds tried to warn him. Because the princess was a princess, and it's not so easy to get to see a princess with your own eyes. But the lonely traveler wasn't going to change his mind. He walked for many, many weeks, until he reached the princess's city, and on the way he dreamed of her daily. She was always passing by in the distance, and never showed him her face. When the wanderer reached the city, he could hardly believe his luck, because there was going to be a festival there that very day, with a great procession going through the streets. And the princess would be carried in a litter in the middle of the procession. Because the king wanted to get the princess married soon, the procession would be a perfect way to mark the beginning of the week when he intended to choose the right husband for her from among all her suitors. Those musicians who hadn't run away played a march, and the people lining the roads rejoiced. But the traveler saw nothing of the princess, because the drapes of her litter hid her from prying eyes."

Or maybe, thought Christopher, she was invisible. The clothes by the stove had disappeared now, but the blanket was back, neatly folded in a distant corner of the room. If Jumar kept this up, Christopher's nerves weren't going to stand up to the rest of their journey.

"However, the traveler fought his way through the crowd," whispered the old lady. "Aha! He fought his way to the very front of it, slipped past the soldiers escorting the procession, and put out his hand to touch the drapes. The princess looked at him for a moment, and her beauty was greater than he had imagined.

"But the princess saw only a man in shabby clothes, with tousled hair, and she called for the soldiers. Before the traveler could say a word, they had seized him and hauled him away roughly. He fell to the ground, and the next moment he found himself alone in a ditch beside the road, while the procession with its bright colors and its music disappeared into the distance.

"Then the traveler was very sad. In the night, he stole his way into the palace garden and climbed the wall, and there he turned himself into a weeping willow that put down roots in the fragrant soil between the flower beds. When the princess was sitting in the shade of the tree next day, she felt the traveler's grief, and began weeping bitterly, without knowing why. She couldn't stop shedding tears and more tears. When people asked why she was crying, she couldn't tell them. She cried day and night. And in the end, her father had to send all the suitors home again. Meanwhile, the princess went on shedding tears. No one could explain how she could shed so many. She wept until the city streets were full of water, and people began poling boats from door to door. And even then, she didn't stop crying. She wept until the water came up to the doors and windows, until people had to climb on the rooftops to save themselves, and finally the whole country was under the water of her tears. Today, there is a sea where that country once was, a sea of salt tears. Some say that the people of the country turned into fish, but I'm afraid that's not true. They all drowned miserably. There is just one lonely island in the middle of that sea, and a single lonely weeping willow grows on it. And the men who sail past the island say that on still days you can hear it sighing like a human being."

The old lady fell silent and nodded her head thoughtfully back and forth.

"What a sad story," said Jumar. "Why does it have to end unhappily?"

"Aha! All fairy tales end unhappily," the old lady explained, with a certain satisfaction. "Only people don't notice. Fairy tales are like reality. But now it's time to sleep, don't you think?"

The family moved closer together and left a bed free for their guest, and soon Jumar and Christopher were both lying on it close together, because it was a narrow bed and there was only one blanket. Christopher slid this way and that, but the bed grew no wider. It was one thing to sit close to someone in a rocky cave beside an underground river; it was another to be squashed together in the same bed.

"Don't worry," Jumar whispered very quietly. "I won't bite you."

Christopher growled. "I'll tell you one lucky thing," he replied softly. "It's lucky that it's so dark, because I bet this blanket and the hard bed are invisible now. Or do you wear gloves and socks in bed?"

Jumar laughed under his breath. "And I'll tell you another

lucky thing: It's lucky that you're not a girl. Have you ever been as close as this to a girl?"

"Are you crazy?" asked Christopher, horrified.

"I was only wondering," whispered Jumar, yawning. "I mean, everything else seems to be different in Europe."

Christopher woke up when someone beside him suddenly stirred. Day was dawning outside.

"Tapa?" asked Jumar's voice.

"Shh!" said Christopher, because three of the children were lying on the floor, fast asleep.

"Christopher?"

"What is it?"

"I was holding him in my arms again," whispered Jumar. "I told you about it, didn't I? How he died? I was holding him up again just now. There was all that blood—more and more of it, and I was afraid I'd drown in it. It rose to just below the ceiling of the corridor, and then I opened the door and it flowed out into the courtyard, carrying me along with it . . . There was nothing I could do, Christopher. There was too much blood. Far too much blood . . ."

"It was only a dream, Jumar," whispered Christopher. "Because of the underground waterfall, and that strange fairy tale."

"No, Christopher," Jumar whispered back. "It wasn't a dream. That blood in the streets of Kathmandu . . . It was so real. Something terrible is going to happen. I saw it."

Christopher put his arms around him the way Arne used to put his arms around the six-year-old Christopher, and suddenly it didn't feel odd to him anymore.

"Go back to sleep," he whispered, as if speaking to a small child. "You're so close to me that we can only dream the same thing. Let's dream about what it will be like when all this is over. We'll be sitting in a meadow in the mountains, you and Arne and me, and the sun is shining, and we've got fruit candy—nasty green fruit candy. Very soon, now. It will be very soon . . ."

But they were not to be sitting in a meadow in the sunlight so very soon after all.

CHRISTOPHER
IN FLIGHT

THE STRANGER LEFT THE VILLAGE ON the steep slope. The people of the house where he had spent the night gave him food and water to take with him, because they had a son aged fourteen, too, and whenever shots rang out in the distance they were afraid for him. He was somewhere up there in the mountains, with the insurgents, and it was best not to know exactly where, because you couldn't tell anyone anyway. He, too, was learning how to shoot. He wanted to change everything, the way one does when one is fourteen: the world, the future, fate.

No one knew where the strange boy was going. They

wondered if he was one of the insurgents after all, or if he was in flight from them.

"Two of them," said the blind old lady with the sharp ears. "There were two boys here."

The village boy's mother thought of that later, when they brought her back her son and she laid him in the grave that had been waiting for him all along. Because then the old lady, whose wits were getting more and more confused, said, "But those two boys who were here, the strangers, they're going to live. I feel it in my bones. They're on the way up to the highest mountains, the iciest peaks. *Aha!* That will surely make a fine fairy tale. It will probably end unhappily."

And she rubbed her spidery-fingered hands and died without a sound on the following night.

However, Christopher and Jumar knew nothing about any of that. They went along the path that had been pointed out to them in whispers. It led out of the village and up the slope in endless winding curves. There was no dead man lying by the well anymore—daylight had changed everything.

"Maybe we just imagined him," said Jumar.

The forest was thinning out; the trees changed shape. The heights reached out for the boys with long, slender fingers. Now there were conifers lining their path, and Christopher

135

was curiously reminded of the Alps. His family had all gone on a walking tour there once.

The boys passed through more valleys in forest shade, and a day later, when they stopped for a rest, Christopher noticed that his shoes were damp. He was surprised, because it was a long time since they had waded through any rivers, but then he saw that the moisture in his shoes was blood. He cried out in horror. Something was crawling over his feet, fat dark bodies like little slugs.

Jumar cast an unseen glance at Christopher's feet.

"Leeches," he identified them. "Interest—"

"Just don't say it," Christopher threatened. "How do I get rid of them?"

"I think you can sprinkle salt on them," said Jumar. "But we're not carrying kitchen equipment around with us, so I suggest you just pick them off."

Christopher looked at the writhing leeches, disgusted. He tried to get hold of one of them. But the slimy body kept slipping away from him. It was some time before he had picked all the leeches off his feet, and now the blood was running freely from the puncture marks they had left behind.

"They leave a substance behind that stops the blood from coagulating," explained Jumar. "Hirudin. Biology. Private tutoring from a crazy expert on invertebrates. Oh, yuck!"

"What's the matter?"

"I—I've got them, too!"

Only then did Christopher see the leeches writhing in the air beside him, just a little way above the ground.

"Oh, no!" said Jumar. "Christopher, help me. How do I get rid of these little horrors?"

Christopher grinned. "I think you can sprinkle salt on them," he said. "But we're not carrying kitchen equipment around with us, so I suggest you just pick them off."

Leeches don't distinguish between visible and invisible prey. They are both deaf and blind. All they can detect is body heat, and they don't care whether they suck noble blood or the blood of a commoner. Leeches are natural Communists.

Just before sunset that evening, the boys reached a strange landscape that reminded Christopher of the moors at home. The jungle had stayed behind, like a timid animal, and the path they were now following led across a wide plain covered with short grass, rough like a pelt. Only the narrow shapes of slender bushes rose here and there dotting the landscape.

"Juniper," said Christopher in surprise. "Those really are juniper bushes."

A strange atmosphere lay over the plain, and when the

sun sank the wind rose. It whistled in the bushes, singing a song they couldn't understand. It swept dry earth up from the grass into the air, raising clouds of dust, and a thousand whistling, hissing, whispering voices seemed to be following Christopher and Jumar.

In the distance, there was a slope without any colors on it. The glowing hues of the setting sun were not reflected on it— it was as if the black-and-white surface of the slope swallowed up the light. The grass and heather growing there were alive, but they looked dead and dry. Christopher kept stopping to look around.

"They could be quite close," he whispered. "The dragons."

"Oh, who cares?" said Jumar. But it didn't sound very convincing.

The colorless slope attracted their eyes, like a finger pointing in warning.

Then the last of the light in the sky flared up like a match, and went out.

"We'd better look for somewhere to sleep," said Jumar.

Christopher was shivering. The grassy plain offered no shelter from the wind, and the spindly juniper bushes were no help, either.

The moon came out from behind the clouds for a second. It was almost full, and cast puddles of moonlight on the path.

Then it veiled its white face with the next cloud, plunging once more into the inky waters of the night.

"Let's go on," whispered Christopher. "After all, this plain must come to an end sometime. Do you have the flashlight there?"

He heard Jumar rummage around in his backpack in the dark. Then there was a metallic click, and a faint circle of light shone on the path. The light trembled, flickered, and went out.

"The batteries," said Jumar. "That's that, then."

"I think there are some matches in the left-hand pocket of my jeans," said Christopher.

Jumar rummaged again. "What are you going to light with them?"

"I don't like these bushes," whispered Christopher. "We might as well use their wood to make torches."

When he came closer to one of the black outlines, it seemed to him for a moment as if the juniper flinched, and then bit Christopher's hands with the sharp little needles of its leaves. Night breathed a strange kind of hostile life into things here.

Christopher struggled with the juniper for a while, and then tore off a large, dry branch. Dead needles fell on his hands.

He broke two smaller pieces of wood off it, and Jumar stuffed the rest into his backpack. A cloud of juniper fragrance surrounded them for a moment, bringing many memories back to Christopher: juniper berries at Christmastime when he was eight, meat broiling in the oven. Arne standing in the front doorway with snowflakes in his hair, spruce needles on his gloves, the Christmas tree outside.

The hiss of the flame brought Christopher back to the present. He was holding a burning branch, and now they could see the path ahead of them again. Jumar went first, his invisible footsteps following an invisible torch. Only, its flame flickered in the darkness. So fire obviously didn't count as an inanimate object, thought Christopher. Did that mean fire was alive, like water? It looked as if a will-o'-the-wisp were dancing over the plain ahead of Christopher.

And then the will-o'-the-wisp began to splutter and throw out sparks—Christopher held his own torch well away from his face to keep the sparks from jumping into it. It must be the resin in the juniper. The flame that at first had been burning yellow like any ordinary flame now looked bluish, greenish— or was it red? Christopher blinked as he stumbled after its light. What a strange light! Was it really juniper wood that they were burning? Was it a special variety of juniper that hadn't yet attracted the attention of botanists? Or was that just his tired imagination at work?

It was impossible to say whether the colors were changing

in rapid succession, or whether the crackling wood spat them all out at once. Part of Christopher thought he had never seen anything so beautiful before, and another part of him was afraid.

It was as if they were walking by the light of a tiny fireworks display.

At first, Christopher was afraid the torch would burn down too fast and singe his fingers. He had always been afraid of fire. But it seemed as if only the resin at the end of the branch was burning, while the torch itself grew hardly any shorter. So they walked on silently in the light of all the colors of the rainbow. Later, Christopher would often dream of it.

After a while, Jumar stopped and whispered, "There, ahead of us, Christopher! Can you see that? What is it?"

Christopher lowered his torch and stared into the darkness, straining his eyes.

Yes, there was something large and jagged rising from the plain. A rock? Among all the juniper bushes?

"It's too far away," Christopher whispered. "I can't quite—"

"Make it out," he was going to say. But a gust of wind tore the words from his mouth. He sheltered the torch with his hand, but it only flickered up higher in the current of air.

It felt like the wind suddenly decided to rise to a gale. The grass was whispering louder, more anxiously. The wood of the bushes creaked. Now there was a rushing and fluttering in the air, like the wings of millions of birds, and something about that sound made Christopher's throat tighten. He tried to figure out where he had heard that rushing before.

Now it was coming closer, growing larger and stronger, roaring and singing—

Christopher looked up.

And then he saw the dragon.

It was flying over the plain with its wings spread wide, and although it was no more than a blurred outline in the night, Christopher couldn't help marveling at the elegance of its movements. Even by night, the dragons were beautiful, with a muted glow of their own shining out of them.

He felt Jumar's hand on his arm. "Stand perfectly still," Jumar whispered. "It can't hurt us. It has no shadow. It's too dark."

And suppose it has something else in mind, Christopher thought, some other way to finish us off?

No, he said to himself as he stood rigid and motionless beside Jumar. The dragon doesn't care about us. Even the dragon in the forest by the spring hadn't really been after him, Jumar had said. The dragons were no more evil than any beast hunting its prey is evil.

But they were just as cruel and just as dangerous as any beast hunting its prey.

But was this dragon making straight for them?

At that moment, the clouds drifted aside and the moon shone through them, large and almost round. It poured its white light down on the travelers like a curse. Christopher saw the dragon's shadow gliding closer over the rough grass.

And he saw the hollow bronze statue of the woman in the paddy field before his mind's eye.

And now he saw the dragon's glowing eyes, unnaturally bright, blazing yellow, hungry. Eyes that had seen their prey. Then he understood.

"The torches!" he shouted. "It must be the torches! The colors, Jumar! That's what it's come for!"

They flung the torches as far away from them as possible, but it wasn't far enough. The dragon wasn't going to halt its swift flight so easily.

"Run!" cried Christopher. He had no idea where Jumar was, but he ran for it himself, along the moonlit path after his own shadow. He stumbled, ran on, with the hissing and fluttering of the dragon's wings in the air behind him. No one could run as fast as a dragon flew. Thoughts exploded in Christopher's head while the effort he was making cut his lungs like a knife. What would it be like to turn to bronze? Did it hurt? Was it quick? Did you feel it?

He thought of the woman who had been brushed by a dragon and came back to life. But what were the chances of having a dragon just happen to come along again?

The air swirling around the dragon sang in Christopher's ears.

He thought he could feel the dragon's shadow on him, like icy breath. His shoulders began to feel rigid and cold. And then that sensation seeped into his arms, his fingers . . . He thought he saw his hands shining like bronze in the moonlight. But his legs were still moving.

He ran toward the big, angular shape.

Whatever it was, it was his only chance. If it offered shade—enough shade to cover him—then the shadow of the dragon couldn't hurt him.

Or so Christopher hoped. Hoping was all he could do.

He turned once, and it was difficult. His neck felt so stiff, stiff as metal. Rigid as bronze. But his eyes could still see.

The light of the torches was nowhere to be seen now. Christopher saw the dragon turning its neck, irritated, looking for the colors that had brought it here. It seemed to hover motionless in the air for a moment, and then it flew on, close above the ground, evidently confused.

He tasted blood in his mouth, and the effort he was making resulted in a throbbing in his temples, but he made himself run on and on . . .

Then he reached the large, angular form.

It was not a rock.

It was a tent.

He had no time to wonder whose tent it was and what he would find inside. The canvas tent flap was open, and Christopher shot in like an animal in flight racing into its den.

"Close the flap!" he gasped, although he didn't know who he was talking to. "The dragon—"

Then his legs gave way, and he found himself on the ground again. Briefly he felt the touch of an invisible hand on his shoulder.

"It's all right," whispered Jumar. "These are my father's men. Let me do the talking."

Looking out through the gap of the tent flap, Christopher saw the dragon fly in a long loop above the plain and finally rise, arching into the night sky, as if to unite its slender body with the light of the pale moon. Then he lost sight of it.

He flexed his shoulders, his arms, his hands.

The rigidity was wearing off. He realized that it had

145

been nothing but his imagination, born of his own fear. The dragon's shadow had not fallen on him.

A group of men in uniform were surrounding him, staring at him as if he were an apparition. A few paraffin lamps shone in the darkness of the tent, and at the back of it Christopher could see the outlines of sleeping figures, lying side by side in rows on the uneven ground. The grass here was trodden flat, but the ground was still the ground of the plain.

There was room in this tent for about a hundred people.

"Who is this," one of the uniformed men wondered aloud, "traveling the country in the middle of the night when no one else is out and about?"

"Who is this," asked another man, "bringing a dragon down on us?"

"Who is this, and how old is he?" asked a third. "He looks to me no more than a boy."

Christopher opened his mouth to speak, but Jumar answered for him.

"I may be only a boy," he replied with dignity, "but I am not just anyone. I am the king's son."

Wry smiles appeared on the faces above the stiff green uniform collars.

"Not very likely," said the tallest of the men. "The king has no son."

Christopher felt Jumar's hand giving him a signal, and he raised his own, palm upward, into the air. The next moment, Jumar's signet ring appeared in the air, sparkling golden in the light of the lamps.

"Do you recognize your king's crest?" asked Jumar.

Christopher saw the men's eyes widen. The ring sailed slowly through the air and stopped in front of the face of the man with the most military badges on his chest. The man stepped back and the ring followed him. It almost touched the tip of his nose, and then disappeared.

A tense silence filled the air.

"Whoever you are," said the man with all the military badges, "there's something uncanny about you. What do you want from us?"

"A bed for the night," said Jumar, satisfied. "A bowl of rice. That's all."

Christopher realized that Jumar was beginning to enjoy the trick of the ring, and that worried him, but he was grateful for the food and the bed. It was a good bed they made for the stranger, with soft blankets and pillows, even big enough for two.

Because after all, the stranger might actually be the king's son.

Christopher had thought he would sleep more soundly

than ever before, because his exhaustion wrapped itself around him like a coat of armor along with the blankets. But he woke when it was still the middle of the night. The darkness seemed even darker since the paraffin lamps had been blown out. The sour smell of sweat and life hovered over the quiet sleepers on the ground.

He lay still where he was, listening. Jumar was breathing the regular breath of dreamless sleep beside him.

Christopher could not figure out what had woken him.

A sound? A movement? His own dream?

He sensed something over by the entrance to the tent. Now Christopher saw the glow of a cigarette in the night. The tent flap itself was slightly open, and a figure in silhouette stood alone outside. There were words in the wind, quiet, whispered words, and a rushing and crackling in the air. It was some time before Christopher identified it. White noise, he thought.

The rushing sound of a radio when the transmitter isn't properly tuned.

But it wasn't an ordinary radio set. It was a walkie-talkie.

Go back to sleep, he told himself in the silence. After all, there must be a reason for someone to be sending a radio message to a military base in the night.

But then he quietly got up from the bed and stole over

to the tent flap. How he wished that, just this once, he could borrow Jumar's invisibility.

Christopher crouched down on all fours near the opening and went on listening. And now he could make out the words.

"Now? Hello! Can you hear me now? What? No. About eleven o'clock. Yes. Yes, that's what I said myself, but he has a signet ring with the king's crest. Of course it could be a forgery. The thing is—What did you say? Oh, damn it all! Now, better? Yes. I was saying the thing is that he can make it hover in the air. I've never seen anything like it. Of course the men are afraid. The general mood is—What? Oh, the hell with this device! What? What was that again? No, no, I understand you. Reception's all right now, but—Did he really run away? Well then, you could call this ironic, because he ran straight into our arms."

For a while, Christopher heard nothing but crackling and rushing.

Then the man said, "Of course. Very good. What? No, I didn't catch that. Say it again. Yes. Of course. In person? When can you be here? The Maoists? No. No, we haven't seen any sign of them. This is a good base. Anyone coming can easily be seen on this plain. Right. We'll keep him here until evening. What? *What?* Invisible? No, definitely not."

A dry laugh mingled with the crackling of the walkie-talkie.

"Yes, well, the king. Forgive me, but we all know the king is a little peculiar these days, and you should know better than anyone that he doesn't have long to live. I'm not surprised he'd say something like that. Of course, you never know. But we can't do more than keep him safe here. Right. Tomorrow. *What?* How? Oh, hell."

He shook the walkie-talkie angrily, and Christopher moved slowly back, still on all fours. He went back to his bed beside Jumar again, staring into the darkness, wide awake.

Something was wrong.

He still didn't have the missing piece of the jigsaw puzzle, but he felt it wasn't one that either he or Jumar would like. Christopher wondered whether it was just a case of returning a runaway son to his father, but it seemed to him that something quite different was going on.

The crown prince of Nepal was sleeping in a tent at a military base camp, under the protection of his father's own soldiers, secure and warm.

But that security was a trap.

Jumar had been dreaming again. He opened the door, the side door in the corridor of the servants' quarters, and once again that heavy, gasping body fell into his arms. But when he looked at the man's face this time, it was his father's. His father put out his hand to Jumar, passed it over his face—exploring his features as he had never done in real life—and then placed it over his mouth.

Jumar opened his eyes. There really was a hand over his mouth.

He tried to cry out, but the hand wouldn't let him utter so much as a squeak.

It was so dark. If only he could have seen it coming—

"Shh," someone whispered beside him. "It's me, Christopher. Keep quiet and listen carefully."

He took his hand off Jumar's mouth, and Jumar let out a sigh of relief.

"We have to get out of here," whispered Christopher, his words hardly more than a breath in the night close to Jumar's ear. "Don't ask me any questions now. There's one of them outside the tent, but as soon as the coast is clear we must set off again."

Jumar pressed Christopher's hand to convey that he understood. Then he carefully sat up. His mind was still caught in the dream of the king, and he didn't understand anything.

He saw the man outside the tent, smoking. He smoked cigarette after cigarette, the glowing tip hovering in the air like a firefly.

Jumar counted fifteen cigarettes before dawn.

The man out there was nervous.

Too nervous to leave the tent flap clear for them.

But when he had smoked his fifteenth cigarette, and dawn came, the light of the new day fell on a stretch of the plain where the juniper bushes had lost their color. The heather was gray now, and the grass swaying in the wind was not like real grass anymore.

A meager, dirty landscape faced the heir to the throne of Nepal.

The dragon must have come back again in the night, angry and cheated of the wonderful lights spraying color. In its fury, it had consumed all the colors it could find.

Jumar's eyes hurt when he looked at the bleak landscape, and he knew that the pain came from somewhere inside him—the place where fear of failure and of being unable to save his country from the dragons also lurked. But he swallowed his pain and fear, and told himself that this was nothing but a little gray grass, and after all, he had already seen plenty of gray grass on his travels.

That morning, they served the heir to the throne of Nepal a breakfast worthy of a crown prince. What a wonderful moment it was! They had laid a table outside on the meadow, a real folding table, and Christopher was sitting on a cushion, while Jumar ate his breakfast sitting on the ground. Dozens of little birds were singing now in the colorless junipers.

They had drawn on all the camp's stores to provide a varied menu, and with his invisible fingers Jumar ate buttered toast with sliced gherkins, fruit salad, and sweet muffins still shaped like the can in which the dough had been shipped. Christopher sat beside him, visible and very pale, just sipping some of the sweet, black tea with milk. Jumar was afraid the soldiers would notice.

He wondered whether Christopher had gone crazy. Or if he had dreamed what Christopher said to him in the night.

Yes, that must be it. Christopher probably looked so pale only because he'd slept badly.

The sky was blue, and the flawless sun shone down in the middle of it. And to see how the decorations on the soldiers' uniforms gleamed and shone in its light!

Jumar thought he might wear a uniform like that later, when he became king some day. He added salt to his egg.

One of the soldiers looked surprised when the salt sprinkler disappeared and reappeared and the next moment the eggcup and egg were nowhere to be seen. But he obviously didn't dare to say anything about it.

The crown prince of Nepal felt that he could almost forget the colorless landscape, and a warm feeling glowed through him: a sense of being at home. He had to admit that it was wonderful to have eaten his fill, and be feeling generally content.

"Excuse me," said the soldier who was standing behind him, hands clasped behind his back, ready to serve him. "Did you say *interesting?*"

"Oh, uh, no," replied Jumar, because he couldn't possibly explain what had been going through his head—not to this soldier.

He finished his breakfast and thanked the soldiers politely, as befits a king's son, for his private tutors had taken particular care with that part of his education. Then he cleared his throat. "And now I'll be on my way again," he announced.

All was quiet around him.

"On your way?" asked one of the soldiers. He was the one with the most decorations on his chest. "Where to, Your Highness?"

"Farther that way." He took Christopher's arm and pointed vaguely along the path. "I'm making for the camp of the Mao . . ."

"Shh," said the soldier, quickly putting a finger to his lips.

". . . for the camp of the terror . . ."

"Shh!"

". . . of the Commu—"

"Shh!" went the soldier for the third time. Jumar rolled his eyes, and was glad no one could see him doing it.

"Well, anyway, their camp," he finished his sentence. "Their base camp."

Did they all think the Maoists would jump out from behind the juniper bushes as soon as one mentioned them? Did they think there was some kind of magic in naming names? He had already noticed something like that in the villages, but didn't expect to find it in the army. Jumar marveled at how fine their three tents looked in the sunlight and how proudly their horses stood, tied up in the shade. Were the soldiers by any chance afraid—afraid of the insurgents?

The heir to the Nepalese throne sincerely hoped not. He had learned that his father's soldiers were fearless and noble, brave and clever, bold and magnanimous, and he wanted it to stay that way.

"No one knows exactly where their base camp is," the man with the decorations replied. "It may not even exist at all."

"I'm going to find it," said Jumar. "Never mind what people say. I have to speak to their leader, because I have an offer to make him. I am traveling in the name of my father, the king, and he has given me a part of his power. I can't disappoint him."

He saw Christopher frowning as he moved his lips in time with these words. He knew what Christopher was thinking, and it made him furious: *Yes, yes, Jumar, that's what you'd like. For your father to think of you and give you part of his power. But it isn't true.*

Jumar noticed that the men were exchanging glances.

He couldn't interpret what they meant.

"If that is so, then we'll escort you," said the man with the decorations. In his mind, Jumar began calling him the lieutenant.

Jumar tried to make a gesture of refusal with Christopher's hands. Christopher, irritated, flapped them around in the air.

"I am used to traveling alone," replied Jumar. But it was a shameless lie. He was so glad to have Christopher's company. "And it would certainly be a bad idea to go where I want to go with the army. As you must understand."

The lieutenant humbly bowed his head. "We will go as far as the big bridge with you," he said. "So far and no farther. We can head out in a quarter of an hour."

And so the crown prince of the country set off—even if no one could see him—this time with a royal escort.

It was a fabulous procession. For the first time since

leaving Kathmandu Jumar was riding a horse—of course Christopher was riding it, too.

The lieutenant with all the decorations rode ahead through the colorless landscape, and at least a dozen more soldiers rode behind the crown prince's horse. Their helmets and weapons shone in the morning light, flecks of color in the bleak black and white all around.

Then came the foot soldiers and then the mules. At first, Jumar wasn't sure what they were for, but the lieutenant explained with a proud smile, "They're carrying the pots and pans. Did you see the little goat we have on a rope? We're going to prepare a royal meal for you when we get to the bridge, before we leave you to go the rest of your difficult journey alone." Then he sighed.

But there seemed to Jumar to be something artificial about that sigh.

He could tell that Christopher wanted to say something to him.

"Come to your senses, Jumar!" hissed Christopher in his ear at once. "All this fuss they're making about you is just for show! They're not the least bit interested in your father having a successor!"

"No, honestly. This kind of fuss is perfectly normal," whispered Jumar. "It's just the way they do these things here."

"You're a pig-headed idiot!" Christopher whispered, and Jumar could tell that he really was furious.

The lieutenant rode past them, put a hand to his cap, and murmured something about "checking up on the mules." Now another soldier was riding at the head of the escort.

Jumar saw Christopher turn, and followed his gaze.

Back at the end of the procession, the lieutenant's ear was glued to a walkie-talkie.

"See that?" hissed Christopher. "See what he's doing? He's sending someone information about where we're riding. I'll bet you everything I have—"

"Which isn't exactly impressive," whispered Jumar. "I wouldn't want to bet anything for this T-shirt. It's sticking to my skin."

"Oh, thanks very much. Last night he was speaking to someone on that walkie-talkie. I overheard him. You'd better spur this horse on. We can make a break for it."

"Why shouldn't the lieutenant speak to someone? Walkie-talkies are military equipment like guns. *You* spur the horse on!"

"I don't know how to ride," said Christopher.

"What *can* you do? Christopher? Christopher?"

But Christopher tightened his lips and said not another word.

Jumar was feeling bad about mocking Christopher's T-shirt and riding, because such remarks were not what a king's son was brought up to say. But he was feeling too defiant to apologize.

The ground was rising again. The plain gave way to the familiar green of the forest and the thin, dry juniper bushes were left behind. The sultry air under the leaf canopy was full of the humming of mosquitoes.

But how thankful Jumar was now for those mosquitoes, because with them the color of the forest came back. The yellow and brown of dry leaves lying on the path, the flicker of a purple butterfly's wings in the sunlight, the red veins in the tremendous leaves, the orange blossom that a tree had dropped on the path from its moss-covered branches.

It was as if his eyes could breathe again, as if his soul were heaving a deep sigh of relief. There were still colors in the world. The dragons still came down here from time to time, but there was no major threat to the road that went through the deep valleys to the capital city—no threat from either the dragons or the insurgents.

He still had time to change everything for the better.

The sun had already reached its highest point in the sky, and was announcing that it was midday when the forest came to a sudden end on the brink of a valley. A rocky chasm yawned ahead like a wound in the landscape. Trees clung to the rock here and there, and orange buckthorn berries glowed among the silvery needles of their foliage.

And there lay the bridge.

It was impressive indeed. The valley that it spanned was wider than any other Jumar had ever crossed by bridge. Down below, rivers foamed.

Then Jumar thought: Oh, no. The river had no color. Its water was gray, but even gray didn't seem the right word.

The lieutenant noticed the glance that Christopher cast at it, and gave a grim nod.

"There's a dragon sitting at its source, drinking the color," he said. "That's what happens to the water."

"Worrying," said Jumar—as an alternative to "interesting."

The lieutenant nodded again.

Behind them, the goat uttered a shrill cry as it was butchered, and Jumar saw Christopher flinch as if feeling the animal's pain. Europeans were odd. He knew that they ate a lot of meat, yet they couldn't cope with hearing the cry of a goat being slaughtered.

The boys sat down on the soft cushions that had been brought specially for this purpose, and soon the air was filled with the aroma of firewood and roasted meat.

But before they had finished the banquet, someone

interrupted the quiet midday peace of the camp. He came galloping up on a black horse with flanks that gleamed like the night. When he brought the horse to a halt, the foam at its mouth was like a crown of white.

The soldiers surrounding Jumar and Christopher bowed very low, and some of them touched their foreheads to the ground. But the lieutenant stood up to greet the rider of the black horse.

"How good to see you, General Kartan," he said. "Now you can greet His Majesty's son yourself."

The general dismounted from his horse and bowed his head in acknowledgment.

Jumar blinked, shook his head, and looked again. Yes, it really was General Kartan. What was he doing here in the middle of the mountains? Wasn't Kartan busy near Kathmandu, training new troops in the east? Jumar had last seen him two weeks before he himself left the palace. He'd been sitting on a seat in the garden deep in a game of chess with the king. Of course Kartan had had no idea that he was watching them.

Jumar couldn't stand the general. And he had to admit that he was jealous—jealous of that successful, good-looking hero to whom his father devoted so much time, playing chess with him, discussing philosophy and literature with him on long walks. It had been the king himself who sent the promising young man to study in America. And in the years after that, he had risen in the ranks to command the army. No decision on the troops was taken without Kartan; no move was made without him.

Christopher and Jumar stood up at the same time, and Kartan sat down.

"Surprised?" he asked with a little smile playing around the corners of his mouth.

That smooth face of his, thought Jumar, it looks as if it had just been ironed! And smiling seemed to be an effort for him, because it meant he had to crumple up a little part of his skin.

"Surprised to see me?"

A cold shudder like icy water ran down Jumar's back. All Kartan had to go on was Christopher's face. And that, to be honest, showed more fear than surprise.

"I am surprised, too," the general went on. "I had no idea that my king had a son at all. And what a fine young man his son is! A word with you, prince."

He took Christopher by the arm and led him a little way from the fire, toward the bridge.

Over his shoulder, he said to his men, "We'll be ready for a good hot meal. But first, I have a few private matters to clear up with this young gentleman."

Jumar followed the two of them to the place where the suspension bridge began.

There was something wrong. But he didn't yet know what it was.

"It's a great strain," said Kartan, looking into the distance on the far side of the valley. "It really wears me down. Always having to be everywhere at the same time. Even I am only human. And when the king's son takes it into his head to run away and travel the world, my life is really hell." He sighed. "Your father is very worried about you. He told me about you so that I would go and search for you, my boy. You are still so young! Much too young to die. It's dangerous up here in the mountains, and I can well understand His Majesty's anxiety."

"Is he anxious?" asked Jumar.

But he received no answer to that.

Instead, there was a flash of metal in the air, and next moment, the blade of a knife was pressing against Christopher's throat.

Jumar gasped for air in his friend's place.

"Very well, crown prince," whispered Kartan. "Scream if you like. Scream for help. Those are my men over there. They are afraid, cowards that they are. They're useless. But they won't stab me in the back. So listen carefully."

He was whispering now, and Jumar saw him forcing Christopher closer to the precipice.

"I have been the king's right-hand man for a long time," whispered General Kartan. "The only man he trusts. I'm the man who keeps the Maoists away from the city so that he can dream in his garden—dream that we live in a peaceful state. I'm the man who makes sure the taxes keep flowing, and they flow into the garden and into his dreams. But they flow into my troops, as well. Wherever you've been over the last fourteen years—you and I both know who's going to succeed to the throne of Nepal. And it's not you, my boy."

Jumar wanted to reply, but the words would not come out.

Christopher had been right all along. Jumar felt like an idiot. A totally pig-headed, invisible idiot.

"No, I'm not," he heard Christopher say, and he looked at him in surprise. "The person you're looking for isn't foolish enough to fall into your trap."

Oh, yes, he is, thought Jumar. Forgive me, Christopher. Please, please forgive—

"The son of the king of Nepal," said Christopher firmly, "is invisible."

Kartan narrowed his eyes in his smooth face, and that tiny movement, too, almost seemed to stretch his skin to a painful grimace.

"That," he replied, "is what the king says, too. I admit I thought he was crazy. Not everything is the way it ought to be in the king's head these days. He does not have much longer to live."

"What is he going to die of?" Jumar heard Christopher ask. Jumar himself couldn't utter a word.

"If you really were his son, I wouldn't need to tell you," answered Kartan. Only Jumar knew how wrong he was. "He's had a tumor growing in his head for many, many months," whispered the general. "It grows slowly, but there's no stopping it. The best doctors in Kathmandu have diagnosed it with the most modern of instruments. He has refused to have an operation, and he is right. It won't do him any good. He takes pain-killers, but they are not strong enough. He finds peace only in the garden beside his sleeping wife."

Kartan spoke without any emotion, like a newsreader saying what the weather will be like next day. Jumar clenched his hands into fists.

"In short," said Kartan, "the king will soon be no more than a sick old man. He'll have to keep to his bed, a white hospital bed, and then he will pass away. I won't even have to lend a helping hand."

He forced Christopher even closer to the precipice.

"Where is he?" Kartan asked urgently. "Where is the king's

invisible son? If you love your life, you'll tell me. I'm not the squeamish sort. I must admit, I don't like the expression, it's such a cliché, but the fact is that there's so much blood on my hands already, it's not worth washing them anymore."

"He's far away by now," whispered Christopher, and a drop of blood showed on the gleaming blade at his throat.

And a pulse of fear ran through him. Jumar could see it, and he felt that the fear was nailing Christopher's thoughts down, keeping him from speaking. He heard his own difficulty in getting any words out, but he spoke.

"He went east. Or south. Or west. Or maybe he went—"

"That will do," said Kartan.

The chasm opened its arms to receive a boy who was not a king's son. Who was nothing and had nothing—except for a Red Hot Chili Peppers T-shirt and a brother who had disappeared.

The colorless river prepared to take him into its waters.

But no such thing happened.

What happened instead was something very, very interesting.

Later, the soldiers who had seen it said it was uncanny, and it must indeed have been the king's son, or, if not, then a saint or a spirit in human form. The few Christians among them crossed themselves, and the rest of the men dropped to the ground, touching it with their foreheads, and did not look up until they could no longer ignore their general's furious cries.

A mysterious power had snatched the knife from Kartan's hand, pushed him away from the boy standing on the edge of the precipice, and tipped him so that it looked as if it was the general who would fall into the abyss.

Maybe some of them even hoped he would.

When Kartan recovered his balance, they saw that his left hand was clutching his right hand, and blood was seeping out between his fingers. His own knife, they said, had turned against him.

The boy had already leaped forward and was now running across the suspension bridge.

"What are you waiting for?" screamed the general. "Don't just stand there gaping. Go after him! Whatever happens, he mustn't escape us! Get moving, you lily-livered cowards—"

He started toward the bridge himself.

And then—the bridge disappeared.

It simply vanished. It vanished entirely, dissolved into a void.

The boy stood still for a moment, as if hesitating. But then he went on again, walking over the void above the abyss until he reached the far side.

Subalpine Steppes

·····

HEIGHT C. 8,850–13,125 FEET

·····

FLORA

Blue pine (*Pinus wallichiana*), East Himalayan fir (*Abies spectabilis*), Morinda spruce (*Picea smithiana*), Tibetan sea buckthorn species (*Hippophae tibetana*), drumstick primula (*Primula denticulata*), larkspur (*Delphinium*), hemp (*Cannabis sativa*), various conifers, mugwort, barley, potatoes, various species of fruit trees

FAUNA

Snow leopard, snow hare, fox, yak

NIYA'S WORDS

CHRISTOPHER SAW THE BRIDGE DISAPPEAR. He was dizzy.

He could feel its metal plates underfoot, but he couldn't see them anymore.

"Don't be afraid," he heard Jumar saying somewhere ahead of him. "It's all right. It's just my bare hand on the parapet. I took my gloves off. I'm going to run my fingers along the handrail, and I won't let go until we're on the other side. And I bet you none of those cowards will follow us."

"Wh—wh—what are we betting for?" asked Christopher, with an uncontrollable trembling in his voice.

"Your T-shirt," said Jumar gravely. "I like it very, very much, and I'd be happy to keep it after this journey is over."

Christopher doubted whether there would be much of the Red Hot Chili Peppers T-shirt left after "this journey" was over, wherever it might end.

"You *must* keep going," Jumar urged him. "Hesitate too long and they might try following after all. Please, go on! Hold on tight to the parapet!"

The bridge swayed this way and that, and the parapet was only a length of wire netting, quite low, probably intended to keep sheep or goats from falling off the sides of the bridge, but it wasn't high enough to give a human being secure support—especially when the wire netting was invisible.

Christopher saw the turbulent, colorless water of the river far, far below him, with sharp rocks on either side.

He felt the chasm pulling at him, and he remembered the dragon's eyes—those fathomless black whirlpools. He forcibly tore his glance away from the depths and looked ahead to the other side of the valley, where the mountain forest waved its green hands to them.

Then he put one foot in front of another and began slowly walking straight ahead, through nothing, through the air—a tightrope walker without any tightrope.

He spread his arms and gritted his teeth. If only the

bridge didn't sway so much! Go straight ahead, he told himself. Just keep going straight ahead. But he could hardly tell where straight ahead was . . .

Jumar was a little way ahead of him. Christopher could hear him whistling to let him know his position. Rivulets of sweat were running down Christopher's neck, even though the air was chilly up above the river.

He heard the soldiers shouting behind him. He couldn't hear exactly what they said, because his head was too busy not thinking about the abyss below. But he sensed their amazement. And then there were other cries, too. Another voice—a furious voice: Kartan's voice. His rage was as unfathomed as the depths below.

Christopher was sure that Kartan was going to follow him—that he wouldn't hesitate much longer before attempting to walk out over the invisible bridge.

He could almost feel Kartan's hand seizing him before he reached the other side of the great ravine.

He wasn't going to turn around.

But he did turn, all the same.

And there stood Kartan, staring. His eyes reminded Christopher of the empty, black eyes of the dragon. And a nonsensical thought came into Christopher's mind: Kartan himself was a dragon. Any moment now he would change, clothe himself in shimmering scales of many colors, spread his wings, and soar over the abyss . . .

Kartan did not change into a dragon. Instead, he reached out an arm and pushed one of his soldiers forward. He moved so quickly that the soldier had no time to resist. Of course, Kartan wasn't stupid enough to try the invisible bridge out first . . .

There were plenty of soldiers, just as there are plenty of pawns in chess. They are there to be sacrificed.

And Christopher watched as one of the soldiers was sacrificed that day.

Kartan hadn't pushed him in quite the right direction. The man stumbled forward, reached out his arms in search of some support to help him—and found nothing.

He fell into the depths.

The world began to turn around and around as Christopher walked over the abyss. He felt as if he himself were falling. He didn't know if it was he or the bridge swaying. He went down on his knees, groped around, found nothing to hold on to—

He closed his eyes. Clung on. He felt that he couldn't go another step farther. He was going to stay here, clinging to the wire netting, swaying back and forth with the suspension bridge until the end of his days . . .

"Christopher!" he heard Jumar calling softly.

I can't do it, thought Christopher. I can't, I can't, I can't.

Arne could have done it. But I can't.

Then, somehow, he slowly straightened up, opened his eyes, and went on.

Because you can do anything when there's no alternative.

He didn't know how he reached the other side of the ravine, but he did reach it. It was like a miracle.

When at long last he had firm ground under his feet again, he was shaking all over. There was still no sign of the bridge behind him.

"Where . . . Where are you?" asked Christopher, exhausted.

"Here. I'll hold on to the handrail a little longer—"

"It would be a good idea," said Christopher, "if a part of you could stay here forever, and then the bridge would never reappear."

"Oh, that would be easy," replied Jumar cheerfully. "How about if I just chop off a finger and we fix it to the rail?"

"Wait a minute," said Christopher slowly, trying to get his head around an idea. "Why not . . . hair? Couldn't we leave a strand of your hair tied to this rail?"

"It's worth a try . . ."

The backpack appeared on the ground. "Would you look for my pocketknife in there? It's tricky for me with only one hand."

Christopher found the knife in the jumble of scratchy juniper twigs that Jumar had packed, the sleeves of jackets, and the flashlight, and soon an invisible strand of hair cut from the head of the crown prince of Nepal was tied to a wire on a certain suspension bridge crossing a certain valley.

Since that day, the bridge has never been seen again.

Many people say that on moonlit nights, they have sometimes seen a mule or a sheep walking through the air where the bridge once stood, right over to the far side of the ravine. But people will say anything.

Only a little way farther along this side of the valley, the travelers' path led them steeply upward, and this time they finally left the green world of the tropical forest behind. They passed other valleys, crossed other bridges taking them over calmer rivers, and the look of the country changed.

Something else changed, too, in secret, and so slowly that you would hardly notice it. The heir to the throne of Nepal stayed silent for long periods at a time. The boys never talked about what had happened, yet Christopher knew that something in his unseen companion had broken—a little cogwheel in the gearbox of his confidence—and when that cogwheel broke it threw off the whole purpose of their journey. They ought to have been discussing so many things, thought Christopher. But instead, they were just walking and walking to the point of exhaustion, going stubbornly ahead.

The bushes were only knee-high now; short, dry grass spread its rough coat over the earth. It was as if the plain with the juniper bushes had been a sign of what was to come in the next few days. The sun burned down on the backs of their necks, but by night it was colder than ever.

Christopher realized that it was getting harder for him to climb.

"It's the altitude," said Jumar. And Christopher was glad to hear him speak. "Something to do with oxygen. You get used to it after a while."

Christopher hoped the Maoists hadn't made their base camp somewhere beyond the reach of any oxygen at all. But Jumar was right: His body did get used to it as time went on.

Christopher was relieved that there were no steps anymore. Where the ground did not rise too steeply, huts were no longer huddled together, but were isolated and far apart, as if a handful of toy houses had been scattered over the landscape. Here and there, the sturdy bodies of shaggy-coated animals towered above the low shrubs. They seemed to be thinking of something deeply philosophical as they moved their horned heads back and forth while they grazed.

"Yaks," said Jumar.

Christopher remembered a photo in the picture book he took home from the library and he wondered if it had been taken somewhere near here; the landscape in the background was the same.

They had left the tourist route; the last scrap of broken English they saw was a sign on the wall of a mud hut that announced: YAK TAIL—YOGHURT FORSEL HERE. LODGE.

It probably meant to say, YAK TAIL LODGE and YOGURT FOR SALE HERE, but it was a nice idea to think they might be selling yak-tail yogurt.

However, the laughter died on the boys' lips when they saw the owner of the lodge. He was sitting alone on his bench, and he was made of bronze, just like the little girl on his lap.

They counted thirteen more bronze statues that day, all hollow and lifeless.

They were approaching the heights where dragons often came, and there were more and more gray patches in the landscape. Christopher tried to act as if he didn't see them.

Toward evening, they crossed a stretch of land where the bushes were no longer green or the grass brown, and Christopher was glad that in the fading light they couldn't see more details.

By now he was used to knocking at any door he saw

when night fell, and he had never yet been turned away. This evening, however, all the doors stayed closed.

"The dragon," whispered Jumar. "The dragon who was here. It's not been gone long. People are scared."

"Dragons don't knock on doors," said Christopher.

Finally, the very last door opened just a crack, a pair of eyes in the darkness beyond it inspected Christopher closely, and he was pulled through the doorway so fast that he was almost afraid Jumar wouldn't have time to follow.

Inside, the remains of a fire glowed in one corner. Two children were asleep there on the bare floor.

"Who are you?" asked the woman who had let Christopher in.

And Christopher had the feeling it would be better if he didn't let Jumar do the talking this time.

"I'm no one special," he replied. "But I need a place to spend the night, and if you have a little rice, I can pay for it."

The woman nodded, but her face remained impassive.

"Then that's all right. No one came here, I'll tell them, and I didn't give anyone a meal."

A little later, Christopher and Jumar were sitting beside the dying embers of the fire, and the woman gave Christopher a bowl. "The rice we have here doesn't satisfy the appetite," she said. "But it's all there is."

Even in the dim light, Christopher could see that the rice had no color. It tasted of nothing, and it didn't warm him. At least it seemed to drive his hunger away.

In the night, Christopher was woken by his rumbling stomach. It was as if he'd eaten nothing at all.

He lay awake, staring at the darkness. The embers of the fire were only cold ashes now, and outside the wind was howling like a rabid dog.

"You can't sleep, am I right?" whispered the woman. "I can feel your thoughts. You're looking for something, aren't you?"

She must be sitting somewhere behind him in the dark, upright and awake.

"No one can sleep in this village anymore," whispered the woman. "Too many nights have been broken by knocking at our doors. First it was the people up in the mountains asking for shelter. Their requests were black and gleamed in the starlight with polished gun barrels, but they were polite to anyone who let them in. However, next came the men in uniform looking for them. And their questions were red as blood and smelled of the cold sweat of fear. Many of the houses here are empty now. They're full of broken fragments. Those are the ones where the men from the mountains slept. The soldiers have left nothing of them intact. And now—now they're looking for someone else. A fugitive, a boy about your age."

"Why are they looking for him?"

"When the men in uniform come, there are no questions beginning with *why*."

Christopher let the silence fill the air for a while. Finally he asked, "When *they* were here, did you hear them talking? Did they say anything about foreigners who . . . who were guests in one of their camps in the mountains?"

The woman seemed to hesitate.

"It's strange that you ask that," she replied at last. "Because when I saw you today, I thought you looked like one of them."

Christopher sat up so suddenly that the darkness swirled around him.

"You thought I looked like him? Who?"

"One of the three foreigners," said the woman. "They were here. They were on the way to their base camp. Nobody knows its whereabouts, and they were taking the foreigners there. I saw them—three tall young men with light-colored eyes. The people whose house they slept in said the fighting men had treated them with respect. When they set off at dawn, they passed my door, and one of the foreigners smiled at me. He had fair hair, almost white, and such a friendly smile. He was the one you look like."

Christopher listened to the thudding of his heart in the

darkness. It was racing faster than ever before, and he had to force himself to breathe calmly.

Arne. It was Arne. He had been here. He was alive, and all right.

And Christopher was on the right track.

"You said his eyes were light-colored?" he whispered. "And his hair was almost white? Then how can I look like him?"

"It was the smile," she said. "You have the same smile."

"I—I—" He hesitated. The same smile? He recalled the stunning, dazzling smile with which Arne enchanted girls by the dozen without ever meaning to, the smile that touched the hearts of ticket inspectors and traffic cops, the smile that everyone wanted in a group photograph.

"I'm afraid," whispered Christopher at last, "that I don't smile very often."

The next morning, the woman looked out at the path before day dawned and asked them to leave. The sunlight must not find any stranger in her hospitable house.

So they walked on, hunger in their bellies and exhaustion in their legs. But there was a song in Christopher's heart.

"Arne was here," he told Jumar. "She saw him. We were talking in the night while you were asleep. He's all right, and it really does look as if they were taking him and the others to their base camp."

Jumar seemed to hesitate.

"I saw him, too," he said after a while.

"What? You saw him? Where? When?"

Christopher stopped, reached out into the empty air, found Jumar's shoulder and shook it.

"Underground, by the river," Jumar went on. "While you were unconscious. The Maoists I saw passing by—they weren't alone. They had three foreigners with them. It was so dark, and only the Maoist leading the way had a light. They'd blindfolded the foreigners. I think . . . I think one of them looked like your brother. The way you've described him to me."

The thoughts in Christopher's head swirled like a storm.

Perhaps it hadn't been Arne. Or perhaps it had. Perhaps he had been very close to him. Close enough to touch. And Jumar hadn't told him.

He had almost found Arne, and then lost him again.

"Why, Jumar?" he asked. "Why didn't you say anything?"

"I wasn't sure what was going to happen to them. The Maoists were carrying guns. That's why I didn't tell you."

Red-hot anger rose in Christopher, burning his throat. He wanted to shout at Jumar, it was what his anger demanded, but he wasn't used to shouting at people, so his voice just dropped even lower.

"It's a great pity," he whispered, "that I can't look you in the face."

"Oh, stop being so angry," said Jumar. "If something *had* happened to them, wouldn't it have been better for you not to know about it? We couldn't have done anything—"

"You're invisible. Forgotten that, have you?"

"So?"

"You could have freed them."

"Guns can be fired at something invisible, too. Christopher—I—I was scared."

"Huh!" Christopher shook his head. There were a thousand things on the tip of his tongue, but they wouldn't do any good. Not now. "Scared?" he finally said. "Nonsense. I know why you didn't do anything. And why you didn't tell me. You don't have to explain."

He felt Jumar twisting in his grasp. "Because—because I didn't want you to be disappointed! Christopher! Disappointed that we can't help them. Not yet. Christopher, I only mean not yet. We couldn't have helped them down by the river. But when we find the camp—"

"Nonsense," hissed Christopher again. "You need me. That's why. You thought if I found Arne, that would be it.

Then I'd leave you. And you'd have to go on by yourself and make your own way to that base camp or whatever it is."

Jumar did not reply.

"And you don't even really need *me*. All you need is my body so that you can talk to people, nothing else."

He let go of Jumar's shoulder and spat on the ground in front of him.

"There," he said, "that's what I think of you. Find yourself someone else to lend you his body."

With those words, he turned and went along the path, the way that his brother had gone. A path that would take him to Arne. He dug his hands deep into his pockets, clenching them into fists, and his anger rang in his head. He felt as if the rage filling him made even the air harder to breathe.

The path grew narrower and steeper, winding its way past boulders and scrubby bushes, and sometimes he wasn't sure whether it was a path at all he was going along, or maybe the dry bed of a stream.

He could see the last huts lying far below him. Otherwise there was nothing to be seen.

"Jumar?" called Christopher. There was no answer.

"Okay," he said out loud. "Good riddance."

So he walked on, alone. And he climbed higher and higher, with no companion but his hunger and his own thoughts. Two hours later, there was no path or even any dry stream bed to be followed. All he found was a long heap of boulders looking like a tumbledown wall. Christopher sat down on the stony ground beside it, leaned back against the wall, concentrated for a while on breathing the cold air in and out, and turned his face up to the sun.

It burned on his cheeks just as the anger had been burning in his heart, but now that he tried to summon up that feeling again, he couldn't find it anywhere. And he began asking himself whether it had been right to shout all those accusations at Jumar.

Maybe he really couldn't have freed Arne. And if Jumar needed Christopher, didn't he need Jumar, too? Jumar might have been able to tell him where the path went on. If it went on at all. This was Jumar's country, and he knew what it was like.

He picked up a smooth, oval, flat stone. It was almost like a small plate. And when he turned it over, he noticed that there was something scratched into it: writing, but not any kind of writing he could read. He might be able to speak the language of this country, for some reason that he couldn't figure out, but he didn't know how to read its writing. Jumar did.

Christopher got to his feet and walked past the long structure of loose stones.

At its far end, someone was crouching on the ground.

He jumped, and stood stock-still. For a moment, he thought it was Jumar. But Jumar was invisible. And Jumar wasn't with him anymore.

It was an old man, crouching there to keep out of the wind. And he was made of bronze.

Christopher shook himself and took a step back. And then another. And then he began to go on uphill in a hurry. He didn't know where he was going, but he knew he was still alone.

The sun was already sinking when he reached the crest of the mountain, still without finding a path. A valley lay before him on the other side. Only beyond the valley did the mountains begin rising again, and in the distance ice glittered on the highest peaks. Christopher stopped and wondered whether to go down into the valley or on along the rocky ridge.

Arne smiled up at him out of the darkness of memory, saying, "If you go down into the valley, we'll go on reading at page fifty-one. If you'd rather go on along the ridge, we'll go on reading at page sixty-seven."

He was holding a book on his lap and sitting on the banks of a stream beside Christopher. The sun was shining, and they let their bare feet dangle in the water. Christopher was still too little to read for himself. What had he answered that day?

"We'll go together," he heard himself saying in the voice of a five-year-old. "We'll go down into the valley together, because there'll be people and something to eat there. Or what do you think?"

But Arne wasn't there, and couldn't help him.

The valley was narrow, and the village in it was the prettiest Christopher had ever seen. The houses here stood close to one another, and prayer flags were hung on their flat roofs—red, green, yellow, and blue, blowing in the wind like paper toys. The walls of the houses were not made of mud here, but of stones piled on each other like layers of slate. The branches of fruit trees rose behind walls of the same stone. Peaches and apples grew from them, and pears and apricots. From a distance, Christopher watched as goats climbed around and up the walls to eat the grass growing between the stones. A flock of chickens scurried along the broadest alley in front of a cheerful little boy, and two men were turning the hay in the low loft of a barn on the outskirts of the orchard.

"It must have been like this everywhere once," he said with a sigh. He was talking to Arne, or to himself, or just to the afternoon air.

"It will be like this everywhere again some day," said a voice beside him.

Christopher jumped.

There was nobody there.

Then he smiled. "Jumar?"

"Mmm, yes," said Jumar. He sounded rather embarrassed. "I—I'm sorry. You were right. Maybe. About me needing you."

"I'm sorry, too," muttered Christopher. "Maybe we need each other. I was going to ask you what the writing on the stones meant . . ."

"Simple prayers. You came off the path and lost your way somewhere."

"And you—you came off the path and followed me?"

"Yes."

"Promise me," said Christopher, "promise, Jumar, to tell me about everything you see from now on. It's important."

Jumar sighed. "Right. I promise."

"And I promise not to leave you alone. Even if I find Arne. I'll help you with finding the base camp and . . . and everything else that happens."

They said nothing for a while.

"This is where the violins come in," said Jumar at last.

"What?" asked Christopher, baffled.

"Violins. There'd be violins playing at this point in an American movie."

Christopher threw a punch into the air in front of him,

187

and something invisible threw a punch back. Then Jumar said, "Wait a moment. Look. Look over there!"

He took Christopher's arm and pointed it the way he meant.

Then Christopher, too, saw the shadow gliding just above the mountain, coming down over the village. Christopher's eyes searched the blue sky, and they didn't have to search for long. The dragon was shimmering green and violet, red and yellow, blue and silver.

He ducked and sensed Jumar doing the same.

For a moment, fear clutched his heart again, but the dragon wasn't heading for them. It had another goal, and soon reached it.

The people in the village streets were running around like ants, doors were slammed frantically, children dragged indoors. In a split second, there wasn't a human soul in any of the alleys. Christopher heaved a sigh of relief. It looked like everyone would be safe.

But the dragon wasn't bothered by the people. The destructive power of its shadow was only a side effect. Its broad wings covered the village when it came down to begin grazing on the colors: the juicy green of the fruit trees, the yellow of the apricots, the red of the peaches, the gold gleam of the fresh hay.

By the time Christopher and Jumar reached the village

in the mild light of early evening, the dragon had gone away. People were venturing out of their houses again and going on with their work—turning colorless hay, picking gray fruits.

The apricots were gray, the peaches were gray, the houses were gray—even the mood of the evening was gray. The village was like a burned-out candle. Its bright, glowing patch of color in the middle of the monotonous brownish green of the mountains had turned into a gray puddle of unwept tears. And suddenly the brownish-green mountains looked almost brightly colored by comparison.

How long would it be before the whole country was gray?

"Oh, it makes me so furious!" hissed Jumar. "If only I already had my father's power! It's time something was done!"

Others thought the same way as Jumar.

And that day, in the village drained of its colors, the journey of the two travelers was to take an entirely new and unexpected turn.

The one broad street in the village led to a little square, and to their surprise, the two boys heard music. The rhythm of drums and something like a lively melody drifted through the air to them from the square, enticing them, luring them on. As they got closer, they also saw the crowd of people who had gathered there.

The boys stood in the back row and craned their necks.

189

Sure enough, there in the middle of the square, two men were sitting on the ground beating drums. A third man stood beside them playing a sequence of notes on an old fiddle, and about a dozen others leaned against the wall of a house. The men wore camouflage-green army jackets and heavy boots, and their cartridge belts glinted under the jackets. It was only too clear who they were.

"I can't quite make it out," whispered Christopher, "because they're not particularly good musicians, but that tune they're playing—I've an idea it's meant to be the Internationale."

"The what?" asked Jumar. This song was not part of the royal education provided by his private tutors.

But Jumar would have to look it up in a reference book when he got home to the palace, because Christopher didn't answer him.

For at that moment, the drums fell silent, the shrill sound of the fiddle faded, and a girl stepped forward into the middle of the square. She raised one hand, and the murmuring in the square stopped as if someone had thrown a switch.

Christopher gasped.

There was something about the girl that held your gaze, something almost uncanny. He guessed that she wasn't much older than he was, yet a movement of her hand was enough to silence the crowd. She looked around, and her glance fell on

Christopher. He sensed heat rising to his face. This girl was different from all the other girls he knew.

Her eyes, shaped like two slender crescent moons, were dark, almost black—but not cold and hard like the eyes of the young guerrilla he had found dead by the rim of the well. There was a glow in her eyes, and a sparkle as vital as the buds on the trees and the wind in the branches, hot as the fire of the sun, and dangerous: You could get burned.

She had the broad, flat, regular features of the people of northern Nepal, and the skin just above her cheekbones was dark, with fine little cracks running through it like cracks in paint. Christopher had noticed this in the children up here— traces left by sun and the altitude, the handwriting of the mountains themselves.

The girl's long hair fell loose around her face, and it was a long time since it had last seen a comb. It was matted in a few places, like the fleece of sheep, and Christopher thought he saw bit of leaves and twigs in it. She wore green camouflage pants, torn at the knees, and a floppy gray shirt. A rifle was slung over her shoulder.

He felt a moment's doubt. Was this a girl at all? A boy with long hair? No. The outline of breasts was clearly visible under her shirt, still small, budding breasts, but they were there, that was for sure. Christopher realized that he was staring at her. In fact, he had been so busy staring at her that he hadn't even noticed when she began to speak. Only now did her words penetrate his mind.

And the same fire blazed in her words as in her eyes.

"Your children are starving, your cattle won't get enough nourishment from the grass in the colorless pastures," she said. "Isn't that so?"

A whisper of assent ran through the crowd.

"But the king demands taxes from you and does nothing to help you in your trouble," she went on. "Isn't that so?"

The people seemed to agree.

"And I ask you: How long will you stand by and watch your animals dying and your children's bellies swelling with hunger? How long will you listen to them crying at night because they can't sleep? How long will you hide from the dragons' shadows in your houses? How long will you tremble before Kartan's troops, who take what little food you have left when they stay with you? How long will you smell the blood they shed? How long are you going to wait, until he, Kartan, rides his coal-black horse to Kathmandu and makes himself king?"

The murmuring grew louder, swelled like a river. No, no. They weren't going to wait for that. And Christopher found himself whispering "No" along with them, very softly.

"My name is Niya," said the girl. "And I am your sister. My father went into the mountains to join those who want to change things," she went on. "Many years ago, when there were only a few of them in the mountains. We found his clothes outside the door, drenched in blood, and a heart was wrapped in his shirt. Maybe it was a goat's heart, but maybe not. Kartan's cruelty knows no bounds. My brothers followed him, and they didn't come back. My mother drowned herself in the river beyond our village when Kartan's soldiers came to ask her about them. But I hid, and I went into the mountains, and they told me that the soldiers had killed my brothers as well. My name is Niya, and I am your sister, because I have no one else left."

The crowd was quiet now, there wasn't a sound to be heard. And in the silence the girl's words sank into the hearts of the people in the village square, and began to take root in them like shoots sprouting from seeds.

"Your children go hungry," repeated the girl called Niya, "because the fruits in your orchards are colorless. The rice in the fields is colorless and doesn't satisfy you. You are caught, like frightened animals in a trap. The dragons and starvation lie in wait on one side, Kartan lies in wait on the other. And the only power that can defeat the dragons and put Kartan in his place is the power of the king. You know that. And I know it. And every guerrilla in the mountains knows it. But the king seems to have forgotten us. So we are going to have to take power for ourselves. We are strong, and we will grow stronger. There are many of us, and there will be even more. And soon, soon we will go down to Kathmandu, we will chase Kartan's troops so far away that they will never, never find the way back, and everything will change. There will be no more rich and no more poor. The palace gates will stand wide open, and the king will shed tears."

She swept back her untidy black hair, and looked around as she had done at first. It was as if she were looking every single person present in the eye. And Christopher felt a spark of her fire kindled in him, too, a tiny, glowing spark. It grew bright and full of hope.

"We in the mountains," the girl finished, "we need you. The Great T.—and I don't have to tell you about him. He needs you. He, too, is your brother, just as he is my brother, and he is waiting for you. Every one of you. Men and women alike. The brave will join us and help us to fight for justice. Tonight, when the moon rises, we'll be waiting for you up on the northern slope."

For a few seconds the crowd was silent, and then some began to applaud. Finally everyone was clapping. Christopher looked down at his hands and saw that he was clapping as well. The girl's words, her glowing eyes, and her wild hair had taken root in his heart.

Christopher stopped for a second and thought, Wasn't it people like this girl who had captured Arne? But suddenly he began to doubt that. Arne would have applauded the girl, too. Arne would have gone with her. Tall, blond, brave Arne, ready to fight for justice.

Maybe that was exactly what had happened. Maybe he'd joined the insurgents as a volunteer.

Maybe, on the way along the underground river, the guerrillas had blindfolded the foreigners only so that they couldn't give away the secret of that route later. Jumar hadn't said that they had been bound . . .

The idea was so extraordinary and so new that it made Christopher feel dizzy. But yes, he decided, that must be what happened. He stood there for a moment, dazed. It was as if this young woman's eyes had bewitched him.

And then he felt as if time were zooming forward like a rubber band shooting through the air. Christopher found himself sitting cross-legged in the dust of the village square. The villagers had served up a banquet for their guests, and it seemed quite natural for him and his invisible companion to join the party. But how different this was from the one that the soldiers had prepared for the crown prince!

It was so much less grand, but so much more honest. Christopher wondered if these were the last provisions in the village—the last that had any color, that still had life and flavor in them: the last yellow apricots, the last green beans, the last rice that left you feeling satisfied. He was almost ashamed to eat any of it, but the people he sat with urged him to have some, and the hunger inside him couldn't be ignored any longer.

He looked for the girl with the wild hair and found her at the other end of the square, surrounded by a crowd of men who seemed to be asking her questions. She had put her gun on her lap while she ate, as if it were a child. Once she seemed to glance at Christopher. He lowered his eyes.

Closer to them sat one of the drummers, and Christopher heard one of the old men from the village asking him, "Is it true that you can give the fields their color back?"

The drummer seemed to hesitate. "Yes, it's true," he said at last. "We give them their color back."

"And the rice plants will be green again? And the apricots will be yellow?"

"They won't be yellow again," replied the man. "But they will satisfy you."

"How about the statues? Is it also true that you change them back to people again?"

"We'll begin to do that soon," he said. "Soon. As soon as they've found a way to catch dragons. So far no one's succeeded, but up there in the mountains, they're working on it. We'll give you back everything you've lost if you help us."

Then he said no more for the rest of the meal. So the apricots wouldn't be yellow again, but then what? Christopher didn't understand. At this moment he didn't understand anything. He felt as if all of a sudden the world around him were speaking another language. He understood the words, he heard the sentences, but they didn't get through to him.

"If we follow them, they may take us where we want to go," whispered Jumar beside him. Christopher jumped. He had almost forgotten Jumar.

"To the base camp," Jumar went on, still in a whisper. "Where we've been wanting to go all this time. Where I expect your brother is, too."

"Of course," he murmured. "We'll follow them."

And he thought he should be thinking about Arne now, but a pair of burning eyes had taken Arne's place in his mind, suddenly and without asking permission.

They left the village ahead of the men, and no one noticed at all.

The wall of a house cast its friendly shadow over them, and the sun sank behind the mountains, large and oval, red as blood, glowing like the girl's eyes.

They waited a long time in silence.

At last a group of guerrillas riding horses and mules passed by. Christopher counted thirteen of them. Their saddlebags were almost bursting with what the village had given them to take away, and the moonlight was reflected on the shiny barrels of their guns. They were singing—not the "Internationale" now, but a slow, soft, melancholy song, with words that Christopher couldn't make out.

"Where—where is she?" whispered Jumar, when the men had passed.

"Maybe she isn't riding back with them," replied Christopher. "Maybe her group divided, and some of them are going on to the next village."

"Yes, maybe," said Jumar. Christopher heard the poorly concealed disappointment in his voice. And sensed a quiet echo of the same disappointment in himself.

"You'd have liked to see her again, right?" whispered Christopher.

He got no answer.

"Jumar," said Christopher, "she's one of the people you want to kill. One of their leaders!"

"Shut up," said Jumar brusquely, and Christopher heard fabric rustling as he got to his feet.

But he also heard something else. Jumar was murmuring, more to himself than anyone else. "And the king—the king will shed tears."

Because that, he thought, was what he, the heir to the throne of Nepal, wanted. He wanted his father to feel sorry for never having taken him seriously.

"We must get moving. If we don't want to lose them."

The slope to the north of the village was bleak and barren as the moon. Broken rock covered its surface, with a few tufts of grass. You could hardly say where the path was. The horses loomed above them in the night and they heard their hooves trying to find firm footing on the gravel. Little stones trickled down toward them.

"If they turn around now," Christopher whispered, "they'll see us in the light as clear as day."

"They won't turn around," Jumar whispered back, and he was right.

The slope ended when it reached a steep wall of rock, and there they lost sight of the outlines of the riders. Their shadows merged with the shadow of the wall. Presumably they were waiting there, under the overhanging rocks, for any brave villagers who decided to join them.

Christopher looked around.

Below them, the slope lay empty in the moonlight. The village seemed to be asleep. Now, by night, you could hardly see that its colors were missing, and it looked as peaceful as a picture.

"Cowards," he heard Jumar muttering.

"What?" asked Christopher.

"Oh, nothing. Come on."

But they did not get much farther, for very soon the peaceful scene with the huts spewed out a troop of mounted men storming up from the valley as if the devil were after them. At first Christopher thought: These are men from the village. They've made up their minds to follow the insurgents after all. Then he thought: But why are they in such a hurry? And how do they all have those fine, tall horses? You don't often see horses like that in the mountains.

And then he thought: They're making straight for us. For me. Because I'm the one they can see.

They could see him very well indeed in the bright moonlight on the barren slope.

He stood on the stony path like a target, like a straw dummy on a firing range.

"Uniforms," said Christopher. He had stopped, because it was no use running away now, and he spoke out loud, because it was no use whispering anymore. "They're wearing uniforms. I can see their epaulettes."

"Kartan's men," said Jumar. "They're not after the Maoists."

The words fell into the darkness.

Kartan's men.

They were coming closer fast, the thudding of the horses' hooves breaking the silence into a thousand little pieces, and it was as if you could hear Kartan's breathing in it, like the breathing of a great beast of prey, a wild cat, coming closer and closer—

Christopher wanted to ask Jumar what they should do, but he knew there wasn't any answer.

He turned pointlessly on his own heel, looking for an answer.

He found it without knowing what he had been looking for.

Suddenly, without warning, there was another rider there—a rider on a small, sturdy horse. The rider was coming up from the side, out of nowhere, in a cloud of pebbles and dust, galloping at an angle over the slope and up to them, with a second horse close behind.

"What—" Christopher began. The rider was beside him, and he was enveloped in the cloud of dust, and someone ordered, from the back of the horse, "Get up on it!"

Then Christopher recognized her.

It was the girl with the wild hair, Niya. He could have sworn her eyes were glowing like live coals in the dark.

"What? I—" stammered Christopher. "I'm not one of you. You've no idea how little I belong here."

"Who cares?" she replied briefly. "Get up on that damn horse."

Christopher felt Jumar helping him up on the back of the riderless horse. The girl had been holding its reins, and now let them go. Seconds later, they were racing together through the dust. They were being chased. Christopher clung desperately to the horse's neck. Jumar had his arms around his waist, and once, when Christopher glanced back, he saw the soldiers were very close.

Niya did not lead them into the shadow of the rock wall where her men were waiting, but parallel to the rise of the slope. Christopher heard the hooves of their pursuers' horses; he heard them shout something, but he didn't understand what they were saying. There was a shot, which missed. A second. He ducked lower.

And then he saw Niya turn in mid-gallop. The gun he had seen slung over her shoulder earlier was like part of her body; it merged with her, became an extension of her burning gaze, and the shot she fired found its mark.

Christopher heard a whinny and a scream. He thought his eardrums would burst. Her movements burned themselves into his memory like a trail of gunpowder, he saw her in slow motion, saw her again and again, long after that day in his dreams.

She fired shot after shot into the night, the bullets like carrier pigeons bearing her deadly message. Answers came back at once, but they became isolated, and finally a great, heavy silence surrounded them. Niya stopped the horses.

There were patches of black on the slope behind them in the darkness. Patches on the ground, lying there like stones.

They were calm now, calm and peaceful. Niya's message had been successfully delivered.

The four horses trotting down the slope had no riders.

"They're useless in the mountains," said Niya. "The wrong sort of horse. Kartan will never learn the laws of the mountains."

She looked at Christopher, and although he cast his eyes down again, he felt her inquiring gaze wandering over his face.

And Christopher didn't know who he was most afraid of—Kartan or Niya.

But she had saved his life. And her glance had buried itself in his heart. It was nesting inside him, and there was nothing he could do about it.

"It's easier to shoot the horses, but I never do," she explained. "It's not their fault." Then she reached her hand out to Christopher and gently raised his chin so that he had to look into her eyes.

And for the first time, he saw a smile there. It surprised him, because it was an almost shy smile.

"Why are they so hell-bent on killing you?" she asked.

NIYA'S REVENGE

THEY RODE ALL THROUGH THE NIGHT.
Waves of sleep swept over Christopher, interrupted
by brief, disconnected dreams. His room at home featured in
them, and his parents' faces, but he couldn't make any sense
of them.

He kept waking in the night, startled and disoriented. He
saw the dark shadow of his rescuer with her wild hair ahead
of him, and he lapsed back into the mists of sleep.

Sometimes in his dream he thought of his reply to Niya.
My story is too long to be told on a night like this.

And it was true.

When he finally woke up, the sun was shining on the coat of her horse, which gleamed with sweat.

Plants with five-lobed leaves grew beside the path they were riding down now, and Christopher thought they looked as if you could smoke them, but Jumar told him in an amused whisper that they were only weeds.

Niya turned her head. "Did you say something?"

"Me? No."

"Strange," she murmured, and a little later they stopped.

"The horses have never been so slow before," said Niya. "It's a miracle that we got here at all. But here we are."

Christopher avoided her eyes. She couldn't know his horse had been carrying two riders all night.

Ahead of them, a handful of huts could be seen emerging from the morning mist. But there were no people outside at all. A strange silence lay over the place.

Niya dismounted gracefully and Christopher laboriously climbed off his horse's back. Every bone in his body ached, and he had never before realized how many bones he had.

He would have liked to whisper something to Jumar, but Niya would have noticed.

"We'll find out here where the others are," said Niya. "We rode a long way around in case someone followed us after all. But I didn't see anyone."

They led the horses through the village, and Christopher expected Niya to knock on one of the doors. Instead, she did something else.

In the middle of the village, a wall along the sandy path rose to shoulder height, with a set of brass prayer drums gleaming along both sides of it. They were metal cylinders the size of hats, engraved with large Nepalese letters—a prayer on each drum. Christopher had seen a photo of a prayer wall like this in his library book, and the caption had told him that a stick ran through the middle of each hollow drum, sometimes with a scroll of paper wrapped around it that featured a long prayer. The drums turned around the axis of the sticks. You had to keep to the left-hand side of the wall so that you could turn the drums with your right hand in passing. Each turn of a drum counted as a prayer.

Niya went ahead, her right hand reaching out to the drums, and in the morning light, Christopher saw the scar of a wide burn mark on the back of her hand.

He watched as she turned the cylinders. *Om mani pad me hum, om mani pad me hum*, sang the prayer drums. They had clearly left the Hindu part of the country behind them. It was uncomfortable for the colorful crowd of Hindu gods up in these heights. Only the Buddha sat with his usual composure in his temples on the peaks. He must not mind the bleakness of the countryside, thought Christopher.

"There!" Niya stopped halfway along the prayer wall. "Hear that?"

She turned one of the drums again.

Christopher listened. There was a faint crackling, a tiny rustling—he would never have noticed it if she hadn't drawn his attention to it.

Niya fingered the upper end of the metal prayer drum where the stick disappeared into a hole in the drum, and when she withdrew her hand, she had freed a piece of thin paper from the spindle.

She unfolded it, read it, nodded, and tore up the paper.

"Come on," she said. "It's not far now."

Christopher held back a groan. Every fiber in his body rebelled against climbing on that horse again, but Jumar helped him up, and they left the village. Christopher looked around. There was still no sound to be heard, smoke rose nowhere from any fire, there was nothing moving in sight.

Niya followed his gaze.

"There's no one there now," she said. "They've abandoned the huts."

"Abandoned them? Why?"

"Kartan," Niya replied. That was all. Then she turned

her eyes to look straight ahead, and Christopher did not venture to ask any more questions. Half an hour later, the path led them over a hill, and beyond it lay a narrow valley with steep walls. Niya stopped her horse and took a deep breath. "We hardly needed their message," she said with a smile, pointing. "There, and there, and over there! Do you see that?"

The valley was gray, almost colorless. A colorless village lay in the middle of it, like the one with the orchards. But there was a difference here: Color seemed to be coming back into many of the fields.

Christopher was confused.

He hadn't been mistaken. Small groups of men and women were moving down the pathways through the fields. They didn't seem to be doing anything but strolling along, yet where they had walked, color began returning to the rice paddies. A few solitary notes of music rose from the valley, the scraps of a song carried on the wind.

"That's—that's them?" he asked. "Your people?"

"Not mine. The Great T.'s people. But, of course, I'm one of them myself."

"Then—then it's true? You can give the fields their colors back?"

Niya nodded. "With our songs. It takes a long time, but it

209

works. Come on and I'll introduce you to them. And it's time we had something to eat."

"Wait a minute," said Christopher. "I—I don't know. I don't know if I belong with you."

"Everyone who's hunted by Kartan belongs with us," Niya told him gravely.

Christopher nodded. He wished he could have read the thoughts of the invisible rider behind him.

It must be best to follow the black-eyed girl. Hadn't they set out to find the insurgents? And here they were, sitting on one of the insurgents' horses, invited to go and eat with them.

Well, no, said Christopher to himself. That's not why I came. I'll go on by myself and find Arne.

But he knew that was impossible now. His own story and Jumar's had been woven together long ago. They couldn't be separated now.

And when he followed Niya down into the valley, he felt like a traitor.

She had saved her own enemies' lives without knowing it.

The farther down into the valley they went, the more clearly did the melody carry up to them, and when they had almost reached the first group of singers, the song wrapped around them.

"That's strange," Christopher heard Jumar whisper very close to his ear. "Look at those rice plants. And the paths. Even the tiny flowers at the roadside, the huts . . . the ones getting some color back again."

Christopher narrowed his eyes.

"They're like a badly developed film," he whispered back at last. "They all . . . they all have a tinge of red—"

Niya turned. She looked at him for a while, but she didn't say anything. They eventually reached the first little group walking through the fields.

There were three women and two men, and they stopped and placed their hands together in greeting. Christopher caught himself looking at the women. They wore the same green camouflage pants and the same boots as Niya; otherwise they had little in common. They hid their hair under patterned scarves, but where any of it showed, it seemed to be well combed and glossy, and they carried no weapons. They were all older than Niya, and their eyes were beautiful and dark and full of determination. But no fire burned in them.

"This is a friend," Niya told them, pointing to Christopher. "I literally plucked him from the claws of Kartan's men, although I don't know why they wanted to kill him. At the moment, he can't be safe anywhere but here with us. They could come after him again."

She turned to Christopher and put a matted strand of hair back behind her ear. "You didn't tell me your name."

"Uh . . . ," said Christopher. He was blushing again, and felt furious with himself. "Christopher. My name is Christopher."

"Kisopa. Kisopee?" The women giggled, and the two men's sunburned faces wore grins of amusement. "Where do you come from with a name like that—a name no one can pronounce?"

"I'll tell you some day," he replied.

The Maoists had pitched camp in a corner of the valley that couldn't be seen from the village—it was hidden from view by a huge rock. Their tents looked suspiciously like those used by the army.

Fragrant rice was cooking over an open fire in the middle of the camp, and Niya gestured for Christopher to sit down.

Arne, said a voice in Christopher's head, and blue eyes struggled with black eyes to come first in Christopher's thoughts. Had Arne been here? Was he near? In one of the tents? Absurdly, Christopher's eyes searched the ground for footprints. Footprints left by rainboots with laughing clown faces. An almost forgotten afternoon in fall boiled over in his memory.

Had Arne sat by this fire?

"You look pale, as if a color dragon had been licking your

face," said Niya, handing him a bowl of rice. The rice was red, but it was satisfying, and Christopher didn't say no when she led him into one of the tents and gave him a blanket so that he could get a little sleep.

Before she left, she looked into his eyes. "When we get a chance," she said, "I really would like to hear your story."

And then she had gone. The tent flap was still moving gently back and forth, like a memory of her graceful movements, and for a moment her presence lingered in the air.

Christopher sighed. "Jumar," he said, "what are we going to do now?"

And when Jumar replied, he was surprised by the clear tone of his voice.

"I was wrong," said Jumar.

"What?"

"You heard me. I was wrong. It's all different from the way I thought. I've spent a long time working out what to do next. And now I know."

"You do?"

"Can you remember what she said in the square, with all those people listening?"

Christopher nodded. How could he forget? Every word was there in his head, burned into his mind. He couldn't extinguish those memories now.

"'The only power that can defeat the dragons and put Kartan in his place is the power of the king . . . But the king seems to have forgotten us.' It's true, Christopher. He's forgotten them. He's forgotten us all. We need his power. The Maoists want the same as I do. They want to get rid of Kartan. They want to drive hunger away. They want peace. I thought I should hate them. But how can I hate anyone who wants what I want?"

"How about the old servant who fell into your arms? Weren't you going to avenge his murder? Isn't that why you left Kathmandu in the first place?"

"I suspect Kartan had something to do with that as well. Maybe old Tapa was talked into believing he'd fallen into the hands of the insurgents, but I don't think it was them at all."

"What are you going to do?"

"Stay with them and help them," replied Jumar. "What else *can* I do?"

"But they're Communists. You'll never get to be king."

"Who cares if I'm king or not?" said Jumar, and his cheerful tone of voice surprised Christopher. "What's a king good for? Maybe I'll be a mathematician or an astronaut instead!" And he laughed.

"An astronaut?" said Christopher doubtfully. Jumar punched him in the ribs.

"Only joking. Maybe I'll go to Europe myself and study there. And maybe I'll even come and visit you. Where did you say you lived? Norway? Sweden?"

"Germany."

"I'll never be able to tell the difference. Anyway, I'll visit you when all this is over."

"When all this is over . . . ," Christopher repeated. If only he could have taken things as lightly as the strange, invisible boy beside him!

"And how about Arne?" he asked. "How about my brother?"

"Oh, of course we'll set him free," replied Jumar. "Do you think I forgot about that? When we've been here for a while, we'll speak to the people. When they trust us. When we've shown that we're to be trusted. We'll explain things to them and they'll listen."

"I've been wondering whether he really is a captive," said Christopher. "Maybe he went with the fighters because he wanted to." That would be just like Arne. "Maybe . . . just maybe he's even here."

"Yes and no," said Jumar. "Maybe he's not a captive, but he isn't here. I looked inside the other tents. Just now, while you were sitting beside the fire. We'll soon find him, Christopher. I know we will."

He yawned, and Christopher couldn't help yawning, too.

"But let's get some sleep now," said Jumar, and Christopher heard a rustling as he stretched out on the floor.

"Yes," said Christopher. "Yes, we'd better do that."

And just this once, he gave his doubts and worries a well-aimed mental kick into the background. He was too exhausted to deal with them.

Everything was all right. They weren't traitors. They would set Arne free without having to creep about on the sly. There'd be no more lies and no fear of being caught in the act.

And they were not alone now.

They want the same as I do. He heard Jumar saying that again.

In Christopher's dreams, he felt the touch of Niya's hand—the hand with the scar of a burn on it. Her hand was warm and alive.

"The first thing you have to learn is how to shoot," said Niya.

A cold wind was driving large, ragged clouds across the sky, and Christopher stood helplessly in front of a wooden frame with rusty cans dangling from it on strings. Sometimes a draft of air moved them gently back and forth. There was a whole row of guns lined up against a nearby rock.

The weapon in Christopher's hands was heavy and black.

It seemed to be resisting his fingers—or maybe his fingers were resisting it.

Niya kept patiently getting it into the right position. The touch of her hands was like her touch in his dream.

He found it hard to concentrate on aiming.

The air rifle fired corks, but none of them hit its target. The cans swung lazily in the afternoon light.

He tried to imagine that they were part of the rifle range at a carnival. But it was no good. His memory of the shooting on the night when Niya had sent the four horses back without their riders was still fresh in his mind.

And the cans changed before his eyes as they themselves thought best. Sometimes when he blinked, they were human heads nodding to him. He saw fear in their eyes. Then they were Kartan's men, uniform buttons gleaming in the sun, laughing at him. Sometimes Arne's face appeared in front of the cans; sometimes Niya's.

Finally he shook his head and put the gun down. His hands were shaking. "I can't do it," he said. "I'm not cut out for this sort of thing."

"Try again," said Niya gently.

Christopher raised the gun and shot without even looking. He just wanted to get away from the weapon, away from the noise of the shots.

When he was about to give up, one of the corks hit the middle of a can, and Niya clapped. Then he hit another. And then another.

But that was wrong. He wasn't hitting the cans. And then Niya herself noticed. Christopher's corks were still missing the cans. The corks that hit them came from a little way to one side of him. Christopher counted the guns leaning on the rock. One of them was missing.

He sensed Niya's eyes on him.

"There's someone else here," she said quietly.

"Yes," said Christopher.

Now she was staring at her arm as if some invisible insect were sitting on it. But Christopher knew it wasn't an insect. It was the touch of an invisible hand.

"Time for the truth," he heard Jumar's voice saying.

The heir to the throne of Nepal had read all the novels in the palace, he had let the poetry of the eastern and western worlds wash over him, he had seen all the films he could get hold of, and heard all the music lying hidden in the grooves of vinyl records and the shining surfaces of his tutor's CDs. He consumed all those novels and poems and films and songs with the same eternal subject: love.

He used to puzzle over that.

Because he had never been in love.

But on the day when he heard a girl speaking in the dust of a colorless village—a girl who didn't fit in with any of the novels, any of the poems, any of the films, or any of the music—it seized upon him like an unknown power. Love had him in its grip.

He didn't know what it was, or where it would lead him, but he knew he stood no chance against that power. When he looked at Niya, he felt as if he had a fever. His cheeks burned, and his head seemed to be floating in the air.

When he put his hand on her arm, he felt the fine little hairs on her skin, and he had to take a breath before he could say anything.

"Time for the truth," Jumar said.

"The truth?" asked Niya. She looked past him, searching and seeing nothing.

Then he took her hand, just as he had taken Christopher's when they first met, and guided it to his face, so that she would understand. But when her fingers moved over his forehead and eyebrows, he was sorry he had done that, because he thought he would burst apart with longing for her.

All this was new to him, and unsettling. He was only fourteen.

"You didn't save just one life, you saved two," he whispered. He hoped she wouldn't notice how his voice trembled. "I'm Jumar, and I was born invisible like this."

Niya was silent. Then she asked, "Why?"

"No one knows."

"Didn't you ever try to find out?"

"No," said Jumar, taken aback.

"Well, you can still do it," she said, and smiled. Then she withdrew her hand. "Anyway, you know how to shoot."

"I was watching you and Christopher."

She seemed to think for a moment. "An invisible man," she said, "is worth gold to us. The Great T. will be over the moon. An invisible man can do all kinds of things that someone visible can't. Will you stay with us?"

"I'll help you and do whatever you want me to," said Jumar, and he could hear how emotional that sounded, but when you are fourteen and in love for the first time, you can't help feeling a certain amount of emotion.

"Is it all right if I tell the others?"

"Tell them I'm invisible, you mean?"

She tipped her head back and laughed, and Christopher joined in.

"That," she said, "is something they'll probably notice anyway if you talk to them."

And Jumar knew he was going red in the face right up to the hairline. It was a good thing no one could see.

It took the Maoists some time to get used to Jumar's presence, but living in the mountains had exposed them to many strange things, as strange as an invisible man.

The group went traveling again the next morning. The fields they had passed, singing, stayed green behind them—green with a faint tinge of red. But the rice was satisfying to eat again.

"We're on our way to the base camp," Niya explained. "Just like many other small groups. And when we get there, we want to be as many as possible. And we want to bring a great many mules and horses. The Great T. is waiting for us. Waiting for new recruits to come and join his ranks for training. He doesn't send anyone into the fight defenseless. He's waiting for you two, as well, even if he doesn't realize that yet. Once we're at the base camp, you'll learn all you need to know."

Jumar saw her winking at Christopher, and he felt a pang.

"Even *you* will learn to shoot there, you can be sure of that," she said, giving him a friendly nudge.

And the heir to the throne of Nepal, whose real identity was not yet known by Niya, sighed silently, deep in his heart. What good did it do him to be able to fire corks and hit a few rusty cans? He was still invisible, and sometimes he felt that Niya was forgetting him. But Christopher was visible. He was the one she talked to.

At this moment, he wished he were like everyone else.

Why was he invisible? Niya's words were still echoing around in his head.

Soon, however, there would be a different way for him to show Niya how indispensable he was.

It was a cool evening, and they had been riding for a long, long time without seeing any human dwellings. When they saw the outline of a village in the distance, they all breathed a sigh of relief. They were hungry, thirsty, and tired; the animals needed rest, and it was going to be a cold night. Niya, Jumar, Christopher, and two other men rode ahead down the streets, and knocked at the door of the biggest house in the village. It was a handsome old building with three floors and balconies running around each of them. The rails around the balconies were decorated with wooden carvings of peacocks, tigers, deer, and plants.

A tiny woman opened the door. She wasn't much bigger than a child.

Jumar saw the fear in her eyes as she stared at the men with guns over their shoulders.

"We're looking for a place to stay overnight," said Niya. "This is the biggest, finest house in the village. I'm sure you have room for a handful of tired guerrillas, don't you?"

"I don't think my master will see uninvited visitors," the woman replied. Her voice shook in the evening air. "I'll go and ask," she said, and tried to shut the door, but one of the men put his foot in the way.

"We'd rather this stayed open," he said with a friendly smile.

A little later, the tiny woman reappeared, but now she was accompanied by several men.

"The master of this house does not open his doors to those who are disloyal to the king," said the tallest of the men. "That's all I can say."

"Wouldn't the master of the house prefer to speak to us himself?" asked Niya politely.

"He doesn't want anything to do with you," replied the man.

"Are those buildings next to the house his stables?" Niya asked peaceably.

"Not just his stables. The storehouses, the well—every square yard of this village belongs to him. Even the road you're standing on. As you can see, it's a fine road. Only a man like our master could have afforded to pave it. The fields are his, so are the pastures, the cattle—whatever you see. He is a great lord. The small farmers all owe him debts, but he lets them go on working on his land."

"I'm glad to hear it," said Niya. Jumar sensed something cold emanating from her, like a wave of anger that she was holding back only with the utmost self-control.

"And could your master spare a few sacks from his lavish stores of food?" Niya inquired. Jumar knew what the answer would be, and he knew that Niya knew. He clenched his fists in the pockets of the shabby old jeans of Christopher's he wore.

At that moment, a door creaked on the floor above, and a middle-aged man came out on the balcony. He wore a smile on his face, and a white shirt draped over a neat little paunch. He had a cloth tied around his waist, and over the shirt he wore one of those vests that Jumar had seen on the police officers in Kathmandu. This man was expecting bullets fired from black guns, expecting hatred and death. He knew who was trying to take shelter in his house, and he was no fool.

Still smiling, he leaned on the carved wooden rail of the balcony, and looked down at Niya and her companions.

"I think you had better get out of here," he told them. "What a pitiful group. Thin and dirty! As guerrillas you've seen better days. You stand no chance against my men. Although I know there are more of you lying in wait somewhere nearby, well, you've come to the wrong house here. You are on my land and my property. Leave this village before I lose my temper. I lose my temper quickly, and I have a good friend in the army. The best friend a man could wish for."

"Kartan," said Niya. Her voice was suddenly strangely flat.

"I did a great deal for him once, far from here," replied the man. Then he suddenly leaned forward and scrutinized Niya.

"We know each other, don't we?" he said after a while. "Am I right?"

"You wore a uniform," replied Niya. "And you didn't have a paunch. I was afraid of you then. The fire you lit burned my fear away."

The man laughed. "Fine words," he said. "As fine and beautiful as your mother was. She was one of the loveliest women I had. You are beautiful, too. I didn't think you were still alive. Perhaps you will come to see me on your own one of these days . . . and then we can talk to each other."

He let his eyes wander, with obvious pleasure, over the body beneath the green jacket, and Jumar thought Niya was going to level her gun at that fat face above the bulletproof vest and fire a shot. He thought she was going to go off like fireworks in an uncontrollable explosion, a whirlwind of red anger.

But she turned in silence and signalled to the others to follow her.

When they were back with the rest, she said nothing. It was as if the words had dried up in her throat.

"Niya—" Jumar began. She shook her head and led her followers around the village until it was out of sight. Then she indicated that they should stop and pitch their camp.

"Aren't we riding on?" asked one of the women. "To the next village? Shouldn't we find a level place for our tents somewhere? And water—for the animals."

Only then did Niya speak again. "You'll have to put up with the wind tonight," she said. "And the dew on the grass will have to be enough for the animals. I have something to do here."

No one dared to argue with her.

When the clouds had passed over, and the stars in their constellations began rising above the horizon, Niya took Jumar and Christopher aside.

"You two must help me tonight," she said. "Really, Jumar's the one who must help me. Tonight I need someone invisible."

"I'm willing," replied Jumar. And there came all that emotion again. He would have said so much more, he would have sworn to do anything she wanted, but she put a finger to her lips to silence him.

"Tonight," she whispered, "a rich man's stables will burn down. His stocks of provisions will turn to white ashes. His horses will smell freedom. And the beautiful carvings around his house will turn to glowing embers. And you're the one who will light the fire."

Jumar nodded, even though she couldn't see it. He nodded for himself. Yes, he would light the fire. He would be the one who took revenge for her.

She pulled two small glass bottles from a box and handed them to him. At first he didn't understand. Then he saw the fuses, and realized that the bottles were explosives.

"Let the horses out before you light the first fire," she whispered. "Don't forget that. And leave the stable door open. Throw the second bottle through the window of the barn. It stands right next to the house, and the flames will easily spread. I'll come with you."

"Can I come, too?" asked Christopher. Jumar cast him a surprised glance.

"Yes, if you like," said Niya. Part of Jumar was relieved. Another part was annoyed. This was *his* task. Christopher wasn't needed. Didn't he understand that?

The heir to the throne of Nepal was far from realizing that he was the one who hadn't understood.

✦ ✦ ✦

That was the blackest night that Jumar had ever known. They had come back on foot so as to make no noise.

The two glass bottles were in Jumar's backpack. He carried a gun, like Niya. Only Christopher's shoulders bore no weight of any kind.

"If we give you a gun, you'll just blow yourself sky-high," Niya kindly explained. "Or shoot me in the guts."

Christopher seemed relieved.

The large, handsome house was a part of the night now, a part of its blackness, dense and sinister. But the owner of the house was not stupid: Three armed men squatted outside the door by the flickering light of an oil lamp, and there were two more leaning against the stables, their watchful eyes gazing constantly into the night.

But even the most watchful eyes couldn't see the boy who came to leave their master's house in ashes.

Niya pressed Jumar's invisible hands, and her strength seemed to flow through his body. He returned the pressure of her hands, let them go, and stole toward the stable door.

He looked around. Niya and Christopher had disappeared as if they, too, were invisible. Only he knew that their outlines on the other side of the street were merging with one of the walls of the house, waiting.

The first glass bottle weighed heavy in his hand. He pulled back the bolt of the wooden door, slipped through, and breathed in the smell of hay and horses. He wished he'd taken a lantern with him. It seemed forever before he had all the horses untied. Their irritable snorting could give him away at any moment; the nervous scraping of their hooves on the stable floor sent shivers running down his back. At long last, he undid the last halter. He left the bottle in the far corner of the stable so that the flames wouldn't come between the horses and the door. He wasn't sure if that was any good. Maybe they wouldn't make it. Maybe they would burn with their stable.

He thought of Christopher, and how he had been so disturbed at the sound of the goat's death cry. Christopher couldn't have done this. Christopher would never understand what was necessary. Sometimes you have to do things you don't like to achieve your ends. They saw things differently where Christopher came from.

The flame of the match flared brightly in the dark, and he saw its reflection in the eyes of the horses standing closest to him. Now the end of the fuse was smoldering.

Jumar blew out the match and ran for the door. He reached the road, stood there for a moment, and listened. Nothing. On past the house to the big barn full of supplies.

The second fuse caught fire. He opened the shutter over the barn window and threw the bottle in.

But now the men had seen something. Or maybe they had heard the bottle fall on the barn floor.

One of them was coming his way.

Jumar moved away, going backward. His heart was in his mouth, and he forced himself to breathe steadily. He could have called out to the man, given him a warning.

He was invisible. No one could do anything to him.

But Jumar didn't call out. He went on walking backward.

The man opened the barn door.

And then the first explosion tore through the air. The second followed. Jumar saw the light in front of him—a huge, bright light. He saw the man flung back, saw the flames shooting out of the building, and behind him he felt the cool of the house wall against which he was now leaning. The night had turned to chaos.

He heard the shrill whinnying of the panic-stricken horses. He heard the crackle of the fire, and screams.

He smelled the burning wood, and the fear in the air. The fire had begun licking at the house now, devouring the beautiful wooden handrail around the balcony, and a stream of people poured out into the night through the doors.

Seconds later, he saw someone running in the opposite

direction, toward the stable. The door had closed again, Jumar couldn't think why, and now someone was trying to get it open: a small, slight figure.

Whoever that is, thought Jumar, he must be out of his mind.

And at that moment, he knew who it was: Christopher.

Christopher, who couldn't bear the death cry of a goat. He was trying to save the horses. He *was* out of his mind.

Jumar saw him struggling with the bolt, and then he managed to open the door. The light on the other side of it made Jumar close his eyes briefly. When he opened them again, the first horses were racing past him. He looked for Christopher in the confused, dancing shadows, but he couldn't see him.

Jumar tried to make his own way back to the stable. Waves of heat pulsed into his face. But the horses wouldn't let him by; there were too many of them. Only when their screams of fear had been swallowed up by the night did he make it. The stable wasn't a stable anymore, it was a single huge, blazing pyre.

"Christopher!" yelled Jumar. He could hardly hear his own voice. People were shouting in the village streets as they all came running out of their houses. The flames crackled, the world was made of nothing but crazy, incoherent noise.

In the middle of all that noise, Jumar heard his name.

231

But it wasn't Christopher calling to him. It was Niya.

And then he saw her—she was kneeling on the ground a few feet away, she had left her hiding place, but no one had noticed her in the confusion.

In a moment, he was with her, crouching down beside her, and then he saw why she was on the ground there: A motionless body lay in her arms.

"Christopher," whispered Jumar.

"We have to get him out of here," said Niya. "Help me!"

Jumar wanted to ask questions. He wanted to know what had happened. Whether Christopher was breathing. Whether he was alive. But he said nothing, and did as Niya wanted. She took his backpack from him and instead helped him load the limp, slight figure onto his back. No one, thought Jumar, seeing Christopher being carried down the street by invisible hands, apparently floating in the air, was going to stop them. The idea almost made him smile.

They turned into a side street, where it was quieter, and the crackling fire was left behind them.

"I'd have liked to see him," whispered Niya. "But I couldn't spot him anywhere. There were too many people. I wanted to watch his face when he saw his house burning."

"I'm sure it was worth seeing," said Jumar, pressing her arm.

"The question is whether it was worth *this*," she whispered, nodding her head at Christopher. "I—I didn't want that, you know. I wanted to hold him back, but he tore himself away. The last thing he said was: 'You said it yourself, Niya. It's not the horses' fault.'"

"He didn't want them to burn to death. He's not like us."

"I know," said Niya. "I know."

When they reached the camp where the men and women were sleeping side by side, wrapped in blankets on the bare, sloping ground, they put Christopher down on a blanket, and Jumar heard his shallow breathing.

"It's the smoke," said Niya. "He inhaled too much smoke. The fire got into his lungs. It's my fault."

"No," murmured Jumar. "No, it isn't."

And he took her in his arms, and felt her heart beating against his chest. She leaned against him as if, for a moment, all her strength had left her, and Jumar thought how wonderful her body felt against his.

But he knew that her thoughts were with Christopher.

NIYA'S SONG

A SONG WOKE HIM.

There were words in the darkness, and he lay there with his eyes closed, listening to them. The notes of a guitar accompanied the beautiful words full of sadness.

At first he didn't understand them. His mind was still in a place where there were no words. He had been dreaming of his parents. A mild evening in early summer. The doors to the veranda were open, and the scent of wisteria drifted in. The old record player was playing a waltz, and Christopher had seen his parents dancing in the living room in the twilight, before they turned the light on.

Arne had been sitting by the open veranda door, reading a book.

The waltz was all that was left of his dream. The guitar, too, was playing a waltz. How odd, thought Christopher, because I'm in Nepal. And are there waltzes here? Well, there are ramen instant noodles, and there are radios and guns, so why wouldn't there be waltzes?

The voice kept repeating its words again and again, and finally he could make them out. The song was a love song—a sad love song with a color like dark blue.

You say that you will love me
As long as the stars shine.
You say that while the winds blow,
You will still be mine.
You say you'll always love me,
But now there is no sign,
My dear, that you spoke true.

The night is dark, without a star,
No wind blows either near or far,
And now my heart bears sorrow's scar,
For I hear no more from you.

235

Over the mountains you went away,
They caught and killed you on that day.
My unseen lover, you would not stay,
By the light of sun or moon.

Rivers you swam, but you were slain.
You will not come this way again,
And so I suffer grief and pain
And sing this sweet, sad tune.

But none have seen me shed a tear,
I, too, will cross the mountains here.
I have not yet wept for you.

All my bridges I will break,
I'll be revenged for your dear sake,
Till Death unites us two.

Now Christopher knew the voice. It was hers. *Niya's.*
Her voice was rough as she sang, like the rusty metal of
the empty cans he hadn't been able to hit. But it was a voice
that suited the melancholy of the song. Christopher opened
his eyes. It was night. Above him was the wide sky, covered
with stars.

He wanted to say something, but his voice would obey him only after a couple of attempts. "Was . . . Was it like that?" he asked. His throat hurt, and his words were no more than a hoarse whisper.

But she heard him. The outline of her face, surrounded by her wild hair, appeared over him, shutting out the stars for a moment.

"Are you awake?" she asked.

"No," Christopher whispered. "I'm talking in my dreams."

"Oh, are you?" she said. "Then let me tell you, in your dreams, you're crazy. Out of your mind. A lunatic."

"Thanks very much," said Christopher modestly.

"But better a live lunatic than someone reasonable and dead," said Niya. "I can't tell you how glad I am to hear your voice again."

"Jumar," Christopher managed to say. "Where is he? Is he all right?"

"He's asleep," Niya whispered. "In the big tent with the others. But I couldn't sleep, and I thought you could do with a little starlight, too. . . . Jumar told me you quite often take refuge in unconsciousness, and it was nothing to worry about. But he was more worried about you than any of the rest of us. He dragged you around with him on his horse for three days, like a dead man. The others thought we ought to leave you behind in a village somewhere. Maybe that would have been better for you. But Jumar refused to ride on without you."

"The others . . . ," Christopher murmured. "And you?"

Reluctantly, Niya shook her head. He couldn't see the expression on her face in the dark. "That's nothing to do with it," she said. "What did you ask before?"

"The song. The song about the man going over the hills . . . Is it true?"

"Oh, definitely," she replied. "It's true for a lot of people."

"Including you?"

She laughed quietly. "You mean, do I have a lover who's gone away? No. But it makes no difference whether the man is a lover or your brother or your father."

"So what you said in the village square that night was true?"

"Every word of it," replied Niya seriously.

Christopher was silent for a while.

"It's all so different where I come from," he said at last.

"Where do you come from?"

He hesitated.

"Even this night isn't long enough for you to tell your story, am I right?" she asked.

"I'm afraid it isn't," replied Christopher.

"We'll reach our base camp in a few days' time," said Niya. "Perhaps the nights will be long enough there."

"What's it like at the base camp?"

"I don't know," she replied. "I've never been there before myself. And I don't know exactly where it is. Nobody does. A group of the Great T.'s people will be waiting for us somewhere to take us to it."

"Have you ever seen him? The Great T.?"

Niya nodded. "He was the one who pulled me out from under the ruins of our house. With his own hands."

"Who else's hands would he have used?" Christopher murmured, and she laughed again.

"It was four years ago," she said. "I haven't seen him for four years. He made sure, back then, that his people would look after me. Otherwise, I'd probably be dead by now."

Niya plucked a couple of chords on the guitar and seemed to be listening to their echo. They rose into the night air like soap bubbles.

"Do me a favor," Niya whispered, almost inaudible. "Don't go rescuing any more horses."

"Did I . . . Did I rescue them, then?"

"All of them. But I'd rather have lost two dozen horses than you."

Christopher grinned. "Can I get that in writing?"

239

"I can't write."

He tried not to look surprised. Luckily that was easy in the dark.

"I can teach you if you'd like," he said, entirely forgetting that he himself couldn't read Nepalese writing. "On one of those nights that are long enough for it."

She nodded.

But neither of them could yet know how long the nights at the base camp would really be.

They passed through only a handful of villages in the next few days, and the huts became smaller and lower, crouching close to the ground on the few level surfaces. Niya made her speech in every village, and although Christopher knew every word, the force of those words seized on him every time. She had only a small audience now, of shy, reserved people who gathered around only after some hesitation. They, too, saw the fire in her eyes, but the mountain wind had made their hearts hard, and they did not open them to her. They had no food that they could give the guerrillas, and only two villagers decided to join them.

As they entered each village, they rode past the prayer drums on the left and turned them, one by one, but there were no more messages waiting inside.

Christopher saw how impatient Niya was.

Their destination could lie around any turn in the road, beyond any mountaintop, or rock—but they didn't know just where it was, and it was entirely up to their leader, the mysterious Great T., to decide when he would send his men to guide them to him.

Once they pitched their tents close to a small Buddhist monastery, and it seemed strange to Christopher that the monks shared their food with the party. Under the stupa, the dome of the monastery, two eyes were painted: the eyes of Buddha. He seemed to be observing the guerrillas with a touch of suspicion.

"Are you Buddhists, then?" Christopher asked Niya, and she laughed and shook her head so that her untidy black hair flew around it.

"We're fighting men and women," she said. "We don't have any religion. You can't afford religion if you want to fight."

"But why are they giving you food?"

"Perhaps they know that what we're doing is good?" replied Niya.

"Or maybe they're afraid," murmured Christopher, so quietly that she didn't hear. The wind blew more aggressively than ever this evening, and two of the monks beckoned to them to come inside the shelter of the monastery walls. Christopher, like everyone else, took off his shoes. It was a strange sight to see all those sturdy, thick boots standing on the walled gallery outside the entrance to the monastery—all those boots, one pair of sandals, and a pair of white sneakers that had been invisible until this moment.

Inside, the monastery was so colorful that it boldly contrasted with the brown and gray of the steppes. The sturdy, wooden columns were painted all colors of the rainbow. Masks of animals and fabulous creatures with unnervingly bulging eyes and crazy expressions hung from the tops of the columns, and a kind of cylindrical windsock made of dozens of tiny silk patches in all imaginable patterns hung on either side of the shrine at the front of the monastery. And inside that shrine, behind spotlessly polished glass, was the huge, framed photograph of a man wearing glasses too large for him, looking gravely out past a whole series of brightly colored cloth garlands and floral decorations, almost threatening to smother him in his picture frame. Christopher wasn't sure if he was the Dalai Lama. There was a certain doubtful timidity in his eyes behind the big glasses that made you like him.

The monastery walls were adorned with scenes from the life of Buddha. Christopher couldn't interpret most of them.

"Why is there a green rat playing the guitar there?" he whispered to Jumar.

242

Jumar made a sound as if he were suppressing laughter, but maybe he was only coughing.

"I think," he whispered, "it's meant to be something else."

Finally Christopher tore his eyes away from all the colors and shapes, all the stories and secrets of the monastery, and obediently sat down cross-legged with the others. They sat in two long rows to the right and left of the narrow central aisle of the monastery, guerrillas and monks side by side, and the youngest monks, who were not much older than eight or nine, went around with bowls and pans to serve their guests.

They ate a strange kind of corn-mush. If you had the knack of it, you could roll the mush into little balls and then dip them in sauce. Christopher did not have the knack of it, and struggled in vain for some time, until one of the little monks took pity on him and, suppressing a fit of giggles, handed him a bent tin spoon.

He felt Niya's eyes resting on him. One day quite soon, he would have to tell her where he really came from.

It was during that strange meal, surrounded by all those beautiful colors, that they heard another fairy tale. Christopher thought back to the old lady with the spidery fingers who had told them a story at the beginning of their journey—and her satisfaction in the idea that all fairy tales ended unhappily.

The oldest monk spoke as if he were talking to himself,

out of the blue, with no introduction, with no reason for telling his story. And this time, it was a tale about a monk.

"Long, long ago," he began in a strange, monotonous voice, "a king ruled a country somewhere in the mountains. He had a garden as beautiful as the night, and a girl gardener as beautiful as the day. The sun dwelt in her eyes. The king was happy, his people were happy. And at that time, they all lived in peace and harmony. Then one day, a monk came down from the peaks, down the mountain that looks like the tail of a fish, and he walked far and wide. He walked for a long time to see the king's wonderful garden.

"When he arrived, he knocked at the gate and found it open. In the garden he met the girl gardener cutting roses. The king sat beside her, absorbed in the charming picture.

"'I have heard of the beauty of this garden,' said the monk, 'and of all the wonderful trees that grow here. The monastery I come from lies high in the mountains where the land is bare and bleak. Not a single flower will grow there. But a flower from your wonderful garden would take root in the little soil we have. Grant me my request: Let me dig up a single flower from your garden, and take it back with me to my lonely life among the windy peaks.'

"The king nodded, but the pretty girl gardener looked away from the roses and shook her head.

"'I have tended your garden and cared for it, Your Majesty,' she said. 'I did it for you, and every minute of my life becomes a flower in this garden. No, I cannot spare a flower from this garden, not a single one!'

"Then the king sighed, because he loved not only the garden, but also the girl gardener. And the girl gardener was closing the gate to the monk's request. 'My flower would freeze in your heights,' she said.

"Hearing this, the palace servants urged the monk to leave the city. 'Once the king has come to his decision,' they said, 'nothing will change his mind.'

"Then the monk turned away from the city, and instead of a flower, the thorny plant of anger grew in his heart, nourished by the fertilizer of humiliation.

"He went back to the monastery he had come from, and there a seven-headed monster grew from his fingers—larger than any monster ever seen in the world before, and a more terrible sight than all the thunderstorms in the mountains.

"The monster left the monastery, prowling around on heavy paws, and made its way down to the king's city and his garden. And anyone its hot breath touched fell into a deep sleep and could not wake up again. Soon the whole city was asleep. The whole valley, the whole palace, the whole of the mountain countryside. The girl gardener slept in the palace garden, the king slept, and the whole court slept with them. Only one little boy managed to hide from the monster. He opened the door of an empty stable and lured the monster in with his calls, and once it was inside, the little boy locked the door. The monster breathed its hot, angry breath into the air until the entire stable was full of it. So then it had to breathe in its own fire, until finally it fell asleep, too. But a little of its breath had seeped through the cracks in the stable walls and touched the little boy waiting outside, and so the boy fell asleep himself. Ever since then, the land in the mountains has been dreaming an endless dream, and nothing more has ever been heard of it. That country has disappeared entirely from the face of the earth. Somewhere in it, however, the flowers grown by the pretty gardener bloomed in the king's garden. But they bloomed for no one, and their beauty is cold, because there is no one left to see them."

The old monk nodded a couple of times, and went on dipping little balls of corn-mush in sauce as if he hadn't really said anything at all. Christopher decided that he didn't like the fairy tales these people told. The old woman had been right: They all ended unhappily. They left him with a queasy feeling. It was as if there were a little grain of truth in each of those stories.

When they left the monks the next morning, Christopher spent a long time thinking of all the colors surrounding the monks where they lived and prayed, and he thought how strange it was that the dragons hadn't discovered them yet.

They were still not entirely out of sight of the monastery when two horsemen emerged from nowhere and came galloping toward them. At first, Christopher was alarmed, but the riders were in the well-worn, green camouflage uniform of the rebels, and he saw the light in Niya's eyes.

"The waiting's over now," she said and halted her men. She dismounted, placed her hands together in greeting, and bowed low when the riders came up to them.

So did all the others in their party.

But the two men threw back their heads impatiently, and clicked their tongues.

"No time for formalities," said one of them. The other added, "Get back on your horses and follow us."

So they did.

The men rode ahead through low, thorny brush, following no path. They led the group steeply uphill, then finally through a narrow pass—like the eye of a needle—between tall rocks. Then it lay before them—a place where no one would ever find it: the base camp.

But it was not a camp. It was a town. And it looked as if it had melted. As if it came out of a picture by Dalí. Arne had hung a picture by Dalí taken from a calendar over his bed.

Christopher almost found himself looking for the inevitable liquefying watches—

"What a strange place," Christopher whispered. "It's like something out of a dream. How can a whole town melt?"

"Mud," said Jumar matter-of-factly. "The houses in the town are made of mud. They haven't melted. The rain has made them into what you see."

As they rode down toward the mud buildings, it suddenly seemed to Christopher as if he had seen the town somewhere before, as if he had known it for a long time. A vague memory surfaced in him—the library book. Hadn't there been a photograph of this town in the book of pictures he had been looking at back home, sitting on his bed? How long ago was that? Weeks? Months?

But he couldn't figure out how the photo of such a secret, remote place could get into a published book of pictures. He shook his head, and put off trying to solve the puzzle until later. He had other things to think of now. Somewhere ahead of him, in this molten town, was Arne. He felt his fingers beginning to tingle and his breath coming faster.

"We've reached our journey's end," he whispered to Jumar, who was sitting behind him on the horse. "Now we'll find my brother. We have to ask them—"

"Not yet," replied Jumar. "Wait a little longer, Christopher."

And Christopher sighed, because he knew Jumar was right. What he didn't know was how often he would hear those words repeated, and how much he would begin to dislike them.

There was no wall of prayer drums at the entrance to this town. There were no stones on which people had scratched their hopes and fears, and no colored flags.

Instead, there were figures standing on a wall, gleaming in the pale light of this cold noon: men and women, children and old people.

"Bronze," Jumar whispered.

The rider in front of them swung around. "Yes, bronze," he said grimly. "We stand them here so that no one will forget. The people touched by the shadow of the dragons. There will be others. The dragons are coming more often now."

And Christopher felt as if a cold breath out of nowhere were passing over him.

He turned on his horse and looked back at the wall. The bronze statues looked lost. Cold, empty, lifeless.

The town itself was full of life, but all of it revolved around one thing: preparation for the great day when the insurgents would finally gather all their forces and march on the capital city. Everything centered on learning, training, and loyalty.

There were no individuals in the molten town. "We are

all one," said Niya as they rode along the streets past the mud houses, and her eyes were shining more brightly than ever. "Look at that! Just look! All these people—they all want the same as we do. There are so many! Far more than I thought! And they all stick together like one large family. They're all brothers and sisters. Together, we'll succeed in changing everything, everything. There'll be no rich and no poor anymore, just as I said. Isn't that wonderful?"

"Yes," said Jumar, "wonderful."

Christopher did not respond.

Something gnawed away at his heart when he saw all those men and women in their green camouflage jackets marching down the streets. It was as if no one ever went anywhere in the molten town without marching and singing. He looked for Arne among the marching throng and failed to find him. There were too many people.

The new arrivals were welcomed with a speech full of fine words about the way Communists stand together all over the world—Maoist Communists in particular. There were fine words about poverty and justice, but they did not move Christopher. They had none of the sparkling brightness of Niya's own words.

They sounded cold and stiff, as if they had been learned by heart and brought out on command.

◆ ◆ ◆

On that first evening, when he was lying beside Jumar in one of the mud houses, in a room with a great many other people whom he didn't know, he whispered very quietly, "I may be a bad person, Jumar, but I don't like all this. I don't want to give up my identity and be one of a crowd. I'd rather stay just Christopher."

"But that's what you *are* doing," Jumar whispered back. "By helping all the others to build a better world. That makes you Christopher more than you were before!"

"You sound like them," murmured Christopher, and he turned over on his other side to go to sleep.

The next day, they were sent to separate groups for training. Everything was organized: time, meals, sleeping, waking. Here there was a precise plan for every hour, every minute of the day. And Christopher was never, never alone. Wherever he went, someone was watching him, not meaning any harm, not even suspiciously. There was simply always someone there.

What he minded most was parting from Niya. For some unknown reason, the men and women slept and ate separately here at the base camp. They trained separately and they went about their daily duties separately. Only after several days did Christopher realize that this measure was for the sake of discipline as well. Anyone who took too much interest in mixing with the opposite sex had no room left for the training they had to do every day, and no room left in his mind for learning what they had to learn.

And so Christopher began learning.

He learned to shake off his uneasiness with a gun and hold it properly. He learned the insurgent songs, he learned what their leaders' orders meant, he learned to react fast enough once those orders had been given.

At first, it was like a game, and for a while he forgot his misgivings.

They got up at first light and began running around the town, and he heard Jumar panting beside him and knew he wasn't alone. They developed a kind of rivalry to see which of them could do the most push-ups, knee-bends, and chin-ups, although he couldn't really check up on what Jumar said he was doing. He sensed his own muscles responding to the training, he felt his body getting fitter.

In the evening, he fell on his bed exhausted, and was asleep almost before he could close his eyes. He had always been small and slight, but that was going to change. He would be a different person when he left this camp. No one would laugh at him anymore. He wouldn't let himself be laughed at. He was tough, and he'd get even tougher. Jumar was right. He would be more himself than ever before.

When he went along the streets, he listened for familiar footsteps, looked for a shock of blond hair, but he never saw any sign of Arne. Once he summoned up all his courage and asked a man running beside him about the foreigner.

He had heard rumors, Christopher said, hoping his voice didn't tremble too much.

"Oh, yes," said the man. "I've heard rumors, too. But only rumors. People say there were three of them—three foreigners. They're in another part of the camp. They're going to fight with us."

"They're not . . . prisoners?"

Christopher sensed the man's glance as he looked sideways at him. "Prisoners? Why would they be prisoners? You're here of your own free will. Are you a prisoner?"

"I'm a . . . a servant of our common cause," said Christopher, choosing his words with care.

A spark of uneasiness began to glow somewhere inside him. It was better not to say what you were thinking straight out.

◆ ◆ ◆

In the second week of their life in the camp, the Great T. summoned Jumar and Christopher.

They were sitting at one of the long tables, eating with the others, when one of his men came for them.

Christopher felt his nervousness rising. "Don't tell him who you are," he whispered to Jumar. "Not yet."

"Don't say anything about Arne," Jumar whispered back. "Not yet."

The man led them to a nondescript mud house on a remote narrow side street. It was a building without any ornamentation or splendor about it. Who would have believed that the leader of such a far-reaching insurgency operated from this house, like a silent puppet master?

He sat in an entirely empty room on the ground floor of the house. The only thing hanging on the wall was a faded photograph of someone who Christopher thought was Chairman Mao, although he could have been anyone. A withered hibiscus flower had been left on one of the nails fastening the photo to the wall.

The Great T. was not great in the sense of being tall. He was a small, lizard-like man: nimble, flexible, and clever. No one could pin him down. He wore a green uniform without any insignia of rank on it. On his desk, beside some papers, lay a fur cap and a revolver, looking as if they had been placed there for no special reason. As they entered the room he rose from his desk, walked around it, and looked Christopher up and down for some time.

Christopher now wore the green camouflage clothing of all the warriors, and sturdy boots in place of Jumar's sandals.

He lowered his eyes, placed his hands together, and bowed.

"You are not alone," said the Great T. "I summoned you because I hear that you travel with someone who is not like other people."

"He's invisible," said Christopher.

"That's what I heard."

"It's a kind of congenital defect," explained Jumar, and Christopher expected the Great T. to jump when his voice came out of nowhere, the way everyone did on hearing it for the first time. But the guerrilla leader didn't show any surprise.

He turned his head just a little so as to look in Jumar's direction. "You can do us a great service," he said. "Do you know that?"

"Yes," replied Jumar.

"Then you will stay and fight for us?"

"Yes."

"It is difficult to have someone invisible among the men,"

255

said the Great T. "It makes them nervous. That could be bad for discipline. Someone invisible can't be controlled—he's always free, always his own master. I hope you know that I am showing great confidence in you by letting you stay. The responsibility you bear is not the same as any ordinary fighting man's. You are responsible for yourself. That's a heavy burden to bear. How old are you?"

"Fourteen," said Jumar. "Like my friend here."

"A good age to learn to fight," said the Great T. "A bad age to take responsibility."

"I will prove myself worthy of your trust," declared Jumar. Christopher might have been compelled to smile at his friend's solemn tone of voice if he hadn't felt so constricted in this bleak room, in front of that quick-moving, lizard-like little man.

"I hope so," said the Great T.

And that was the end of their conversation.

He hadn't once asked whether there were ways of making Jumar visible. And Jumar hadn't mentioned it, either.

Three days later, it began to snow.

The first flakes fell as the afternoon light disappeared behind the mountains, and icy cold spread over the town. That afternoon, Christopher had hit the target for the first time during shooting practice, and a warm euphoria kept him from feeling the cold at first. The leader of their troop ended the training session sooner than usual. As they marched back along the streets to their houses, he looked up at the rapidly darkening sky and opened his mouth to catch snowflakes and let them melt on his tongue.

And memories from long ago surfaced in him again.

He and Arne in the snow. Gloved hand in gloved hand. Footprints left in the garden by the smiling clown faces on the soles of their boots. A snowman with a cucumber for a nose because they couldn't find any carrots. A blue snowsuit. Arne lying on his belly on a toboggan while Christopher sat on top of him, shouting with glee. The toboggan flipping over halfway down the slope so that they went tumbling through the snow like puppies. He could hear their laughter—the laughter of children from far away, so very far away.

He had been bringing up the rear of the procession, and only when he emerged from his memories did he realize that he had stopped marching. No one had noticed. He looked around.

"Jumar?" he whispered. But Jumar seemed to have gone on with the others. He saw the men disappear around a bend in the road ahead.

I should run after them, he thought, because they wouldn't

like it if they noticed him hanging back. At that moment, he saw the little boy. The child was standing in one of the alleys, catching snow on his tongue, just as Christopher had been doing. Christopher waved to him, and the little boy waved back shyly. What was a small child doing in the insurgents' base camp? Christopher went over to him, and for a moment it looked as if the boy would run away, but he stayed where he was.

"Do you live here?" asked Christopher. The little boy stared at him with big, dark eyes. Those eyes reminded Christopher of Niya. Niya. How long was it since he last saw her? If only he could meet her in the street! But he never did. Perhaps she wasn't even in the molten town anymore, perhaps she'd long ago gone out with her men to recruit more guerrillas.

"Over there," said the little boy, pointing to a house in the alley.

"Then your parents are guerrillas?"

The little boy shook his head vigorously. Christopher saw how thin his body was under his big woolen sweater. He was almost drowning in it, yet his lips were blue with cold.

"But why are you all here if your parents aren't guerrillas?"

The child looked at him in surprise. "We live here," he said.

"You mean there are people living all over this town?"

"Not all over it anymore. A good many people went away when *they* came. Others moved closer together. *They* need a lot of space. *They* need our houses. And our food. *They* need all sorts of things. There are so many of them."

Christopher nodded slowly. "I'll have to go on," he said. "See you soon."

After that encounter, he began seeing eyes behind windows—faces, movements. The Maoists had occupied the town, and the people behind the windows, unseen in the shadows, lived crowded together and went hungry.

They weren't going hungry in hopes of a better future. They were going hungry out of fear.

He wanted to tell Jumar about the other villagers, but they were separated that evening. Christopher was moved to different quarters, a long way from the house where Jumar would be sleeping, and put in a group where he didn't know anyone. Perhaps it was just chance. Perhaps these things happened. Perhaps it had something to do with organization, although Christopher couldn't see any special point in it. Perhaps they'd noticed that he had lagged behind that afternoon, had stepped out of line, broken away from the rest.

From that day on, there was no one he could talk to. He tried, but no one seemed to want to say anything to him.

They had noticed that he was different. He, too, began to stay away from the others, mark himself off from them, keep himself to himself. The training was harder now; it wasn't a game anymore. It was deadly serious, and the sharp, cold air bit into his lungs. It was as if the outer, protective layer of his body had developed a leak like an old coat and the snow were penetrating his heart. He was missing Niya more than ever—the fire of her eyes that could have melted the snow, the touch of her hand on his shoulder when she wanted to show him something, her laugh, her words, the notes of her guitar. When he lay alone on the hard ground by night, freezing under his thin blanket, he thought of her and imagined she was with him.

And where was Jumar? He was invisible, always free, responsible for himself. Christopher almost wished he'd come to find him and talk to him just for a few minutes. But Jumar never showed up.

So Christopher wondered if Jumar had suddenly turned so faithful to the Great T. that he wouldn't act against any of the leader's orders. Christopher suspected that was it. The Great T. had given Jumar what his father never had. He had accepted him, so Jumar himself accepted the Great T. as his commander. But it was a dangerous kind of acceptance . . .

♦ ♦ ♦

When his troop marched in the snow now, Christopher lagged behind more often. A persistent cough settled in his lungs, and he couldn't keep up with the others. The leader of his troop didn't like that, and Christopher had to keep his head down and let the man's shouting pass over him. Then he would find himself alone after the others had marched off to eat, forced to jog around and around under the same leader's supervision, in an exercise that did no one any good and made his cough worse. The man seemed to be developing an active dislike of Christopher, who bowed to the leader's will out of fear—the same fear that he saw in the eyes of the people behind the windows.

The wind drove snow down the streets like pages torn from a book. It was a long time since he had seen a book. Christopher began to long for books, for stories, for some way out of this cold, regulated, organized, and supervised world into which he had fallen.

Only Arne still visited him in his dreams, but when he was woken by his own coughing, Arne, too, would disappear, and all that was left was the sense of helplessness. Christopher felt that Arne was close, yet there seemed to be no chance of meeting him.

Dragons flew over the molten town three times. It was here that Christopher saw them flying in a group for the first time. And here he learned that they could breathe fire. He first saw that at night. The colorful flames coming from their shimmering bodies were a hot blaze in the black sky like a signal being passed from dragon to dragon.

But the roofs of the molten town remained unaffected by the dragons' fire and untouched by their claws. They flew overhead only on their way down to the valley. For there was nothing for them to eat in this town. Nothing cheerful existed here. There were no flowers, no colors. They were not yet hungry enough to eat the grayish-brown of the rooftops. Christopher learned to squeeze into the shadows of the house with the others at a sharp, barked command. He trembled with them when the shadows of the dragons passed over the icy alleys, slowly, seeking, as if the shadows themselves were living creatures hunting for prey.

On one of those dragon mornings, when they were standing lined up against the wall of a building again, afraid, watching, crowding under an overhanging roof, he saw a man and a little boy running down the alley. The dragon's shadow moved along the alley after them. The man wasn't wearing the guerrillas' camouflage clothing. He must be one of the townspeople.

Christopher saw the fear in his eyes. He saw the man run toward the wall, slipping on the frozen slush, and holding the boy's hand tightly. But the guerrillas were standing against the wall in the shadow of the roof. There was no room left for the man and the boy. Christopher tried to move aside, and noticed that none of the others were doing the same. He saw the man put out a hand and Christopher reached out his own to draw the man into the shadow—

Without a word, the guerrilla beside him struck his hand down.

At that moment, the dragon's shadow fell over the strange man and his son. Then it was gone, and the rushing of its wings disappeared into the distance. With a lifeless clang, two bronze statues fell into the snow in front of Christopher.

He stared at them for a moment, numb with horror. Would his own hand have touched the shadow of the dragon if he'd really reached it out? Would he have turned into bronze? Could he have saved the two of them?

There was no time to think about it.

The others had already moved away from the wall and were marching on. Christopher hurried to catch up.

And a few days later, on a training march around the town, he saw two new statues on the mud wall.

Only then did it strike him that he knew the little boy. It was the boy he had spoken to earlier. From then on, the bronze statues followed him into his dreams.

263

+ + +

In these weeks, he began to think he would die. One day, he would simply come to the end of his strength, and he would fall down dead. It wouldn't bother anyone. They would hardly notice.

But he didn't fall down, and he didn't die.

Instead, he found someone. It happened on the night it finally stopped snowing.

Christopher was lying awake as usual, fighting back his cough. He felt feverish. He had thought that evening that he would never move a muscle again. Yet now his body felt light, almost weightless, and he got up, very quietly, and clambered over the others. He felt as if he were floating, as if he were walking on the moon and might take off at any moment.

The dormitory door wasn't locked. Where would anyone run to from here? There was nothing beyond the molten town, nothing at all, and anyone who didn't know their way around the mountains would be hopelessly lost in them within a few hours. If only he could find the way out of this secret valley, where for some reason, long ago, people had taken it into their heads to build a town out of mud.

He left the house where the others were sleeping in silence, without waking anyone. When he glanced back at the outlines of figures lying side by side on the floor, wrapped in their gray blankets, he suspected that he might not have really climbed over them. He might not really be standing at the door. Of course they couldn't hear him, because he wasn't really there. His body could still be lying somewhere among them, dead. Nothing stood here but a kind of memory of himself.

He wandered down the street without knowing where he was going.

He was going nowhere.

Christopher raised his head and saw the moon high in the sky. The clouds had moved away. How beautiful the night was! Even the wind had died down as if it didn't want to spoil the picture of the molten town. Now, under the soft blanket of white snow shining in the moonlight, it lay as still as a dream. Maybe it *was* a dream?

The narrow streets were empty.

He went to the end of the alley, to the end of the town, on and on, and there, sitting on a rock in the snow, he saw someone. Christopher told himself he ought to feel afraid, but all he felt was a certain curiosity, and he went toward the person on the rock without haste. When he was very close, he heard the notes of a guitar in the night air. Notes rising like soap bubbles, clearer than ever above the unwritten page of the snow. And a memory rose in him of other notes on another night—a night that seemed to be an eternity ago.

"Niya?" he asked the night, and the night answered him with her face.

She turned to him and smiled. But her smile was full of grief. It was a new kind of grief, not the melancholy he had heard in her song before.

He sat down beside her on the rock in the snow.

"Niya," he said again, and that was all. He wanted to say, "I'm so glad to see you! Where have you come from? Where have you been all this time? I thought about you so often—"

But he said none of that. Instead, he coughed.

She put the guitar down beside her and gazed at him intently for a long time.

"You look terrible," she said at last.

Christopher tried hard to grin. "Thanks a lot."

Niya put her hand to his face and touched his cheekbones, and he felt her warmth soaking into him.

"You're so thin!" she said. "I remember that you once had a face, but all I can see now is a collection of bones and shadows."

"As bad as that?" asked Christopher.

"What happened?"

"I'm afraid I'm not strong enough for your struggle."

"Where's Jumar?"

"I don't know. They separated us. Where have you been all this time?"

"Here," she replied. "I've been here in the town all along. I'm nothing special here anymore, not a leader now. They sent me off to a training troop, too. And I've been learning."

"Learning what?" asked Christopher. She had moved closer to him to keep out the cold. But he sensed that there was something else she would like to keep out. He had never felt so close to her before. He had never yet felt so close to anyone before.

"I learned that this isn't what I want," Niya whispered.

"It isn't?" he asked, surprised.

"No," she said. He felt her warm body, and what he had dreamed so often was true. She melted the snow in his heart. It was as if a huge, icy clump of snow deep inside him were dissolving and beginning to flow away into nothing.

"The Great T. has changed," she whispered. "He has too much power now. Back when he pulled me out from the ruins of our house, his face was still full of life. Now it's turned cold. I've seen him—if only from a distance."

She leaned her head against Christopher's shoulder and said with conviction, "I hate this camp. It's not the training—I don't mind that. I'm strong and I'm tough. But the people! They look at me with suspicion in their eyes. They say I'm no good at submitting to authority. They're probably right." She sighed. "And I've seen the townspeople."

"So have I, Niya. So have I. Hardly any of the guerrillas takes any notice of them."

"Sometimes I think my own people here don't care about justice and helping others. Or giving color back to the fields and creating a peaceful land. When I look at all the group leaders and deputy group leaders, when I hear the orders they give, I sometimes think they don't care about anything but power," she went on. "Power for its own sake, for no other reason. No other purpose. That wasn't the idea of Communism, not as I understand it. Sometimes I don't know what to do. I don't belong here. But then, where *do* I belong?"

Her hair was tickling Christopher's chin. He ran his hand through it as if it were an animal's fur, weaving strands of it between his fingers and losing himself there as if lost in thought. All his shyness had left him. This night was too unreal for anything like shyness.

"And I've seen your brother," she said.

He started. "You've seen—?"

"He says he's your brother. He's fair-haired and tall and his face isn't like yours, but his smile is just the same. He saw you, but you didn't see him. He can't figure out how you got here. He told me where you both come from. From so very far away."

"Where is he? asked Christopher. "And *how* is he?"

"He's all right . . . all things considered," she replied. "He's alive and in good health. Me and the rest of the women in my troop were given the job of taking the three prisoners their meals for a week."

"They really are prisoners?"

"What else would they be?"

Christopher swallowed. "I was told they were here of their own free will. I was told they were going to—they'd joined us to—they were going to—"

He fell silent.

"You were told they were here to fight?" asked Niya quietly.

Christopher nodded. At that, Niya laughed. Her laughter was as rough as the wind and very angry. "They're in the cellar of one of the houses on the western outskirts of the town," she whispered. "It's too cold there. And one of them is sick. Not your brother, one of the others. They're being held hostage so that the powerful people in their own countries won't intervene when the king asks them to. If he ever gets around to that."

"That's what I thought at first," said Christopher in a low voice. "That's why I came here. To find my brother. But then—"

"Then you fell for the dream," said Niya. "The dream that

the Great T. pours into us like snake venom. You fell for it just the way I did."

"But Arne—my brother—is he *really* okay?"

"I think so. Well, I don't like the way they're being treated. I told the leader of my troop that they need a doctor. He told me not to meddle with what's none of my business."

"Niya, can we go there? Can we free them?"

She said simply, "No. Not yet. But we will."

"We? You mean you'll help me?"

"You can rely on me for that," she replied grimly. "I'll do everything that the Great T. says we mustn't. Just wait."

Her hand sought his, found it, and held it firmly in the white twilight of the icy snow.

Christopher took a deep breath. "Maybe this night is long enough for me to tell you my story," he said. "Maybe it's time you heard it."

She moved a little closer to him.

"Then tell me later," she whispered. "It's so cold, much too cold to be alone . . ." She closed his eyes gently with her hand, and then he felt her lips on his. It was strange.

Christopher had never kissed anyone before. One hasn't necessarily had much practice kissing at fourteen. Not that he had anything against kissing her. It was a wonderful feeling. He felt her tongue, warm and a little rough, and the night seemed to spin around him. He forgot which way was up and which way was down.

At the beginning of the night, he had thought he was going to die, and now here he sat on a rock in the snow, kissing a girl for the first time in his life—the girl he loved. Because he did love her.

Of course.

He had known it all along without wanting to admit it.

NIYA'S HANDS

ON A CLEAR NIGHT, UNDER THE MOON, somewhere at the foot of the Himalayas, just outside a molten town built of mud—on a night too cold to be alone— two bodies found each other and merged into a tiny, warm spark in the endless, cold expanses. If anyone had passed by, they might have seen a light, a strange light in the snow. Or maybe they would not have seen anything at all ...

But nobody passed by that way. The night gave the two lovers freezing in the cold their own private place, and then they weren't freezing anymore.

Christopher felt Niya's hands searching for a way under the green layers of camouflage clothing, and in a kind of quiet amazement, he let her do as she liked. Her fingertips brought warmth back to his body—a warmth he had never known before. And Niya's hands knew just what they wanted.

In a country where you are old enough at the age of fourteen to fight and to fall down in the snow, then at fourteen you are also old enough to make love.

"Have you ever done this with anyone?" whispered Christopher.

"No," she whispered back. "But I don't know what might happen tomorrow, and then it may be too late ever to do it with anyone. I've been thinking about it as I lay awake on my own all these nights. Thinking I wouldn't want to die like that."

"But you're *not* going to die. Why would you die?"

"Over these last few days, I thought I will surely die because it's all so pointless," she whispered. "But there are a thousand reasons to die. And a thousand reasons not to."

He let his own hands search for a way under her layers of clothing, and everything they found was alive with warm, pulsating life.

"Niya . . . I don't know much about this . . ."

"Nor do I," she whispered. "But these things know about themselves. That will be enough."

And so the things that knew only about themselves took their course that clear night, under the moon, somewhere in the foothills of the Himalayas. Christopher was surprised to find how natural it all suddenly seemed.

Everything had to be exactly as it was. Everything was all right.

When the moon had moved a little farther across the sky, they lay close to each other in the snow, breathless and without feeling the cold. There was no cold for them anymore.

And Niya listened to Christopher's story. This time, he told her everything, from the beginning to the end—from Arne's disappearance and the way Jumar's ankle was caught in the trap to their first meeting in the village without any colors. The only thing he left out was who Jumar really was. "Someone who had set out to change the world," he told her. When the last words of his story had died away, they kissed again, to make sure of each other. Then Niya picked up her guitar again.

My heart longs for peace, her husky voice sang, quietly now, very quietly.

> *My heart longs for peace,*
> *Peace in this land of our fate.*
> *My heart longs for peace,*
> *But they tell me: Peace must wait.*
>
> > *First comes action, be on your guard.*
> > *First we must strike, and let us strike hard.*

"Another of those songs telling a story with a sad ending," he whispered. "Like the fairy tales. Don't you have any cheerful songs and stories in this country?"

"No," she replied, putting a finger on her lips before she went on playing. And Christopher closed his eyes and listened to her voice:

My heart longs for quiet,
Quiet in this land of our fate.
My heart longs for quiet,
But they tell me: Quiet must wait.
 First we must speak, first comes the word,
 And let it be loud, or it will not be heard.

My heart longs for dreams,
Dreams in this land of our fate.
My heart longs for dreams,
But they tell me: Dreams must wait.
 First come deeds, first comes the sword,
 With its sharp edge to mow down the enemy horde.

My heart longs for sleep,
Sleep in this land of our fate.
My heart longs for sleep,

But they tell me: Sleep must wait.

First comes waking, first comes the light,

We shall make our mark by day, not by night.

My heart longs for life,

Life in this land of our fate.

My heart longs for life,

But they tell me: Life must wait.

First Death must free us, low we must lie.

And they ask me: Are you ready to die?

For quiet, dreams, and sleep,

For peace in this land of your fate?

And I say: quiet, dreams, and sleep

And peace, all of these must wait.

Her words followed him back to his quarters, where no one had noticed him going out, and into the dreams that he had dreamed in the few hours left before dawn. The next morning, he wondered whether he hadn't also dreamed that incredible encounter with Niya.

But the soft fragrance of her skin still clung to his clothes, and so he had to believe his memory.

And although he was so tired that he could hardly put one foot in front of the other, the coming day sang a song in his veins. He had a plan. They would set Arne free. Jumar would get the key—and Niya knew where he must look for it. No one would notice them leaving on a night like last night. Now they just had to find Jumar.

However, they did not find Jumar; Jumar found them.

"I need someone I can trust in these matters," said the Great T., as he walked over to the window of the bare room to look out over the town. Snow lay on the irregularly shaped walls and roofs of the molten mud-brick houses. The snow itself did not melt. If this winter was the same as every year, it would lie there until they had left the town.

"You could never trust someone invisible," replied Jumar.

"Who knows?" murmured the Great T., turning. "Something like today's incident must not happen again. Never again. If those three go back to Kartan, we're finished. I am grateful to you for coming to me. But if this alone had been your job, you could have come sooner. Then they wouldn't have left camp in the first place."

Jumar shifted uncomfortably from foot to foot. He felt pride rising in him, but something else was lurking there, too—something acrid and cold.

Two of the men in his troop had been lying all along. Kartan had sent them as spies. A third man had joined them, and Jumar had heard them whispering. They foolishly had thought they were speaking so softly that he couldn't hear them.

Last night, he had felt that something was wrong. There had been tension in the air—faint and barely perceptible. He had removed the blanket that kept him visible, and stayed awake, leaning against a wall and waiting. So he had seen the three of them leaving the house, quietly, furtively. An invisible shadow followed them and overheard their whispered words in the night.

"There's one of Kartan's men waiting for us in the first village," said one of them. "With horses and weapons. We only have to reach that village."

The man who had arrived at the camp late was afraid—Jumar could hear it. But the other two reassured him.

"He'll pay us well for what we do," they said. "Just wait. Soon you won't have money worries, and you won't have to obey the Maoists' orders in the snow anymore."

"I'll go back to my family," the man had whispered. "They're waiting for me. I have five children. I'm doing this for their sake."

That had given Jumar a pang, but he knew what would happen if the men managed to see Kartan and speak to him. It wouldn't be only the base camp and the lives of all the men and women there in danger. Within seconds, the whole great plan to get the power of the king from the city, drive Kartan away, and defeat the dragons, would turn into the dust and ashes of memories, like sand blowing in the wind, nothing but a dream that had burned out.

Followers of the Great T. would be sent to look for the traitors, and the crackle of tension that had been in the air of the dormitory would take over the whole town. From this day on, guards were posted at every way out of the town and the steep-sided valley. No one could leave the base camp now unless he was on a mission from the Great T. himself.

"And yet I still need invisible ears to listen," he said. "Invisible eyes to keep watch. An invisible mouth to report back to me. I have to know what our people are thinking. Who is dissatisfied and spreading discord among the others. Who is no longer in tune with our aims. Discipline is not yet strict enough."

"I didn't come here to be an informer," replied Jumar. "An informer among our own people! I came to fight Kartan and his followers with my own hands."

"Sometimes one thing is right and sometimes another," said the Great T. His voice showed there would be no contradicting him. "If you want to stay with us, you'll do as I ask."

"Aren't you afraid that I might go over to Kartan myself and give you away? No one could prevent me."

"I know he tried to kill you," said the Great T. "I know more than you think. I know who you are."

Jumar felt the blood drain away from his body, and an icy chill spread through him.

"And I know," said the Great T., "that there are two people who are dear to you in the camp. If I want to lay hands on you, I can do it, just like that. What could suit the king's enemy better than for his only son to run into that enemy's arms? Now, do you understand?"

Jumar did understand. Yes, he could certainly leave the camp this very day. But then something would happen to Christopher and Niya. He was caught in a trap.

"I could use you to put pressure on the king," said the Great T. "But I am not doing that because I know you're on our side. Because I know that you will help me. You *are* going to help me, aren't you?"

Jumar took a breath and replied, "I'll do as you ask. But what kind of a man are you?"

The Great T. smiled. It was a sad smile. "A man," he said. "An ordinary man. Not a saint. Now go—and I expect results."

"But suppose they were the only traitors? Suppose there's nothing more for me to overhear?"

"There's always something to overhear. This is a hard

winter, and there will be discontent. We need to make an example of a few people to strengthen discipline. You will find me those people, and before next week."

In that moment, a clear idea came into Jumar's mind. The pride he had felt turned to hatred. He had had to give up his gun at the door where the Great T.'s guards were standing.

But what is a dead, inanimate weapon against living, breathing hatred?

Jumar took an invisible and barely audible step toward the Great T. There was an ornate letter opener lying on the desk beside a stack of papers. He reached his hand out to it. His breath was coming unsteadily.

He had never killed anyone in his life.

The Great T. was looking at the doorway, where he thought Jumar was standing.

He waited for the door to open and Jumar to go out. He seemed to suspect nothing.

Jumar's hand hovered in the air.

"You are still there," said the Great T.

Jumar hesitated. "Hasn't it ever occurred to you," he whispered, almost inaudibly, "to be afraid of me because I'm invisible?"

"If you were visible, I might be afraid of you," replied the Great T.

Jumar's question hovered silently in the cold air.

"If the king had a visible son, that son could speak to the people," said the Great T., breathing vapor into the cold air as he spoke. "And he could try to be a better king than his father," the Great T. went on. "But they would never accept an invisible king. They'd be afraid of him, they would hide from him, no one would listen to him. He couldn't change anything. You need me in order to change things. Much more than I need you."

Jumar's hand had still been hovering over the letter opener. Now he let it drop to his side.

Then he turned abruptly and left the room.

282

The Great T. was speaking the truth, and the truth tore a painful wound in Jumar's guts.

When he was out in the street again, he took deep breaths of the cold, crisp air. The sweat was beginning to freeze on his forehead. Even if he had picked up the letter opener—even if he had thrust it into the Great T.'s heart—it wouldn't have done any good. The Great T. was right. An invisible prince could teach people the meaning of fear, but he could never be one of their own kind.

At that moment Jumar came to a decision: He would become visible.

Not that he knew how.

But he knew he would do it.

Suddenly he was breathing more freely. Suddenly he felt as if he had been almost suffocating in that bare room with Mao's faded photograph and the withered flower on the wall. He decided that he would read what Mao had really written someday so he could learn what he had really wanted, because this couldn't be it.

He had to find an opportunity to talk to Christopher. He had so often watched over his friend's sleep in the first nights after they were separated! But in the end he had taken to making his nocturnal excursions to that other part of the town, and it was at least a week since he had set eyes on Christopher or Niya.

They brought the three men back around midday. They could hardly sit on their horses, and there wasn't much life left in them, but the Great T. had given orders to bring them back to him alive, and what little life was still in them would have to do.

Jumar didn't want to think what the Great T. would do to them.

There were things you didn't have to know.

Late that afternoon, the men were dead.

He watched another troop trying to dig a hole in the hard,

frozen earth. The Great T. stood beside the men, smoking. The tip of his cigarette glowed in the clear, cold air when he drew on it. After a while he shook his head and signed to the men to put their spades away. There was no point in it; the ground was already too hard.

They put the three motionless, naked bodies over the backs of mules, and Jumar accompanied them, unseen, to the rocky eye of the needle—the pass through which they had arrived at the camp. There, a small, agile man clambered on one of the rocks and pulled the bodies up by a rope, one after the other, to lay them on the bare stones up at the top.

Jumar stayed with the guards on the rocky pass for a while. He watched the black silhouettes of birds soaring down from the mountain ridge. First there were only one or two, then more and more, circling lower and lower. He heard their cries and he saw their huge wings in the last light of day: bearded vultures, the largest birds in this country. They had come to dispose of the dead men. When they settled on the rocks, the heir to the throne of Nepal turned away and went back down into the valley. The first lights were flickering on in the molten town.

The three traitors were dead, but they had obviously talked to someone outside the camp, for the Great T. was still nervous. There were rumors that he had decided to get his three Western hostages away from the town. Their time had not yet come, but they were a treasure, the most valuable weapon he had.

Jumar knew where the prisoners were being held, at the end of a narrow, winding street. It was quiet and empty. Only when it was deep night would the Great T. send his men to take the hostages away. Four mud-brick steps led down to the tiny cellar window that Jumar had only recently discovered.

Someone was already standing there. Jumar recoiled. Then he whispered, "Christopher!"

Christopher spun around.

"It's me, Jumar!"

"Oh, what luck!" whispered Christopher. There were tears in his eyes.

"People say they're going to take the prisoners away, hide them even farther up in the mountains," said Jumar softly. "This very night."

"I'd almost reached my journey's end," said Christopher tonelessly. "Niya knew where they keep the key. But it's not there anymore. If they take them away tonight, we may never get another chance."

Jumar laid an invisible hand on his shoulder. "It's high time we left, too," he whispered. "We won't lose sight of your brother."

"We?" whispered Christopher. "You're not staying with the Great T.?"

"No," said Jumar, "it was all a mistake. But this isn't the time for explanations."

"Where are you planning to go, Jumar?" Christopher whispered.

"Ask me again the day after tomorrow," Jumar replied. "I've got no idea. I just know one thing: I'm going to become visible. Somehow or other. I have to do it."

"What?" asked Christopher. "How—?"

"Shh! Later."

Jumar tried to laugh, but he couldn't.

He moved to Christopher's side and looked into the darkness in the cellar beyond the barred window. It was like the window of a wagon carrying wild beasts in old pictures of circuses. A musty smell came from the room inside that mingled with the cool cellar air and mud walls.

But right behind the bars he made out a face in the darkness that was now coming into focus: a face surrounded by light, untidy hair and hidden by a growing blond beard. But the mouth and eyes in the face were smiling. They were smiling Christopher's smile. Jumar was so excited.

"I—I'm Jumar," he stammered, and something like shame formed in the prince of Nepal's mind. He was ashamed of his country, where a foreigner could end up in a cellar behind iron bars. Not that he or his country could do anything about that. All the same, he felt ashamed. "And you—you must be Arne."

"That's what I tell myself every day," the young man with the blond beard said. "Although yesterday, I found a piece of mirror glass in a corner here, and then I wasn't so sure."

He frowned. "Christopher's told me this weird story about you, and how he comes to speak your language! It took me so much hard work to learn it, but he speaks it just like that! And the way he came here is weird, too. And you being invisible! I wouldn't have thought it possible, but I can see that he's here, and I can hear that *you're* here. But as for understanding all this—I can't begin to do that."

His voice sounded amused, as if he had just read a good book telling a story that he couldn't quite believe. It didn't sound like the voice of someone who had been locked up in a dark cellar for weeks while it was snowing and freezing outside.

"How are the other two in there with you?" asked Jumar.

At that Arne's voice grew serious. "Not too good," he said. "They're asleep at the moment. They're both sick, and I'm really worried about one of them. It would be great if we could get out of here and put those two on a plane for home."

"Yes," Christopher sighed. "It would be great. But we don't even know how to get out of this place ourselves."

287

"Hey," said Arne, and the laughter in his voice sounded forced. "If they take us away tonight, you two won't just go off and leave us, will you? I mean, here my little brother pops up in the Himalayas out of nowhere. Maybe he'll simply disappear again?"

"Don't let that bother you," someone said behind them, and Jumar and Christopher spun around at the same time. There in the narrow alley behind them stood Niya, her black hair wilder than ever, her arms crossed over her chest. The glow in her eyes was bright again now. And she had brought her smile with her.

"We can't set you free," she said. "Not yet. But we'll go with you. I have an idea."

When Christopher lay awake that night, staring into the darkness, he felt as if everyone else in the dormitory must hear his heart thudding. It was almost bursting apart with joy that he had finally found his brother, and that Jumar and Niya had turned up again, ready to go with them. And with fear as well. His mind was full of questions.

Would Niya's plan work?

Would they succeed in getting across the narrow pass outside the camp without being seen?

When the wind that never slept began sweeping through

the streets, Christopher slipped out from under his blanket and through the door without a sound, just as he had done the night before. The memory of that unreal night still gave him strength. And he needed all the strength he could summon. He suppressed the cough in his throat with all his might. A cough could be deadly dangerous—it could give them away.

Christopher followed the wind, knowing that it was Jumar. And while he made his way swiftly through the starlight, keeping in the shadow of the walls, he thought of what Niya had said when they parted. "I'm the only one who knows what happens to anyone they bring back," she had said. "And it can't happen to us. If they catch one of us, the others cannot hesitate. We must shoot anyone who gets caught."

"*Shoot?*" Christopher had asked.

"Shoot to kill," Niya had replied. "That means kill you or me. Believe me, it's better to die than be brought back to the Great T."

"Niya—I could never, never shoot you."

She had looked at him intently, with a burning glow in her eyes.

"Promise me to do it if it comes to that. Promise."

"I promise."

The words stuck in his throat like a leaden lump as he followed Jumar through the night. He didn't look around, for if you look around you are showing your fear. How good were their chances? Had anyone noticed that he wasn't at the barrack with the others anymore? Even the few minutes he had spent talking to Arne, Niya, and Jumar had been an almost impossible risk to take. He knew there could be eyes behind him in the darkness now, eyes watching, mouths that would report back, just as the Great T. had ordered Jumar to report back.

They reached the shed beside the cellar where the captives were held. Jumar, who had stolen a key, got the shed door to open without a sound. Inside, they could see the dark outlines of crates and sacks. This was one of the storehouses for provisions. The baskets that the guerrillas escorting the prisoners were to take with them that night stood packed and tied up by the door, heavy with bottles of water, food, and ammunition. No mules would accompany the party, for mules could not go where they planned to climb. Bearers from the town who had served the Maoists for a long time would carry the equipment, and they were not just used to heavy loads, but also knew every path farther up in the mountains. Christopher had seen them wrapping straps around the baskets and tying the ends of the strap to their foreheads; they carried astonishing loads in that way.

Niya greeted Christopher with a nod and a finger to her

lips. She was already emptying two of the baskets and hiding the contents farther back among the crates. Christopher helped her in silence. Cold sweat was running down him, and his fingers were trembling uncontrollably. He kept stopping to listen for any sound. The night was still quiet in the street outside; there were no footsteps. Every minute, every second counted. At last, the first basket was empty, and Christopher obediently curled up in it, arms around his folded knees, a gun beside him. He hadn't wanted to bring it, but Niya had insisted. They were closing the lid of the basket over him as footsteps approached outside.

He heard Niya swear softly, and then a rustling sound. Then all was quiet around him. She and Jumar had hidden somewhere. The only sound was the footsteps, and Christopher's panic filled the night. If anyone came in now, they would see the ropes and straps that had been tied around the basket earlier lying on the floor. The footsteps were right outside the door of the shed. Christopher was caught in a trap.

Then the door opened. It squeaked very quietly and then the footsteps crossed the room. Those footsteps, as he noticed now, were also quiet—even if they seemed to him louder than any other sound in the world, they were stealthy and careful. The footsteps stopped in front of the basket. Someone bent and muttered something.

Christopher's heart was racing.

Their escape would never work now.

He thought of the three men who had run away and been brought back. He didn't want to think about what had been done to them. He closed his eyes in his hiding place like a child who believes that by doing so, he can't be seen.

The footsteps lingered beside the basket for an eternity.

But in the end, the lid wasn't lifted after all. The footsteps went a little farther. Someone seemed to be picking something up, and then they stole away through the room. Once again the door squeaked quietly and the footsteps went away down the street. Only then did Christopher realize that he had been digging his fingers into his hands, and when he cautiously let go he could feel the blood that his own nails had drawn on his palms.

A little later, Christopher heard Niya and Jumar whispering.

"A thief," whispered Jumar. "Someone stealing the supplies. He must have been happy to find the door open. Come on, quick . . . !"

Then Niya and Jumar tied the strap and the ropes back around the basket, while Christopher tried to control his trembling inside it. He heard the rustling sound of human contents settling into another basket, and knew that Jumar was securing Niya in by himself.

Then more footsteps approached. He could count the footsteps of several men, and he took care to breathe in and out without any sound. He hoped he wouldn't need to cough.

He felt himself being raised in the air, heard the men cursing the weight of the baskets—and the world around him began to rock slowly back and forth like a baby's cradle.

After a while, exhaustion overcame him, forcing him to close his eyes, and the Great T.'s bearers had no idea what an unusual load they were carrying out of the molten city and up into the mountains that night.

They made slow progress, for one of the foreigners could hardly keep on his feet, and if the one with the fair hair hadn't supported him, they would never have reached their destination.

The guards at the narrow pass like a needle's eye placed their hands together in greeting. The bearers and the guerrillas who were leading the prisoners returned the greeting. There was a smell in the air of stale blood and vulture droppings, and so they made haste to move on.

When it was nearly morning, something strange happened to the little group as they made their way.

They had stopped for a short rest and taken off their

loads to make tea over a small fire. The foreigner who was limping on so painfully had limped into their hearts. A cup of hot tea, they felt sure, could do him no harm. They made tea in the same way as the Tibetans, who were not so very far away from here. Tibetan tea was strong, with a piece of butter and a pinch of salt in it, to give strength to anyone taking the steep paths up to the heights. They were quite amused by the faces of the three foreigners, who had never drunk this kind of tea before.

They were still laughing when the inexplicable happened: two of the baskets suddenly began to move and roll back down the slope. The bearers jumped up and ran after them, but the heavy baskets rolled faster and faster, and ended up in a crevice, too steep here for the bearers to climb down after them without losing too much valuable time.

So they just cursed. From then on, the bearers took turns to carry the remaining provisions. What they had left would have to be enough.

"Maybe it's just as well that we didn't catch up with those two baskets," said one of the men. "Maybe there was something unnatural about them. The mountains are full of spirits up here as the land rises higher and higher. They came with the Tibetans who fled here from the politics in their own country, and the spirits have stayed—"

✦ ✦ ✦

Christopher felt more bruised and battered than he had ever been in his life when at long last Jumar freed him from the basket. He had difficulty getting to his feet, but when he was standing there stretching, the sky above him seemed higher and the air clearer than ever before.

"We made it!" he said in amazement.

Niya was standing beside him. She was carrying her gun over her shoulder, and handed Christopher his. Black and heavy, it nestled close to his body; a faithful companion now, although he could not return its affection.

"Yes," said Niya. "We made it."

"We made it," agreed Jumar.

And they all hugged each other, which must have looked odd, since one of them was invisible.

"Time to put the rest of our clothes on," said the invisible one, "because it's going to be cold now. Do you have the bundle I gave you there, Niya?"

And then the invisible one put on two pairs of socks with the boots that he had been wearing on his bare feet until now, for purposes of invisibility, and another pullover, another cap and a green camouflage jacket, a second scarf and another layer of warm gloves, as well as another pair of pants . . . and that second layer of clothes and the boots became visible, standing beside Christopher and Niya. That was all. From a distance, you might have taken Jumar for an ordinary traveler—a traveler wearing many layers of clothing, but up close he looked very strange, because he had no face.

"A walking heap of old clothes," said Niya, laughing.

"Ha, ha," said Jumar.

"But now," said Christopher, "there's no time to lose. We must get out of this valley and find the path they took."

However, the valley was unwilling to let the three travelers go again.

It fought them with rocky teeth and sharp claws, it fended them off with jaws full of small stones that rolled away beneath their feet, it veiled itself in dark cloud to keep them from seeing where they were going.

When the landscape's hostile, rugged face was behind them at long last, day had dawned. However, there was no path for them in sight.

They made their way along the rim of the valley, and through scrubby undergrowth. For a while, they followed a narrow, winding track that petered out into nothing again. They thought they saw a path in every stretch of debris, every track trodden by game, and they were disappointed every time. Christopher felt himself beginning to despair.

He stopped and looked around. No, no sign anywhere

that anyone had been this way before them. And the distance of the mountains spread out before them without a sign of human life. He saw snowy peaks clearly now, against the blue sky of a beautiful morning that cried out to be captured in a photograph. This was just how the summits of the Himalayas had looked in the book of pictures that he had taken to his room at home, half an eternity ago.

He had admired their beauty at that time.

Now he was beginning to hate them. They had swallowed Arne up. He had disappeared for the second time.

Niya began singing softly as they walked on:

You say that you will love me
As long as the stars shine.
You say that while the winds blow,
You will still be mine.
You say you'll always love me,
But now there is no sign,
My dear, that you spoke true.

Over the mountains you went away,
They caught and killed you on that day.
My unseen lover, you would not stay . . .

"I've heard other people sing that song," said Jumar. "In the molten town. Was—was the unseen lover invisible?"

"I think he just can't be seen because he's gone away."

"Hmm," said Jumar. "Yes, that's what I thought, too."

Christopher felt that Jumar was thinking something over. Suddenly he remembered what Jumar had said when they met again in the molten town.

"Jumar," he began, hesitantly, "is what you said true? Do you . . . do you really want to become visible?"

Niya stopped so suddenly that Christopher bumped into her.

"What?" she asked.

"Yes," replied Jumar. "I . . . I came to a decision."

The others waited in silence.

Jumar cleared his throat thoroughly. "If there's one thing I've found out on this journey," he said, "it's that you can't get anything done unless people can see you. I'm tired of making things float through the air, like some kind of tacky conjurer, just to impress someone. I'd like to impress people with what I do and what I say. I'm tired of borrowing your body, Christopher . . ."

"Thanks very much. I've always been reasonably satisfied with my body until now."

"That's not what I meant! I'm tired of putting you in

danger. I . . . I want to have a body of my own, not a body that I can only feel. I'd like to walk through a door into one of the huts and say: Here I am, this is me, Jumar, and nobody else. I'm tired of being a phantom, a ghost. Sometimes I almost doubt if I exist! I'd like to look in a mirror and be sure that I do. I'm tired of doing things back to front, going around thousands of corners, having to rely on thousands of people like a baby. And I'm so tired of telling lies. If I want to get anything done, then there's only one solution: I have to become visible."

Niya raised her hands and clapped slowly. The sound echoed among the peaks, perhaps announcing the heir to the throne of Nepal's decision to the tallest crags. A touch of solemnity blew through the air with the wind.

299

"Just a minute," said Christopher. "First you want to kill the Maoists, then you want to be a Maoist . . . and now you want to be visible?"

"We can't always know everything in advance," Jumar admitted awkwardly. "I'm only fourteen, and how are you supposed to know what you want when you're fourteen?"

That was a good question, and Christopher said no more.

"And it's not important what I am," said Jumar. "What's important is what will become of this country."

"Wise words, very wise," said Niya.

"Don't make fun of me," snapped Jumar. "It's true! Everyone's trying to do this country and its people some kind of damage. The dragons want to eat it bare, and Kartan and the Great T. want to leave what's left of it in dust and ashes. Only someone who is visible can stop all that."

"And only someone of fourteen," whispered Christopher, "can believe that's possible."

But he was whispering so quietly that Jumar didn't hear him. And he himself was too much of a fourteen-year-old not to go on hoping.

"How are you going to set about becoming visible?" he finally asked.

"I'm still thinking that over," said Jumar seriously. "Niya once asked me why I've never tried to . . . well, find out why I'm invisible. Maybe that's what I have to do first."

No sooner had he spoken than it began to snow again. They watched as thick flakes covered the trackless countryside, muting all sound.

"If we set out to do that just now, we'll lose a lot of time," said Niya. "Should we work on a plan for how—"

A gust of wind blew that made the dancing snowflakes swirl. A second gust followed. Niya said no more, but looked up at the sky that now consisted of gray-and-white streaks of low-hanging clouds.

Nothing was left of the bright blue morning. A curtain of whirling snowflakes descended and they couldn't see where they were going anymore.

The snow was bitterly cold on Christopher's face. Their clothes would keep them warm—but only for a certain length of time. And they would soon be beyond it.

Christopher was trudging along behind Niya with his head bent. Jumar's words mingled with his own thoughts and made a brightly colored kaleidoscopic pattern of crazy bits and pieces.

The dragons . . . Arne . . . Only someone visible . . . Dust and ashes . . . The Maoists . . . Kartan . . . The Great T. . . . Stop all this . . . The cold . . . The cold . . . The cold . . .

He stopped and looked around for the camouflage jacket and the thick gloves hovering over the snow behind him, worn by someone without any face.

"What do we think we're doing in these darn mountains anyway?" he shouted against the snow and the wind. "Saving the world, or what? Defeating dragons? Keeping back armies? Three fourteen-year-olds alone in the mountains? It's pointless, it's a total waste of time! It was pointless all along. We'll never find them, we won't even find our own way! What use is a gun to me if I freeze to death? Can't you admit it, Jumar? Niya? We don't have a real plan anymore. We've lost track of Arne. We've got no idea where we are! What are we really doing here?"

"Surviving, you idiot!" shouted Jumar. "Nothing else matters at the moment!"

"Oh, yes, surviving. We might just as well stay here and wait for the snow to cover us up, and then it will all be over."

"You stay if you like," said Jumar. "I'm going on. Niya?"

Christopher felt Niya's arm around his shoulders.

"You need sleep," she whispered. "You need it badly."

Christopher tore himself away. "Sleep?" he cried, his voice hoarse. "Don't you realize, Niya, sleep is the one thing we're all going to get, and very soon at that? A long, long sleep that's so long, we'll never wake up again."

"Keep your mouth shut," said Jumar. "If you're giving up, you can do it on your own."

"And what about you?" said Christopher. "You don't even know where you're going. First you want to smash the insurgents, then it's Kartan . . . Now you suddenly want to get visible, and the next idea you think up will be that we're really wandering around these mountains because you need a pair of sneakers!"

That made Niya laugh in her own unique way, and it was as if a shell of ice that had formed around Christopher were breaking. He laughed, too.

Finally, even Jumar laughed.

"Yellow sneakers with black polka dots," he said.

They walked on and not much later, Niya's expert eyes spotted a kind of natural cavern under an overhanging wall of rock. They found shelter from the snow in there, huddling together like animals. And it was there that Christopher had the strangest, most vivid dream of his life. A dream much more like real life than the story in which he was stuck.

INTERLUDE

H E WAS SITTING ON THE LIVING ROOM carpet, his legs drawn up, his head resting on his knees.

At first he couldn't make out what the unsteady flickering that filled the room was, but in the end he realized it was the TV, painting strange shadows on the walls with its swiftly changing pictures.

The news was on. Christopher looked around. The big clock on the wall said five past eight. His father's upright figure sat in an angular blue armchair, Christopher's mother was sitting on the sofa behind him. Oddly enough, he himself still had the book about Nepal open in front of him.

It was already getting dark outside. The long, mysterious shadows of fall stole through the garden, and the wind threw faded leaves and handfuls of rain against the glass of the veranda door.

"Now!" said Christopher's mother. "He'll be on any minute now!"

He turned his eyes back to the TV screen. What was she talking about?

The pictures behind the anchor changed.

"There he is!" whispered Christopher's mother. Yes, there he was: Arne. He was in a slightly blurred photograph, standing between two other young men of his own age who looked smaller and more frightened than he did. The others had unkempt hair and stubbly beards. Their eyes looked dull, and Christopher remembered how Arne had said the other two weren't well. But Arne was smiling at the camera, as if he had actually *asked* someone to take this photo of him. His smile was like a message sent home. He had known they would see this picture.

The anchor explained that the photo had been published on the Internet half an hour ago, along with the official statement from a Nepalese guerrilla group of Maoists who said that the three young men in the picture, who had been missing for several weeks, were alive and well.

"If there are ongoing hostilities around the capital city, Kathmandu," the anchor announced, "the Maoists are calling for complete neutrality and no foreign intervention; no kind of support from other countries for the Nepalese army. Two of the men in the photograph are from the United States of America, one is from Germany. So far it is not known exactly where they are being held, or whether the Maoist group plans to make a concerted attack on Kathmandu to depose the king of Nepal by force . . ."

The picture changed again. A weather map appeared.

Christopher slowly breathed out. Of course his parents had known in advance. Someone must have called them when the picture was first published. He watched their faces in the light cast by the TV, and it struck him how small his mother looked all of a sudden. As if she had shrunk during the time Christopher was away. But—was he here now? And if he was here now, where had he been before?

Why was the book of pictures lying on the sofa in front of him?

A tear-off calendar hung on the wall under the clock. Today's date showed the tenth of November . . . Christopher calculated nervously. This was about four weeks from the day when he had sat on the bed in his room and opened the book about Nepal.

"That beard," murmured Christopher's father. "A beard suits Arne, don't you think?" Christopher could hear how hard he was trying to sound cheerful and positive.

His mother nodded faintly. Then she shook her head. In the end she said, quietly, "I don't know."

Christopher's father rose from his chair, sat down beside her, and put his arms around her. She rested her head on his shoulder.

"If only Christopher would at least start talking again," he heard her whisper. "At least that would help."

"He'll start in his own good time," said his father. "He just has his own way of coping with these things."

"It scares me," she whispered. "It's like losing both of them at once."

Christopher opened his mouth to say something. What made her think he wasn't talking? But what was he supposed to say? He couldn't think of anything, and he closed his mouth again.

The book was open at a page that struck him as familiar. Of course. That was it. The molten town.

He turned the page and found himself looking at a picture of a mountain with a pointed peak like an equilateral triangle with slightly curved outlines. And there was a fishtail without any fish attached to it. The mountain looked very close in the picture, and the ice of its glaciers glittered in the sunlight. The side of the mountain turned to the viewer didn't look as if anyone could climb it. It didn't look as if the peak would be kind to climbers who wanted to scale its heights. The clouds coming up from the left in the sunny sky of the photo promised snow.

"I'll light the fire," said Christopher's father. "A little warmth won't hurt any of us on such a dismal November evening."

He rose from the sofa, smiling at Christopher. Christopher smiled back. He knew he ought to say something, because they obviously thought he had lost the power of speech. But the only thing he could think of was to ask: How did I get here?

And he didn't feel as if this question would reassure his parents at the moment. He had a feeling that they hadn't even noticed he'd been away.

His mother was clattering pots and pans in the kitchen now, and he could smell a casserole.

Then he heard the fire crackling on the hearth and a wonderful warmth spread through him.

But even as he felt the warmth, he realized that the whole scene was slipping away from him—the soft carpet on the floor, the suppertime aroma, his father in front of the fire; it was as if someone were pulling all this from under his feet.

He tried to reach out his arms to hold on to something in the scene, but all his fingers felt was the smooth, cool pages of the book of pictures in front of him.

He opened his eyes.

Above the Snowline

·····
HEIGHT C. 13,125–29,500 FEET
·····

FLORA (ABOVE THE TREELINE)

Arctic bell heather (*Cassiope*), pink mountain heather (*Phyllodoce empetriformis*), huckleberry (*Vaccinium deliciosum*), edelweiss (*Leontopodium*), white-flowering sandwort (*Arenaria bryophylla*), saxifrage (*Saxifrage saginoides*), glacier buttercup (*Ranunculus glacialis*), map lichen (*Rhizocarpon geographicum*)

FLORA (THE ONLY FLORA LIVING ON SNOW)

single-celled algae (*Chlamydomonas nivalis*)

FAUNA

Snow hare, snow pheasant, Himalayan marmot, bearded vulture, Tibetan blue sheep

JUMAR, UNDERSTANDING

THE SOUND OF CRACKLING FLAMES WAS still there. So was the warmth. Christopher sat up, feeling dazed. Sure enough, there was a fire burning in the middle of the cave now.

Niya was sitting cross-legged beside it, feeding the flame with little bits of wood and dry leaves as if it were a timid animal.

"Good morning, Christopher," she said, looking up and smiling.

"Is it morning?"

"No, but I thought it would be a nice way to say hello. Come closer to the fire. It's warm."

"Fires usually are," replied Christopher, obediently moving

over to her and taking off his cap. "I've been dreaming," he said. "There was a fire in my dream, too—a fire in my parents' fireplace at home. It was a strange dream. Where did you get the firewood?"

"Someone stacked it in one corner of this cave," said Jumar. "There are a whole lot of sheep droppings lying around. I expect a shepherd slept in here before it started snowing."

Christopher flicked off several of the droppings Jumar had mentioned from his green camouflage jacket. Jumar laughed at him, and pretending to be surprised, Christopher cried, "Hey, you're still invisible! Weren't you going to turn visible while I was asleep?"

Niya had been right. He really did feel better. Nothing had changed, they were still stuck in a cave, snow was driving past outside like a scurrying white phantom figure; they had lost Arne, and they had no plan in mind anymore. But sleep—and perhaps his dream, even more than sleep—had restored his will. He was going to bring Arne home.

Somehow.

It was almost as if he had found a small part of Jumar's fierce determination in himself.

Jumar's backpack appeared briefly near the fire and then disappeared again, and he could be heard rummaging around in it. Finally he pulled out a can of sardines.

"I took some of the provisions from the baskets," he said. "It's a pity there wasn't a can opener . . ."

"I could shoot a hole in the can," Niya suggested. But when she saw Christopher's horrified expression, she laughed and opened the can with her knife. Using their fingers, they ate sardines in oil that had gone a little rancid and watched the snow. And then they began to wait. With the snow falling so heavily, it made no sense to set out in search of a trail leading to the Great T.'s men and their captives.

"I don't like to sing without my guitar," said Niya at last, "but I could tell you a fairy tale."

"Is it another of those stories that end badly?"

"I'm afraid so. I heard it when I was a little girl. It's about an old magician and a queen . . ." She looked into the fire, lost in thought. "The magician in the story lived on a mountain that looked like a fishtail—a fishtail without any fish attached, like a triangle with three equal sides. He lived high up on this mountain. One day, the magician climbed down into the valley to sell his harvest. But what is there to be harvested on such a high mountain? The magician's whole harvest fit into the breast pocket of his jacket.

"There was a young queen living in the most beautiful city in the valley, and the old magician went to see her and offered to sell her his harvest. He put his hand into his jacket pocket and pulled out a single tiny seed. The queen eyed the seed suspiciously. She couldn't believe it had any value, and she refused to buy it from the old man. Then the magician was angry, and he secretly planted the seed outside the palace gates and climbed back up his mountain—the mountain that looked like a fishtail without any fish attached.

"But he was a magician, and the seed he had planted had magic of its own. Wonderful things would have grown from it if the queen hadn't annoyed the magician. As things were, it grew into a great fire. Yes, a great fire grew from an insignificant little brown seed. However, it was a secret fire; you could feel it, but you couldn't see it. When the queen left the palace, soon after that, she felt the fire reaching out for her with sudden strength. The queen was carrying a child in her belly, and she felt the invisible fire that had grown from the magician's seed burning her child. No one believed her. But when the time came for her to bear her baby, it was nothing but a little heap of white ashes."

Niya fell silent, and fed the fire another handful of leaves and twigs. They, too, were turned to white ash within a very short time.

"Is that—is that all?" asked Christopher. "Was that the fairy tale?"

She nodded.

"The fairy tales I've heard here so far are all so bizarre," said Christopher.

"And unimaginative," said Jumar. "They all tell the same story."

"Do they?" asked Christopher. Maybe he should have listened more carefully.

"In a way. They're always about beautiful women and strange old men."

"Who don't get what they want," said Niya, and smiled. "Maybe that's just how old men are in the old stories."

"They always come down from the mountains," said Christopher thoughtfully. "Maybe that means something."

"It means that life in the mountains is uncomfortable, so the old men aren't happy with it."

Niya laughed.

"No," said Jumar, and suddenly he sounded serious. "Wait a minute."

Niya and Christopher stared at the place where his face must be, roughly above his jacket—as if that would help them figure out what he was thinking.

"What is it?"

"I have to think this over," said Jumar. "These stories . . . they remind me of something. If only I knew what . . ."

"They reminded me a little of the dragons," said

Christopher. "Maybe because of the great fire. The dragons breathe fire, too."

"And then there was the garden . . ." muttered Jumar. "A garden like my father's garden at home."

"Your father has a garden?" asked Niya. She still had no idea who Jumar was.

He did not answer her. So they all sat in silence and looked into the fire as it slowly burned down.

"It's a test," Jumar said at last. "Couldn't that be it? In all three fairy tales there's a test. And the beautiful woman doesn't pass it. She doesn't want to see the lonely traveler. She rejects the monk. She sends the magician away. It's always the same story."

"If you say so," said Christopher. "Right, so it's a test. Which means we've interpreted the fairy tale correctly. Are you going to write an essay on it now, or what?"

Jumar grunted.

"Let's go," said Niya. "It's stopped snowing, and there's no wood left."

"Go where?" asked Christopher. "Where are you planning to go?"

She shrugged her shoulders under her thick parka. "That doesn't matter. We have to keep warm."

And as Niya was the one who knew her way around

the mountains, they followed her out into the endless white expanse and went on, not really knowing where they were headed. There was nothing to help them get their bearings. No tree, no shrub, no sign of life. The shining expanse of newly fallen snow dazzled Christopher, and he almost wished a dragon would appear on it.

But only almost.

Jumar trotted along behind them, silent and brooding— Christopher thought he heard him muttering from time to time.

"One and the same story, one and the same story . . ." he murmured. Then, suddenly, he grabbed Christopher by the hood of his parka. "It's not just all the same story," he said. "It's all the same *woman*."

"What?" asked Christopher.

"One and the same woman. The princess. The girl gardener. The queen. But that's not quite right. She's always a queen. The rest is made up. I think . . . I think parts of the story are true. Or like the truth. In one of the fairy tales there's a monster that sends everyone to sleep. A monster is almost a father, right? But in real life, it's not everyone who goes to sleep, only the queen. In Niya's story, the woman is pregnant, but instead of a baby she bore a heap of ashes."

"Yes?" asked Christopher.

"In real life," explained Jumar, his voice trembling with excitement, "she bore an invisible child."

Niya looked up. "An invisible child? What queen? *The* queen? The one who's said to lie sleeping in her garden in Kathmandu while people starve to death outside?"

"That's her," replied Jumar. "And I'm her son."

Niya looked at Christopher. He nodded.

"That's why Kartan is after him."

At that, Niya threw back her head and laughed. She laughed and laughed until there were tears running down her cheeks. They left pale trails in the dirt on her face.

"That's incredible," she gasped at last, mopping up the tears. "That is just plain incredible! I've left the Great T., and now I've been wandering around here in the snow with the rightful heir to the throne of Nepal. And I call myself a Communist! What's happened to the world? And as for you, Jumar—so you wanted to be one of us, did you? Was that true, or was it just a trick, and we fell for it?"

"Oh, it's true," said Jumar seriously. "Of course it's true. Only it didn't work. But that's not what matters now. It's the fairy tales that matter! The queen in those stories, or the princess—she's my mother. And the monster from the fairy tale is a color dragon, I'm sure of it. And the magician—or the lonely traveler or the monk—he exists. He must exist.

Something happened before I was born. She must have made him angry. I wish I could ask her about it! I didn't simply come into the world invisible like this. It has something to do with that old man in the stories. And something to do with the color dragons. People say they weren't always around."

Niya shook her head, and her wild black hair came loose from under the thick cap and flew around her head like a flock of birds.

"So what are we supposed to do now?" she asked. "Go looking for an old man sitting all alone somewhere in the Himalayas? Such a small place, the Himalayas. It's so easy to see everything at a glance! Maybe you're wrong. Maybe the old man doesn't even exist. Or maybe he died long ago. This is fourteen years in the past."

She trudged on, marching through the white void of the snowy mountain range.

As afternoon approached, the last clouds cleared and the sky turned a clear, pale blue.

When they stopped, Christopher shielded his eyes with his hand and watched the peaks emerge from the mist one by one, as if shedding a coat of white vapor. Suddenly they were no longer hostile and frightening.

Now they were beautiful.

The distance was beckoning, showing them mountains of all shapes and all shades of glittering color. But some had colorless patches that seemed to swallow up the sunlight. Traces of dragons.

Christopher tipped his head back and looked up at the great massif with the cave at its foot. The clouds were just leaving the peak of the mountain. It was shaped like an equilateral triangle. Christopher had seen it before.

A long, long time ago, in a book with pictures of Nepal.

Then he remembered the name of the mountain.

Machapuchare. The Fishtail.

The mountain that looked like a fishtail with no fish attached.

It rose above them like a gigantic beacon. It had been waiting for them all the time. The sun played on the ice at the very top of the faraway mountain, painting patterns there like frost flowers on a window: flourishes, tendrils, petals—and among them, once again, there were those colorless, lightless patches, more of them than ever before.

"Jumar!" called Christopher. "Niya!"

They came up to him—and now, in the snow, Jumar's crunching footsteps were visible for the first time. Tracks appeared, although no one seemed to be making them. Christopher smiled.

In silence, he pointed up.

"Christopher," whispered Jumar solemnly. "That's it. The mountain from Niya's fairy tale. We've found it without even looking for it."

Christopher laughed. "Maybe it has found us."

"If the mountain exists," said Jumar seriously, "so does the monk. He's sitting somewhere up there. He's old, but he's still alive. I can feel that he is."

"Nonsense," said Niya. "You won't let yourself believe he's dead."

"Sometimes," said Jumar, "I'd like to be visible just so that someone can write of me: He cast an irritated glance at her. So where . . ."

"You were saying, 'He's still alive, I can feel that he is,'" said Christopher.

"Right. He must still be alive. He's the one who can tell me why I'm invisible. Once I know that, I'm sure I'll manage to change somehow. And then I'll return to the city and go to my father, and he will give me the key to his power. And everything will be all right. No more dragons, no hunger, nothing bad like that."

"Amen," said Niya, who didn't believe in any religion. Then she sighed. "I'm afraid you want to go up there, right? And I'm afraid it'll be no use for me to tell you it's impossible. They say no one can climb the Fishtail."

"I vaguely remember reading somewhere that Reinhold Messner climbed it," Christopher objected.

"Are all you Germans crazy?" She sighed a second time. "What a question. I know you are. I know that only too well."

At that moment, Christopher wanted to take her in his arms—it was the way she stood there, shaking her head, wise but resigned. Yet her heart was young and inexperienced, and it had been seriously hurt back in the molten town. He reached out a hand, but then let it drop again. They were not alone.

And he guessed that they never would be alone again.

A thousand thoughts were swirling around in the crown prince of Nepal's head as he set off that afternoon to climb Machapuchare, the Fishtail—the mountain where fairy tales came from. The only path had come to an end. They were leaving it behind them with their own tracks in the snow, and new snow would cover those up.

But for the time being, the sky was blue—bluer than all the flowers in the garden where the queen had been sleeping for fourteen years, bluer than the water in the king's blue-tiled pool.

What will it be like, Jumar wondered. What will it be like when I am visible? Will I feel it? Will it hurt? Will my steps be heavier?

And what will I look like? Who will look back at me from the mirror? Will I recognize myself? Do I look like my father? Will Niya like what she sees? Will it change something between us if I'm visible?

Yes, of course, it was bound to change something.

But suppose I can't do it? What if that's what the old man on the mountain tells me?

The snow crunched underfoot, and the wind swept gusts of fine, icy dust toward them like ghosts scurrying over the slope. Jumar put one foot in front of the other, the visible outlines of Niya and Christopher ahead of him, and soon his thoughts were lost in the heights. He was finding breathing more difficult.

They were at a very high altitude now, and had to stop to rest more and more often. Just before darkness fell, they came upon a rough track, but Jumar had never been so glad to see a track in his life. They wouldn't have found it but for a torn plastic sandal lying there—a sign of human life. That night, they found a hut standing empty, a makeshift shelter cobbled together from thin boards, but like the track, the hut seemed to Jumar the best thing he could imagine.

The wind whistled through the cracks between the boards, and the door wouldn't shut properly. They slept on the rough wooden floor, and the heir to the throne of Nepal dreamed. He dreamed of a color dragon flying over the hut with its gigantic wings spread, its black, hollow eyes seeking, waiting, on the lookout—as if it knew someone was on the way to discover the secret of the dragons and destroy them. But the snow had covered up their tracks again, and all that the color dragon in Jumar's dream found was a hut that had been standing there for ages.

The next morning, they shared another can of sardines and left the hut. Outside the snow was matte, not glittering white anymore. It looked dull and dim, like snow in a bad photograph in a cheap newspaper.

324

"It was here," whispered Jumar. "I dreamed of the dragon, but it was really here."

He looked up the slope and a shudder ran through him.

"If we meet one of them here by day," he said, "there's nowhere we can hide from its shadow."

"Then we'd better not meet one of them," said Niya. "Do you still want to climb this damn mountain?"

"Of course," replied Jumar. "More than ever."

But on this second day, he had a bad headache and felt wretched. There was a thudding and hammering in his head as if the dragon had found a way in there and couldn't get out again.

"Great," said Niya, "it's the altitude. You know that yourself. We'll go back."

"Back? We can't go back. We've come so far!"

She felt in the air for him and grabbed him by the shoulders of his green camouflage jacket to give him a little shake.

"If you go on in this state, we'll never get anywhere. We stay in the hut until you're used to the altitude, understand? Or can't a crown prince bring himself to believe a girl who's only one of the common people?"

"No . . . I—" said Jumar, twisting and turning in her grasp.

But when she let go of him, he wished she had held him longer.

So they spent another day in the hut, and Jumar felt time running through their fingers. When would the Great T. send his people down to Kathmandu? How much time did they have left? He began hating the mountains, hating his head, hating the snow, the cold. Christopher coughed again.

The day slipped by in silence. Even Niya's songs had died away.

And when on the next morning they went on back to the track, he sensed that the others, too, were relieved. The throbbing in his head had stopped, and it didn't come back. They were climbing more slowly than ever now. Jumar thought that from a distance they must look like three snails climbing the mountain, making their way in slow motion along curve after curve of the winding track.

That day mist rose among the mountains and took the view away. White swathes of mist hovered ahead of them, like ghostly guides, and they kept thinking about what the bearer had said in the molten town: the spirits that came with the Tibetans . . . Jumar told himself that this was nonsense, and the mist was only mist, but it didn't help. He kept seeing arms and legs in it, dissolving, unsteady, eerie. But no, it wasn't mist; these were clouds. They were climbing through the clouds.

"Christopher," he whispered.

"Yes?"

"I just wanted to hear your voice. It's so quiet."

"We could sing," Niya suggested. "Singing calms the spirits."

"So you were . . . thinking of spirits as well?"

"Oh, they're here," said Niya seriously. "Every mountain has its spirits. It doesn't mean anything. They just have to let us through. If they don't want us to reach the peak, then we won't. It's as simple as that."

"I thought you didn't believe in such things? I thought you people didn't have any religion?"

"Spirits have nothing to do with religion," stated Niya. "So, let's sing."

So they sang.

For some reason, the only song they all three knew was the English version of "Silent Night," and it was strange to be walking through snowy mountains in Nepal singing that carol when it was the silence that they wanted to drive away. But it did help.

The next night, however, was far from silent. They found shelter in a hollow in the ground. The wind couldn't get into it, but its whistle rang around their ears, howling and wailing, as if it were disappointed that it couldn't reach them. They tried to close their ears to the voice of the wind, but it found its way into their ears, and deep into their hearts, too, whispering tales of other, stronger, greater spirits than those that lived in the mist during the day.

Jumar took Niya's and Christopher's hands—almost without noticing. They crouched there like small children, listening and trembling, and at last their exhaustion cast them into a restless sleep.

In the morning, the sun exploded near the peaks in a firework display of colors, and every tiny crystal in the snow reflected the sky. That morning, they saw the shadows of birds high above them against the background of the light.

"No," said Christopher. "Those aren't birds. They're dragons. A whole flock of dragons."

And Jumar saw that he was right. The movements of the creatures up there under the sun were too supple for birds, too beautiful, too unique. Too dangerous.

The flock of long-necked shadows disappeared from view, and they breathed a collective sigh of relief.

Soon the path became even narrower than before, leading directly along a rock face. Crags rose to their right, the mountain fell steeply away to their left, and Jumar avoided looking down into the depths. Years ago, when he was little, he had sometimes climbed up to the palace roof and looked out over the city from that vantage point, feeling like its ruler, so high above its rooftops. Now he smiled to think of it. His world had changed so much since those days!

He saw that Niya and Christopher had stopped.

"What's up?" he asked. "Why aren't you going on?"

Niya turned to him. "There's nothing left to go on along," she said. "The path stops here. It just stops short."

"You were right," said Christopher. "It's impossible to climb the Fishtail."

Jumar remembered that the servants had also thought it

was impossible to get up to the palace roof. But he had found a secret way over the stone carvings on one side of the wall and along a gutter. He had never told anyone about it. Only the pigeons had known that he sometimes sat up there.

"There must be some way," said Jumar. "Someone laid out the track up to here, and no one lays out a track leading nowhere."

He pushed past Christopher and Niya and narrowed his eyes, trying to read the secret of the rock. And then he saw it: The secret lay in the shadow of the overhanging ledges. And he smiled.

"Yes, there is a way," he said. "See those iron hooks? There! The path goes on, but it leads up through the air."

When he turned around, he saw all the color draining from Christopher's face. "You mean . . . there's only the hooks? The hooks are the way to go?"

"There are two rows of them. One row to put your feet on, another row above it for you to hold on to. Of course they're the way to go. Someone drove them into the rock here for that very purpose."

"Then you two will have to go on without me," said Christopher. "I . . . I can't do that. I'm sorry, but I can't. Arne could have done it. But you have the wrong brother with you. Sorry."

"Of course you can do it," said Niya. "I'll climb up first, and you'll see how it's done."

Christopher shook his head. Jumar saw small beads of sweat on his brow.

"We don't even know how far it is! Or whether the path leads anywhere!"

Jumar laid a hand on his shoulder. "No one can force you to come with us if you don't want to," he said quietly. "But please come, Christopher. Whatever is waiting for us up there . . . I don't want to face it without you. Remember when we were in that tent with the soldiers? When you told me I was an idiot?"

"I'm sorry about that," muttered Christopher.

"No!" cried Jumar. "You were right. I *am* an idiot. I keep falling into people's traps. You knew Kartan wasn't interested in saving the life of the heir to the throne. You knew not everything in the Great T.'s camp was as wonderful as it seemed. And you knew we were already at the foot of the mountain we were looking for. Please, Christopher. I need you."

Christopher smiled. "You're good with words, did you know that? If you ever get to be king, the people's hearts will melt when you speak to them."

"So you will come with us?"

Christopher hesitated. "I guess it's inevitable," he said at last. "I'd be done for in these mountains without you two anyway."

"Thank you," Jumar whispered.

Then Niya reached for the first hook in the wall of rock, put her foot on the first piece of metal below it, and began climbing up the path that someone had made in the rock that stood vertically before their eyes.

"It's . . . actually easy," she gasped. "The rocks go around a curve here . . . I can't . . . can't see where we're going yet . . ."

Jumar saw Christopher take a deep breath.

Then he began climbing after Niya, and Jumar followed him . . .

The wind had left them in peace for a little while. Now it came back. Perhaps it was curious to see why the climbers were clinging to the vertical wall like insects. It sang its song in the cracks of the rock, a song of heights and depths and ancient times.

But even the wind didn't tell them where the hooks in the rock were leading.

The rock did indeed curve, and soon they could no longer see the end of the path—they were hanging in the air, in a void, without anything for the eye to rest on. The hooks led upward. They climbed on and on, and Jumar's hands began to hurt. That frightened him. If he lost his strength before they reached the end of this strange path, if his hands refused to hold on to the iron hooks anymore—then he would drop into the depths like a stone. And it would be no use to him that no one could see him falling. He would hit the hard rock far below, and never, never find out what had happened before his birth.

And never, ever be visible.

At that moment Niya cried out, and he started.

He saw that she was looking up. And from high above them, one of the color dragons came soaring down. It was the biggest and most beautiful dragon that Jumar had ever seen. Its wings glittered turquoise and dark blue in the sun, its body had a violet sheen, and its long neck gave off a golden glow that was almost too bright for the eyes to bear.

It was coming closer and closer.

Jumar saw Niya take one hand off the rock, level her gun, and take aim. She managed to cock it one-handed. Jumar heard the click more clearly and distinctly in the empty air than he had ever heard such a sound before. The dragon was very close now. The sun cast its shadow on the rock wall a little way above Niya. If it came down a little lower, the shadow would touch her . . . and then she fired a shot.

Jumar held his breath. He had expected the creature to cry out, stagger in the air, fall—but nothing of the kind happened. The dragon was still hovering in the same place, and he saw something brightly colored, like feathers falling out of the air. Had the bullet just grazed it? One of the feathers caught in the hood of Niya's parka—Jumar saw its blue glitter there, like a splash of color. He saw Niya reloading the gun laboriously with one hand, and heard her fire for the second time. Once again, he thought she would hit the dragon, and once again nothing happened. It was as if Niya had suddenly lost her talent for marksmanship.

Now the dragon raised its mighty, brightly colored wings, gained height again, then let itself drop once more— as if it were watching them as it hovered above. It spewed out a jet of fire into the air. And then once again its shadow came gliding toward them from above, passing over the rock. In a panic, Jumar climbed two hooks higher. The dragon's dark shadow traveled over the rock like a patch of fear. Had it brushed Jumar's right hand in passing? Seconds later, the dragon was below the three climbers. It flew in a circle, then rose again in a perfect loop, and finally disappeared as if it had seen enough. Jumar stared at his hand.

Then, very slowly, he moved his fingers. It was all right. They hadn't turned to bronze. Nothing about Jumar had turned to bronze. The dragon's shadow had missed him by a mere fraction of an inch.

He took a very deep breath.

Then he climbed on, following Christopher and Niya.

How could Niya have missed the dragon—Niya, who always hit her target?

What luck! If the dragon had changed the course of its flight only a very little, the bronze statue of an invisible crown prince would have been blocking the way through the air up Machapuchare forever.

Although it's very likely that no one would have seen it.

Christopher's hands hurt, and he was sure it couldn't be much longer before he had to let go. He tried to think of everything that gave him strength.

He thought of Arne's face in the photograph behind the anchor on TV. He thought of his mother, who had looked so small in his dream. He thought of Jumar saying he needed his help. He thought of Niya's hands, and that cold night in the snow outside the molten town. Her lips. Her tousled hair that felt like an animal's fur. The notes of her guitar. Her words. Her voice . . .

"We're there," said Niya's voice, and he blinked incredulously.

Ahead of him were the last two hooks. And beyond those, the track went on, looking almost innocent, as if it had never come to an end. When Christopher's feet touched it, he was so relieved that he was tempted to just fall to the ground and stay sitting right there.

Niya put her finger to her lips, and he listened.

"What is it?" whispered Jumar, who was on the level ground of the path with them.

"Shh! Listen," whispered Niya. "Voices!"

And then Christopher, too, heard them.

From far away, voices came to their ears—high, clear voices—and he heard laughter as well.

"Maybe we're dreaming," he said. "Maybe none of this is real."

Niya cast him a glance of amusement. "Oh, come on," she said. "Just for *once*, can't you be optimistic? I'd say, we've done it!"

"Done what?" asked Christopher suspiciously.

"We've reached them."

"Uh . . . who have we reached?"

"That," she said, "is what we'll see if we go around this bend."

335

JUMAR, SEEING

AND THEN THEY DID SEE. IT WAS AMAZING. Christopher might have expected almost anything beyond the bend in the path—but not what they actually found there.

They climbed a snow-covered slope, and there, on a level surface above them, was a group of little boys in dark red robes in the middle of a soccer game.

Christopher blinked, but they were really there. He and the others stopped at the edge of the soccer field, and he felt the same astonishment that he saw on Niya's face.

Wooden posts marked out the goals at each end. The soccer ball wasn't a normal soccer ball, but a bundle of tightly wound, brightly colored fabric. However, there was no doubt at all what these boys were doing. The boys' heads were shaved bald and gleaming, and they wore sandals on their feet. Their voluminous dark red robes kept getting in the way of their legs as they ran, and some of the players fell down in the snow. Then they would beam as if it was the funniest thing ever to happen to them.

Christopher put the smallest player's age at four or five, and the two oldest must be a little older than he was. In between were boys of all other ages.

"Monks," whispered Niya.

Only then did Christopher see the monastery a little farther up the slope, right under the peak of the fishtail without any fish. It was like a monastery he had seen in the Nepal book, but he supposed all monasteries looked the same. Its white dome rose into the blue sky of the mountains beyond an equally bright white outer wall, and rows of colored prayer flags ran down from the top of the dome. Buddha's painted eyes welcomed the travelers with a gentle smile from far above. It looked to Christopher as if they were twinkling—but only for a moment. It was probably just the clear light here making him see things.

The young monks were so deep in their game that it took quite a few minutes before they noticed the strangers.

So the strangers stood and just let the peace of this surprising scene sink deeply into them.

Christopher put out his hand and removed the shining blue feather from Niya's hood.

But it was not a feather.

"A dead butterfly," he said in surprise. "It must have been hidden somewhere in a fold of the dragon's skin. Maybe your bullet swept it off."

Niya gazed thoughtfully at the wings lying motionless on Christopher's hand.

At that moment, a shout echoed over the monks' playing field, but it wasn't the triumphant shout of someone who had kicked a goal. It was a cry of surprise. One of the boys had spotted them, and now the little monks were all standing still as if rooted to the ground, staring at them.

"Jumar," whispered Niya, "your face!"

"What about it?" asked Jumar.

"You don't have one," she replied quietly. "At least, not a visible one. They'll be scared to death. Do something!"

Jumar turned the collar of his jacket a little higher over the neck of his pullover, wrapped his scarf around them, and pulled his cap down. Not a second too soon, for now the curious soccer players were back in motion. The three companions were suddenly surrounded by dark red robes and friendly eyes, and dozens of hands reached out to touch the camouflage green fabric of their clothes. Presumably the little monks had never seen such garments before. They giggled, put their hands to their mouths, and whispered behind them. Christopher gave them the nicest smile he could manage.

"Who are you?" the biggest boy asked. He was a good three inches taller than Christopher. "Where do you come from?"

"We come from a place where no one's played football in the sun for a very long time," replied Niya, "and we have walked a long, long way to reach a place where something as wonderful as that is still possible."

A smile spread over the boy's face. "You're welcome, then," he said.

"You must be tired," cried a very small boy. "And I'm sure you're hungry." He turned to the other monks. "Why don't we take them to our master? I can lead the way!"

"And me! And me! And me!" they all called, pushing to the front of the crowd.

The biggest boy silenced them with a wave of his hand.

"I'm the oldest, so it's my job to show these travelers our monastery," he said with dignity. "The rest of you can stay here and finish the game. There's still half an hour to go before evening prayers."

He nodded to the visitors, and they followed him up the slope. When Christopher turned once to look back, the boys were still standing on the playing field without moving, watching them go. It was obvious that none of them wanted to do anything but talk about the appearance on the mountain of the mysterious strangers until it was time for evening prayers.

Behind the monastery walls, flowers grew in metal containers that had been painted blue. Here and there you could still see the lettering on the metal from their original use: They had once held cooking oil.

But if there was no real path up the Fishtail, wondered Christopher, only those metal hooks, how could they bring canisters full of oil up here? What did they live on?

How had the children come up to this place?

"Wait here," said the young Buddhist. "I'll see if the Master has time for you."

Until now, Jumar's scarf had been hiding the face that wasn't there. At this point it slipped. The young monk stared, and Christopher prayed that the boy wouldn't believe his eyes and would take the whole thing for an optical illusion. But optical illusions were not included in the training of young Buddhist monks.

"I thought there was something strange," whispered the young monk. For a while no one said anything. There was nothing to say. Something that is inexplicable can't be explained.

"The Master says I may go far," murmured the boy. "And he says I'll see things that other people don't see. But he never said I'd fail to see things that other people *do* see . . ."

Other people don't see it, either, thought Christopher. That's why we're here. Because people tend to see too little.

However, he did not say that out loud. Out loud, he said, "Don't tell anyone."

The boy nodded. Then he left them where they were, and crossed the courtyard to disappear through the side door of one of the buildings crowded together behind the wall like a small flock of well-groomed white sheep. He was walking a little unsteadily. Of course he would say what he had seen later, much later. And yet another story would be added to the thousand strange tales of the Himalayas. In the Himalayas, such tales are a part of life.

Not far from where Christopher, Jumar, and Niya were standing, there was a washbasin against the wall, and a shining mirror that reflected the sunlight.

Christopher went closer and looked at it.

It gave him a shock. The boy looking back at him was a

stranger. He had eyes sunk deep into their sockets, and the little veins in one of them had broken, so that the white of the eye was tinged with red. Shaggy brown hair hung around the face in the mirror, and a layer of dust and dirt covered the boy's skin. His cheeks looked hollow and angular, and there was a covering of light down that you could barely see on his chin.

Another face appeared behind him in the mirror—a face he knew. But only now did he see that it looked like his. Niya. They were both dirty and disheveled, and they both wore the same green clothes.

"I look like you," said Christopher, smiling.

And then, all of a sudden, he saw someone else in the mirror: Arne. It was true, he *did* have Arne's smile. And the face wearing that smile wasn't a child's face anymore. He had begun growing up.

"I wish I could see myself in a mirror, too." Jumar sighed behind them. "I wish I could say, 'I look like you.' Or at least, 'I look like me.' But I haven't got any idea what I look like! The people we've talked to on our journey all see Christopher in their mind's eye when they hear about the crown prince of Nepal." He was silent for a while. "Well, maybe it's just as well," he said in a subdued voice. "Maybe I look hideous. It doesn't feel like it, but maybe I have a hooked nose and crooked teeth and—"

"Oh, come off it!" said Christopher, laughing. "Princes in fairy tales are all, without exception, handsome young men with straight noses, and their teeth are perfect."

At that moment, the young monk came back. He cast a quick glance at Jumar, who had pulled the scarf back in front of his face, and just as quickly looked away again.

"The Master will receive you," he announced with a grand gesture. He seemed to be enjoying his task, even if he was still unsure of the mystery that had just come into his life with that task. "There are not many minutes left before evening prayers, but he will receive you. It's a great honor. Follow me."

They crossed the courtyard and entered a simple, square room, its only furnishing consisting of a few straw mats and the floor.

For a moment, Christopher thought of the Great T.'s bare room, but except for the absence of furniture the two rooms had nothing in common.

The Great T.'s bare room had looked plain and unwelcoming, as if everyone who entered it was a nuisance.

This room spoke a different language. It was plain so that a visitor would have all the space he needed to unburden his heart.

In the middle of it, an old monk sat on one of the straw mats with his legs crossed. It was hard to say how old he was. He wore a large pair of rectangular, horn-rimmed glasses, his white beard fell softly from his chin to the floor, and his head was shaved like the heads of the boys out in the snow.

The monk who had brought them in bowed deeply and stepped out of the room, and the door latched behind him.

Christopher and Niya bowed as well.

The silence in the room surrounded them like clear water. It was not a sinister silence; it was calm and inviting.

"Sit down," said the old monk, smoothing his orange garment over his knees. "Sit here, opposite me."

They obeyed, and only when Christopher was seated did he realize how tired he was. Exhaustion washed over him like a gigantic wave, and he had to struggle hard against his wish to drop to the floor and lie there without moving.

A pleasant warmth filled the room, although there was no fire burning in it. It was as if the warmth came from the old monk in his orange robe.

For minutes on end, the monk said nothing. He looked at Christopher, and then he looked at Niya, and then he looked at the face under the cap, the face that no one could see.

"Take your scarf off," he said gently. Jumar obeyed, and the monk smiled. "There, that's better. How else am I to see the expression in your eyes? No honest person hides his eyes from an old man."

"But—" stammered Jumar.

The monk cut Jumar's objection short, as if it were a silk ribbon offering no resistance.

"Your eyes are seeking something," he said. "And they will find it. Don't let it trouble you that I can see them. I do not see them with the sense of sight, but with my mind. I saw the three of you coming as well."

"You . . . You saw us coming?"

"I see many things," replied the monk, with the hint of a smile. "You heard the spirits of the wind and hid your fear deep within you. You came through the snow and through the air, along the path that is no path. You met a dragon, but your bullets could not harm it. Am I right?"

"Yes," said Niya, "that's how it was."

"You risked everything," the monk went on, straightening his horn-rimmed glasses. "Every minute could have been your last."

"There was nothing else we could do," murmured Christopher.

"No," said the monk, "maybe not. You are the first to come up here in a long, long while. The monastery has been forgotten. Only the man who flies the airplane knows the way through the air."

An aircraft, thought Christopher. So that's how they get their provisions up here. Once again the silence surrounded them. Finally, the old man said, "You whose eyes are seeking something. Tell me what it is you want to find here."

Jumar took his time before answering. Suddenly he who always had words ready didn't seem able to find the right thing to say.

"I . . . I came . . . ," Jumar began, pulling himself together at last, "I came to ask you what really happened all that time ago. When you came down to Kathmandu and spoke to my mother."

Then the old monk heaved a deep, heavy sigh—a sigh deeper than the deepest abyss and heavier than the heaviest rock. He took off his glasses and began cleaning them with the hem of his orange robe, and finally he asked, "Why do you want to know?"

"I've decided to be visible," replied Jumar. "So that things will change. My father sits in his garden, and he has forgotten the people outside the garden walls. But I haven't forgotten them. And I want nothing so much as to be able to talk to them at long last, and be seen, and be one of them."

"A wise decision," replied the monk. "Almost too wise for someone as young as you." He smiled. "I will be honest. I admire your courage. You have come up all this way, without knowing that it would lead to any destination. You did not hesitate in spite of the snow, in spite of the dragons. There are reasons why the way to this monastery is so hard to travel. There are reasons why the path leads through the air. Only those with enough courage and enough faith can reach this monastery. It is more than fourteen years since anyone found us. Even the boys who come up here to learn are brought to me by the man with the airplane. But you took the way through the void. And so I will tell you the truth that you came for."

The muted sound of a gong was heard out in the courtyard, and the old monk put his glasses on again.

"Time for evening prayers," he said. "Time for prayers and for rice. Come and eat with us. After that we will talk about the past."

He rose to his feet and went ahead, and Christopher noticed that he moved with remarkable agility for his age. Christopher would have liked to stay on the straw mat in this comfortable, warm room forever and ever. He would have liked never to move again, but he guessed that wasn't an option. So he and the others followed the rustling folds of the monk's robe, and soon they all entered the prayer room of the monastery.

The walls were covered with bright, colorful pictures, the wooden columns were painted in glowing hues, and the floor was covered in patterned rugs.

The monastery must be the only patch of color that the

347

dragons could find here in the middle of the snow—and what an explosion of color it was! The many colors of the prayer flags on the dome of the stupa, the flowers in their containers, the young monks' dark red robes . . . How was it, Christopher asked himself, that the dragons spared this place?

The visitors sat down on the floor with the monks. Evening prayers and supper turned out to be the same thing. Christopher watched, fascinated, as the boys each held a scroll in one hand, reading the words from it in a strange singsong chant. Now and then they'd use their other hand to roll the rice on low desks into little balls. Their murmuring filled the room like the humming of a beehive, and there was something soothing about it, like it could lull you to sleep.

Christopher wondered what would happen if he asked the old monk whether he could stay here. He would put on a red robe, tie a yellow cord around his waist, and shave off his tousled hair. He would learn to read the texts on the scrolls— and then he could be sitting here, murmuring, eating, day after day, and he could play football with the others out in the snow; the sun would shine above the mountains, and nothing bad could ever happen to him again. It was tempting.

But no. No, none of that would help him rescue Arne.

So he ate the monks' rice, and drank their cold, clear water, and listened to their prayers, as a stranger.

The snow was already reflecting the starlight when the old monk finally led them back across the courtyard to the room with the straw mats. He lit a kerosene lamp and placed it in the middle of the room.

"The time has come," he said. "The time for the truth which you have journeyed here to find. But telling the truth is difficult. All that is told turns into a story, and then it is no longer true. I would like you to see the truth yourselves."

"See it ourselves?" Jumar echoed him, puzzled.

"Yes," said the monk. "Sit down, cross your legs, and close your eyes."

They obeyed, and Christopher remembered how they had once meditated in a yoga exercise in gym class. The coach had put on some lame, monotonous music, and after five minutes Christopher had gone to sleep. Here it was different.

There wasn't any music. Only the special silence that he had already noticed in the room.

"Keep your eyes closed to what is outside," said the monk softly, "and open them to what is inside. Then you will see."

Christopher had no idea what he was talking about. He sat there with his eyes closed tight, and felt the weariness in him, heavy as lead. And just as he was thinking he was about to fall asleep again, he felt his weariness leave him. It flew away—like a bird spreading its wings and rising in the air—flew away and left Christopher alone by himself; alone and wide awake.

And then a picture formed in front of him. He wasn't dreaming. He knew perfectly well that he wasn't dreaming, but there was a colorful and chaotic picture, like a kaleidoscope of colors and metallic glitter swirling around, and finally slowing down to show . . .

A city.

Its buildings had tall wooden balconies. Clothes were drying on lines stretched from balcony to balcony across the narrow streets. The roofs were covered with reddish shingles, and here and there tin, wet with rain, shone in the sun. Christopher saw children playing in puddles and dogs lying outside the doors of houses; he saw bells, prayer flags, clothes, metalware, plastic bowls, lengths of piping, statuettes of gods, silk cushions, incense sticks, carved wooden figures, cartons of medicinal tablets, ramen instant soup packets, woolen gloves, umbrellas, prayer drums, embroidered rugs, and bicycle-powered rickshaws making their way over the bumpy street surfaces, hooting cars, bikes, pedestrians, vendors, the old, the young, the lame, beggars—

Kathmandu.

Everything in the city seemed to be on its way to the same place, a part of the city center where the jam-packed streets were even more chaotic. There was no room to move, the crowds came to a halt, people craned their necks—it was as if he were standing among all these people, but at the same time hovering bodiless just above their heads. He heard the noise, the shouts ringing through the air. "Where are they? Are they close yet? Just around the corner? Reaching this street? There! There they come! There!"

And then he saw the procession.

The soldiers marched ramrod-straight at the head of it, rank upon rank, in their dress uniforms. A band played, and the children in the crowd danced around among the grown-ups' legs to its music. After the soldiers came the courtiers from the palace, men and women alike, flanked by more soldiers. The women's saris glowed red and gold, the men walked solemnly along in their smart suits, like members of a regal delegation. And then, in the middle of the procession, came the litters.

There were three of them—two large and one small—with their carrying poles resting on the shoulders of magnificently costumed bearers whose expressions conveyed a sense of solemnity beyond words.

The drapes of the litters had been drawn back so that the precious cargo inside could wave to the crowd. A man sat in the first litter, in the second came a woman hardly visible under all the jewelry she was wearing. The third litter seemed to be empty; no one waved from its windows. Christopher caught a glimpse of the contents. There was a small, richly ornamented box with gold fittings inside. It was locked.

The power of the king.

People threw rice and flowers. They cheered and reached their hands out to the three litters, although they could not touch them.

Then someone broke through the ranks of soldiers, a man in an orange robe with only a simple cord tied around his waist, his head shaved bald. Christopher recognized him at first only by his clothing, because he was younger. It was the monk.

And Christopher realized at last that the Kathmandu he saw before him now was Kathmandu fourteen years ago. When Christopher caught a glimpse of the monk's face, he was left with no doubt. He had the same way of wrinkling his forehead, the same grave expression. His long beard was only just beginning to turn white; he was a man on the threshold of old age.

The monk reached the queen's litter before anyone could stop him, and he walked along beside her, his head level with the window. It looked as if the soldiers couldn't make up their minds what to do. This was a monk, a wise man. They left him alone.

As if in a film, the scene moved nearer, and now Christopher could see the faces of the queen and the monk in close-up. How beautiful the queen was under all the ornaments she wore! Her features were as delicate as if someone had spent many hours modeling them out of porcelain, and the eyebrows drawn on her face curved up, giving her a slightly surprised expression. She must be more than ten years younger than the king.

"Today, you are queen of this country," said the monk. "Do you remember me?"

"I remember you," replied the queen quietly, and no one except Christopher and the monk heard her words. "But what was true then is not true now. It's so long ago."

"Time does not change the truth," said the monk. "It is dangerous to forget. You were a little girl in the village playing in the dirt at the foot of the mountain when I first saw you. Never forget the dirt where you were playing; never forget the hunger. And don't forget how you begged from us monks when we came down to your village. I still see your dirty, outstretched hands before me—"

"Be quiet," the queen ordered.

But the monk was not obeying orders. "We always gave alms," he went on, "even when we didn't have much for our own needs. Until one day I saw in your eyes that you would come to something more . . . I sent you to the city, remember that."

"I am the queen," whispered the queen, barely able to suppress her anger. "I am happy and beautiful. I have all I need. I am going to give the king a crown prince."

"And no one knows about that village and the dirt and hunger, do they? The past doesn't exist anymore, does it? You have forged yourself a new past out of the metal of dreams, and the king helped you."

"What is it you want?" hissed the queen.

"I want you to remember," whispered the monk, and then he said out loud, "I will give you a piece of advice, Your Majesty. It won't cost you much."

"I don't need an old monk's advice," she replied in a loud, clear voice that everyone could hear. "I am not giving you a single rupee for it!"

She nodded her beautiful head to the soldiers, and two of them took the monk by the shoulders to force him away from the procession. "Get out," spat the queen. "Take the past back to your mountain with you, and never, never come here again."

There was confusion in the crowd when the monk in his bright orange robe, which was visible from afar, landed among all the people. He fell, and those around him scattered.

Dozens of hands helped him up, but it was as if no one quite knew where to look. What had happened between this monk and the queen?

They asked him, but he did not answer. He picked up the hem of his robe, which had fallen into the dirt, and disappeared down the street and out of the city. Christopher saw him as a patch of orange disappearing into the shadows among the houses. And he felt the monk's disappointment and anger.

It was from the hearts of the people who had helped the monk up, he thought, that the fairy tales had sprung. That's why fairy tales all have a grain of truth in them.

The picture abruptly changed, and Christopher found himself in a garden again.

Green shadows lay on the gravel path, and beyond the trees he saw the walls of a magnificent building rise: the palace. The sky above was blue. Jumar had said something about a huge glass dome cutting off the garden from the outside world, but of course this was fourteen years ago. There was no glass dome yet.

A beautiful woman sat on a wooden chair in the garden, her eyebrows drawn in with black kohl, giving her a surprised expression. Now she was wearing a plain red sari, and just one narrow gold bangle on her arm. It was the young queen.

The fabric of her sari curved over her belly, where the life of a crown prince was waiting to see the light of day. The queen was humming to herself, reading a magazine, and seemed to think she was alone—but she wasn't. Christopher saw the figure of a man hidden in the deep shadows of a banyan tree, standing there watching and waiting. It was the monk.

Just as Christopher saw him, he raised his right hand, his outstretched forefinger pointed to the queen, and then a strange thing happened: the air above the place where the queen was sitting began to bubble as if something were gathering there, as if thousands of tiny scraps of different colors were flying up and joining into a single whole, uniting to become a figure—there was a rushing in the air like thousands of wings. Where had Christopher heard that sound before?

Now the queen was looking up; he saw her eyes widen with horror. The magazine slipped from her hand and fell silently to the ground. The queen opened her mouth to say something, but no sound emerged from her lips. A moment later, she was enveloped in the cloud of color. Christopher tried to focus, but he still couldn't make out an outline to the cloud.

Then the flickering and fluttering, the swirling and whirling rose into the air, and now it began to take shape. It grew and stretched sideways, becoming taller and wider, bigger and bigger, and finally it unfolded two huge, shimmering wings, and curved a long and graceful neck.

A dragon.

The first color dragon.

The queen put one hand to the curve of her belly, and there was a look of fear and disbelief on her face. The dragon flew a loop and then soared away toward the northern mountains. Christopher looked at the banyan tree. The shadows around its trunk were dark, mysterious, and deserted. The monk was nowhere to be seen.

Christopher opened his eyes.

The light of the kerosene lamp was flickering, casting shadows over the white walls in an unsteady dance. He could feel Jumar's hand on his knee, and felt for the invisible fingers to hold them tight.

"The heart of the first dragon," said the monk, and Christopher could hear that in those fourteen years his voice had grown old and tired, "that heart is made of your colors. And to make that heart, it wasn't enough just to take away the colors. Every single, tiny scrap of visibility flowed into the dragon's heart. That was the only way it could be born. At first it was timid. At first it didn't know how powerful it was. So it flew to the mountains. But gradually it understood that no one could harm it. It divided, and multiplied, and over the years the dragons ventured farther and farther down from the peaks."

"Then it's not my fault," whispered Jumar. "All this time I've thought it was my fault, but that's not true."

The monk smiled. "How could it be your fault? Life is unjust. Injustice is never the victim's fault. It isn't Niya's fault that Kartan killed her parents. And it isn't Christopher's fault that his brother was held captive by guerrillas."

"You . . . You know . . . ?" Niya whispered.

"I know a great deal."

"It's not our fault," said Christopher slowly, "but it's up to us to change things. Is that what you wanted to tell us?"

"I don't want to tell you anything. I do not judge, and I am not giving you advice. You came to find out the truth, and I have shown you the truth. That's all."

"You called the dragons to life," said Jumar. "Can't you call them back again? Can't you make everything the way it was before?"

Then the monk smiled again, and did not reply.

And they knew what his silence meant.

No.

He had not forgiven. Perhaps he never would forgive.

Jumar's voice was soft and low when he asked, "Is what

they say about the people changed to bronze true? Can they be brought back to life again if a dragon touches them?"

"I have heard what they say," replied the monk thoughtfully. "You hear so many strange stories in this country, don't you? You hear that what the dragons have changed they can also change back again. You hear that the scales of their wings do that. Oh, you hear all kinds of things. But no one has ever heard of anyone catching a dragon."

Silence fell on the room, like the shadow of a creature even larger and more powerful than all the dragons.

"I must find the first of them. The oldest," whispered Jumar, squeezing Christopher's hand so hard that it hurt. "I need its heart to make myself visible. If only I knew where to look!"

"That is the only question of yours that I can answer, my boy," said the monk. "They live at the peak of this mountain. You haven't reached the peak yet; you must go a little farther. High above, there on the glacier, they have their caves in the shining ice. They can't hurt the monasteries, and we watch their flight on clear days. I cannot tell you how to defeat the dragon. I don't even know if it is possible. But it will be waiting for you up there, in the ice at the mountain peak."

"It's late," said Niya. "Can we stay the night in the

359

monastery? If we're going to be victims of a dragon, I'd like to get some sleep first."

The monk nodded. "It is warm and out of the wind here. Stay in this room."

With those words, he rose, took the lamp, and left them in the dark.

Christopher got up and went out into the courtyard . . . and there it was in the night, white and narrow: a thin crescent moon, hardly more than a line in the sky.

"Tomorrow night," said Christopher, when he had curled up on the floor beside Niya and Jumar, "tomorrow night must be the new moon. Do you realize? The night of the new moon! There'll be no moonlight to give us away. No moonlight to cast shadows! We must reach the peak tomorrow night."

"You mean you two are coming with me?" asked Jumar.

Christopher snorted. "What a question!"

And so the day came when the heir to the throne of Nepal set out to face the largest and oldest of the color dragons.

The murmured prayers of two dozen monks of different ages accompanied him, and the monks themselves went with the travelers as far as the place where the mountain sloped more steeply again and glittering ice lay under the snow. The monks stayed behind there, and when Jumar turned a little

while later, they were still standing on the white sheet of the
snow, as if someone had drawn them on the landscape in red
pencil, the smallest monks waving at them for a long time.

The way was icy and dangerous. Sometimes they had to
move forward on all fours to keep from slipping. They helped
to haul each other up, supporting one another, gasping and
swearing—for the crown prince of the country had learned
how to swear on his journey. The effort made them forget the
cold, which was just as well, because the cold up here was the
coldest cold in the world. Nothing could live in it, no animal,
no plant, nothing but the dragons.

Christopher was grateful for every fiber of the clothes
he wore. But the cold still found its way through their caps
and jackets, and would creep into their boots and settle there.
This was a deadly cold.

As evening came, they saw the caves, black circular holes in
the ice, like swallows' nests.

"They look like the dragons' eyes," whispered Jumar.
"Deep and dark and empty."

No dragons were in sight, and they waited below the
caves until sunset.

"What luck, too," said Niya, "that they haven't taken the
precaution of turning us to bronze on the way up here."

But Jumar could hear that her brusque tone hid fear, fear as naked and sheer as the ice over which they had come.

"What are you going to do?" she asked him. "We've been walking all day to find a dragon whose heart you have to tear out if you're ever going to be visible. But you haven't yet told us how you're planning to do that. And when you do, we can't even be sure it will work."

"I don't know what I'm planning to do yet myself," replied Jumar, truthfully. "I'll think about that when I see the dragon."

Christopher sighed. "That's the way he does everything in life," he said.

"And does it work?" asked Niya doubtfully.

Jumar felt that Christopher was thinking hard. "Difficult to say. But we did find the monastery, and we did learn the truth . . ."

"Get down!" cried Niya.

Jumar looked up. And there it was—the dragon. The same dragon that had nearly turned him to bronze on the way up Machapuchare. He recognized it: the turquoise wings, the violet body, its claws, its shadow on the snow. But even as it was soaring up from below in great curving loops, the shadow paled. The whole world paled. Night enveloped them. Even the stars were hidden behind a covering of cloud, and all they could still see was the dragon, the faint shimmer of its body, glowing and terrifying, and in the middle of that shimmer of menace and uncertainty were the burning eyes. Now, in the darkness, they blazed like fires.

Jumar settled the gun on his shoulder. He had been carrying it ever since they left the molten town. "Jumar, you can't shoot the dragon," Niya whispered. "I've tried. The bullet went straight through it, and all that fell from the sky was this."

He looked at the motionless blue butterfly on the palm of her hand.

Then he looked up again to where the dragon had landed outside its cave. He saw its eyes disappear.

"I'm going up after it now," said Jumar, swallowing. "I don't know what will happen. Maybe it will tear me to pieces with its claws. Maybe it will turn me into bronze or something. Don't you two go any closer than the mouth of the cave."

They nodded silently, and Jumar heard their breath in the night air behind him. This last part of the way was the worst of their entire journey. He put foot in front of foot as if wearing lead shoes, and his heart was racing.

I am the crown prince, he told himself in the silence, heir to the throne of Nepal. The king's son. I will do it. Whatever has to be done, I will do it. I will be the boy who killed the greatest of all dragons. Or if I don't, then I'll be the boy who tried.

The mouth of the cave could hardly be made out in the black night. But Jumar saw the faint shimmering glow coming from inside. The dragon's colors glowing with their own faint light. Jumar took a deep breath.

"Good luck," whispered Christopher when they had reached the cave. Jumar went over to hug him. He felt silly, but there was no one to see but themselves.

He hugged Niya, too, only very briefly, but in that single second, he held her as close as he could. He felt her warmth and the life coming from her, and he felt that she herself would have liked to hold him a little longer—that she didn't want to let him go. He sensed both her hope and her fear.

She didn't say anything, and he finally let go of her. Then he turned and stepped into the dragon's cave.

Darkness.

Light.

Colors.

Green. Blue. Turquoise. Violet. Gold.

Ice under Jumar's feet. Hard. Smooth. Chilly.

Then that rustling, like the sound of tiny wings. Thousands upon thousands of wings.

He took everything in, because it could have been the last thing he would ever see, ever feel, ever hear.

The glimmering body before him turned, stretched its neck, and from above looked down at him with its burning eyes.

And the dragon looked at him. *Looked at him.*

It didn't just look his way. Those eyes, the eyes that weren't there, that were only bottomless, burning holes, saw what was invisible.

Jumar was going to level his gun, but he knew it was hopeless. Instead, he put it down on the ground at his feet.

Then something happened that he had not expected.

The dragon spoke to him. Its voice was low and soft, like the colors that it had united in its body.

"I have been waiting for you," said the dragon. "Since the beginning of my existence."

Jumar was alarmed. "You knew I would come?"

"No," said the dragon. "But I was waiting for you all the same."

The dragon rose, rustling its wings again. It took a step toward Jumar, and he wanted to retreat. But he stayed where he was. Some strange power had clamped his feet firmly to the ground. It was like one of those nightmares where you want to run away, but you can't move from the spot.

And then you wake up.

But Jumar wasn't dreaming, and he wasn't going to wake up.

He was here, and above him the head of the greatest, oldest, and most powerful of all color dragons swung its long, graceful neck.

A jet of colored flame shot out of its mouth, hissing into the dark air of the cave. It cast the dragon's shadow on the back wall. If the dragon turned a little way, only a very little way, then part of that gigantic shadow would fall on Jumar.

The dragon turned a little way.

Jumar's feet still wouldn't obey him.

But the shadow did not reach him, and no more flame came from the dragon's mouth.

"You are my heart, and my heart is you," said the dragon. "We belong together. Yet there can only be one of us." The dragon brought its head even closer to him. "What are you going to do, little human?" it asked.

"I—I—I don't know," stammered Jumar.

"You have come to get your colors, haven't you?" asked the dragon. "You have come to kill me."

There was a desperate "No!" on the tip of Jumar's tongue. But he said nothing.

"But you don't know how," the dragon went on. "Am I right?"

In silence, it looked at Jumar for a long time.

"I was afraid you would come wanting my heart back," it said at last. "And I also hoped you would."

Suddenly the glow in the dragon's eyes by night reminded Jumar of the glow in Niya's eyes. They, too, were full of sadness.

"You can't live without your heart," said Jumar.

The dragon moved its slender neck as if it were shaking its head.

"As I told you, there can only be one of us," he said. "Either me or you."

Jumar took a step toward the dragon, and put out his hand to its glittering coat of scales. "Even if I knew how," he said slowly, "I can't kill anything so beautiful."

It was as if he had fallen into a strange trance. His fear was still as great as before, but he felt it in a different way. This cave might have been lying outside time, outside reality, in a dream that the dragon and he were sharing. All of a sudden, he was sure he was going to die, but it no longer seemed important.

His hand sought the dragon's smooth, armored coat, but it found no surface to rest on. He felt a movement, light and gentle, and once again he heard the fluttering of many tiny wings.

"I am not what you think," said the dragon. "I don't exist at all. I am neither good nor bad. I don't exist, I *consist*. I consist of many separate beings. Only the monk's power holds me together. And the heart containing your colors allows me to speak. The other dragons who split off from me later have no hearts. They can't speak and they cannot understand your words."

"You . . . *consist*?" asked Jumar. "Of many separate beings?"

And then he saw them.

The butterflies.

There must have been millions of them, billions, hovering close together in the air, fluttering, dancing, coming together to form the body of the dragon. That was why, when Niya's shot grazed the creature, nothing had come sailing down from the sky but a single dead butterfly. The dragon itself had no body. Its body was a cloud of colorful, shimmering wings, more beautiful than all the butterflies there were in the world—improbably beautiful, shining with all the colors the dragon had eaten during its life.

There was no chance of defeating this being. Jumar's hand passed through its body without inflicting any wound.

He looked up into the deep, glowing sockets hovering over him instead of eyes.

And he forced himself to think beyond the trance that

threatened to hold him in its spell. He forced himself to think of what was outside this cave. It had almost faded from his mind.

He closed his eyes for a moment. The snow was the first thing to come to him. The red robes of the young monks, The tracks of two pairs of feet that had crossed the glacier . . .

"Christopher," Jumar whispered, and he remembered a face. "Niya."

They were waiting for him, out there in the icy cold.

He had almost forgotten them.

He thought of the path through the air that Christopher hadn't wanted to take, yet did after all because he, Jumar, had asked him to. What had Christopher said?

369

"You are good with words, did you know that? If you ever get to be king, the people's hearts will melt when you speak to them . . ."

And then, suddenly, he knew. He knew what to do. It was his only chance. Words were all he had, all that he could control.

He opened his eyes and looked at the dragon.

"I'd like to tell you a story," he said.

"A story?" asked the dragon, folding its wings with a thousand-fold rustling and sinking down on its back legs like a cat. "No one's ever told me a story. Is it a beautiful story?"

"Beautiful and terrible," replied Jumar. "Good and bad, wonderful and cruel. Will you listen to me?"

"I've been waiting for fourteen years," replied the dragon. "Maybe I was waiting for a story."

And so the heir to the throne of Nepal sat cross-legged between the dragon's claws and began to tell the story. At first he chose his words carefully, weighing them up, tasting them all on his tongue before letting them cautiously out into the expectant night air. But then he felt more sure of himself, and the words fell from his mouth like supple creatures with lives of their own, cascading out like glittering, golden waterfalls, spreading their wings like shimmering songbirds, unrolling from his tongue like snakes, growing out of him like rare plants never seen before.

They enveloped the dragon, and it turned its neck this way and that as if watching them.

The crown prince's words told the tale of the sleeping queen, they fluttered with the wings of the pigeons in Durbar Square, they were caught in a trap in the depths of the jungle, they climbed steep flights of steps up into the mountains— they trembled with the fear felt by the village people, they tore at the villagers' guts with hunger, and fell to the depths with the water of the underground river. The words bit holes in the air with their sharp teeth, burning with hatred and shaped like General Kartan, they made a bridge disappear into nothing, and spoke of love for a girl with wild hair.

They told the story of a friend who came from far away, they echoed like shots in the night and crackled like flames in a stable, they leaped like sparks to kindle enthusiasm for something that was not what it seemed, they rode into a molten town full of snow and full of wounds, they looked out at the world from a cellar with the eyes of prisoners, they fled in panniers on horses' backs. The words towered up into the blue heights with the Fishtail mountain, and whispered with the spirits of the icy winds, they pressed air out of living bodies with the hard fist of the heights, and climbed on their ringing syllables up a vertical wall on iron hooks ... until they saw the red specks of robes in the snow ... until they sighted the brightly colored prayer flags on the solitary dome ... until they turned into the truth about the past.

And then they fell silent.

Jumar listened to their lingering echo in the cave.

It was not the echo of letters and words—it was the echo of scenes and pictures, smells and sounds, of every second he had experienced on his journey.

A very slight movement ran through the dragon's huge body, a quiet tremor, as if all the butterflies were moving closer together.

371

"If that is so—" said the dragon.

Jumar kept still and waited for it to go on. He waited for a long time, never moving.

And finally the dragon continued. "If that is so, then you'll need your colors to bring everything to a good end."

It bent the head on its long neck down very close to Jumar again.

"I will give it to you," it whispered. "I will give you my heart."

"You'd do that?" whispered Jumar incredulously.

For fourteen years, this dragon had stolen colors from the country and turned human beings into bronze. And now—?

"I told you, I am not bad," said the dragon. "And not good, either. Because I am not real. Take it. Take the heart. I would like to see how you free this country."

"But then—then you *are* good."

"Who knows?" said the dragon. "Things change. Things come into being. Just don't forget what I told you. The other dragons have no hearts. You won't be able to win them over. They will go on doing what they've always done."

"But then you won't be there anymore."

"My heart will be there." The dragon spoke so quietly now that Jumar could hardly understand its words. However, he heard the fear in them. The fear of the void. Of nowhere. Of never again.

"My heart will be there, in you," whispered the dragon. "And with my heart I shall see how your story, let's hope, takes a turn for the better."

"What—How can I—What must I do?" asked Jumar.

"Stand up," said the dragon, "and walk through me. There, right in the middle of me, you will find my heart."

Jumar rose from the icy floor of the cave. He didn't feel the cold.

The dragon sat still, waiting.

"Thank you," whispered Jumar. And then he walked into the middle of the cloud of butterflies. Their shimmering bodies surrounded him. He saw nothing but their colors, heard nothing but their fluttering, felt nothing but the soft, fleeting touch of millions of delicate, fragile wings. And right among them he found something intangible, glowing, inexplicable, and it joined with him. Perhaps it, too, was nothing but butterflies whose bodies disappeared when they touched his. Or perhaps it was something entirely different. A strange feeling ran through Jumar, a sensation that couldn't be compared with anything he had ever felt before or was ever to feel again.

He closed his eyes and looked for words to describe what it was like—words such as those that had saved him—but there were no words for this sensation.

373

And when he opened his eyes again, the cloud of butter-flies was dispersing. They were scattering, flying out of the mouth of the cave and fluttering into the first light of the new day. Jumar must have been telling his story all night.

Only now did he realize how rough and dry his throat felt.

He followed the last butterflies to the cave mouth, and watched as they fluttered down the mountain, separating, parting, tiny flecks of color above the glittering surface of snow and ice.

Two figures in green camouflage jackets were huddling together there, looking up at Jumar, and one of them pointed to him. They waved.

Jumar waved back.

And then he looked at his hands.

JUMAR, VISIBLE

CHRISTOPHER THOUGHT THE COLD NIGHT would never end.

Now and then, he and Niya ran back and forth, chased each other through the snow, forced themselves to keep moving. Then they sat down again and waited, their thoughts with Jumar in the dragon's cave. Not a sound came out of it to meet their ears. Niya leaned against Christopher. At some point in the night, later, her lips came toward his again, but Christopher's heart was with Jumar, and when her hands wanted to do what they had done back on the rock outside the molten town, he shook his head.

"But we have to keep warm," she whispered. "Somehow. Otherwise we'll freeze."

"We can just hold each other very close," whispered Christopher. "That will have to do. I'd have a guilty conscience now if—you see . . . Jumar, he—he loves you. I know that."

"What about you? Do you love me?"

He put his finger on her lips.

So they held each other close and waited all night. But there was still no sign of Jumar.

"How long do we wait?" asked Christopher. "How long do we wait before we go up and see what's happened?"

"Until morning," Niya decided.

And when the sun rose, driving away the shadows of the night, Christopher thought he would go crazy with impatience and anxiety.

"I can't stand this a minute longer," he said.

"You don't have to," replied Niya, and a broad smile lit up her face like a special kind of morning sun. Christopher's glance followed her outstretched arms.

"There he is," said Niya.

And there he was.

"But what's that?" asked Christopher. "There's something in the air—"

"Butterflies," she cried, staring at her hand. One of the fragile creatures had settled on it. "Millions of butterflies."

Following the butterflies, a figure in a green camouflage jacket and pants flecked with green came down the slope, a gun over its shoulder, thick boots on its feet.

"If I didn't know for certain that you're standing here beside me," said Niya to Christopher, shaking her head, "I'd say it was you there."

"Uh, yes," said Christopher, baffled.

It was true: The figure approaching them looked almost the same as he did.

It was not particularly tall, rather slightly built, had dark hair and flat features.

And then the figure was beside them.

"Jumar?" asked Christopher incredulously.

"I'm afraid so," said Jumar.

Niya looked from Christopher to Jumar, from Jumar to Christopher, and back again. Finally she flung her head back just as she had done when Jumar told her who he really was, and laughed and laughed and laughed.

"So here's one of you making out he's the other the whole way here," she said, "and all the time—all the time you two look just the same! Well, except maybe for your noses. Christopher's nose is a little too European. You—oh, you've got to see yourselves! I'd be surprised if you couldn't pass as twins!"

Jumar and Christopher looked at each other, and Niya laughed more heartily than ever. "And you both make the same silly face," she added happily.

"Hmm," said Jumar.

"Hmm," said Christopher.

And they set off down from Machapuchare, away from the deadly cold. But the mountain hadn't finished with them yet. It still had a surprise or two in store.

The first was that they couldn't find their way over the glacier again. They had come up along a path, but the path had disappeared—even though it hadn't been snowing.

"You've been leading us astray, Jumar," said Christopher. For a change, Jumar was walking in front. In fact he had insisted on it.

"Nonsense," said Jumar. "I can see a bit of the path down there."

Christopher strained his eyes, but he couldn't see anything.

And after a while, Niya said, "We really should be on your path now, shouldn't we, Jumar?"

Jumar grunted. "Hey," he said, "what's that over there?"

"Sheep, if you ask me," said Niya.

Sure enough, a little farther down the slope, a small flock of sheep was on the move. Their fleeces looked blue against the white of the mountain, and Christopher remembered reading about blue Himalayan sheep.

"They have a bronze tinge in their fleece," said Jumar.

"Nonsense," said Niya. "They're moving. They haven't been turned into bronze. They're perfectly ordinary sheep."

"Perfectly ordinary sheep? You must be joking," said Jumar. "Look! Where they climbed down the glacier, the path disappeared! They—they're taking the path with them! The dragons," he whispered. "The dragons' shadows have fallen on them. Nothing good ever comes of that."

The blue sheep gradually disappeared behind a projecting rock, and Christopher shook his head in disbelief.

"We've lost our way," he said. "We're truly lost."

It was as if their upward climb had never been: no path, no vertical rock face with hooks in it, no monastery, either.

Finally they clambered, slid, and scrambled their way down the mountain. Jumar tramped through the snow ahead of them, still claiming that the blue sheep had a bronze tinge in their fleeces, and had taken the path away.

Finally Niya and Christopher pretended to believe him, because you don't insult the honor of an heir to the throne on the very first day of his visibility. At least, not if he's a friend.

379

And so, on that day, one of the strangest phenomena on earth came into being, something you can find only at great heights or among anglers: a one-man rumor.

"Where are we going anyway?" asked Christopher a few miles farther on. "I mean, what are we going to do once we're out of the snow and ice. Then what?"

"We'll go to Kathmandu," replied Jumar, as if it were the most natural thing in the world. And Niya nodded. "Wasn't that obvious?" she asked.

"No," said the confused Christopher. "Not at all. Once I was on my way to find my brother, set him free, and take him home. But now I don't know where I'm going. We lost track of my brother anyway, didn't we?"

He was hoping someone would contradict him, but neither of them did.

"When the Great T. is ready, he's going to Kathmandu," said Jumar instead. "Kartan will be waiting for him there. And then comes the bit about the dust and ashes, and so on. We need to get there first to prevent the worst of it."

"What are you planning to do?" asked Christopher.

"I'll know that," said Jumar thoughtfully, "when we arrive."

◆ ◆ ◆

Farther up in the mountains, an old monk sat in a room with brightly painted walls. He had closed his eyes, and you could have said he was meditating. He had sent his soul on a weightless journey and was free of all thought. He remained in that state in which the mind hovers, unimpeded, beyond all the bonds of earthly events and emotions.

Or perhaps he hadn't.

Perhaps he was simply thinking.

Or perhaps he, too, was entangled in ideas and emotions . . . Perhaps his hovering soul saw a boy trembling in a dragon's cave, perhaps it met three travelers later on their way down the mountain.

Perhaps his soul was inclining toward a feeling that he had forgotten long ago—a feeling like the color blue. Perhaps that soul was thinking of forgiveness.

Of offering one last chance.

Perhaps.

381

It was afternoon when they saw the vultures.

Their gigantic bodies were circling alarmingly low in the blue of the sky, and Christopher saw their beaks flashing. One of the birds flew in a wide curve and then away over them, and its wingtip almost touched Christopher.

He shuddered.

"There must be something lying ahead there," said Niya. "Probably a dead animal."

And then they saw the dark patch on the white slope, with vultures gathering around it. But it wasn't a dead animal. It was a man.

Niya fired a shot into the air, and the birds scattered in alarm. However, they didn't turn away, but hovered in the air and waited until they could return to their meal, flying loops as they waited, their plumage gray and brown.

The dead man was not lying on the snow, but on an improvised bier of branches tied together. Lengths of green tent canvas held the branches in place, and at one corner of the framework a piece of red cloth fluttered in the wind like a flag. Christopher didn't want to go any closer, but he followed Niya and Jumar, and suddenly he found himself standing right beside the bier.

The vultures must have begun their work some time ago. Pieces of the dead man were missing.

Christopher turned away, fighting down his nausea, and took several steps back. He heard Niya's voice as if she were speaking through cotton wadding.

"That red flag and the tent canvas tell us enough. It's one of them. One of the Maoists. They were here, and they may not be far away."

Above them, the vultures' cries sounded, shrill and impatient, so they left the corpse to them and walked on through the white snow of the heights. But now they were more on their guard. There could be someone lurking in every hollow, looking out for them, a figure crouching on the ground behind every hilltop in the range. Niya kept looking around nervously.

And then it began to snow.

At first, Christopher felt only movement in the air, then he saw single, tiny flakes dancing, still unsteady, hesitant. Finally, the barriers broke in the white sky. The snow dropped like a curtain between them and the world, a cold, compact wall in the air, moving back with every step they took, letting them through but not showing the view ahead.

383

"Damn it," said Niya. "I don't want to stumble over any other bodies—living or dead."

And Christopher remembered that "they" had once been "us," and thought how strange life was—a dense wall of strangeness that seemed to give way but never let them see ahead. Any attempt to go forward was mere groping in the dark.

"We can't get lost," said Niya's voice from the veils of snow around them. Jumar's outline was walking through the snow behind her. "Give me your hand, for goodness' sake. And take Jumar by your other hand."

Christopher obeyed without a word. And so they wandered like children through the white void, through the faceless depths of a scene. Three children lost in an absence of colors and sounds. Niya's hand in Christopher's was slim, and wore a woolen glove. Through the swirling snow, he saw that the ends of the fingers of the gloves had been cut off, showing her own bare fingertips red with cold. Fingertips left bare on the hand she used for shooting. He felt how cold she was, and remembered that night outside the molten town, when the cold had turn to warmth, sudden, blazing warmth.

Or had that only been a dream of warmth? But what a beautiful dream it had been. He could still feel the movement of her ungloved fingers . . .

. . . and then he was lying flat on his front in the snow.

His outstretched hand was still clinging to Niya's, and her fingers were clutching his painfully. Jumar stumbled, let go of his hand, fell half on top of him.

Christopher looked up, bewildered, puzzled.

Niya was gone. Her hand was still there in his, but he couldn't see her anymore. Her whole weight was dangling from his hand. And he heard her gasping breaths, muted by the snow. Her voice shouted something he couldn't make out . . .

The rock face. It was the rock face. The same wall of rock

that they had once climbed on the way up. They had been bound to come to it again at some point.

Niya had stepped over the edge into nothing.

And there she hung, from Christopher's hand, and the snow fell and fell and fell.

Christopher shouted and pulled. He pulled with all his might, working his way backward, feeling himself slipping toward the abyss. He felt Jumar holding on to him, felt himself gaining inch after inch . . .

His scream died away, and he struggled in complete silence against the force of gravity. All he heard was his own gasping, filling his head right up. His hands were so cold. But he couldn't let go. He managed to grasp a second hand, at last his knees were holding firm on the ground beneath the snow—and then, with a final effort, he had done it.

The next moment she was lying beside him in the snow, breathing heavily. He counted four heavy breaths.

Then she swore.

And then she sat up and brushed the snow off her face. The flakes were not falling so heavily now.

"That was—" said Niya, and couldn't think of the right way to describe it.

"A long way down?" suggested Jumar.

Christopher laughed. He felt relief flowing through his

veins, soft and warm. When they stood up, the snow gave them a view of the chasm below. It was just a glimpse of it, far from clear, but good enough to see the edge.

They turned right and walked in silence along the top of the precipice.

"There," said Niya. "There they are."

"Who?" asked Christopher.

"The people who left that dead man on the bier," she replied quietly.

"What dead man?" asked Christopher, puzzled. But then the image came back. Flapping vultures' wings. A lifeless body. Niya had been right. The Maoists were here.

The tent was a stone's throw away, white as the snow; only its shape gave it away. It was hard to see why it had been pitched so close to the precipice, with only a few yards separating it from the depths.

The last snowflakes hovered down silently. And there was something else to their left, on the side where the precipice lay, something that was still hidden behind fibrous veils of mist left behind by the snow clouds. The three travelers stood there without moving and stared at the tent.

"It's so quiet," Jumar whispered. "I get the feeling there's no one in the tent at all."

Niya nodded and put a finger to her lips.

And before anyone could say anything else, two figures appeared out of nowhere.

But of course they didn't really appear out of nowhere. Until now they had been crouched in a hollow halfway between the tent and the three friends, and now they both stood up at the same time. One was tall, the other short.

After that things happened too fast.

Christopher felt someone flinging him to the ground, cold snow in his face, yet again, and an explosion in the air just beside him. A second, farther away. Something warm was running down his arm. He turned his head. The snow beside him was red, and the red was spreading. On the edge of his field of vision, he saw Niya. She was kneeling, and had leveled her gun to shoot again. Christopher struggled up and looked in the direction she was aiming. He heard the next shot, saw the taller of the two figures fall silently back like the cut-out metal figures in a carnival game. He remembered the night when Niya had fired at Kartan's men. This was not something he could ever get used to. He felt the same icy triumph as before, and the same burning shame.

But there was still the other figure, the smaller one. A boy. He couldn't be more than eleven or twelve, and the gun he was carrying looked grotesque. As if that occurred to the boy himself, he flung his gun away, turned, and ran toward the tent. The barrel of Niya's gun followed him calmly, with certainty. He could run as fast as he liked, but her bullet would find him.

Christopher saw her finger on the trigger. He put out his right hand, with the warm blood running down from his arm over it, and an agonizing pain went through him. But his hand reached its target. It struck the barrel of the gun and knocked the shot aside. Niya swore again. The bullet landed somewhere in the snow, doing no damage. Wasted.

She didn't look at Christopher until she had reloaded.

Her eyes were flashing angrily; she couldn't understand him.

"Don't!" begged Christopher. "Don't do it. Don't fire again."

"Why not?" She spat the words out into his face, and he instinctively warded them off with the hand that now had a pattern of red lines on it.

"He's still so young," said Christopher. "And he's running. Look. He's running for his life."

"He'll give us away."

"If there's anyone in that tent, they've already heard the shots by now," said Christopher.

They both looked at the tent at the same time. But there was no one to be seen there.

"Those were the only two," said Christopher.

The boy hesitated outside the tent flap for just a second. He seemed to be wondering whether to go in.

But then the boy changed direction, left the tent behind, ran away from the precipice. His dark figure disappeared, a tiny dot in the white of the snow.

"Well, there's nowhere he could run," said Niya. "He'll freeze to death out there. My bullet would have been kinder to him."

Jumar clicked his tongue. "It's no use arguing with him, Niya. I've told you already. He's different. Let's take a look at the man over there in the snow."

"Wait," she said. "Christopher? Show me that wound."

Christopher grunted as she examined his arm. The pain was growing and spreading, hot and red. The fabric of the jacket over his upper arm was in shreds, and the blood was still flowing from the place.

"A glancing shot," said Niya. "But we have to wrap something around it to stop the bleeding."

With her knife, she cut a strip off her shirt, and he flinched when she wound it around his upper arm.

"Keep still," hissed Niya. "Why do these things always have to happen to you? You wouldn't shoot a fly—not that you could hit one—but if anyone's going to be grazed by a bullet it's you. If there's a fire anywhere, then you're the one who breathes in the damn smoke, and if it's cold enough to fall sick, you're the one coughing your guts up . . . We're always having to save you from something or someone . . ."

She tightly knotted the strip of fabric in place, and Christopher gasped with the pain. Then his pain turned to anger.

"Then stop it!" he spat back. "Stop rescuing me. Just leave me to lie and bleed to death. I really wouldn't mind. One of these days, your temper will get the better of you, Niya, and then you'll get so carried away, you'll shoot me as well. Just like that. You like seeing people fall down dead, right? You love the blood and the sense of power. You're cold and cruel. You have no heart."

"That's right," she said. "I have no heart because Kartan tore out my heart with his claws when he killed my family. Where you come from, maybe people can afford to have hearts, but not here."

Jumar cleared his throat. "I don't want to interrupt you two," he said, "but could you continue arguing later? I can hear something. Something odd . . ."

They fell silent to listen. Jumar was right.

There was a sound in the air, very quiet at first, then louder.

"Someone's singing," said Niya. "But where?"

"It's as if it came out of the mist on the other side of the precipice," said Jumar. "Out of the air. Right out of midair. And it's not a song I know."

Christopher tipped his head to one side and tried to force his concentration away from his wound and into his ears instead.

"I know it," he said at last, slowly. "It's a German nursery rhyme."

Then he heard it clearly. The words came out of the mist and seemed to push it aside, old, familiar words. And perhaps it was not just a nursery rhyme. Whoever was singing it had begun again at the beginning.

The golden stars are shining
In the sky so clear and bright . . .

Christopher closed his eyes, and a cascade of memories fell over him like a waterfall. Arne holding their dog, that old black dog who died in his arms, and he was singing, singing the same song: "So let your brother lie, In God's name say good-bye, Cold is the evening air." Arne sitting by the campfire with his guitar on a summer's evening, children around him, the bulky shadow of a church behind him. Some kind of holiday, Christopher had forgotten what it was for. There was a girl with Arne as well, one of the girls from school, and Arne was singing the song for the children, but she thought it was for her. "May God our suffering ease, and let us sleep in peace . . ." Arne holding Christopher's hand, years earlier; Christopher was sick and couldn't get to sleep again, and Arne was singing for him . . . "Our poor sick brother, too . . ." And he had laughed. "The moon has risen . . ."

Again and again. It had always been like a magic spell. Christopher had never known why. Maybe it had been the first song that Arne ever sang. Perhaps it would be the last.

He opened his eyes.

There they were again, those words, and it was Arne's voice singing them.

And now the words had driven the mist away. The white swathes of mist that had been floating through the air in front of them were being drawn aside as if by invisible hands pulling back a curtain.

The snow was gone, the clouds were gone. The sun was shining like a spotlight, the only true spotlight on the only true stage in the world.

It shone on the abyss, which wasn't an abyss at all but a ravine. On the other side of the ravine, opposite the tent was a gaping hole in the wall of rock, a dark patch: the mouth of a cave. It was a cave like the one Jumar had entered at the peak of Machapuchare. But someone had helped to shape this one; the entrance was too regular to be natural, and the rubble left by the blast of an explosion lay on a ledge outside the cave like the scab of a wound.

The ravine was about four yards across—too wide to be jumped. But not too wide to have a long board laid over it.

And there was a board nearby, a rough, gray, weatherworn wooden plank. It was not lying across the ravine; it was on this side of it, lying in the snow near the tent. They found the body of the dead guerrilla a little way from the abyss, and his head had dropped on the plank. Niya pushed him aside with the toe of her boot. Brown blood on old wood.

"A bridge," she said. "A bridge to their prisoners over on the other side."

393

A bridge, thought Christopher, to the song in the air. Arne's song.

Christopher was afraid, for a moment, that he had imagined it all. It could have just been an illusion conjured up by memory, wishful thinking.

Had the words really come out of that wall of rock?

A bridge to their prisoners . . . were the prisoners really there?

"Of course they are!" said Jumar, sensing Christopher's doubt. "They're there, nowhere else. It's the perfect place if you don't want to leave too many men guarding your hostages."

Christopher looked at him and sighed. He wanted to call out, but all of a sudden his mouth was unbearably dry, and not a sound would emerge from his throat. Only the pain throbbed in his arm, and suddenly he felt so tired—but there wasn't time to feel tired yet, because this was what he had come for. The end of his long journey.

Christopher lost himself in thought for a moment. It was Jumar who finally called his name. Jumar who bent down to the plank and pushed it across the dangerous depths until one end was lying safely on the ledge outside the cave.

"Arne!" he shouted across the ravine. "Arne? We're here! Arne!"

And then a figure appeared in the black jaws of the cave mouth. A bearded face, and Arne's broad smile in the middle of it.

"Well, well," he said. "Looks like there's a way across again at last."

And then the rigidity went out of Christopher's body, the dryness out of his throat. The throbbing pain in his arm seemed slight and retreated into the background. There was a song inside his head—a loud and happy song, and he thought that this was the best day of their journey.

He didn't think about the depths below. He nodded to Jumar—and to Niya, too, although there was still tension in the air between them. Then he put one foot on the plank, brought his other foot up after it, and with five steps he was on the other side, standing on the ledge outside the cave.

"Hi," said Arne.

"Hi," said Christopher.

Arne was still taller than he was, and still broader and stronger, but at the same time everything had changed.

"Would you mind very much if I gave you a hug?" asked Arne. "I know people don't like that sort of thing when they get to be fourteen."

"Shut up," said Christopher, and then they hugged each other for a long, long time.

And Christopher noticed something wet running down his face. He tried to wipe it away surreptitiously, because when you get to be fourteen, you don't cry. But there was something wet on Arne's face, too. Arne was making no attempt whatsoever to hide his tears.

"Have you any idea how worried I've been about you?" he whispered. "My little brother with the Maoists! Damn it, and I didn't want to tell you when we saw each other back there. My little brother who takes it into his head to rescue me!"

"Hmm," said Christopher. "I always thought I was the one worrying about you. They all were. Mama, Papa, everyone at school . . ."

"Yes," whispered Arne, "but you're the one who's here."

His voice sounded hoarse, and he was clearing his throat a little too much. "If anything had happened to you when you were with those Maoists," he said sternly, "I'd never have forgiven you."

Christopher grinned.

"Oh, nothing much has happened to me since we last saw each other except pneumonia and a bullet wound," he said. "Before that, of course, there was a bridge and Kartan wanted to push me off it. And—"

Arne held his mouth closed. "I don't want to hear about all that," he said, hugging Christopher even harder than before. "At least, not now."

"So here I find you after all this time," said Christopher at last. "In a cave in the middle of nowhere."

"Yes, here you found me," said Arne. "Who'd have thought it?"

Then he turned serious. "I'm not alone," he said. "The other two are here as well. The boys from the U.S. Come on."

There was a fireplace in the middle of the cave, and stacks of firewood and rusty cans of food.

"I guess they didn't want us to die of starvation or cold," said Arne. "They told us we'd be very useful to them yet. And they were as worried as I was about the other two. But they said there was nothing they could do for them. One of them's been coughing up blood for the last two days, and the other one's running a temperature as well."

It was a little while before Christopher's eyes were used to the darkness, and he saw the two bodies lying on the floor. "Are they—are they alive?" he whispered.

Arne nodded, and they knelt down beside the two boys on the floor. Their breathing seemed calm and regular. They were asleep, but one of them woke up, and, for a moment, Christopher saw alarm in his eyes. It was the alarm of a child. They must both be about Arne's age, but fear and sickness had made them seem so much younger. They were helpless, with no strength left.

"What's happening?" whispered the boy. "Who's that? One of them?"

No. Not one of them. Not one of the Maoists, not anymore.

Christopher knelt beside the sick boy and tried to explain.

"I don't understand," said the boy, his sweating forehead showing his bewilderment.

"Well . . . ," said Christopher. "That's okay. Probably no one can understand."

"We can't take them with us," said Arne.

Christopher looked up at him. "We can't?"

But he didn't need an explanation. Arne was right. They were too sick to travel. The older boy bent down and talked to the others in a whisper. His smile promised that he'd be back, that they needn't worry. There were enough provisions, the firewood would hold out, and soon everything would be all right, soon . . .

And finally, still smiling, he said, hesitantly, "Maybe I should stay here. Maybe it's better if I stay and look after them."

"No," said Christopher. "Arne, come with us. There's nothing you can do for them here, but you can help us."

"What with?" asked Arne. "What are you planning?" His smile had disappeared.

"I don't know," said Christopher. "But Jumar will think up something. He has to change everything. The city of Kathmandu is waiting for us. Jumar says . . . He says there'll be chaos and turmoil and death, but when that's all over we'll come back here to get these two out."

"Do you believe that?" asked Arne, looking at him.

Christopher looked at the ground.

"Come on," he said.

As Jumar waited for Christopher by the tent across the ravine from the prisoner's cave, his gaze fell on the rock wall opposite, and for some reason his eyes then moved up the rock wall.

And at the top of the wall, his gaze stopped.

The heir to the throne of Nepal took a step back and reached for his companion's arm.

"Niya," Jumar whispered. "Niya, look! Up there!"

"Shh," said Niya. "Keep perfectly still. Don't move. Maybe they haven't seen us yet."

At the top of the rock wall, above the cave, two huge dragons were perched, shimmering blue and silver. They were sitting perfectly still, wings folded on their backs, like enormous, lazy cats on a windowsill. Only their heads were moving back and forth on their long, flexible necks, watching, waiting, in no hurry.

"We must warn Christopher," whispered Jumar.

Niya nodded grimly.

But at that moment, Christopher emerged through the snow from the mouth of the cave itself and stepped onto the plank with Arne following him. This was a first. The heads of the blue and silver dragons swept from left to right and back again for the last time. Then they made up their minds to leave their posts. They spread their shimmering wings and rose into the air with all the elegance of disaster, and their great, dark shadows hovered over the ravine below them.

◆ ◆ ◆

Christopher felt the wind of tremendous wings passing above them in the cold air. Wings that were so close that they almost touched the brothers. But only almost.

What did touch them was the shadow of those wings. A deadly shadow.

Christopher looked up and glimpsed shimmering blue and silver out of the corner of his eyes, but before he really saw the dragons, he saw their shadow passing over Arne. The sun came right through the veil of snow, and he saw the bronze glittering in its light. And then what was once standing behind him on the wooden bridge that had no handrail lost its balance and fell.

Christopher staggered and reached out for Arne. He found himself lying flat on his belly again. Though he'd done this very same thing before, this time, he wasn't lying on snow—this time it was a hard plank, and the fingers closed around his were made of bronze.

He looked down.

As the dragons above disappeared into the distance, cruel sunlight was reflected on cold metal below him.

Horror hit Christopher like a strong fist. He wanted to let go, wanted to stop holding the thing he was clutching so hard. It wasn't Arne. It was something strange, something he didn't know, something hollow and without feeling.

But here was this hand, looking exactly like Arne's hand. He couldn't bring himself to let go of it.

So he hauled the hollow, cold bronze statue up, got it on to the plank, fought to keep his balance, and won the fight. He worked his way carefully backward, inch by inch, until he reached the end of the plank, and reached firm ground and frozen snow with a bronze statue in his arms.

And then he closed his eyes and lay perfectly still in the snow, unable to believe what had happened.

JUMAR, GONE AWAY

CHRISTOPHER," SAID A VOICE ABOVE him. "Christopher. It's all right. You must stand up now. You can't lie here for ever."

He heard the voice—it was Jumar. But he didn't react. He didn't have enough strength to react. Everything was pointless now. His brother was covered with a layer of gleaming, unfeeling bronze, as if the metal were in himself, in his heart, in his mind . . .

"Christopher, you can't just freeze to death here. It's all right. It isn't your fault. Please, we must go on!"

He opened his eyes. Jumar's face was leaning over him, with a ridiculously blue sunny sky behind it.

And when he saw that blue sky and felt furious with it, the rigidity gradually left his heart and his mind, giving way to a memory. Not a memory of Arne this time, a memory of words. Words spoken by a woman in a dark hut, on an evening that now seemed an eternity ago.

"The woman in that village," he said quietly. "They put their statue out in the fields because they felt it was eerie. And then the dragon came back and touched it. And the monk . . . what was it the monk said?"

"You mean—?" Jumar asked. "What the dragons turn to bronze they can turn back again?"

Christopher nodded and then he sat up suddenly. "The scales on their wings," he said, in a louder voice. "We didn't know what he was talking about, not then. But now, Jumar, now we do know! It's the scales on butterflies' wings, the scales they use to keep their balance in the air! When I was little Arne explained it. He told me you shouldn't touch their wings . . ."

His glance fell on the snow beside him, and he stopped talking. There lay the bronze statue of a boy with long hair and a shaggy beard. And there was a smile on the statue's face. Christopher stood up, determined now.

"We'll take him with us."

Niya narrowed her eyes and looked at the statue in the snow.

"We can try," she said. "But don't be too sure it will work."

"How are you going to get at the scales?" asked Jumar. "Remember what the monk said: 'No one has ever been known to catch a dragon.'"

"Even I couldn't hit one," said Niya, "so how are you going to?"

"I don't know," admitted Christopher. "All I know is that this is my brother, and I came to take him home. Never mind how. Never mind what I have to do. Let's go."

He heard Niya growling under her breath. He could see she still didn't agree with him. There was something in the air between them, and then there was the young guerrilla boy's blood that had not been shed. And now the weight of a bronze statue, too.

Or perhaps it was something quite different standing between them? Something invisible, something incurable? Something for which there were no words?

They carried the statue in turn, two of them at a time, while the third carried Jumar's backpack. The precipice led them along its edge, refusing to show them a path. It was evening before it gave up and took them to a pathway leading down. It isn't easy to carry a six-foot-tall bronze statue hiking downward—even if it's hollow.

They took turns carrying it, and swearing.

Night found them halfway down the slope. They slept briefly and badly, without speaking to each other. Christopher put both arms around the statue so that it wouldn't roll downhill while he was asleep.

Where was Arne now? Could he feel the cold on his bronze skin? Could he hear with his metal ears? Did he see with his cold eyes that were no longer blue?

In the morning, they ate some canned meat that was going bad—and then they were on their way again, going on and on, down, down, and down. Matters improved toward evening of this day, for the effects of the altitude that had been with them until now dissipated, and the snow came to an end. The white gave way to a colorless, stony landscape—colorless not because of the dragons. It was country into which no dragon would roam, for there was nothing to see here and nothing to eat.

Christopher was brooding, waiting for an idea. But no ideas came to him.

A time came when there was grass once more, growing sparsely at first, then low bushes, and then came the day when Jumar suddenly, unexpectedly, said, "We're going too slowly."

And Niya, who barely had anything to say anymore, replied, "That's because as well as three guns and a backpack, we're dragging a six-foot bronze statue along with us."

405

They stopped. There was tall grass waving and a strong wind around them, but the midday sun was already shining with the promise of warmth in the valleys and by the rivers.

Jumar sighed. "Whatever happens in Kathmandu, we aren't going to get there in time to do anything to stop it."

He and Niya had been carrying the statue, and Christopher the backpack, and now they put both down for a moment.

Christopher sighed. He put out a hand to support the hollow statue and keep it from falling. The bronze hand in his seemed to be pleading, as if it wanted to reach out and beg them: Don't leave me alone.

"We can't do it," said Christopher. "We can't leave him. We could always leave the guns here."

"Christopher," said Niya. "Be reasonable. Listen—"

"No!" He shook his head frantically, and felt he was being childish. "I don't want to listen to anything! He's my brother! You got us to set a house on fire to avenge your family, remember? None of us is reasonable! Human beings aren't reasonable! Nothing in the world has anything to do with reason! I—"

Niya had come so close to him that her nose was almost touching his. The fire in her dark eyes was the same fire that had destroyed the stable on a night long ago.

"That," she said, pointing to the statue, "that, Christopher, is not your brother. It's nothing. It's lifeless, cold. It doesn't feel anything. It has no heart beating inside it. It feels no grief, no fear, no disappointment. There's no one who needs your help inside that thing anymore. Even if we had the scales or the dust of millions of butterfly wings in a bag with us, I don't believe it would change anything. All that's only a rumor. And as things are, we have no dust from butterfly wings. Are we going to give up on a whole country because we can't leave a dead statue behind?"

Christopher let go of the bronze hand and clenched his fists. He felt that his breathing was labored—as if he had to struggle against some resistance that stood between him and Niya.

"So you two think," he said, "you can save a country because you turn up in some city at a certain point in time? What are you going to do there? Change everything just by snapping your fingers? How? Why not save the whole world while you're about it? You still don't have a plan!"

"Yes, we do," said Jumar. "I'm working on it."

"Oh, yeah?" said Christopher. "I just can't wait!"

For a while, a cloud of heavy silence sank over the three travelers, and the tall grass itself stopped moving as if the wind, too, had fallen silent.

Then Niya said. "Fine. Maybe it *is* nonsense. But it

matters to us. You don't have to care about this country. It isn't yours."

There it was again, all of a sudden. We and us. You and I. A country that wasn't his.

A mission that had nothing to do with him.

Christopher put out his hand, in a faint attempt to salvage something.

"Okay," he said. "I didn't mean it like that. Can't we try—together—"

He reached out and touched her arm in a gesture of appeasement, but she pulled it away.

"Don't touch me," she snarled. "We can't try anything together. There isn't any *together*. There never was. You said so yourself. You never believed in our cause."

Something snapped in Christopher, with a crunch like breaking glass, although only he could hear it.

"Right," he cried, "so now it's *don't touch me*, is it? May I remind you it wasn't always like that? Maybe you'd rather forget it, but there was a night outside that molten town where it wasn't *don't touch me*, it was the opposite. It was *do touch me*, here and there and there, too, almost like an order, Sergeant Niya. You were the one who began it all. So now it didn't mean anything, there was never any *together*? Well, that's nice to know."

Niya stared at him, her face as stony and frozen as the lifeless bronze face of his brother.

He stared back and then let his eyes wander aside and meet the eyes of Jumar, who hadn't said anything all this time. He had nothing to do with this fight. And at that moment, Christopher realized that they were somehow taking out their anger on Jumar. He should never have known about their night together. He ought never to have known about it.

But once words are spoken, they can't be unspoken again.

"Ah," said Jumar. "So that's it. Yes, you're right. Nice to know. And yes, there never was any *together*."

With that, he turned and went on along the downward path, going away. Away.

Niya cursed at Christopher through gritted teeth, turned around, and ran after Jumar. "Wait!" he heard her call. "Jumar, wait! It's not—it's not what you think."

And Christopher was left alone, with only a bronze statue beside him, watching the other two go.

"This," he said quietly, "is the end of our journey. This is the end of everything. Or anyway," he added after a moment, "the end for me."

The hand he was pressing was made of cold bronze and did not respond.

It couldn't. It would probably never be able to respond again.

He guessed that Niya was right. But all the same, he picked up the statue, and as he slowly made his way down the path, he felt as hollow as it was.

Evening came, and the light of the setting sun was caught in hundreds of cobwebs spun between the waist-high grasses like a natural filigree. Christopher saw them breaking as he walked through them, and for some vague reason, that made his grief even worse. Nothing remained whole. Nothing lasted.

He put the statue and his gun down in the grass and waited for the sun to set. And when it did, he lay down to sleep with his head on Jumar's backpack, which he was still carrying. There was something in the backpack sticking into him through the fabric. He undid the zipper and reached into it. And there, at the bottom of the backpack, under cans and ammunition, wax matches, damp Nepali rupees, pieces of string, and a pair of gloves, he found the crumbling remains of bark and branches. He took his hand out and stared at the twigs in the last light of day. Then he remembered.

Juniper wood.

That special, strange kind of juniper that they had used

as torches: resinous juniper torches spraying colored sparks like fireworks . . . And a dragon, lured by the glowing colors . . . Christopher took a deep breath.

"That," he said to the lifeless bronze statue beside him, even though it probably couldn't hear him, "that's the answer. We can lure the dragon with this. The dragon we need for the scales from the butterfly wings. We have it! Almost, anyway."

He set his gun aside. The matches. The largest complete juniper twig he could find. His hands were strangely calm.

"Jumar said they're only made of butterflies," he told Arne who wasn't Arne anymore. "And that's why it's no good shooting a dragon. That's why Niya couldn't hit it. But even Niya isn't perfect. Perhaps she really did miss. After all, she was hanging from a vertical rock face at the time. And, well, this is the only opportunity I have to hit it. The dragon I'm going to lure here. And then I can catch the butterflies. There'll be enough of them for me to catch a few, surely. And then you'll feel the dust on your skin when you wake up. And if you don't wake up . . . if you stay bronze, then . . ."

He didn't finish his sentence.

Instead, he struck a match. He used up seven of the thin wax matches before he managed to light the juniper twig. But finally, with the eighth match, he did it. And with some difficulty, Christopher rammed the burning, crackling twig as it sprayed color into the hard, cold ground where the grasses grew. Dew was sparkling in the cobwebs now, drops of dew glowing like a thousand jewels, lit up by the miraculous juniper torch.

It was dark all around. Hopefully dark enough to keep the dragons from casting shadows. He wondered if any dragons would even come.

Christopher waited at a little distance from the torch.

"This," whispered Christopher, "is our only chance."

The word "chance" was still in the air when that air itself was churned up by the movement of something huge up above.

First Christopher was triumphant, and then the claws of fear closed around his heart.

He crouched lower in the tall grass, felt the lifeless metal body beside him.

The faint glow of the dragon in the night reminded him of the dragons in the molten town. It gave off a little light, just enough for him to see it coming—a mere outline moving with mysterious grace. It was bright, gleaming gold with a red tinge to its wings.

Christopher was always surprised by how beautiful the dragons were. Why does evil have to be ugly? And were the dragons evil? Deadly, yes, and destructive, but evil?

"Now you're feeling sorry for a dragon," he scolded himself. "They're right. You *are* crazy. A totally hopeless case."

And now the dragon was upon them! It was flying straight toward the torch, its claws outstretched. Christopher took aim and pulled the trigger. The sound of the shot tore into the night, and Christopher staggered back. For a moment he closed his eyes, but now he made himself open them. And there was the dragon, still in the air, unharmed.

It went on flying down to the ground, toward the colors sprayed out by the torch, as if nothing had happened. Christopher had no time to take aim again, and he knew it would be no use anyway. It didn't work. It was impossible to shoot a dragon down. You couldn't kill enough butterflies at the same time to stop it in its tracks.

A little slow-motion effect would have come in very handy here, thought Christopher. Then I could crawl backward to get away from the dragon. Because, no, it is not dark enough. I can see the stars, and they *are* bright enough for a dragon to cast a shadow, and, yes, it *is* going to fly right above me, leaving two gleaming metal bodies lying in the grass, resting harmoniously side by side.

Brothers.

But there was no slow motion.

It all happened at merciless speed. There was no time for

him even to shut his eyes. The dragon dropped straight down to the ground to seize the torch in its claws and then fly away over Christopher. But it never reached the torch.

A sound like the fluttering of thousands of butterfly wings filled the air—from thousands of butterflies whose flight was abruptly braked. And then thousands of butterflies, most of them gold and red, were struggling in a dense net of cobwebs glittering with dew in the tall grass. Christopher gasped for air. The dragon was stuck.

It was still a dragon, but as soon as the spiders woke up and set about killing and digesting butterfly after butterfly, it would fall apart. And the dragon knew that. Christopher saw it desperately struggling to break loose, but becoming ever more hopelessly entangled. It was a struggle of gold and red, like a table full of gift-wrapped Christmas presents running wild.

"Now," whispered Christopher. "This is it! We must—"

And he picked up the bronze statue that wasn't Arne, and carried it very close to the struggling dragon—the dragon on whose wings, made of captive butterflies, were the tiny scales that might turn Arne back into Arne.

Maybe.

If the rumors were true.

Christopher dragged the statue close, very close, in spite of the fear singing in his ears. In spite of the doubts tormenting him, he took care to approach the dragon so that its starlight shadow couldn't fall on him. And then he was close enough to plunge one of Arne's bronze hands into the swirl of butterflies caught in the webs, into the helpless body of the dragon. It was close enough for the metal fingers to touch the butterfly wings—maybe even to crush them. Close enough for the miraculous scales from those fragile creatures to trickle down, like colored dust, on the smooth bronze surface of the statue.

But the dragon knew.

It lashed its tail and tried to flap its wings in vain.

And then, in panic, it opened its mouth and spewed a jet of fire into the air. An angry jet of fire spraying sparks of color—just as the dragons that flew over the molten town one night had done. But the flame that came from its jaws was far higher and far stronger. It was as if the dragon were crying out for help with the force of desperation.

Christopher leaped back, shielding his face with his arms. He found himself back in the grass, and cursed his panic, felt the heat, and smelled burning grass. And something melting.

Metal.

Bronze.

When he looked up again, the dragon was lifeless in the

cobweb trap. Perhaps breathing out so much fire had taken too great a toll on its strength.

Many of the butterflies were still moving their wings a little. A fat black spider was climbing, in amazement, toward a particularly beautiful red butterfly flecked with gold, shining like a Christmas tree bauble.

Another fat black spider was smoldering on the singed ground.

Where the cobwebs had stopped burning, a few butterflies, astonishingly unharmed, were fluttering up and flying away into the night. And then what was left of the dragon lost its shape, leaving nothing but a large mass of dead, sticky insects caught in a few cobwebs somewhere in the foothills of the Himalayas.

None of this was logical.

Later, people would say that the spiders on that slope spun fiery cobwebs. They blazed in symmetrical patterns and wonderful colors among the tall grass, and singed the eyelashes of anyone who dared to look at them.

That day, the two halves of a bronze statue that had burst apart lay among the charred grass where the cobwebs were torn and the fire was going out. Christopher knelt on the black ashes of what had once been grass, extended a trembling hand, and cried out. The metal was too hot to touch.

The bronze still kept its shape, but you could see that its extremities had begun to melt. Had it changed first? Just for the fraction of a second? Was that the smell of burnt flesh in the air? Of blood that had flowed and charred?

"No," whispered Christopher. The word was there in his head, glowing red like the first that had now gone out:

No, No, No, No.

Did Arne's hand ever touch the butterflies? Or not? But that wasn't important anymore.

Christopher stood up and, in a pointless gesture, brushed the ash off his legs.

And the word in his head was replaced by other, harsher words.

I have killed him. My own brother.

Staggering, he moved away from the broken statue and stumbled. When he recovered his balance, he wondered where was he going. And why.

He was all alone.

Jumar and Niya had gone, and Arne . . . Arne was dead.

An image of a night: A boy, maybe fourteen, standing among a clump of tall grass. And two other figures.

They were watching him from a distance.

"I told you he was crazy," whispered Niya. "I told you so

when he enticed the dragon down. But what's he doing now? He's just running around in circles—"

"Not a bad idea of his, about that dragon," whispered Jumar. "We've got to do something, Niya. He really is running around in circles. And where's that statue?"

Christopher didn't see the two figures watching him. He saw something else. Mist. Mist rising from the grass, or smoke from the fire. And something was stinging his eyes, making them stream.

He heard Arne's voice in his head. Those damn memories. He wished that now that it was all over, the memories would finally leave him in peace.

Arne's voice sang on as it had sung for him when he had been small and sick in bed—as it had been singing when they found Arne in the cave in the rock wall.

> The woods stand black and silent
> And from the meadow rises
> White mist this evening fair.
>
> So let your brother lie,
> In God's name, say good-bye.
> Cold is the evening air.

But why, if the voice was in his head, why was it moving? It had just been some way off, and now it was closer . . .

Hesitating, he turned—and collided with someone.

That someone was taller than him, broader, and stronger. He smelled of soot and charred fabric. And he put his arms around Christopher.

Christopher looked up.

"Hey," said Arne. "Hey, Christopher! What's . . . I don't understand what—"

Then Christopher began crying like a child. His tears fell and Arne murmured, "Hey, hey," and, "Now, now," and, "If only I knew what—"

⋮
419
⋮

"I don't believe this," said Jumar, and he realized he had begun jumping up and down like a little boy. "He was right. He was right all along, Niya! He did it!"

"Well," said Niya. "Yes. Damn it, so he did!"

They said nothing for a moment. "And about the rest of it—" Niya began.

"The rest of it?" said Jumar.

"Things happen," said Niya.

"But . . . are you . . . Do you think, you and Christopher?"

"No. Things happen."

"Unfortunately . . . ," said Jumar. "Unfortunately I'm . . .

Would you . . . This is, kind of, how should I put it . . . kind of a new experience for me. But I collect new experiences."

Niya held him firmly by the shoulders and looked at his face. She couldn't see much, because it was dark.

"I'm afraid I'm in love," said Jumar.

"What, with Christopher?" asked Niya, laughing quietly.

And Jumar barked, "No."

"We really should go to them," she said. "And . . . uh . . . make up with Christopher. Maybe."

But on the way, her cheek touched his—or was that just the tall grass?

420

"And I have an idea," said Jumar later, after apologies had been spoken and accepted, as they walked through the night. "An idea about Kathmandu. The chaos. The end."

"Yes, sounds like you need one," said Arne in friendly tones.

He had asked them no questions. He would go to Kathmandu with them, into the chaos.

The city was calling to them strongly now.

There was nothing to keep them in the mountains. The time had come to change the course of things.

And far from the four figures making their way down a wall

of rock, General Kartan sat on his black stallion, watching his men train for the last time.

In a bare room in a molten town, the Great T. ground out his cigarette and went to the window.

It was the beginning of the end. Soon the curtain would rise—the actors were ready.

Central Hill Country

· · ✦ · ·

· · ✦ · ·

FLORA

Tulip tree (*Magnolia*), pipal tree, sacred fig (*Ficus religiosa*),
eucalyptus, banyan tree, elephant grass, hibiscus, jasmine,
mimosa, bananas, papayas, guavas

FAUNA

Rhesus monkey, jackal, Danfe pheasant, ringdove

ARNE IN THE RIVER

THE WAY SOUTHWARD WAS LONGER THAN any hike that Christopher had ever gone on before. Time clung to the soles of their feet, keeping them from feeling like they were going forward, the last peaks refused to give way, and suddenly they no longer seemed to be losing height. It was one of those endless journeys that you make in dreams, never arriving anywhere, marking time, moving but never leaving the spot.

"And what if we don't make it?" Christopher kept asking. "What if we don't arrive in time?"

No one was talking about "we" and "I," "you" and "they," "together" and "alone" now. They had reached the limit of their discussions, the limit of fighting and blaming each other. They had simply left that behind.

"In time to do what?" asked Arne.

"We'll arrive in time," replied Jumar. "And we'll do what has to be done."

"I bet," said Niya, "you don't have any idea what that is yet. You're just assuming that you *will* know by the time we're in Kathmandu."

"No," replied Jumar simply. "I told you, I have an idea. I know *exactly* what we're going to do."

When twilight fell, he told them his plan.

They had left the grass behind again, and one of those moonscapes of rubble and rocks surrounded them. They built a fire among the rocks, and opened a can of meat pâté. No one complained that its expiration date was two years ago.

"Juniper," said Jumar. "Christopher's juniper."

They all stared at him.

He nodded. "Christopher was right. That's the answer. We must find those juniper bushes again. Juniper bushes of some kind, anyway. We need more juniper wood."

"When we go farther down, I can show you where some bushes grow," said Niya.

"But why on earth do you need juniper rather than any other wood?" asked Arne.

Jumar smiled. It was still strange to see him there, smiling, instead of just hearing a smile in what he said.

"You wouldn't be here but for juniper wood," he told Arne. "It was juniper wood that Christopher used to entice the dragon down into the cobwebs. The resin in it gives off colored flames, and they lure the dragons," he explained.

The little group beside the fire waited in expectant silence. The flames rose high, crackling. They were not burning juniper, and reassuringly the flames were not very colorful. A few single sparks shot up to the sky.

"I had a dream," Jumar went on at last. "Well, a daydream. I had it today when we were climbing down the mountain. My legs were climbing but my head was dreaming. It was dreaming that I saw the city from above. The streets were full of guerrillas. They filled the city like ants. I heard screams in the streets, shots, sirens howling. I saw dogs running away and pigeons flying up. I saw the people's eyes behind their windows and their fear. And I saw the palace. It was dark with soldiers. The tanks in Durbar Square were ready to fire their guns. And then I realized that I'll never get inside the palace. Not now I'm visible. Not even with the signet ring on my hand. No one's going to have time to bother with something like a signet ring. I'm visible, but the gates of the palace are closed to me. The power of the king, the locked room, the box—all of that's out of my reach."

He looked around.

Then he said, "There are only four of us. We can't do anything, but I know who can. We'll lure the dragons into the city. The same way Christopher did it."

"You're crazy," said Christopher.

"But what use will that be?" asked Niya. "And where would you get enough cobwebs?"

Jumar slowly shook his head. "This isn't a joke," he went on. "It's the only logical conclusion. We'll lure them in on the day when the streets are full of chaos. The day when the Maoists storm the city, and Kartan sends his men to fight them. The day I've dreamed of. The dragons' shadows will turn all the men into bronze—the soldiers, the insurgents, everyone who is outdoors fighting, never mind which side he's fighting on. And when all the soldiers are turned to bronze, and the palace is guarded only by statues, like an army of tin soldiers, then no one will keep me from entering it. Then I can talk to my father. And then, at long last, he will give me the power. The power we can use to defeat the dragons."

They said nothing for a long time.

The darkness beyond the fire was denser now. The future lay in wait in that darkness.

"This is a fairy tale," said Niya at last. "One of the stories people tell at the fireside. Just that, no more. But I admire your courage, believing in fairy tales."

"Yes, it is no more than a fairy tale," said Jumar. "But it's also no less than a fairy tale."

"I don't know—" Christopher began.

And Arne said, "We have to try. It's . . . our only chance."

Later, they sat there looking at the stars, and Niya sang her songs for them, even without her guitar.

"My heart longs for dreams," she sang. "Dreams in this land of our fate . . ."

And Arne, who was good at such things, listened for a while and then joined in with his bass voice. Later on, Christopher would remember how the two of them had sung together. It was a beautiful night, so beautiful after all the terrors of the last few days, and he saw something in Jumar's eyes that was reflected in Niya's. Something in the night quietly asking him to go away. It hurt, but the night was right. He wasn't the one who belonged with Niya. A whole world smelling of blood and heavy boots lay between them, a world in which they could never entirely meet. When the fire had burned down that evening, he stood up and asked Arne to come with him.

"Let's go for a walk," he said. "It's a fine night."

And Arne followed him unquestioningly.

When the fire was only a dot in the distance, Christopher turned and looked back. But apart from the glowing embers, there was nothing to be seen there.

Christopher walked a little farther and finally sat down on a rock, looking down into the next valley. Somewhere there in the distance, other dots glowed; other fires, far, far away.

Arne sat down beside him in silence.

"I thought it would be a good idea to leave them alone together," Christopher said after a while.

"I've been thinking about that all this time," admitted Arne. "But I couldn't decide which of you two she—"

Christopher put a finger to his lips. He looked at Arne and smiled.

"I missed you so much, Arne," he said. "I've always admired you. Everyone does. And of course you're older than me, and . . . but the world is more complicated than you think."

"Maybe," said Arne.

"Not that I understand it myself." Christopher laughed quietly. "I don't understand anything at all. I don't understand

Niya, either. She loves life, but she also loves death, and sometimes it's as if she still has something to do before she embraces it. Kill someone. Save someone. Sleep with someone. As if she knew she didn't have much time left."

"But, why? Why wouldn't she have as much time left as all the rest of us?"

Christopher shrugged his shoulders. "Maybe there'll be no place for her in the world that comes after the chaos," he said. "Maybe she isn't made for peace."

Arne stretched out his hand and touched Christopher's cheek.

"You're crying," he said.

Christopher angrily shook his head. "It's the dew in the night air."

Arne put his arm around him as he used to, and so they sat there looking ahead into the future, but it couldn't be seen in the dark.

"Here's my little brother sitting in the dew," said Arne, "and he has grown so wise, he's almost a stranger to me. If it didn't sound so condescending, I'd say I was proud of you."

Christopher rested his head on Arne's shoulder.

"Do you remember," he whispered, "the time I sprained my ankle just before Christmas, and you carried me piggyback to church?"

"Of course I remember. We were giggling the whole way, and I almost slipped and broke my leg."

"It's nearly Advent again now," said Christopher. "And soon Christmas will come. I wonder if our parents will celebrate it without us this year. It will be so empty and so sad at home. Will they have a tree if we're not there?"

"Oh, they'll have a tree," said Arne firmly. "And we'll both decorate it, and if I know you, you'll fall off the stepladder and break something."

The crown prince of Nepal slept soundly that night, a deep and dreamless sleep. A girl with tangled black hair slept in his arms.

When he woke up, she wasn't there.

He sat up with a start and looked around him.

Two people lay asleep not far away, beside the cold fireplace, wrapped in their jackets: Christopher and Arne. Then he turned and saw her.

She was standing in an early ray of sunlight, holding her knife. Its blade sparkled in the morning light. He was startled, but she smiled. Black, matted animal fur lay at her feet, and the hair on her head was short.

Jumar quietly got up and went over to her.

He took her chin, turned her head a little way, looked at

her, examined her face, and finally said, "You're beautiful. But why did you . . . ?"

"I could never have managed to comb all the tangles out," said Niya, laughing. "And maybe I wanted to be beautiful."

"Come away with me," he said. "When all this is over. I'll go to Europe. For a while. Or maybe to America. Come with me. I mean it."

She ran her fingers through her short hair thoughtfully.

"Who knows?" she replied vaguely. "Let's wake the others up. It's time to set off."

They breakfasted on a can of fruit in syrup and some dried meat. And on their endless way downhill, the heir to the throne of Nepal began dreaming of the time after the chaos, after the day when they call the dragons to the city—a time full of peace, full of books, full of bathtubs and bowls of fruit.

In his dreams, Niya no longer wore her green camouflage parka and her tough boots; she walked lightly beside him, in clean clothes, through the corridors of the palace, down the central aisle of an airplane, along streets in distant lands—and he had only to put out his hand to touch hers. In his dreams, there was no gun over her shoulder anymore. In his dreams, everything was different.

Leaving the barren landscape behind, they reached the

steppes again. There were a few villages here, the first bushes and stunted trees appeared, then there were more. Here and there a grazing yak or mule looked up from the low scrub and gazed at them in surprise. They found juniper, too. They almost stumbled over it, but as the heir to the throne of Nepal filled his backpack with the wonderful wood of those fragrant bushes, he went on dreaming. He dreamed of his mother walking through the garden, listening as he told her about his adventures, shaking her head incredulously from time to time. He dreamed of his father sitting opposite him in a restaurant in the capital city, not a king anymore but only a father, telling him how proud he was of him. In his dreams, his father was younger and healthy again. In his dreams, Kartan had been lying, and the king had never had a tumor in his brain.

His dreams saw the colorless patches on the landscape, and the bronze statues in the fields through which they were sometimes walking now, but they already seemed to belong to a terrible past.

On the fourth day of their descent, Jumar was abruptly wrenched out of his dreams.

There were tall trees along the way now, and they were moving around the rim of a green valley where rice grew on the slopes, and a blue river flowed in the depths below. A village clung to one of those slopes, and Jumar sent his dreams on ahead of them.

"We'll get something to eat that's never seen the inside of a can there," he said. His steps carried him after his dreams, swift and light. And when he turned around, he had left the others far behind. But he didn't feel like stopping. The path was wide and easy to walk on here, and his feet went on as if of their own accord. He waved back to his friends, and kept on walking. He would wait for them among the houses.

He saw something blue and white in the distance, something like one of those notices meant for tourists. He would sit on a chair in a garden, and someone would dig out an old, dog-eared, laminated menu in bad English, dating from the time when tourists came. And the villagers would see him. They would see his real self. For the first time, Christopher wouldn't have to lend his body to Jumar's voice.

Jumar thought of how wonderful that would be.

The path wound its way down the slope, and then Jumar reached the first houses. But they lay there in a strange silence. He sighed. Another deserted village.

No chair in the garden, no laminated old menu. Only melancholy, and times past in the empty streets. Somewhere a horse snorted.

CHECKPOINT, Jumar read on the blue-and-white sign that had looked so tempting in the distance.

TO REST PEAS REGISTER HER.

He suppressed a grin. The idea of giving the peas a rest was funny, but it probably meant *Tourists Please Register Here.*

However, there were no tourists, and there hadn't been any for a long time. And there was no one here to check them in, document them, count them—there was no one around at all.

A wooden door was banging back and forth in the draft beyond the blue-and-white sign, and Jumar opened it and entered an empty room. Big windows without any glass in them formed the whole back wall, and far below lay the river valley.

Jumar went over to a window and looked out, down into the valley where green grass beckoned once more. Outside this room there was a small terrace, also perching over the drop below at a daring angle. Two weathered chairs stood on the terrace, looking at the scenery.

The door to the terrace was open. Jumar went through and saw someone standing by the rail of the balustrade. He was standing so still that Jumar almost missed him completely.

At that moment the wind slammed the terrace door.

Jumar froze.

The man by the balustrade was tall and had a face as smooth as if it had just been ironed. No. This couldn't be. This was impossible.

A mocking smile crossed the man's face.

"Well, what a surprise," he said.

Jumar took a step back, felt for the door handle, and already knew it was too late for that. I'm visible, he thought, and it hit him like an electric shock: He can see me, I'm the same as anyone else. No more tricks, no more objects hovering in the air, no more surprise attacks.

And suddenly, he also knew whose horse he had heard snorting.

Kartan's fingers closed on his arm before he even had time to think of the gun he carried. They were cold fingers, hard as steel. They swiftly and expertly twisted his arms behind his back and hauled him over to the rail around the terrace. It was a long time since Kartan had done any fighting himself; he was used to giving orders, standing on the sidelines, directing events. But he hadn't forgotten anything.

"Well, well. So I come up here to take a last look at the country," he said, and his voice was calm and unemotional. "A last look before it's mine. And what do I find? The friend of our little heir to the throne. Chance plays strange games, don't you agree?"

Jumar didn't answer. It was a little while before Kartan's words sank in. *The friend of the heir to the throne.*

"Do you see them down there?" he asked. "Those are my men. They're leaving the mountains. I don't need them here anymore. There's no point in taking land from the Maoists now. Not in the mountains. They'll come down to me in the valley, because they think they can beat my men there. I know their plans, which of course are nonsense. Do you see how many of my forces are already on the march down below? I am withdrawing them, assembling them in the city ... thousands and thousands and thousands of them."

And Jumar did see. From where they stood, all you could make out was a few bends in the path running through the trees. But that path was thick with people, mules, horses. He saw uniform buttons flash in the sunlight, he saw the barrels of guns gleaming, saw medals shining on some of the men's chests, and the horses' glossy, well-groomed coats. And he hoped that Christopher, Niya, and Arne were going slowly— too slowly to catch up with that endless caravan of soldiers.

"Now I have you in my hands." Kartan went on, "I don't need you anymore. The king's invisible son may be alive, but that won't do him any good now. It's too late for him."

"Too late?" said Jumar, and then bit his lip.

"Yes, much too late," Kartan nodded. "I assume from your

presence that he's not far away, is that right? The Maoists will be attacking the city in four days' time. I have eyes and ears everywhere, in their ranks, as well. Even an invisible man can't change the course of history in four days. I'll let you go if you give me your gun. I need no more information from you. I have a kind heart."

Kartan shook his head. "Tell your friend with the signet ring I'm sorry. He has nowhere to go back to. His father won't hear anything he says now."

Jumar forced himself to keep silent.

"Sad but true," said Kartan. "The king is dying. It won't be much longer, and if the fighting for the city cuts short his sufferings, so much the better for him. The doctors who say they never give up on any patient . . . Well, they've given up on him. Only the nurses keep watch by his bed in the palace now."

Jumar gritted his teeth, pursed his lips, and told himself not to speak. But the words came out of his mouth as if of their own accord.

"How much longer does he have?"

Kartan shook his head thoughtfully. "A day? A week? I'm not one of his doctors. For all I know he may be gone already."

Then the heir to the throne of Nepal saw his father before him, saw him in his great bed—the bed he had not shared with the queen since she began her long sleep, saw him lying in cool silken sheets among all the magnificently embroidered cushions, heard the ventilator above him humming. And his father looked so small, so tiny. So lost.

"He asked about his son," said Kartan. "But no one could give him any answer. He will probably never speak to the boy again."

Something hot and unfamiliar rose in Jumar, something that frightened him. It was as if the pain inside him were rising and wanted to get out, and since he was keeping his mouth closed and refused to let any more words emerge, it chose to use his eyes. The view of the green river valley blurred, and Jumar blinked. Something warm ran down his cheek, found his mouth, and tasted salty.

Niya's words came into his mind.

But none have seen me shed a tear,
I, too, will cross the mountains here.
I have not yet wept for you . . .

It was true: he had shed no tears. That surprised him, and so did the strength of the tears pouring out of him now. He struggled to keep it in, but it was in vain. His eyes were burning, and behind the blur of tears he saw the big bed and his tiny father, and he knew that Kartan was right. It was too late.

The king would never speak to his son again. He would never know why he had left the city, and how much he had learned. And he would die without ever seeing Jumar.

"Just a moment," he heard Kartan saying. "Are you crying? You're not crying, are you?"

His cold fingers passed over Jumar's cheek, and found the tears there.

Through the veil before his eyes, Jumar saw Kartan staring at his fingers.

"You are not his friend," he said slowly. "You are not the friend of the heir to the throne."

Now that smooth, well-ironed face was very close, the eyes in it were searching Jumar's face . . . and they found what they were looking for.

"No," said Kartan. "You look like him, but you're not his friend. You are the king's son himself. The heir to the throne. The crown prince." He shook his head incredulously. "You—you're visible."

At that moment, Jumar knew that he couldn't pretend to Kartan anymore. And he knew he had just this one second left—the second in which Kartan's astonishment made him loosen his grip.

It cost him all his willpower to force the image of his dying, shrunken father out of his mind, and then, with a sudden jerk, he escaped Kartan's clutches.

Kartan's hands did not follow him. Instead, they went to his pocket, and Jumar was looking down the barrel of a revolver.

But he was already beside the handrail.

As Kartan pressed the trigger, the king's son, the heir to the throne of Nepal, the crown prince, took a step backward into the void. A step into the future.

He fell without a sound.

440

Kartan watched him go, shook his head, and put the gun away again.

Then he left the tourist checkpoint, mounted his black horse, and rode after his men. It was time for them to get down to Kathmandu, where he needed them.

They were only a hundred yards from the first houses in the village when the shot rang out.

"What on earth—?" asked Christopher.

Niya put a finger to her lips and listened. A horse snorted. Someone spoke soothingly to the animal, and then they heard hoofbeats swiftly moving away along the stony path.

They ran without knowing why. Niya was first to reach the bend in the path, and from there they saw him: a rider on a black horse.

And behind him, farther down, the long lines of endless ranks of soldiers.

"I'll be damned if that's not Kartan," whispered Niya. "Riding as if the devil himself were after him. Or Death."

She seemed to be listening to the echo of her own words.

"Where's Jumar?" asked Arne.

No one replied. Niya leveled her gun and aimed at the rider on the black horse, but Christopher's arm prevented her from firing.

"Shoot him now and we're all dead," he said quietly. "There's half an army on the move down there!"

This time, Niya nodded in agreement, and lowered her weapon. Then she stood in the middle of the path for a long time, silent, watching Kartan until he disappeared around another bend in the path.

"Jumar," she said at last. "He asked if I'd go away with him. To Europe. Or America."

She smiled, her eyes empty of tears. "Looks like he's left without me," she said.

They searched the tourist checkpoint and the other houses without finding any trace of Jumar.

And when they finally gave up and went on with their descent, Christopher clung to a hope that he knew was pointless: Something had happened that forced Jumar to hide. He suspected that Jumar had escaped Kartan and maybe he'd even turned invisible again. But the more rational part of his mind understood the irony of that. After so many brushes with Death, so many escapes in the nick of time, it had been chance, nothing but stupid chance that had cost Jumar his life.

He said, "But what are we going to do without him? How are we going to reach Kathmandu and carry out his plan?"

Even Jumar's backpack containing the resinous juniper wood was gone beyond recall.

"It doesn't matter how. We'll do it," said Niya. "That's all that matters. Do you remember what Jumar always said? 'I've got no idea, but I'll have thought of something by the time we get there.' And he always did think of something, am I right?"

Christopher nodded.

"We're not leaving him in the lurch," said Niya. "We're leaving only because he's not with us anymore."

But every step they took that day pierced Christopher like a knife—and he knew it was just the same for Niya, even if she would never have admitted it.

The water was cold. Colder than he had expected.

Just a moment. Had he been expecting to land in water?

Well, maybe. Maybe in some hidden corner of his mind, where the important decisions were taken without him.

He went under, came up to the surface again, fought for air, and found himself in tumultuous eddies.

Well, he thought, at least this river doesn't flow underground. There's light, and a bank that I can see. This is nothing.

This is the luxury version of something I survived long ago.

He wanted to laugh, but he got water in his mouth and coughed and spat instead, in a way very unsuitable for the heir to a throne, on the way to that throne, but his lungs told him to do it and wouldn't be contradicted.

The eddies were strong. Stronger, he had to admit, than the pull in the underground river.

They took him in their arms and pushed him down below the surface, threw him up again, whirled him around, and sang of times past—when they had carried inflatable boats on their wet surface. Times when they hadn't been hostile, but an attraction, filling pages and pages of descriptive writing in tourist guidebooks in English, something the country was proud of, something easily turned into dollars. *White-water rafting in Nepal, so close to nature* . . .

Jumar fought to keep his head above water.

443

Rocks came into his field of vision, breaking the surface of the river, their hard edges threatening him. He let the eddies carry him around the rocks, but it wasn't easy, and his arms were beginning to ache. His whole body hurt, in fact, and he prayed that the last of his strength wouldn't leave him. This water had a will of its own, and it didn't care whether it submerged a tree trunk, a beggar, or a crown prince.

Like leeches, the water had certain Communist qualities: a wet death in its clutches was available to one and all, like the life it gave back to those who escaped it.

It took a long, long time deciding which side it would come down on in the case of the crown prince of Nepal.

But he surfaced at last. Finally, someone was pulling him out of the water. Arms were tugging at him to retrieve the river's unusual cargo . . .

The last part of the way down into the valley was steep, and it was some time before they were level with the river. Until now, Christopher had thought climbing up would be more of a strain, but his knees were beginning to shake, and sometimes he thought he was losing control of his feet. He saw them walk on all by themselves, imagined them falling over each other and taking a shortcut to the depths below.

"Take it easy, go slowly," said Niya. "That's the secret."

Down by the river, houses beckoned like an oasis. The long, winding line of soldiers had long since wound its way out of sight, but there was still life down there—people were scurrying about, and there was the possibility of finding a bed for the night.

"How long do you think it will take us to get down to the village there?" asked Christopher.

"About an hour if we get a move on," said Niya.

Arne grinned and said, "A pity the village won't come up to us here instead."

It was already getting dark when they heard the roaring of the river.

"That's the best sound I've heard in a long time," said Arne, and no one disagreed. They were back in a part of the country where rivers flowed, where green trees with huge leaves and trunks strung with clinging creepers grew, where birds called in the forest, where monkeys screamed in the undergrowth and where cicadas chirped nonstop.

The heights were only a vague, unreal, faded memory now. The travelers could hardly conjure up a picture of the snow, the ice, the moon landscapes.

The village had a broad bridge of strong wooden planks, and part of the village stood on it. Houses crowded close together above the water, flowers grew in old tin canisters and

445

broken pots, and somewhere the disjointed bawling of a TV with bad reception floated out of a window. A chicken was nesting in its satellite dish on the tin roof.

Outside one of the huts on the bridge was a sign grandly announcing, HOME MAD MOMOS FRESH.

Beside the wording was a picture of a squinting individual with legs too short for him and very long arms, sitting in front of a plateful of pale half-moon shapes. The picture was black-and-white, although it looked as if it had once been colored.

"If they really make momos here, that would be wonderful," said Niya. "For one thing, I never want to eat food out of a can again, and for another, the backpack disappeared . . . with Jumar."

Christopher thought how hungry he was, and how sad it was to be thinking of food when Jumar would never eat with them again. But his hunger insisted on getting the best of his emotions.

"What are momos?" he asked.

"A kind of ravioli," Arne explained, obviously glad that they weren't pursuing the subject of the backpack and its owner any further. "They really do look like the picture. Except that you don't absolutely have to squint when you eat them."

A woman carrying a child appeared in the doorway of what might be a restaurant and gave them a distrustful look.

Presumably she recognized Arne as a tourist from his fair hair, but without understanding what he was doing here or why he was in the company of two young Maoists. Her face reflected mingled fear and curiosity, as if she couldn't quite decide between them.

Arne decided for her.

He gave her his most dazzling smile and said, "We're incredibly hungry. Have we come to the right place?"

At that, she nodded and led them into an empty room where there were three tables with plastic flowers gathering dust on them.

"Sit down," said the woman, and the child in her arms stared at them wide-eyed, with its nose dripping. "This is the strangest day for a long time. No one comes here for ages and ages, and then . . . there's a stranger here already. My husband and his brother pulled him out of the river."

Only then did they see that the room was not empty after all.

Someone was sitting in the farthest corner, in front of a plateful of pale half-moon shapes made of dumpling dough, and the scene was so like the picture on the notice that for a moment Christopher thought the person sitting there was squinting.

447

But he was only grinning. A grin they knew.

"I ... uh ... took a shortcut," said Jumar. His grin reached from ear to ear.

Jumar told them his story four times in all as night came.

They slept in the house on the bridge, feeling well fed again for the first time in ages. The river rushed by below them. Jumar's backpack, rather beat-up now, was drying beside the fire, and a cat was making itself comfortable on Christopher's feet.

They whispered in the dark for a long time like children.

Into their relief at being together again came Jumar's own grief over the coming death of his father, creeping on soft but prickly feet.

"Maybe," he said, "maybe it isn't true. Maybe Kartan just made the whole thing up."

But although they all murmured in agreement, none of them believed it.

Christopher dreamed of the big bed full of silken cushions where the dying king lay—just as if he shared Jumar's sorrows by sharing his dreams. Once, a long time ago, he had thought their stories had woven themselves together too tightly to ever be taken apart again. And he had been right.

A day later, they reached a valley more parched than any of

the places they had passed through before, and dustier than their dustiest thoughts. Even the dragons seemed to avoid this particular valley, where the only color was a dull pale brown.

But if you were not a dragon, there was no way to go unless you walked through this valley. It wound its way through the steeply rising mountains, and the river that had once flowed here was now at one with eternity, with no water in it.

Not even the hungriest color dragon could have felt tempted to come down in this valley.

The green of the jungle had respectfully retreated from the mighty clouds of dust, leaving the four travelers alone in the middle of a bleak, waterless, landscape, in the middle of crunching gravel hostile to all life. Winds carrying dust swept along the dried-up riverbed. The sun beat down unmercifully on anyone going through this valley, as if to discourage them and tell them, "This may look like the broadest road in the whole country, but it's only the grave of a living river, Death itself with its tears all dried."

This must be the Kali Gandaki Valley. Christopher vaguely remembered reading about it in that book about Nepal.

They walked from sunrise to sunset along the dead riverbed, without seeing a single plant. They came upon

449

mule dung and bones, scraps of faded fabric, and bits of paper blown along on the wind. But nothing living.

Every gust swept handfuls of dust into their faces, so that they had to narrow their eyes in the scorching heat.

At first, Christopher welcomed the heat, but then it became unbearable. They took off their jackets, carried them for a while, and finally left them behind. Little cascades of sweat were running down Christopher's back, mingling with the dust and making his clothes stick to him. They shed their heavy shoes as well, and Jumar fished his long-forgotten sandals and Christopher's sneakers out of the backpack. Niya went ahead of them barefoot.

She looked so different with her hair short.

"This is taking too long, damn it," said Jumar in the afternoon. "It's taking too long! There's a whole lot of country to cross beyond this valley before we find a paved road of any size and a bus to Kathmandu. If there are any buses still running when we get there. Kartan said three or four days . . . I don't know how we're ever going to make it."

They were sitting down on the gravel of the riverbed to rest, because there was no shade anywhere.

And to their surprise, this time it was Arne who shook his head.

"We don't need a bus," he said. "Where we come out of this

riverbed again, there's a town with an airfield. A tiny airfield, providing local transportation by air over the mountains and back to the city.

They all stared at him.

"Tourist know-how. Sometimes it helps. I'd thought of taking the shortcut on my own way back so I'd reach the children's home where I'm working."

"You're a bit late now, aren't you?" said Christopher.

"Oh, just two months!" said Arne with a grin.

And so they planned to take to the air.

Before that, however, something quite different happened. Something moved the airfield into the distance of the unattainable and cast doubt on all their plans.

"The river!" cried Christopher, baffled. "It's back!"

"How kind of it," commented Niya. "To come back, I mean."

They were standing at the side of the valley, and in the middle of it, where the bottom of the riverbed went deeper, clear water was trickling and glinting among the pebbles. It began as a handful of tiny channels, like thin, cool, wet strands of hair among absolute dryness; a winking of blue eyes in the blind void of the desert landscape. Then the channels joined, gained courage and the lust for life, leaped boisterously from stone to stone, and grew wider and broader.

It eddied and whirled with shining, rushing water. Yes, the river was back.

To stick to the facts: The river was reaching huge, cool hands into the valley, and in its arms lay an island. Just beyond the island, the river divided into two.

And not just the river; the valley divided as well. And with the valley, so did the travelers' route.

They looked at each other and knew they were all thinking the same thing.

"Which is the right valley?" asked Jumar. "The one that will take us to the airfield? We don't have time to lose our way."

Arne shrugged helplessly and pointed to the island.

"It looks almost as if someone lives there," he said. "We could ask the way."

Though nothing grew on the riverbanks—nothing at all, not a single tiny tuft of grass, not a prickly thistle, not even a cactus—a luxuriant green garden grew and flourished on the little island.

Maybe all the plants had emigrated from the riverbanks to this garden because there was someone there to look after them, thought Christopher. He saw neat furrows of dark soil; sheltered green shoots; dark-leaved bushes giving generous shade; the long, thin branches of oleander with its pink flowers. And in the middle of the pumpkin and potato plants, between lines of tall corn blowing in the wind and blades of grain nodding their heads, stood a single gray stone hut.

From here, the island, created by the flowing of the river's current, was like a green eye: a wise, never-blinking, never-sleeping eye with a stone-gray pupil.

"Someone definitely lives there," said Jumar.

"And we're going to pay them a visit," said Arne.

As they went down to the river, words hung in the air—words that had nothing to do with making haste, words that seemed to murmur themselves. With the voice of a crown prince, for instance, whose last meeting with a river had been less encouraging. "Fresh tomatoes . . ."

And from a renegade Maoist guerrilla, too young for that life, "Rice . . ."

And then they had reached the bank and were standing in the water with their shoes in their hands, the legs of their pants in the water, drenched by the current.

Christopher bent down, dipped his hands in the water, and closed his eyes for a moment. It was as if he hadn't seen, felt, smelt, or tasted water for years.

The dust and the heat and the sun at its height above the apparently endless Kali Gandaki Valley had buried his memories of water under a world of dry pebbles, animal bones, scraps of paper. Niya's voice cut through his thoughts.

"If we want to get to the island, we'll have to swim there," she said. "The water's getting deep."

Christopher sighed longingly. "There's nothing I'd rather do."

"Do we all swim over?" asked Jumar. "It would probably be enough for one of us to go and ask the way."

"Suppose the island isn't as peaceful as it seems to be?" suggested Arne. "Shouldn't we go together?"

Jumar thought it over and finally nodded. Then he stuffed all their shoes into his backpack. Thinking they might ruin the juniper wood, he found a plastic bag in the depths of the backpack, and filled it with the vital part of their crazy plan, knotting the bag to keep the wood dry.

Arne put the backpack on and signaled for Jumar to follow him into the river. Jumar did, and Christopher slid into the wonderfully cool water after him.

Halfway between the bank and the island, he turned to look for Niya.

What he saw startled him so much that for a moment he forgot to swim.

He saw Niya's head, and then he didn't see it anymore. Up came an arm, a second arm, a shock of black hair again, fingers trying to grasp the empty air, helplessly, desperately.

Niya the freedom fighter was now fighting for her life with

the Kali Gandaki, a gasping, gurgling, undignified struggle. An idea emerged in Christopher's mind. It could be a cramp in her foot, or maybe she slipped. But no. The awful, clear truth forced itself on him.

Niya couldn't swim.

ARNE IN
THE DUST

NIYA, THE INSURGENT WHO COULD RIDE better than the Devil, who could shoot the top button off a soldier's uniform from a galloping horse at a distance of fifty yards, Niya who knew all the secrets of the Himalayas and the jungle valleys, and every track, every star, every stone—Niya couldn't swim.

And she had been too proud to admit it. She had followed them into the river for the sake of a stupid green island full of tomatoes, throwing herself into a struggle that she couldn't win. Was she was trying to prove something? thought Christopher.

He thought all this in the time it takes to draw a deep breath—the time it takes to swim a distance of three yards.

He extended an arm to the panic-stricken eddies in the middle of which, somewhere, there was a head with short black hair, and thought: Arne has a water-safety certificate— but he is already ashore.

He caught hold of something—a shoulder—but it slipped away from him again, and he thought, I don't know how to—

He treaded water, paddling on the spot, and felt the current he had hardly noticed before. It greedily tried to carry Niya away with it. This is the third damn time someone's almost drowned on this journey . . .

I don't know how to, but I must.

He swam after her, against the current, reached into the chaos of arms, hands, shoulders—and grabbed.

She struck out, hitting him now and then, flailing around blindly, aimlessly. But Christopher wasn't letting go. He found the back of her neck, got an arm around her rib cage from behind, and began hauling her toward him. And he found a determination in his movements that wasn't his own. A blond, blue-eyed determination: Arne's.

Was he as crazy as Niya, trying to rescue someone when he couldn't do it? A blind will brought him to the surface again and wouldn't let him give up. It made him swim on, despite her resistance.

And then there was the current that threatened to carry them downstream and right past the island!

Were those figures on the bank waving? Were those shouts? Was that someone jumping into the water to swim toward them? Christopher didn't have time to look. Inside, he swore extensively at Niya. Keep still, you idiot. Are you tired of life? Keep still, you monstrosity born of a sick country, will you? But he didn't loosen his hold, didn't let go of her, didn't let her win her struggle with him and lose her fight against the river.

And he sensed that this determination wasn't Arne's anymore; this was his very own.

Then, unexpectedly, his feet reached gravel. The riverbed.

He braced against it, defying the current's last efforts, and waded and staggered his way to land.

Suddenly there were arms and hands grabbing him, pulling him up—and Niya—and then he was lying on the stony bank of the island where fresh green grass was sprouting among the pebbles. He felt it under his cheek.

He closed his eyes for a moment, concentrating entirely on his breathing and the feeling of the current in his body. It still seemed to be pulling at him.

"Christopher? Christopher?" That was Arne.

"Yes," murmured Christopher, dazed.

"Everything okay?"

"Yes, thanks," said Christopher in an uncertain voice. "No resuscitation needed. Give me a minute . . ."

He opened his eyes, sat up, shook some water out of his hair.

Niya was sitting on the ground beside him. Her baggy shirt was sticking to her like something in a low-budget collegiate YouTube video. Christopher thought back to a snowy night in the mountains, on the outskirts of a molten town . . . an immensely long time ago.

Niya didn't seem to need resuscitation either, only a moment to find her way back to herself after the wild confusion of the last few minutes. And Arne looked almost disappointed.

"The things you two do," said Jumar, shaking his head. "The things you do."

Christopher ignored Arne's outstretched hand, stood up, and wrung out the hem of his shirt.

"I think," said a frail old voice behind Jumar, "this is the moment when a certain young lady says thank you for being rescued."

A sinewy arm, flecked with age spots, pushed the heir to the throne of Nepal out of the way, and thin, weather-beaten fingers were extended to Niya. She let the stranger pull her to her feet without resisting.

When she was standing beside Christopher, she ran her

hand pointlessly through her wet hair, which was too short now to hang over her face, and for the first time in her life she looked embarrassed.

"Well?" said the old man.

He was wearing a faded black, floppy pair of pants, a shirt of an indeterminate color that looked as old as he was, and a small round beanie with a zigzag pattern.

"That's all right," said Christopher.

"No," said Niya. "He's right. I . . . oh, damn it all!" She looked at him. "Thank you."

Christopher smiled, and when Jumar began saying, "Why didn't you tell us you couldn't sw—" he abruptly stepped on his foot.

"Would this by any chance," said the old man with a lurking grin, "be the time for introductions?"

"Uh, yes," said Arne. "I'm Arne, and this is Christopher, and that's Niya, and that's Jumar."

"Names are such nice anonymous things," said the old man paradoxically. "They don't tell you anything, they are not at all dangerous. But they satisfy the demands of civility. So let's leave it at that. My own name is Tarmin. And I would be glad to invite you into my humble house."

Christopher looked at Jumar, and the heir to the throne of Nepal shrugged his shoulders.

♦ ♦ ♦

There was something strange about the old man, but Christopher still couldn't figure out what it was. He had a glitter in his eyes just beneath the surface of his gaze, a flickering in his voice just below the surface of the words.

"We really just wanted to ask the way," said Jumar. "The way to the airfield. The valley divides not far from this island, and one of the two parts of it must lead to the airfield."

"All in good time," said the old man.

He led them down a narrow, sandy path, framed by the green of his garden. Leaves danced in the wind coming over the water, green stems bowed softly, insects hummed among flowers, buds stood dreaming, and unripe oranges hung waiting in the branches of an orange tree.

"A beautiful garden," said Jumar. "But we don't have much time. If you would just tell us which way to take . . ."

But the old man would not respond to him.

"This garden and I," he said, with the pride of his sprouting seedlings, "have been living together for—let me count—for forty-six years."

He pulled aside a curtain over the entrance to the roughly built stone of his hut, and they went inside. The smell of incense sticks hung in the air here, heavy and sweet. Christopher saw their bright eyes glowing on the walls in the dark—there must be a dozen or more. He wondered if after a lifetime of flowers and vegetables, the old man had tired of the fragrance of his garden. Didn't he like the scent of the flowers anymore?

"Sit down," he said. There was a single low table in a corner of the hut, knee-high, with cushions to sit on around it. "I will tell you the way you must take, but I don't often have visitors. Allow me the pleasure of entertaining you."

Jumar sighed. But they sat down on the cushions in their wet clothes, and the old man nodded, satisfied.

"It is good that you came today. I was away until yesterday. I value visitors. We have always valued visitors. It gives one the feeling of still being useful. When I see travelers coming through the valley, I bring them away in my boat. I didn't see you in time. Some pay for my services, others have no money. That makes no difference. The river has always given us its fish, and the garden has provided everything else."

He smiled and placed a jug of water and five metal cups on the table.

It was odd that he kept saying *we* and *us*.

"Be my guests. There is not much left." He began to get busy with plates. "Here's a little rice, and some vegetables . . . that's all I still have. They wouldn't leave me more. I still had a little hidden away. You never know . . ."

Hidden away from whom? Christopher wondered. Who wouldn't leave him more?

"This is the last food in this house, and you will share it with me."

"The last food?" asked Niya.

The old man nodded. "Everything is about to change. We are on the verge of a new age. Maybe even the years will be counted differently. Maybe we will begin again at Year Zero. Who knows?"

Maybe he is crazy, thought Christopher. Maybe it would be better not to eat his food. But even as these thoughts occurred to him, his right hand began shoveling rice and vegetables into his mouth. They had been living on the rationed contents of cans past their expiration dates for too long. Hunger was stronger than their haste to carry on with their journey.

"I have been away for two days," the old man continued. It was as if the words had been dammed up inside him, and now they had to come out or he would explode. How long had he been living alone on this island? And whoever "they" were, why didn't he get rid of all those words on them? Maybe they had been in a hurry as well. Christopher could sense Jumar's nervousness, and he himself began to feel uneasy.

"The river, you must know, runs dry again just after the

next bend. Both parts of it. No one knows where it goes. It just seeps away into the ground. Maybe it doesn't like this valley."

Jumar had already cleared his plate, and now he was beginning to drum the knuckles of his left hand impatiently on the tabletop.

"Thank you very much for the food," he said stiffly. "But please tell us, which of the two ways should we go?" This was the third time he had asked, and Christopher felt that he almost ready to jump up and storm out to find it for himself.

"We kept cows, as well," said the old man, as if he hadn't heard what Jumar said. "On the little patch of pasture. Two of them. They didn't leave us the cows."

And once again Christopher thought of "them," and how he was eating old Tarmin's last meal. A stale taste came into his mouth, a taste of dark forebodings. A sense of tomorrow and the day after tomorrow, and his fear of what was coming. He forced himself to swallow it down.

He sought Arne's blue eyes, and the fire in Niya's determined gaze. The river had not put out that fire in her eyes.

"I will make some tea," said Tarmin. "I'll just fetch some water. Just stay sitting where you are. There should be tea with a last meal."

He bent a little and slipped past the curtain to go outside.

The colored fabric brushed his cap, rustling softly. Jumar stood up. "We're never going to get away from here," he said. "I have a feeling this old man doesn't know which way we ought to take. He just wants someone to talk to. Let's just go."

Niya nodded, and pointed silently to the back of the room, where a second curtain could be seen. There were more incense sticks in the wall next to it than anywhere else.

"Maybe we can get out that way," Niya whispered. "Then we won't have to argue with him."

She lifted a corner of the curtain to slip past it, and Jumar, Arne, and Christopher quietly followed. The food and the heavy fragrance of the incense sticks had poured leaden weariness into Christopher's limbs. His thoughts were moving slowly, sticky like honey, and so he stood there for a while without understanding what he saw.

The opening in the wall did not lead out into the garden.

A second and even darker room lay beyond it.

It had a tiny window, with a densely woven piece of cloth draped over it. And here, under the fragrance of the incense sticks, there was another odor as well, an odor that was like the stale taste in Christopher's head. He drew it in. It was the stern, sweetish smell of decay.

"A . . . a bedroom," Jumar whispered. Niya nodded. A broad double bed took up most of the room. And on that bed lay shapes, dark and difficult to make out in the absence of daylight; motionless outlines. The shapes of sleeping figures.

Christopher heard footsteps, and Jumar came up behind him. Then there were more footsteps, the quick footsteps of the old man.

"Shh," said Tarmin. "Don't wake them. They are asleep. They're sleeping so soundly."

"What—?" whispered Jumar.

"Deepa," whispered Tarmin, "was the last to fall asleep. Yesterday evening, just after I got back. Then they were here. They took everything away and slaughtered the cows. So much red everywhere—it took me a long time to clean up. Then I knew the time had come. I had gone downstream at just the right moment."

Christopher couldn't stand it any longer. He put out his hand, pulled the heavy curtain over the window aside, and a ray of light found its way through the tiny opening.

He heard Jumar gasp.

Tarmin put a finger to his lips, and said in urgent tones, "This is not the time to wake them!"

Christopher's knees were giving way. He put one hand on the cold wall of rough stone blocks to support himself.

On the big double bed, under an embroidered bedspread, lay five people and a dog side by side—close together, as if seeking warmth and protection. But any warmth would be too late for them. None of these people would ever rise from this bed again. He counted three young men, a little girl, and an old woman. At their feet lay a dead dog. The bodies seemed to have died at different times, and Christopher was grateful for the bedspread that spared him the sight of further details.

"What—what happened?" he whispered. "Who are they?"

Tarmin drew the fabric over the window again.

"Our eldest son was the first," he said. "He was a police officer down in the valley. The Maoists shot him, and his friends brought him back to us. I rowed him over the river. I thought he was dead, but my wife, Deepa, said, 'Look, Tarmin, he is only sleeping.' So we laid him on our bed, and went to sleep in the other room so as not to disturb him. Next was our youngest son. We knew he would be coming because he was in the police force, as well. He always wanted to be like his big brother. All the police officers at the checkpoints in the streets are frightened—too frightened to sleep at night.

"That's why he fell asleep," Deepa said. "Our sons were just too tired. Not two days later our, third son came. He had been with the insurgents. We discovered that only on the day when they put him in my boat. He was already asleep. The insurgents are too frightened to sleep when they lie down there in the mountains . . . They all feel the same fear.

"It's the evil thing they are afraid of," Deepa said. "When the evil thing has gone, they will wake up again. But who can catch and kill the evil thing? Neither the Maoists nor the soldiers nor the police officers. Someone else must do it. I dreamed that the evil thing will come through the Kali Gandaki Valley. Everyone must past through this valley, including the evil thing. And so I began . . ."

He lowered his voice to a whisper. "I began to build a trap. A trap for the evil thing. I worked on it for two weeks and thirteen days. And I had to build it on land, in the drought and the heat. Because it was heavy, heavy as the task before me, too heavy for the boat. Four days ago, I hauled its separate parts with our last mule and the cart along the valley on the right. The one the evil thing will have to come down when it wants to go to Kathmandu. That is where I have set my trap. It was difficult, it was hard work. I had built a pulley system to lift its parts . . . Yes, my trap to catch the evil thing weighs too much for a single man. But I am not stupid. The evil thing wants to kill, and I baited it with life . . . Shh! That's a secret. You won't tell anyone, will you?"

The four travelers, dazed, shook their heads. Too many thoughts and feelings were whirling in their minds in confusion, and even Jumar had forgotten his haste for a moment and was standing there, frozen.

"The insurgents came toward me first as I returned home. Later, in the dark, Kartan's troops came. I hid behind rocks on the rim of the valley, twice. When I came back here, I found only the red everywhere, and the remains of the cows. The dog lay on the threshold, and inside, on the floor, lay my wife, Deepa, and little Anita. They were asleep . . . so fast asleep . . . Soon, when the evil thing has fallen into my trap, they'll wake up. Then the new time will begin. Now I'll put the water on for tea . . ."

"Don't . . . Don't bother, thank you," Arne interrupted old Tarmin's flood of words. "We really must go on. So it's the right-hand valley we need to take? Does the right-hand valley lead to the airfield?"

Tarmin tipped his head to one side and seemed to be thinking.

"Yes," he said. "I'll take you to the bank in my boat. Be careful. Maybe the evil thing will pass through the valley tonight."

When they climbed out of the boat that afternoon and said good-bye to old Tarmin, they all breathed a sigh of relief. And Christopher thought that the evil thing had already been there. And had not fallen into Tarmin's trap.

Many-headed, on marching feet, darkly moving, it had passed Tarmin by.

It might already be in Kathmandu.

✦ ✦ ✦

Tarmin was right: After the next big bend in the right-hand valley, the blue water of the river disappeared as surprisingly as it had appeared. Rushing and gurgling, the Kali Gandaki sank into the ground, seeping away in dozens of separate veins of water, as if drowning in the overwhelming dust of the desert. And if it ran on underground, its hidden life produced no life above the surface. Nothing grew, there was nothing green, there wasn't the smallest chance for a garden anywhere.

They walked through the burning heat in silence, with the brisk sand-laden wind whipping at their faces again, the blazing sky dazzling their eyes again, the pebbles crunching underfoot again. Their clothes soon dried on them, dirty and dusty, like a kind of crust, a second skin stiff with the salty sweat of their first skin. Only when the sun went down behind the mountains, casting sudden shade over them, did the first of them dare to speak.

The first of them was Jumar. He said, "Maybe we just dreamed that island. Maybe there's no garden there and no river. It's too unlikely. Much too unlikely."

"Nothing in this country is too unlikely to happen," replied Niya bitterly.

The sky grew colder, the shadows darker. The fingers of

the wind were sharp as knives now, and it wasn't just the sand and the dust that cut at the travelers, but the biting cold of the night as well.

"Let's find somewhere to sleep," said Arne.

The sides of the valley rose steeply here, and there were no caves offering shelter from the wind. Only a jumble of rock faced the travelers, and from time to time pebbles rolled down from the mountains as if worked loose by footsteps. But there was no one there.

"Look!" said Jumar at last.

Niya asked, "Where? What? Do you see any shelter for us?"

Jumar shook his head. "No, not that. But there's something there—something surprising. Look. Something's growing, over there in the middle of nowhere."

He took a few steps and they all followed him, amazed. Because he was right.

Hardly a yard from the steep, stony side of the valley grew a tall, slender plant. In the last of the light before nightfall, it waved thin, flexible twigs at them, and on those twigs nodded pink flowers that looked like windmills . . .

"An oleander!" said Arne in surprise. "How beautiful! But its leaves are drooping."

"No wonder," said Jumar. "Where would it find water here?"

"But where did it find water before?" asked Niya. "It looks as if it still had plenty of water not too long ago . . ."

Christopher said nothing. He had that stale taste back in his mouth.

The taste of danger.

Jumar went toward the oleander, put out his fingers to touch its leaves—a friendly green sign of life here in this deadly, dusty, cold void. Niya followed close behind him.

"Don't!" said Christopher for no good reason, helplessly unable to explain why. His hand found Arne's shoulder, and Arne stopped.

The other two had reached the oleander.

And the ground opened up.

The ground of the Kali Gandaki Valley showed a gaping hole going down to fathomless black depths. Stones fell, sand slid, dust swirled up, and in that confusing cloud, the hostile valley swallowed up the heir to the throne of Nepal and a short-haired, fiery-eyed Communist.

They sank like the river itself.

Then a huge man-made contraption suddenly came into view on the slope beyond the oleander—a metal plate, until now carefully hidden, emerging from the rubble. A secret mechanism under the ground crunched and creaked. Wheels turned, ingenious machinery began to move . . . The huge iron plate fell with a dull thud on the hole that had opened up in the ground, covering it entirely. Gravel, rubble, sand, and loose soil came trickling down the steep slope, and before anyone had time to shout or say a word, a rock fall had covered the place.

The dust didn't die down for several minutes. The oleander had disappeared, and, with it, Niya and Jumar.

"That . . . that—" Christopher gasped.

His hand was still on Arne's shoulder, the hand that had held his brother back.

"The trap," said Arne, in a voice as flat as the metal plate now hidden under the stones. "That was the trap. Tarmin's trap. Very ingenious mechanism."

Oh no, thought Christopher. "The evil thing wants to destroy, destroy all life," he whispered. "I baited the trap with life . . ."

"The oleander," said Arne. "Tarmin left it there."

Christopher nodded. Suddenly his head felt as heavy as if it were made of iron itself.

"Arne," he whispered, "Arne, how far did they fall? Far . . . far enough? The metal . . . and the weight of all those stones. You don't think . . . You don't think it's crushed them, do you?"

It was so quiet in the valley.

A memory of driving on the freeway: a little bird flying

into the windshield of the car, their father at the wheel. Christopher, just six years old, sitting in the backseat with Arne beside him.

"Arne," he had whispered, "Arne . . . It didn't . . . ?"

And Arne had shaken his head. "It flew away, that's all, here on my side where you couldn't see it."

And everything had been okay.

But it was all different now. Christopher was no longer six years old.

Arne slowly turned to him. His face looked strangely pale in the very last of the evening light. "I don't know," he said. "Christopher, I just don't know. We'll have to find out. We've got to clear the stones away."

Christopher nodded. He was wondering if he really wanted to know what lay under the iron plate. But suppose they're alive, whispered a voice in his head. Suppose they're alive and waiting for us to get them out . . .

So they began shoveling rubble away with their bare hands in the darkness of the early night, working frantically, desperately. And the night grew with the moonlight, and became older and wiser, and in the Kali Gandaki Valley, two figures were still on their knees, digging their way through a mountain of dust and stones. They dug until their fingers were bleeding, and they didn't even notice. Christopher's back ached, his knees hurt, and his weariness sang in his ears. But there was no time for weariness now.

"*My heart longs for dreams,*" sang his weariness. "*Dreams in this land of our fate.*"

My heart longs for dreams,
But they tell me: Dreams must wait . . .
First comes waking, first comes the light,
We shall make our mark by day, not by night.

But would day ever come? And if it did, would light come with it? Would it come for Jumar and Niya?

Would they ever see it again? He refused to think further on this, just as he refused to feel tired. He allowed himself only one thought: The rubble must be cleared, leaving the iron plate exposed. And finally, when the moon was growing pale, they had done it.

Before them, under a final layer of dust, gleamed hard, cold metal.

Christopher fell back and simply lay there, looking at the stars and thinking of nothing whatsoever for a minute.

"Christopher," said Arne after that minute. "The plate— remember what Tarmin said? It's too heavy for one man on his own. Tarmin was clever with his trap."

He paused, and then said quietly, "We can only do it together."

Then Christopher hauled himself to his feet, looked for a place where he could take hold of the plate, and grabbed it.

"One, two," murmured Arne. On "three," they began heaving. But nothing happened, Nothing at all. This trap wasn't made ever to open again. It was a final trap. A trap that the evil thing could never escape.

If only it had caught the right prey!

"Again," said Arne. "One, two—"

This time, the iron plate moved a little, only a very little, but enough to give them hope. And a third time. Now Christopher did the counting. "One, two—"

They heaved and pushed, braced all their weight against that of the iron . . . Christopher felt the stretched muscles tense in his body until it seemed as if they would tear. He was breathing fast and irregularly, like someone with a high fever. Inch by inch, the plate rose. He heard Arne gasping beside him, saw his smile, covered with dust, sweating, dirty.

We can only do it together, thought Christopher. Arne had said that. And it was true, for at that moment, neither of them was more important, neither of them mattered more than the other. Neither of them led, neither followed. He needed Arne, and Arne needed him. And they were both needed by someone else, neither more than the other and neither less.

They were half of a four-armed creature, gasping and groaning in the dust of a night somewhere in a lonely valley, raising an iron plate.

It wasn't about whether Christopher was as strong as Arne. It wasn't about proving something.

And as he was thinking that, the plate allowed itself to be lifted with a last, desperate effort—and suddenly the iron folded back like the cover of a book. Fear shot through Christopher. A part of him wanted to call out, to lean forward and look down into the depths. Another part wanted to close his eyes, never to know what had been waiting there under the lid. But he was too exhausted to do either of those things. All he could do was gasp for air.

Later, he kept two pictures in his memory that, like so much else on this journey, were never to leave him. The first is of Arne's smile under a layer of dust, at the moment when he is just Christopher's brother, not his older, stronger, more important brother.

The other picture is different and larger: Above the Kali Gandaki Valley, the morning sky is turning red, and the first daylight falls into a rectangular, black shaft. Two figures are visible at the bottom of that shaft, reaching up to arms above.

The picture is taken from a great height, too high for a sound to be heard.

Farther north, a dragon was flying over the Kali Gandaki. The morning sun shimmered on its emerald wings.

The dragon was hungry.

In the middle of the river, it saw a green, almond-shaped eye with a gray, stony pupil. The strong scent of incense sticks rose from the eye. The dragon breathed it in. Surprised, it sank lower in a spiral of perfect beauty, and saw that the eye was an island: an island full of colors.

It flew close above the island, and its shadow flew with it. It came down in a pasture where cows might once have grazed. From there, it began destroying the green of the island.

It took the dragon three hours and sixteen minutes to finish its meal.

Then it unfolded its wings again—their color had now shifted slightly from emerald green to grass-green—and flew away through the valley.

It left behind a colorless island, a blind eye in the river, an eye that could see neither good nor evil. At one end of the island stood the bronze statue of an old man looking out at the water, his head covered with a cap like a small tea cozy.

ARNE IN
THE AIR

WHEN THEY SAW A SCRAP OF GREEN IN the distance, Christopher breathed a sigh, relieved that they would soon leave the troubled valley behind.

Around midday the four travelers had found some shade and tried to catch up with the sleep they had missed the night before, but none of them could manage to lie still for long. Like the soldiers in the undergrowth, like the police officers at the checkpoints, like the rebels up in the mountains, they were too anxious to sleep peacefully. It was a vague, unfocused anxiety. And an open, island-shaped eye kept watch in their minds, never blinking.

Evening was already creeping down from the mountains,

and the sides of the riverbed were casting deep, deceptive shadows, as if water were flowing there again. The travelers kept close to the shadows so as not to miss the path leading them out of the dry river, and when they finally came to its bank, and saw the leaves of a spindly apple tree rising above a nearby wall, it seemed to Christopher that this apple tree was the most beautiful thing he had ever seen. They had finally left behind the Kali Gandaki Valley and the monstrosities born of its madness.

A broad, inviting path led past the walls, and more and more fruit trees welcomed them by waving their branches. There was a gentle melancholy about this place.

Somewhere a rooster whose sense of time had gone wrong crowed.

"He's right, all the same," said Niya. "For us, it's morning. Time to board one of those tourist planes and get away from here."

The path came to a broad, sandy road; the gardens gave way to two-story houses, with flyers plastered all over them, offering TICKETS AIR OF PLANE, SLEEPING BACK FOREST, BEST FOOT BEFORE EVEREST, KODAK FILM ROLCE, CHEAPIEST SUN GLACE AND BINOCULARS, and so on and so forth.

This place was merely a tunnel, a shell of restaurants and

shops, selling equipment for travelers. For a moment, Christopher wondered if the aircraft landed on the street here, but soon they noticed a gate among the houses. Beyond it, a runway ran parallel to the road. A small check-in hut made of rough planks stood at the entrance, but it was silent and dark. The runway was empty. There wasn't a single plane in sight.

"Maybe they're all in some kind of hangar," suggested Jumar without conviction. There was no hangar in sight, either.

Niya pointed silently to the little wooden hut. Then she said, "There's someone there."

And Christopher also saw the silhouette in the shadows—the motionless outline of a human being.

They cautiously went closer. Something was wrong. The wooden hut was like those where people checked your passport at other small airfields. There was a soldier sitting at the little window. But he wasn't moving. He seemed to be looking at them, but his eyes were strangely fixed.

Niya reached through the window, which had no glass in it, and took him by the shoulder.

He didn't react. He slipped slightly her way, that was all. She put her hand to his cheek and shook her head.

"Dead," she said. "Dead as a doornail."

Christopher sensed eyes looking at his back, other eyes, and turned around.

The sandy road was no longer empty. Several figures had come hesitantly out of their houses, keeping in the shadows of the walls, watching them.

"Hey!" called Christopher, and half of them instantly disappeared again through doors that closed without a sound. The others stayed put and went on staring.

"What happened here?" asked Arne.

No one answered.

Then Arne went up to the figure standing closest. He walked carefully, stepping softly, as you might approach an animal that could easily be frightened and run away. It was an old man, with his back bent, who stood there leaning on a stick. Christopher saw alarm flickering in his eyes, but he held his ground. Arne still had it: the spell he cast on people. My smile might be like Arne's, he thought, but I'll never be able to exert the same magic.

Arne was very close to the old man now, and he asked again, quietly, "What happened here?"

"They came," said the old man. "They were here this morning. The guerrillas. They said they needed the airplanes. There are only four. Three of them flew to Kathmandu, with too many men on board. The pilots didn't like it, but they were afraid. The soldiers guarding the airfield were afraid, too. It did them no good. They begged, but the guerrillas didn't leave a single one of them alive. We carried their bodies to the eastern end of the airfield. Except for the one you've found at the entrance. Sitting there in the shade, he was forgotten."

"Four," said Arne. "Four airplanes, did you say? There were four?"

The old man nodded.

"And three of them took off for Kathmandu with the guerrillas?"

He nodded again.

"I don't understand. Where's the fourth?"

The old man thoughtfully shook his head. "The fourth pilot was in the air when they came," he replied. "They didn't know there was a fourth. It's so long since any tourists came, the pilots were beginning to go strange. The fourth was the strangest of them. He bought fuel with all his money and started flying trips over the mountains, all on his own, no passengers. They say he stopped eating, he just flew, and every evening he came back and fell on his bed like a dead man. It makes no sense. He's lost his mind. We thought he would try to leave the country. You can do a lot with a plane. Many of the people began making plans. But not him. He came back every evening."

"Until today," said Arne.

At that moment, they heard the sound of engines. They

looked up at the same time, at the evening sky growing swiftly darker.

The plane was flying without lights, hardly more than a shadow against the gray of the night that threatened to fall. They watched as it flew in a loop over this little place, and Christopher was reminded of the dragons. But this was nothing but a plane, silvery gray, made of metal, without beauty, holding no terrors, meaningless.

However, the farther down it came, the more meaning it gained. And when its wheels came down and touched the ground of the runway, it became the bearer of the most valuable thing under the evening sun, not that its pilot knew: the bearer of hope.

Niya opened the barred gate, and they ran to it.

The pilot of the last airplane had only just touched solid ground under his feet when he saw four figures running toward him. He blinked, bewildered. Where are the other airplanes? Why does the place look so quiet? And who are these four strangers?

He took a step back, shook his head, and stood there in astonishment.

Now they had reached him, gasping, breathless.

"What—?" he began.

"You have passengers again," said the girl with short hair. From a distance, he had taken her for a boy, but now the pilot saw how beautiful she was, so beautiful that he shook his head again, marveling.

"It's worth flying again," she went on. "It's really worth it, maybe for the first time. How many passengers do you have room for in your plane?"

It was crazy. Absolutely crazy.

But then people called him crazy anyway.

So the fourth pilot climbed back into his plane that evening, and four passengers climbed in after him.

Their story was confused and confusing, and he had only just begun to get the hang of it. His mind was still in the peaks above which he had flown that day. His thoughts were still caught in the glittering snow, the shimmer of evening light on the glaciers, the summits of the mountains that he could not leave.

"It's too dark," he said, in a last attempt to make them change their minds. "No one flies when it's as dark as this. Not in these tiny planes. It's not allowed."

"No one's going to bother about what's allowed in this country and what isn't anymore," said Jumar. "Chaos is coming. You'll see. The king is dying, and the Maoists are—"

Alarmed, the pilot put a finger to his lips.

"Keeping quiet makes no sense now," Jumar went on, almost angrily, and Christopher laid a hand on his arm: Calm down. Take it easy.

"Names are nothing but soap bubbles," whispered Jumar. "They're hollow. They don't mean anything. I can say it a thousand times and nothing will happen. The Maoists are outside Kathmandu—the Communists, the guerrillas, the terrorists, the insurgents."

The pilot flinched at each word.

"But if this plane doesn't fly tonight, their names will change—into blood, into bullets, into fire. And Kartan will write his own name on the wall of the palace in that blood. And it won't make any difference who wins the battle in the streets."

The pilot sighed, resigned.

"You know a lot of fine words," he said. "Who are you, speaking like that?"

Christopher saw Jumar grow uneasy. "I'm no one," he replied. "I'm an orphan without any family. I'm nothing. It doesn't matter who I am."

The pilot started the engine, turned around, and looked at them all one by one.

"You know people say I'm crazy," he cried against the

noise of the engine revving up. "And I must be to fly you where you want to go tonight. But the crazy see clearly. You are young. Much too young. However, Death climbed into this plane with you. I can feel it breathing down my neck. And it's not me that Death is after. Death will find one of you there in Kathmandu."

With these words, he turned to look forward again, and soon after that the last, solitary plane was rolling over the only airfield in the Annapurna region. It lifted off, pointed its nose into the night, and climbed—climbed, climbed, climbed up to the stars until it had gained enough height, and then traced a course through the air parallel to the ground, making for a distant destination that none of those in it could yet see.

The city of the kings of Nepal.

Kathmandu.

The plane did not reach Kathmandu complete.

It lost its colors on the way.

They met the dragon beyond the starlight. Clouds had gathered over the night sky, dense and thick, and the aircraft's running lights were the only source of light far and wide. They were flashing red and green on the wingtips when Christopher woke up to find Niya's shorn head lying on his shoulder.

He hardly saw her, he just felt her: her warmth, her soft hair against his throat, her breath on his skin. And then he saw the glow in the night. It was a faint, almost invisible glow, yet it united all the colors of the rainbow in it.

The pilot saw it, too.

"What the devil is *that?*" he asked.

"A dragon," whispered Christopher. Apart from the two of them, no one else seemed to be awake. "Their colors glow. Only a little, just enough for us to see them."

Now they could make out the dragon's wings, spread wide. Soon after that its graceful neck, its serpentine body— and it was flying straight toward them.

The pilot swore and wrenched the nose of the plane upward, but the dragon, too, altered its course slightly, so that they were still making for each other.

"Nothing will happen," said Christopher, putting as much confidence as he could in his voice. "We'll simply fly through it."

"Fly through it? What do you mean?"

"Its body isn't solid. It's made of butterflies. Thousands upon thousands of butterflies. That's all."

"You surely don't expect me to believe that?" asked the pilot.

But by then, it was too late for belief or disbelief: The shimmering body was racing toward them, or they were racing toward it, and the pilot prepared for an impact, a collision, an explosion—

Nothing happened. Nothing at all. They passed through the dragon as if it were a cloud. Jumar had been right. It had no body. It really was made of butterflies. How they could all fly at this height was to remain a mystery to Christopher forever. But compared with so much else that had happened on their journey, it was a small and insignificant mystery.

The dragon's jaws snapped, out of sight of anyone inside the plane, and it ate the gleam of the metal and the colors of the running lights without a sound.

Then it was gone. They saw it turn its neck to the plane once more, and spew a nervous jet of fire into the night. But by then, it was too far away to be any danger.

Christopher heard the pilot breathe a sigh of relief.

The lights on the wingtips were blinking as they had before, but now they were blinking gray.

A colorless blinking, no difference between right and left, front and rear.

So they landed under cover of night on a road outside Kathmandu, and the colorless lights went out.

"I can't go any farther," explained the pilot. Christopher ran his hand through Niya's short hair, and she woke with a tiny yawn.

"We're here," he whispered.

"Have a nice nocturnal walk," said the pilot. "It will take you about two hours to reach the city."

Soon after that they were standing on a deserted asphalt road full of potholes, watching a small plane with colorless running lights rise up into the night sky again to fly north.

The fourth and last pilot in the Annapurna region did not get far. As he approached the rim of the Kathmandu Valley, the needle of the fuel indicator fell to zero, and he just made it over the first tree-grown mountaintop before the metal body of the plane dropped through the air, heavy and exhausted.

Those who saw it said that while it was still in the air, the plane crashed into an invisible obstacle where there had once been a bridge over the rushing river.

The last thing the pilot saw was the snow-covered peaks in the blue distance, the peaks he hadn't been able to bring himself to leave, although there wasn't a single snow-covered peak in the Kathmandu valley.

They walked along the asphalt road as if in a dream.

The wind moved the clouds aside, and the constellations walked with them.

"I'm going to miss them," said Arne. "Those stars. They're different at home."

And Christopher imagined sitting on the terrace with Arne at home, looking up at the night sky and thinking of the stars of Nepal.

But the pilot's words echoed in his ears, almost drowned out by the noise of the plane: *The crazy see clearly. You are young. Much too young. However, Death climbed into this plane with you. I can feel it breathing down my neck. And it's not me that Death is after . . .*

They slept in a ditch on the outskirts of Kathmandu for a few hours until dawn. When the sun rose, they saw hundreds of checkpoints set up in the streets. Dozens of soldiers guarding the roads into the city. Every tiny street that led into Kathmandu was lined by a troop of soldiers.

Many of them were afraid, as you could see by the way the earthenware mugs and plastic cups from which they were drinking tea at the roadside stalls shook in their hands. Many of their eyes were uneasy: At last something was going to happen. At last the years of impatience, the endless hours spent at bus checkpoints, the restless waiting was coming to an end. Many seemed unable to decide if they feared or welcomed it.

Those they were afraid of, whose appearance they ardently hoped for, those for whom they didn't want to wait any longer—were out of sight. They too were waiting—waiting in hiding, waiting for the right moment.

For an order.

For the Great T.'s decision.

"They will attack by night," said Niya. "It's their old plan. It will be under cover of dark, when there's only moonlight to give them away."

"All the better for us," said Jumar with a wily smile.

The days of defensive city walls had been gone for hundreds of years; the days when you could see besiegers and besieged from a long way off, like toy soldiers in their different uniforms; the days of the fairy tales and the great conquests, when everyone knew who belonged where and it was all clear and simple; the days when proud fanfares blown on polished brass instruments gave the signal to attack.

This would be a soundless attack, and no one whose ears it wasn't meant for would hear the order given. And none of the checkpoints around the city would be any use, because there were ways into it that not everyone knew.

And the four travelers on the asphalt road had become shadows themselves. They, too, slipped into the city without a sound.

They came through one of the sewer tunnels like rats. And one real rat, with its little eyes and its nervously twitching nose, met them as they waded through mud and the garbage, bending low. It watched them go, suspiciously, its whiskers quivering. But there was a knowing light in its eyes before it disappeared into a hole in the side wall of the tunnel.

"Where are we going to light the wood, and when?" asked Christopher in a whisper.

Jumar shook his head. "We're not going to light it at all," he said. "If we do manage to light it without anyone interfering and we make a big bonfire of it, a tall flame will shoot up, but burning only in one place, and that won't be enough. We don't want to entice just one dragon, we need to lure them all—every last one of them. So what they see shining in the distance must look as big as possible. The whole city must be glowing and sending out sparks, even if it's only for a few minutes."

Christopher looked at him with a question in his eyes.

"We're going to distribute the wood," explained Jumar.

"Distribute it? Who to?"

"The people of the city. When the insurgents are in the streets, there'll be torches burning in the windows of Kathmandu. Thousands of torches sending out colored sparks. We want the city to be a carpet of light and colors. A carpet giving off light seen all the way off in the mountains, so that none of the dragons can resist it."

"And how are you going to get people to light the juniper twigs? I mean, it won't make any sense to them—"

"Yes, it will," said Jumar. "We're going to explain what happens."

They crouched there in the sewer tunnel in silence for a while. "You surely don't think," said Christopher at last, "that people are going to light torches voluntarily when they know they'll entice the color dragons?"

"It's our only chance," said Jumar.

"He's right," Niya agreed. "It's a case of getting everyone to join in. Nothing can change without the will of the people." And she nudged Jumar gently in the ribs and laughed softly. "At heart the heir to the throne of Nepal is a good Communist."

They broke the juniper branches into as many small pieces as they could, and each of them stuffed their pockets with the pieces. There wouldn't be enough for all the houses in the city, of course not, but one torch in every street would have to be enough.

Jumar's words rang in Christopher's ears like an endless echo. *It's our only chance, it's our only chance, our only chance . . .*

"Today we'll be working harder than any other four

people in this city," said Jumar. "By evening, we have to have convinced as many of the local inhabitants as we can. Tell them they must light the torches when they hear the bell ringing in Durbar Square—the bell in the largest temple there. I often used to hear it from the palace. When it rings, that will be our signal for all the torches to burn at the same time. When the fighting begins, we must all be up there in the largest temple. Until then we'll separate, we'll swarm out like the rats racing out of this sewer, and we'll meet again there."

He stopped and looked at each of them in turn.

And they all nodded.

It's difficult to hug in a sewer where the ceiling is low, and the ground covered with garbage and brackish water. But somehow they managed to.

Christopher noticed that his hands were shaking as he pressed Jumar's hands, and Niya held him close a little too long for someone who never seems to feel afraid.

"Don't you three get lost in the streets," she whispered, laughing again. "And don't forget that what we're doing is sheer Communism!"

But then, she suddenly turned serious. "And remember," she said, "the Maoists know we've turned against them. The Great T. makes sure that everyone knows what traitors to

495

them look like. Remember the men they brought back that time in the molten town."

They all nodded.

"If one of us falls into their hands in the chaos tonight," Niya went on, "and it's impossible to rescue him—then the others must kill him. I told you so before, but I'm telling you again. Death is better than what they do to traitors. I've seen it. I know. And that's what I'm afraid of. Death itself is not so bad as long as it comes quickly."

"What—?" Christopher began, but she shook her head.

"Let's go," she said. "It's high time."

No one saw the four figures who climbed out of the sewers into a dark alley that morning. Or anyone who did see closed his eyes and told himself he hadn't really seen anything. There were too many things that no one could explain going on in the shadows of the city these days—too many things that it was better not to see.

Four tanks were waiting among the temples in Durbar Square. They, too, had been waiting a long time. They would come to life this evening, and the few people who passed them thought they saw the sides of those mighty metal bodies quivering like the flanks of nervous animals. It was all imagination, of course. The air in the city itself was quivering, and when it stood still, you could have cut it with a knife, it was so dense and thick with tension and fear. No one knew anything for certain, but everyone felt a foreboding.

No one spoke, but everyone was thinking.

No one admitted it, but everyone sensed it.

Nothing was normal in this city anymore.

And through that quivering, trembling air Christopher moved, his pockets full of the scent of juniper. This is nonsense, he told himself. This is totally crazy. This will never work.

It's our only chance.

The first door he knocked at opened only hesitantly, and he slipped into the dark corridor inside.

"What do you want?" asked a young woman. "I don't know you."

Christopher put a piece of wood in her hand. She stared at it blankly.

"There's a story to this piece of wood," he said, "a story too long to be told here and now. When the bell of the largest temple in Durbar Square rings today, you must light this wood and put the torch in your window. It will be at evening or night. And the same torches will be shining all over the city. Kartan's men will be fighting the insurgents in the streets. You know that, I don't have to tell you."

A man had appeared in the dark corridor behind the

woman and was inspecting Christopher, listening attentively. The words Christopher spoke were not his own. They were Jumar's words—Jumar's clever, well-turned phrases. They came to his aid as if naturally, although he could not have said how.

"The light of the torches will be no ordinary light," he continued. "It will sparkle and spray fire in all the colors of the rainbow, and it will entice the dragons."

"The dragons?" asked the man.

"Their shadows will fall on the men fighting in the streets and turn them to bronze," said Christopher. "I don't have to tell you that, either."

The man nodded. "We know about it. There have been no dragons in the city yet, but the stories reach us in the baggage of people coming out of the mountains."

"As long as you light the torch and stay safe indoors, where no shadow can fall, no harm will come to you. When the shadows of the dragons have done what we are summoning them to do," finished Christopher, "they will go away. It will be the power of the king that makes them go away. Forever. The king has a son, and his son is here, very close. I can't tell you more."

For a while, the couple said nothing, standing there in the dark corridor with paint peeling off its walls. Christopher expected them to turn and disappear through one of the many doors into separate apartments in the building, without a word, without believing him.

But finally the man put out his hand and said quietly, "We'll need more of the wood to hand it out in the street. We will close our doors when evening comes, but even the strongest lock won't hold in the end against Kartan and against the insurgents. I don't know what you're talking about, or whether it's true. But that makes no difference. It's our only chance."

Jumar's own words sounded small, and his phrases seemed shaky. And all of a sudden he felt that heart-fluttering, weak-kneed sensation you have just before an exam. But the heir to the throne of Nepal had never had to take an exam. His private tutors had been gentle, friendly, and yielding, and a good student like Jumar, they had said, didn't need to pass any tests.

Of course, entering the dragon's cave had been a test. A special kind of test. But no one had been watching him at the time.

Now he felt as if the whole city were watching him with a thousand eyes, to see what had become of its son. All at once he felt lonely and helpless without Christopher and Niya— with only his own plan and his own courage to rely on.

In every house, behind every door, he was afraid people would chase him away, laugh at him, refuse to listen to him. But they did listen to him. They were friendly. They invited him to eat with them, pressed a cup of tea on him here, a handful of rice there, and that surprised him every time.

He didn't tell them who he was. Once he had thought that important. Now it seemed entirely meaningless.

The little pieces of wood went from hand to hand, were examined, felt, smelled.

And what an aroma it had, the wood that this strange, shy boy brought them. They had never come across such a fragrance before. They knew there must be something special about it—and he explained hesitantly, they almost had to beg him to tell them: This was wood that would change the city's history. Their own history. It was miraculous wood. Dragon wood.

"The words you speak are strange," they told the shy boy. "They are hard to believe. But we will think of them when darkness falls and the great bell rings, and we will put the torches in our windows. We will listen and watch from behind bolted doors—to see what happens. If anything happens."

They clapped him on the back, and urged him to stay, but he said he must go on, and on, and on . . .

Arne handed out the wood with a smile.

He didn't need to say much. The language he had taken such trouble to learn didn't give him enough words to explain, to tell the story, to convince people. His smile would have to do. And it did—that broad, magical smile on his friendly face, the beaming smile in his bright eyes, it cast a spell on them without words.

Of course they got the idea of what he wanted them to do, and they promised to do it. This fragrant wood must be something good, something that would have an effect, although they had yet to see what kind of effect. They would light it for the young man with the blond hair and the beaming smile as soon as the evening air carried the first note of the bell through the city, and then they would wait . . .

Niya was exhausted. The evening was fast approaching. She had been into so many houses, talked to so many people. For the first time in a long while, her body was demanding rest, a place in the cool shade, and silence, complete and utter silence.

It was as if she were empty, as if all her words and gestures had flowed out of her, leaving nothing behind but a huge, empty space in which she wanted to lie down and rest for a little. Only for a little . . .

She had given away the last piece of wood, closed the

last door behind her, and she was going down the last street. It looked like all the others: narrow, with laundry hanging from lines slung across it, with garbage in the corners, music coming out of an open window, dogs dozing.

When she came to the end of that street, someone barred her way.

She didn't know where he had come from—it must have been somewhere in the shadows. Her attention had lapsed.

He grabbed her arm, hard, and the shock of the unexpected jolted her like an electric shock. Then she looked into his face and recognized him: one of the drummers who used to travel in the mountains with her. One of those who had accompanied her fiery speeches.

"Niya—" he said. There was hesitation in his voice, and regret. And perhaps she might have managed to tear herself free of him. But now there were two other men behind him, two men she didn't know, and then a third came up. She had seen him at the base camp. She looked from one to another of them, and worked out her chances. They were slim.

The man from the base camp spoke to her. She saw his mouth open and close, but it was some time before the words made their way into her mind.

"Did you think we wouldn't recognize you if you cut your hair and went about barefoot, like a beggar?" he asked.

"I thought you had more sense than that, my girl. The Great T. has had people searching for you for a long time. A traitor can't just be allowed to go. There was a lot of bad blood in the camp after you disappeared."

He smiled a smile that Niya didn't like. "But now you're here again, right?"

Niya twisted and turned in vain in the grip of the two men holding her.

"Let me go," she spat, and her eyes flashed. "The Great T. has other things to do this evening without bothering with me. Let me go. I have nothing to tell you."

"Oh, but I think you do," said the man from the camp. "I think you do have a few things to tell us. Like what you're doing here, for instance."

Niya bit her lip and said nothing.

He raised her chin and looked into her flashing eyes. But Niya herself knew that not even the fire of her glance would do her any good now.

"Bring her with us," said the man, turning to lead the way.

She tried to break free one last time, kicking, biting, and scratching, a wild beast of the mountains, but a fist punched her in the stomach, and next moment she found herself back on the ground, in the dust of the alley. Kicks rained down on her like a promise being fulfilled.

She had guessed it long ago.

Finally, she stopped defending herself and lay still, protecting her head with her arms. And deep inside, she hardened herself, turned to stone, put on armor that no one could get past, steeled herself against the pain.

The men hauled her up and dragged her away with them like a lifeless object.

Niya saw eyes behind the windows that they passed. Eyes in the shadows, eyes in the dark. No one came to help her.

They didn't drag her far. Two streets away the door to a yard opened, and someone let them in.

"They think all our people are waiting outside the city," said the man from the camp. "But I hope you're not as stupid as Kartan's men. You must have known that the city also has eyes and ears to keep us informed."

Niya turned her head once more before they pushed her through the gateway. At the end of the alley, she saw two figures. And she brought a tiny spark of hope through the gateway with her, faint and flickering. But it was there.

ARNE IN A LAST MEMORY

CHRISTOPHER'S POCKETS WERE EMPTY. He turned them out and found only bits of bark smelling of juniper, and of a distant memory of Christmas.

He set off for the city center, for Durbar Square outside the palace, where the wooden temples stood at the top of broad flights of steps. He had seen pictures of them . . . Someone tapped him on the shoulder, and he spun around, ready to fight, ready to run away, ready to scream if necessary—

"Jumar," he gasped.

Jumar grinned. "Looks like it," he said softly. "Did you get rid of it all? Did everything go well?"

Christopher nodded, a question in his eyes, and Jumar nodded, too. Everything was all right.

They went down the street together. The sky was already turning red, and the streets of the city center were almost empty now. At sunset the curfew that had been imposed on Kathmandu for weeks, like a sword hanging over it, would come into force.

Anyone still out and about then was outside the law, and the soldiers regarded him as an enemy. They must hurry.

"This way," whispered Jumar. "Down this street will be quicker."

But a moment later, he stopped suddenly and pressed close to the wall of a house. Christopher copied him. And then he, too, saw what Jumar had seen.

Niya.

Two men in the jackets and boots worn by the guerrillas were dragging her along the alley and away from Jumar and Christopher. Before Christopher could think clearly, a gate in the wall opened and swallowed up the two men and Niya.

They stood there without moving.

Christopher felt his heart begin to race as if it would burst inside him, leaving nothing but broken pieces.

"We must do something," whispered Jumar. "Anything. We've got to follow them."

Christopher nodded. "We can't just abandon her," he whispered. The rigidity in him gave way, and now his feet moved of their own accord, although he didn't know where he was going. His feet seemed to know. Like all the yards in Kathmandu, the yard behind the gate was surrounded by tall buildings with balconies. The whole city was a labyrinth of balconies, verandas, flat roofs, outdoor stairways, and Christopher's feet carried him into this labyrinth. They found whitewashed steps leading upward that led to a dead end. They came down again fast, as if hunted. He rounded the block of buildings, found another stairway, and that one went up to a balcony. Jumar's footsteps raced up behind him. There were more steps, up and up; a flat roof, buckets, mattresses laid out to air, an old broom forgotten there, loose twigs tied together—

Christopher looked around.

"The way, Jumar," he whispered. "Which way?"

But Jumar had already understood, and was running ahead. Christopher followed Jumar, leaping from roof to roof, ducking under clotheslines, and in his head he heard Niya's voice calling his name soundlessly: *Christopher, Christopher.*

And then they had reached the roof next to the yard. They flung themselves down on their stomachs, side by side, crawled forward to the edge of the roof and peered down.

And for a selfish second, Christopher wished they had never found the right roof.

Down there was one of the guerrillas' bases in the city.

Christopher counted twelve men in the yard.

Twelve men and a girl with short black hair.

He reached for Jumar's hand, and felt that he was quivering with anger.

Niya was lying on her side on the ground, curled up like an embryo. She was naked, and her body was smeared with blood. The picture burned itself into his memory, never to disappear again. One of the men was crouching down in front of Niya. He was holding something in his fingers, something small and brown: a piece of wood. And when he spoke, his words also reached the two watchers on the roof.

"What is this?" he asked, loud and clear, as if speaking to someone hard of hearing.

Niya did not reply.

The man took a drag of his cigarette. "Tell us what it is and where the others who came with you are," he demanded. You could hear that it wasn't the first time he had asked her that question. Niya said nothing. Christopher saw her ribcage rising and falling. She was breathing. But she kept silent.

The man reached out his hand with the burning cigarette, and pressed it at his leisure against his victim's cheek. Christopher shut his eyes, felt a savage pain—as if he were the one lying down there, helpless and alone. Niya still made not a single sound.

Coward, Christopher told himself angrily in the silence. He forced himself to open his eyes again.

"Tell us your plan," said the man, lighting another cigarette and blowing the smoke into her face. She raised her head, only for a moment.

But it was enough to show Christopher the marks that the men's unanswered questions had left on her face. Later he tried not to think of it, but the picture would come back. Later he was told he must remember before he could forget, and describe what he saw before he could be rid of it. But he never found the courage or the words, and he never did describe what he had seen down in the yard that night.

He did not see Niya. All he saw was her pain.

"We have time," said the man. "This is only the start. This is nothing. You know that. You'd better talk."

He put out his hand to her again—and once more Christopher couldn't look. He let his eyes stray—and saw a man standing on the balcony below them, watching the scene in the yard. He was a small man, and now, as he began walking back and forth on the balcony, his movements were swift and supple. He stopped again, shook his head regretfully, and

509

finally said, "I didn't pull you out of the rubble from the fire for you to betray me. I thought highly of you. You may not think so, but I am almost sorry myself to see you end like this."

The Great T. The man without a name who would always hide behind an anonymous initial. Here he was, in the middle of the city, where no one suspected his presence, watching his men at their work.

"When we've finished with you," he said, and his voice was friendly, almost affectionate, "our fight will begin at last. The fight you wanted to join. Do you remember, little Niya? Tell us how you planned to harm us. We can still put your mistake right. If you talk, I'll call my men off. You are going to die one way or another, but there are different kinds of death . . ."

She raised her head once more. And this time she saw . . . not the Great T., although he thought she was looking at him. She was looking at the two of them on the flat roof above him.

And her burning eyes looked right into Christopher's heart.

They were pleading for help.

If one of us falls into their hands in the chaos tonight, said her voice in his memory, *and it's impossible to rescue him—then the others must kill him. Death is better than what they do to traitors . . . Death itself is not so bad as long as it comes quickly.*

He saw the fear in her eyes. Sheer, naked fear.

Her strength was all gone.

The man down in the yard was holding the tip of his cigarette right in front of her eyes now.

Christopher looked at Jumar, and Jumar returned his glance.

At exactly the same time they took the guns off their shoulders, quickly, never faltering. They had practiced these movements a thousand times in the snow, in the cold, in the anonimity of the base camp. And Christopher was finally grateful that, in spite of his dislike of it, he had learned to shoot. He could shoot while he lay in the dust, he could shoot even if someone kicked his legs out of the way, he could shoot while he trembled with cold.

Now he felt as if he were choking, yet his hands moved calmly; only his heart was fluttering. He heard her song, and the notes of her guitar again, on a clear night in the snow:

> *First Death must free us, low we must lie.*
> > *And they ask me: Are you ready to die?*
> > > *For silence, dreams, and sleep,*
> > > *For peace in this land of your fate?*
> > > > *And I say: silence, dreams, and sleep,*
> > > > *And peace, all of these must wait.*

He took aim. So did Jumar beside him. At the same time. That click. He hated that click. He couldn't see anything. Tears were blurring his eyes. He blinked them away. He could do without tears now. He took aim.

The tip of the cigarette in front of her eyes. She was trying to twist aside.

The glow of it. The metal in his hands. Then the crack of the shot, the explosion.

There were images in his mind like chapter headings: Niya's words, Niya's revenge, Niya's song, Niya's hands.

The two shots tore through the air like one.

The man's hand did not find its victim; it hovered in the air, baffled. He dropped the cigarette and put his hand out to the blood in front of him. Only then did he turn and look up—they all looked up to the place where the shots had come from. To the roof.

But there was no one on the roof now.

Jumar had pulled Christopher to his feet with him. They ran, crouching low. They ran for their lives.

Christopher's thoughts and perceptions mingled, loose scraps of ideas:

The white steps of the stairway flashed through a veil of tears. *My heart longs for peace.* Christopher almost stumbled, but caught himself up again. *Peace in this land of our fate.* The road. Another road. So dark now, almost night. *My heart longs for peace.* No one among the buildings now. *But they tell me: Peace must wait.*

Steps on the paving stones. Where? Don't turn to look. Go on. Double back. The outline of a shrine by the roadside, at the foot of an old tree. A sacred tree, with a yellow sari wrapped around it, hung with garlands of flowers. Of course, they were back where Hinduism ruled. In the shrine, the size of a chest of drawers, a god shaped like a monkey, painted orange. Hanuman. Jumar's hand. *Now where?*

First comes action, be on your guard.

Then he was crouching down behind the statue, motionless, knees drawn up, with Jumar beside him.

The steps approaching along the street passed by.

First we must strike, and let us strike hard.

They sat there like that for a long, long time. Motionless. Just two shadows in an old shrine.

Their tears dried up.

Tears always dry up eventually.

Someday you are parched and dry inside.

"We must get to Durbar Square," Jumar whispered. "It can't be long now until the guerrillas appear in the streets."

But they didn't get that far.

513

The heir to the throne of Nepal had predicted chaos. He had said it without knowing just what that meant.

Chaos.

Soon after they left the orange god under the sacred tree, they heard the first shots. Christopher hesitated, but Jumar made him go on.

A pointless memory surfaced in his mind: New Year's Eve. Arne in the snow, kneeling beside a bottle with the wooden stick of a rocket in its neck. All around them, the first fireworks were going off, and Arne shook his head disapprovingly.

He was maybe ten at the time, and Christopher, aged five, holding their father's hand, was standing in the drive leading up to the house, looking at the rockets.

"You're not supposed to let rockets off before midnight," said ten-year-old Arne very seriously, and Christopher admired his grown-up tone of gravity. His father laughed.

"Maybe their watches are wrong?" he suggested.

But Arne waited until his own watch—its big hand showed Speedy Gonzales running around in a circle (Christopher was to inherit it a couple of years later)—Arne waited until his watch said midnight. Until Speedy Gonzales had reached his destination on the number twelve. Only then did he let off the first rocket. Christopher could still see it clearly in his mind's eye. How it rose to the sky, how it exploded like a ripe fruit, and its shining seeds spurted out into the darkness. They had been green and red.

But these were gunshots—not New Year fireworks, and somewhere beyond the firing Arne was sitting on the steps outside the largest temple waiting for them.

First the shots came from outside the city, then from the city center, and finally Christopher couldn't tell where they came from anymore. They were everywhere, and soon he was hearing the sound of running feet, voices calling. He ran after Jumar down dark, empty streets, but no one was asleep inside the walls of the houses.

They were all awake, all listening, watching, trembling.

And then the streets down which they ran were no longer empty. A troop of men ran past them without seeing them, disappeared. The lights of car headlamps swept over the walls, searching. They pressed close to a wall, dazzled, but the lights were not looking for them; the sound of engines crawled past them as they closed their eyes in fear, and died down. They ran on, keeping close to the walls, ducking low, moving from shadow to shadow.

"How far?" gasped Christopher. "How much farther to go?"

But Jumar had no chance to reply. A shot hissed past them and struck the wall behind them, and as if that were the grand overture to a play, the streets filled with figures. Shadows, first furtive, scurrying by, then more and more of them, impossible to overlook in the dark, and finally no one seemed to mind who saw whom anymore. And the chaos that the crown prince of Nepal had predicted began.

Uniforms gleamed in the beams of flashlights. Orders were shouted. Horses' hooves galloped on the streets. The clatter of gunfire disturbed the rhythm of a group of men on foot marching in time; shots flew in panic, at random. The night seemed to writhe like the body of some huge, shapeless monster, divided up by searchlights, torn by screams. No one could tell what direction they came from.

Any of the inhabitants of the city who ventured into the streets that night were never seen again. Doors were barred, yards lay deserted in the moonlight.

And how Christopher, too, would have liked to hide, bury his head in his hands, see no more, hear no more. But he knew they had to find a way through all the confusion and get to Durbar Square.

There were men everywhere, their feet running, their raised arms holding guns, their backs bent. He stumbled over a body on the ground, cried out, was hauled on by Jumar again. Jumar wouldn't let him rest. Anyone who stopped running was lost.

Once Christopher looked up and saw that the rooftops, too, were populated by marksmen in camouflage green, marksmen in military uniform, marksmen whose identities he couldn't determine. Did they know it themselves? Did they know which side they were on? Or were they just firing at random? Was it a game of aiming at everything in sight?

Surely there must be some kind of plan. But he couldn't see what it was.

There was nothing around him but a sea of movement, light and shadow, explosions and echoes. It was getting harder to tell the difference between up and down. He saw doors that had been violently forced open, heard screaming from houses. He saw men fighting without guns, he saw knives flashing, and men wrestling with their bare hands, with teeth and nails in the night. And there were more and more bodies lying in the streets. He stumbled over them. Some were still moving and reached out with weak arms. Some lay still. Gunsmoke coiled in the brightly lit wounds of the night; Christopher smelled fire, smoke, blood. His feet didn't want to go on; without Jumar hauling at him he would have stopped a thousand times. Fear sang its song in his heart.

He didn't even know how large this city was. How long had they been running through this chaos? Minutes? Hours?

This was what they had wanted to prevent. They had hardly rested on their travels, they had made such haste. They had flown to Kathmandu, and still they were too late.

Arne, he thought. Arne. Ring the bell. The bell in the biggest temple. Ring it so that the colors burn in the night—the torches. But suppose he really did? Suppose the bell rang while they were still on their way and the shadows of the dragons came sailing through the air under the deep gold of the half-moon?

But did it matter whether two more human beings turned to bronze statues? What were two among so many? Nothing, nothing at all, hardly worth counting. All the same, you can't think like that when you are one of the two.

Wait, Arne, wait! Just a little longer! Keep your fingers off the bell!

But how was Arne to know how long he could wait? How was he to know whether they were still coming? Or whether their bodies had long ago joined the others covering the ground in the streets like a sinister carpet? And suppose Arne, too, was already among those on the ground?

Finally, he saw a square spreading out before them, a wide, empty place without people, without chaos—only a handful of temples stood there, with many steps up to them, tall wooden temples.

The other side of the square seemed to be at the center of the explosion; there was movement there, people there, and the palace. But the square itself lay empty in the moonlight. Jumar stopped for a moment and looked around. And Christopher understood why the square was empty. It was too large, too wide, too brightly lit by the moon. Anyone crossing this square would be a living target.

"Which one?" whispered Christopher. "Which is the temple with the bell?"

To his eyes, they all looked the same size—solid, angular buildings crouching there, silently watching the spectacle before them.

Jumar pointed.

And then they ran.

Christopher had never run so fast in his life. The blood sang in his ears, he tasted it on his tongue, he hardly had time to breathe. He was waiting for an explosion somewhere close, the impact of a bullet, burning pain. But nothing happened.

No one fired at them.

Perhaps simply because no one had been expected to venture into the square.

They reached the temple, climbed its five gigantic steps, and soon after that, dropped flat on the floor of the top platform.

Christopher was still struggling for breath as he saw Jumar straightening up, but it wasn't Jumar who raised his arm to ring the bell. It was Arne.

Arne's hand lured sound from the bell.

His fair hair showed in the darkness, like a phantom in the shadow of the temple, and his smile hung in the night.

A second later, the notes of the temple bell were on their way into the city, ringing loud and clear over the gunfire, the screams, the sound of engines and horses' hooves—a message that was understood.

Later, the people said that when the bell began to peal the blood in the streets had almost reached the lowest window openings. They said they had seen the soldiers and the guerrillas wading up to their knees in it, up to their waists.

But what they said doesn't matter.

What matters is what they did.

They looked for something to strike a light; their fingers trembling, they struck the tiny wax matches used in Nepal. And wooden torches burned in all the windows of the city.

At first, they only glowed, then they blazed up, spraying sparks in all colors of the rainbow, their strange resin crackling. They shone, they sparkled—there aren't enough words to describe the colored fire of those torches. The city had turned into a single surface of tingling colors. Seen from above, it looked like a huge, blazing diamond.

Seen from above. What about how it was seen from the mountains? From their highest peaks, from the glaciers, from the snows? From there, it looked like a huge, blazing diamond. Far away, so enticing! The colors! The sparkling! The blaze! A sudden, unexpected apparition of mysterious origin in the night.

The diamond must be swallowed up while it's still there. It could disappear again. Quick, quick!

And soundless, bodiless dragon paws impatiently clawed the air, eyes that are not eyes glowed with greed, and then broad, weightless wings unfolded.

A rushing and a rustling like the sound of millions of tiny wings filled the air.

The dragons left their snow-covered mountain peaks. For the first time, they all flew together. And they came down to Kathmandu.

To the king's city.

They did not hear dragons' wings—the wings of thousands upon thousands of butterflies. The noise of the chaos was too loud, too violent.

All of a sudden, the dragons simply appeared.

Arne saw them first. Silently, he pointed to the sky, and the three boys on the tallest temple moved farther into the shadows of its pointed wooden roof.

"How many of them are there?" whispered Jumar. But there was no counting them. Maybe there were two dozen, maybe a hundred, maybe more. Their shadows glided over the roofs of the houses on the outskirts of the city, and the men fighting in the streets didn't notice them.

The dragons craned their necks, amazed, seeking. Where was the great, sparkling, diamond surface they had seen from afar? Were the separate lights diamonds? Could you eat their colors?

Then the shadows of the dragons fell on the fighting men. By the time the first of them looked up, it was too late. They tried to run for it, break down doors, throw themselves, panic-stricken, into the few moonlight shadows offered by the walls. But it did them no good.

The shadows of the dragons touched them without a sound, like delicate fingers, and one after another froze in mid-movement, gleaming an unnatural bronze in the moonlight, like statues. And that was what they turned into. Whole armies of statues made of bronze.

Flashlights fell from hands, bullets landed in ditches,

knives gleamed as they fell to the ground, green camouflage jackets changed color, terrified glances were fixed in metal.

When the shadows of the dragons reached Durbar Square, and Christopher saw what horror the men felt, for a moment he felt sorry. But then he thought of the doors they had broken down, the screams coming from the houses, the blood. Most of all, however, he thought of Niya. He clenched his fists in silent triumph, for Jumar's plan had worked. Silence fell in the streets. The fighting men stood motionless, frozen in the middle of their battle.

They saw one man jump out of a car in the middle of the square, look up at the sky, and he stayed where he was standing and did not move again. The starlight played on the polished, gleaming metal of his face. It was a well-ironed face, without any movement in it.

"Kartan," whispered Christopher. And Jumar nodded in silence.

The torches in the windows had burned out. The dragons, disappointed, circled above the city, looking for colors, colors, colors—and finally they came down into the city itself, among all the bronze soldiers and guerrillas, and began eating what few colors they could find. The streets turned black-and-white, the houses lost the color of their paint, the shrines and temples their bright decoration. The dragons had not found a diamond, and they grew angrier and angrier. They grazed brown dust, for there wasn't anything worth eating in this city.

"To the palace," whispered Jumar. "Quick! It's time to get rid of the dragons before they find the garden!"

"The garden?" asked Arne, and Christopher said, "But isn't it surrounded by a wall? And doesn't it lie under a dome?"

"Yes," replied Jumar, "that's right. But dragons are dragons. And there are a lot of them. More than I thought . . . Who knows what they can do besides eating colors and turning people into bronze? They're all descended from that first dragon, and somewhere in them, the memory of the garden must be sleeping . . ."

He shook his head and interrupted himself. "This is no time for fine words. Come on."

They left the temple fast, without a sound. An army of bronze statues was waiting for them outside the palace. Ghostly, sightless eyes seemed to be watching them from metal faces. Four abandoned tanks stood uselessly around. Jumar pushed one of the metal soldiers aside and opened one wing of the magnificent door that the man had been guarding to the end.

They slipped through it, almost silently, and inside thick carpets swallowed up the sound of their footsteps. Jumar

524

went along the dark corridors first. Arne and Christopher followed him, stumbling, hesitating. Christopher feared to see movement around every corner, a gun, a man in uniform still left alive.

But the palace was deserted.

Only silence waited in its corridors and halls.

"Father?" called Jumar, and he stopped. No one answered him.

As he went through those empty rooms and down those empty corridors, the power of memory pounced mercilessly on the heir to the throne of Nepal, squeezing the air out of his lungs. He had taken his first steps here, he had gone up and down these corridors holding old Tapa's hand, he had looked down from these windows at the square without ever setting foot there. This was the vase that he had once knocked over and had been stuck together again. This was the chest of drawers that he liked to pull out when he was little so that he could search them for treasures, although he had never found anything but safety pins and buttons. This was the sofa you could hide under if you'd forgotten you were invisible. This was his mother's picture on the wall in the gold frame that he hated so much, and her smile that he loved so much.

This was the door that was always kept locked. The door

to the room with the special box with its gold fittings. It was waiting for him.

When he was outside his father's bedroom, his courage failed him. He turned to look at Christopher and Arne and searched their faces for support. They both smiled—an identical, encouraging smile.

Why don't I have a brother, wondered the heir to the throne of Nepal. Why am I all alone?

But there was nothing to be done about that. He himself, no one else, must do what had to be done now. He put his hand out and pressed the handle of the door down.

The bed in the king's bedroom was empty.

There was no head to be seen among the embroidered cushions, no body lay under the silken covers. His dream had deceived him.

A breath of wind moved the floor-length drapes over the windows aside, and then Jumar saw someone standing there, almost at one with the drapes over the farthest window.

He went closer. From up here, you could see the dragons in the streets and squares, see them craning their long necks, turning their heads and burning eye sockets, crawling over the rooftops on their short, shimmering legs . . . They were coming closer in their search for color. They were coming closer to the palace.

"Hello?" whispered Jumar.

The man half hidden in the light and airy fabric of the drapes turned.

He was wearing an immaculate suit and a silk tie. He was dressed for a reception. Or a farewell ceremony. It was him. The king. But his eyes were hidden behind a veil induced by the tablets he took to keep his head from breaking apart with pain. Hidden behind a network of confusion, a mind still held together, but with a great effort. He looked old. So immensely, unimaginably old.

Too small for his suit. It was as if the weight of the tie would drag him down to the ground.

"Who—who are you?" he asked fretfully. Exhausted. Tired. Bewildered.

"Don't you know my voice?"

The king closed his eyes. "Say something else," he asked. "Just one word."

"Father," said Jumar quietly.

Then the old man nodded, and a smile crossed his face.

"Jumar," he whispered, opening his eyes. "What happened?"

"Too much to explain now. Tell me just one thing—you're not really sick, are you? That whole story about the brain tumor was just something Kartan made up? He was lying, wasn't he?"

The old man by the window was still smiling.

"I'm afraid, Jumar," he said, "that he was telling the truth."

Jumar came a little closer and put out his hand to touch his father's arm. "Are you . . . are you going to die?" he asked.

"I am dying now," replied the king. He kept smiling all the time as he spoke. "But it's time I did. It's almost too late. See what's going on outside? It's my fault."

"No—"

"Yes, Jumar, yes. You know it is."

Jumar gathered all his strength together and said, "Father. I need the power. I need it to defeat the dragons."

A frown replaced the old man's smile. "The power?"

"The key," said Jumar, "to the locked room. And the special box inside it. Don't you remember?"

For a moment he was afraid that his father's memory had deserted him.

But then the king nodded, slowly, as if it was difficult for him. "Come with me," he said.

And Jumar followed his dragging footsteps through the moonlight filling the room, down the hall . . . Arne and Christopher joined them, but he hardly noticed them.

The old king put a hand in the pocket of his immaculate, perfect suit, pulled out a tiny key, and turned it in the lock. The door opened with a sound you could hardly hear, and a light in the ceiling came on of its own accord.

Jumar entered the room alone. He crossed it with two strides.

The box stood on a little table. Its metal fittings felt cool to his fingers. The catch was no trouble. It opened easily, with a click.

Behind Jumar, the king said, "Take it, my son. It is yours. But it's empty."

Jumar stared at the velvet lining of the box. There was nothing else inside it, nothing at all, not the smallest grain of sand.

"The magic of kings," said his father, and his voice cracked like old leather, "the magic of kings sleeps in human hearts. You must win those hearts to rule a country. The hearts of your people. I have lost them."

Jumar turned, empty-handed.

"You've won them already," said Arne. "They lit the torches for you, even though they knew the dragons would come."

"But . . . I . . . how—" Jumar raised his hands helplessly. "How are we ever going to defeat the dragons now? The magic, the power, it was the only chance! If it doesn't exist, then everything is lost."

The king slowly shook his head. "I'm sorry," he said. "I am sorry, my son."

Then he turned and went back down the hall, his dragging footsteps muted by the soft carpets, with his hand on the wall, feeling for support.

He went to his window. There was nothing he could do now but look out of it, and see the city dying with him.

NEPAL, DECEMBER

ONE NIGHT IN EARLY DECEMBER, THREE figures stood at a window in the palace in Kathmandu.

"We must do something," said one of the figures. "*Anything.*"

They were looking out of one of the windows at two shimmering dragons that now stood among the temples at the other side of the square. The dragons' eyes burned holes in the darkness. The city behind them had no colors left.

"They've found the garden," whispered Jumar. "They remembered it."

"We *will* do something," said Christopher. "Come on. There are two floors full of stairways between this window and the gate into the garden, and we'll think of something on the stairs."

He had no idea what was going to happen, but he felt that he had to go ahead now. His feet flew down the carpeted stairs, and he sensed Jumar and Arne following him.

When he opened the palace doors, two more dragons had come down in the square, looking like huge lizards with wings folded on their backs. They seemed to be waiting.

Then one of them opened its mouth and did what dragons are expected to do. It breathed a jet of fire into the air. An angry fountain of colored sparks.

Two bronze bodies lying in front of it on the ground melted within seconds.

"The garden gate is made of metal," said Jumar in an expressionless voice.

Christopher saw the second dragon spew fire, and he noticed something strange. His fear had gone away. The cold, clammy, choking fear that had had a grip on him ever since he came to the city was gone.

The fear just under the surface that had followed him all his life, everywhere, wherever he went: at school, in the streets, in the bus or train, in airplanes—the fear of doing something wrong, losing someone, being left alone.

It was gone.

He searched himself, every corner of his being, but it was nowhere to be found.

He still had no idea what they ought to do, but he went ahead, along the walls of the palace with the bronze guards outside, to where the garden walls began. Green palm fronds shimmered in the moonlight beneath the glass dome. The fragrance of jasmine and roses made the air sweet and heavy. A nightingale was singing behind the wall; he heard it clearly.

The gate was made of metal, as Jumar had said, with metal fittings and ornate decorations.

Christopher placed himself in front of it and looked at the dragons.

"What are you going to do?" asked Jumar.

"I haven't the faintest idea," Christopher admitted.

The first dragons unfolded their wings made of butterflies to rise from the ground, soar over the square, and fly toward them.

"The garden is the last beautiful place left in the city," whispered Jumar despairingly. "Our only hope."

Then something moved in the shadow of the wall, and a bent old figure rose from the ground. A beggar. The shadow of the wall must have sheltered him from the dragons' shadows when they circled the square on first arriving.

He was clad in rags and dirt, his eyes blinked as if he

were half blind, and now he reached a thin, claw-like hand out to them.

"Do you need advice?" he asked in his thin, dry voice. "It won't cost you much."

Christopher sensed that Jumar was about to say something.

He saw the dragons flying in a great loop in the air above the temples. They had all gathered there now, all of them, to melt down the garden gate together with their fiery breath and destroy what was left of the glories of the city.

"Now, how would you—?" Jumar began.

But at that moment, something inside Christopher clicked into place. An invisible gear engaged, a tiny wheel turned. Christopher, whose memories were always getting in his way, remembered an earlier time. *Do you need advice?* the monk asked the young queen in her litter. *It won't cost you much.*

That was when it all began, with the young queen's arrogant rejection.

He nudged Jumar, and Jumar stopped. Christopher looked urgently at him. He didn't say anything, he just looked at him. And Jumar understood, in some way he couldn't explain, he understood what Christopher was trying to tell him, and what he had very little time left to do now.

"Yes," said Jumar to the ragged old man. "We do need advice. More than ever before."

The old man nodded thoughtfully. The dragons were rising higher again, to fall on the square all together out of the sky.

"Open the gates," said the old man.

"What?" Jumar stared at him incredulously.

"Open the gates to the garden," repeated the beggar. "It is not the king's garden anymore. The garden belongs to everyone."

And in his head, among all the other memories, Christopher heard Niya's words. *There will be no more rich and no more poor. The gates of the palace will stand wide open. And the king will shed tears.*

535

His hands found the bolt of one wing of the door almost of their own accord. Arne helped him to free it from its keep, where it had rusted over the course of time. No one had entered the garden from Durbar Square for fourteen years, and it had just kept on growing. Anyone allowed to go into it had come from inside, from the palace. Out of the corner of his eye, Christopher saw Jumar at work on the other wing of the gate. Flying fingers pushed back all the bolts and bars, and pushed the wings of the great gate back.

They folded out like the covers of a book.

Beyond, the garden lay in the moonlight under the glass dome, green and mysterious.

The old beggar nodded and stepped aside.

Jumar, Arne, and Christopher jumped back back from the gates as well. Then Christopher felt the springy earth of the garden underfoot, he smelled the fragrance of the flowers.

And then the glowing, shimmering bodies of the dragons swept through the broad gateway, a storm of wings, necks, heads, flexible bodies, lashing tails, sharp claws. Christopher felt the wind of their passing, and heard the leaves of the trees rustling in it.

This was the end.

The end of the colors in the garden. The end of the fragrance. The end of the flowers.

The end of everything.

He closed his eyes.

But then he felt a hand on his arm, and Jumar was whispering, "Look, Christopher, look!"

Christopher opened his eyes, and he saw. But it was a little while before he could believe what he was seeing: There were no dragons left in the garden. Not a single one. Only millions of butterflies fluttering among the trees and shrubs, the plants and the rosebushes.

They settled on the flowers to drink their nectar, but they

couldn't take the colors of the garden; their shadows were tiny and harmless.

The old beggar leaned against one of the trees and watched the butterflies.

Then Christopher recognized him. He had sensed it all along. The old man was not wearing rags now. He wore the orange robe of a monk.

The monk nodded again.

He had forgiven.

Then he simply disappeared.

The first faltering light of dawn tinged the horizon pink with timid fingers, fell on no beggar in the palace garden, no monk in an orange robe.

But there were the wings of all those butterflies, and the first light of dawn was now playing on them, faltering and timid no longer . . .

A new day was dawning.

The night was over.

And the king, up at his window, who had not been able to see all this, must have sensed it.

For the king was shedding tears.

He said good-bye to life at 6:54 A.M. in his son's arms.

He didn't die until five days later, in a white hospital bed, surrounded by tubes and pieces of medical apparatus, but that was unimportant. He had last been conscious at 6:54 that morning.

Jumar did not tell him he was never going to rule the country with any kind of power.

The city slept for a long time the next day, exhausted and drained, under colorless roofs. Only the garden watched over all the people, humming and fluttering, fragrant and green.

And in the middle of the garden, the queen slept on in her pavilion, on soft cushions.

The three friends breakfasted together late in the morning, but not on canned food. They did not say much. None of them felt like talking. And anyway, the TV was on.

Kathmandu made headlines over the next few days, and took pride of place in the news. But the news never tells the whole story.

Of course the pictures in the newspapers did not surprise anyone, because most newspaper pictures tend not to have much color. But a great many people took their TV sets to be repaired, since when the capital of Nepal came on the screen the pictures were always in black-and-white. The TV repairmen could make nothing of it, since there was nothing wrong with any of the televisions.

And when news from Nepal retreated into the background, people forgot about the odd problem their screens had developed.

The Great T. was never seen again. Perhaps he is still around, he and his supporters, somewhere in the mountains. But it is said that the people now rule themselves. They elected a parliament, and now they are responsible for their own fortunes, good or bad. Of course one can't be sure whether that is true, and if it's working all right. No heir to the throne ever turned up.

There are rumors, but then there are always rumors.

Isn't this story a single, long rumor?

It is a fact, however, that for a short time in those months after the change of government the export of bronze statues from Nepal rose rapidly. Most of them were about the size of a hand, but very realistic and detailed, as if in some strange way they had shrunk from natural human size to their present form.

And much later, travelers sometimes mentioned paths that all of a sudden simply weren't there anymore. Travelers who swore that they never usually lost their way. And that they saw the famous blue sheep of the Himalayas, but with a touch of bronze in their bluish fleece.

The dome over the garden was torn down, and the gravel

paths were opened up to everyone. People walked among the fragrant flowers, marveling at them, and went home with ideas for repainting their houses and temples. The pavilion in the middle of the garden had also been open to the public for some time. To make that possible, the sleeping queen had to move, and she was put to bed—carefully, but finally—in a room on the third floor of the palace.

She was uncomfortable there for the first time. A tiny fold in the sheet was pressing against her somewhere in the region of her fourth lumbar vertebra, and it woke her up.

Since then, the queen has been tolerated as a guest in her own palace. It is said that she may begin organizing guided tours for tourists there, because she is bored. But wherever she is seen, she always looks a little absent, as if she had missed a large part of her own life, and never found her way back to it again: a lost ghost in her own time.

Not everything can end well.

Two days after that night of many shadows, Jumar was sitting with Christopher in one of the small tea shops in the city. Arne had gone looking for an Internet café with a working connection.

An emergency generator was chugging away outside the entrance to the tea shop, because there was a power failure, as there so often is in Kathmandu, and the ventilator overhead was rattling, fed with uneven current. Two flies were on their way through a small puddle on the plastic tablecloth. Jumar was drinking lemonade, Christopher was drinking tea.

They were talking about Europe, and what Jumar ought to see there.

The smell of ramen instant noodles drifted from a pan over an open fire.

Jumar was playing with his thin green drinking straw, and looking at a glossy poster on the wall which, for some strange reason, showed the high-rise buildings of Frankfurt.

He was opening his mouth to say something, but when he turned, Christopher had disappeared.

The chair opposite Jumar was empty. The tea in the tin cup was cold, and had not been drunk.

He looked at the door hanging crooked, with the words BATH RUM on it in large letters. But the door was open, and Christopher was nowhere to be seen inside.

Jumar propped his head in his hands, lost in thought about Europe. Someone must have cleared away the teacup, because after a while he noticed that it wasn't there anymore.

And when he was going to pay for the tea and the lemonade, the little boy wiping down the tables with a grubby cloth shook his head, puzzled.

"You only had lemonade," he said.

"My friend," Jumar insisted. "My friend who was sitting here with me. I want to pay for his tea."

The boy gave him an odd look.

"You came on your own," he said.

Jumar sat there for a long time, waiting, but Christopher didn't come back.

So finally Jumar got to his feet and, with a barely audible sigh, plunged into the hustle and bustle of the streets.

GERMANY

CHRISTOPHER SAT ON HIS BED, BLINKING. There had been a knock on the door.

A book of pictures lay open in front of him.

Outside, large snowflakes were falling from the sky.

He shook himself, feeling confused. He had been sitting cross-legged, and one of his legs had gone to sleep. There was another knock.

"Yes?" said Christopher. "Hello?"

The door opened, and there stood his mother. She looked at him for a moment with an odd expression in her eyes.

Then she raised her hand and waved a piece of paper in the air.

"Arne e-mailed!" she said. "Oh, Christopher, think of that—he's free! And he says he's fine. The other two boys are on their way home, as well, and Arne's flight lands at eight-thirty in Munich tomorrow morning."

"That's wonderful," said Christopher, getting up with some difficulty. "My leg's gone to sleep."

He took the book off the bed and put it on his desk. The back of the jacket showed a picture of a little tea shop, with a Nepalese boy sitting at a table drinking lemonade. The only non-Nepalese thing about him was the faded Red Hot Chili Peppers T-shirt he was wearing.

"I've got to remember to return that book to the library sometime," said Christopher.

"Yes," said his mother. "By the way, when did you get that white shirt?"

Christopher smiled and she forgot the shirt. "Has anyone ever told you that you look just like Arne when you smile?" she asked.

"Oh, yes," said Christopher. "To be honest, quite a lot over these last few weeks."

They all went to the airport together to meet Arne. His flight was two hours late, and Christopher assured his parents again and again that they really didn't need to worry.

When Arne emerged from the baggage reclaim area, he waved as cheerfully as ever. His hair was short again, and he had shaved off his beard.

"What's he carrying under his arm?" asked Christopher's mother in surprise.

"Good heavens, it's a little bronze statue," said his father, smiling. "A goddess or something. Is he suffering from a sudden lapse of taste in his old age?"

On the way home in the car, Arne and Christopher sat in the backseat. Arne had the little statue on his knees.

It was the figure of a girl. She had short hair, and was lying stretched out on her back, wrapped in a cloth. Her eyes were closed as if in sleep. And although there were some strange irregularities in the bronze, her face was the face of someone deep in a wonderful dream.

Christopher carefully caressed the girl's bronze forehead. What had happened? What was real?

"My heart longs for dreams," he murmured.

His mother turned to look at them. "What did you say?"

"Oh, nothing," Christopher replied.

But he saw Arne nodding to him, barely perceptibly.

Afterword

For Political and Geographical Correctness

THERE IS NO SUCH PLACE AS THE NEPAL of Christopher's adventures.

It was explained to him, later, that the places through which he had passed lie in different parts of the country, many of them a long way from each other, many in different directions: photographs from a book on the lap of a quiet, reserved boy, loosely fitted together.

He never entirely believed that.

And it was also explained that the Maoists never had a leader addressed exclusively by his initial. And that they do not play the violin when they make speeches, not even during the "Internationale." It was explained to him that the army had no intention of deposing the king, that juniper wood burns very badly, and that Kartan is not a Nepalese name.

As mentioned above, he always had his doubts about all those points.

He remained a doubter, which is no bad thing.

All that is certain is that one day in April, long after Christopher came home, a king gave way to pressure from his people and finally allowed them to rule themselves.

Not until April? What happened to the timing of the story? What was the truth?

Some day, Christopher plans to go back to the scene of his adventures and see for himself what the truth looks like, and the geography, and the politics. Later. When he is grown up.

But there is a little while to go before that yet.

Acknowledgments

I WOULD LIKE TO THANK THE NEPALESE FAMILY who took us in in the middle of the night, in the middle of nowhere, in the middle of the mountains when we were so badly lost on our way to the tiny hospital at Amppipal, carrying heavy medical operating instruments.

I would like to thank Ole H., who made me eat some horrible fruit candies when I started crying on the way up a steep flight of stone steps, because my blood sugar was low and the stairway was endless. If he reads this, I hope he will forgive me for not bringing the Ghurkhas into this book. He wanted me to have them in my last book, as well, but they simply wouldn't fit into it.

And I would like to thank the Nepalese nurses and doctors whose language I speak too badly to thank them in it.

And the Maoists who let us go at the foot of Poon Hill just after sunrise, even though we paid them less money than anyone else, because we didn't have any more.

And everyone somewhere up there, in the Amppipal hospital and elsewhere, still listening to shooting practice.

Because there will always be someone firing a gun.

About the Author

ANTONIA MICHAELIS was born in Kiel, Germany, and has taught in southern India and traveled to Peru, Ghana, Syria and the British Isles. She lives in northern Germany. Her work has been translated into a dozen languages.

ANTHEA BELL is a freelance translator from German and French. Her translations for young people include books by Cornelia Funke and René Goscinny. She has won a number of translation awards in the U.K., the United States, and Europe. She lives in England.

This book was designed by Maria T. Middleton and art directed by Chad W. Beckerman. The text is set in 13-point Adobe Jenson, an old-style typeface designed by the fifteenth-century French printer Nicolas Jenson. Redrawn in the 1990s by type designer Robert Slimbach, Adobe Jenson remains a highly legible face with a distinct calligraphic character. The display type is Requiem and Zephyr.